LOVER'S TALK

"What do you wish to talk about?" Night Wind asked before settling down again.

Rebecca shifted uncomfortably. What did she want to talk about? "I don't know . . . I—" Her cheeks became several shades darker.

Suddenly, Night Wind was there, closer than before, his large hand cupping her chin. He turned her face up for his inspection and gazed into her eyes . . . at her mouth. "You want to talk?"

She blinked and gazed back. She nodded.

"You want to talk or do you want to touch mouths with Night Wind?"

Her gasp of protest was cut off when he leaned forward and captured her lips with his mouth. Rebecca moaned and returned his kiss. She'd forgotten how wonderful it was to feel his mouth on hers.

Night Wind muttered something in his native tongue and she wished she could understand him, for his tone was strained, emotional . . .

His voice thick, he said, "You are much of a woman, Reb-bec-ca."

TODAY'S HOTTEST READS
ARE TOMORROW'S SUPERSTARS

HEAVEN'S FIRE

CANDACE McCARTHY

ZEBRA BOOKS
KENSINGTON PUBLISHING CORP.

ZEBRA BOOKS are published by

Kensington Publishing Corp.
850 Third Avenue
New York, NY 10022

First Printing: April, 1995

Printed in the United States of America

Prologue

August 1701

The naked woman groaned with pain as her belly tightened with the contraction, pulling her abdomen taut. The groan became a shriek as the pain intensified, and her muscles stretched, seemingly tearing her insides apart. The contraction eased, and the woman quieted, but her face bore the remnants of her agony. Her skin wore a fine sheen of perspiration. Her normally glistening dark eyes were dull.

Rebecca stood by helplessly, watching White Flower endure one contraction after another until the Indian woman's body was nearly sapped of all strength. Again White Flower cried out with pain, and Rebecca tensed with concern . . . and the terrible foreboding the English woman had felt earlier returned.

Rebecca's gaze met White Flower's dull eyes. "The babe should have by now been born," she said anxiously. "Something's not right. Let me go for the shaman."

"No!" White Flower had barely managed to open her eyes when the contraction returned, harder, faster, making her gasp and then scream, a wild shrill shriek that sent chills down Rebecca's spine and brought the hairs on her arms up on end.

The Iroquois woman grabbed Rebecca's hand and squeezed, crushing her slave's hand in a bruising grip. Rebecca winced but didn't withdraw, for she knew her pain was only a fraction of what the woman must be feeling. White Flower was strict, but she wasn't a mean master to her, and Rebecca hated to see the woman suffer.

White Flower's grip relaxed as the pain subsided. She stared at Rebecca with suddenly clear eyes. "To give birth is woman's work. The shaman knows little of such things."

"What of your sister?" Rebecca asked, uncertain whether she could deal with the complications of birth alone. "Shall I get Doe Eyes?"

Rebecca had to wait for another pain to pass, before White Flower could speak. The Indian woman nodded, her eyes glimmering with tears. "Yes. Doe Eyes will know what to do," she gasped.

The two women had come to the lake to wash and gather the berries that grew along the shoreline when White Flower had gone into labor. Rebecca didn't need the Indian woman to tell her that the babe was early, or that something was dreadfully wrong. She hurried back to the compound, silently praying that Doe Eyes could help White Flower.

The two women returned to White Flower quickly, and the labor continued until the baby was born a half hour later. Doe Eyes's face was grave as she cut the umbilical cord that held child to mother and then cleaned out the boy's mouth and nose. Next, White Flower's sister turned the baby over to give him a sharp rap between the shoulders to dislodge any remaining mucus. The women waited for the loud, lusty cry that would ring about the forest with joy, but the child displayed no signs of life.

Exhausted from her labor, White Flower barely

managed to open her eyes to look at her still child. She began to cry silent tears as she realized that her son had been born dead.

Doe Eyes handed Rebecca the dead child. Rebecca felt her throat tighten as she stared at the tiny boy, and then, without thought, she moved to the lake to wash the dead baby so that he would be prepared for his funeral ceremony.

While wading into the water, Rebecca stumbled and lost her balance, and was horrified when the baby was submerged fully into the lake. She quickly righted herself; her heart thundering wildly in her chest as she recovered the child from the cold water.

And the child gave out a lusty cry that was heard throughout the forest. The sound was a gift from the gods, a celebration of life.

$O_{n\varepsilon}$

November 1701

Hoo—*oo-ooooo! Hoo-oooooo!* The call of the owl rent the stillness of the night and was answered by the echoing hoot of its distant mate. Night Wind crouched beside the tall stockade fence surrounding the Indian village and listened expectantly. The owl calls were signals from the Lenape brave's friends; if the sound came again, he would know that it was safe to enter the camp of his enemy. The sentinels guarding the Iroquois compound would no longer be a threat.

Hoo-oo-oooo!

Night Wind smiled with grim satisfaction. Deer-That-Runs and Raven Feather had successfully killed the two Cayuga guards. The time had come for Night Wind to enter his enemy's village and kidnap the White Medicine Woman. He crept toward the compound entrance.

The air was crisp with the cold of late autumn, but Night Wind didn't feel the chill as he slipped past the gate into the Iroquois Cayuga village. There was barely enough moonlight to see, but the Lenape warrior preferred the darkness. If one of the Cayuga woke and spied him moving about the yard, Night Wind would be strung up and tortured until he was dead. The risks in entering his enemy's compound were high, but a young boy's life depended on Night Wind's success. He was determined to succeed at all costs.

The Indian paused several feet from the gate. Staying near the fence, he studied the circle of longhouses. The structures were huge, built of spaced vertical wooden poles covered with bark. The buildings housed up to twenty families, depending on their size, and differed greatly from the single-family wigwams of the Lenni Lenape.

Which one held the woman healer? Night Wind wondered, his gaze narrowing on the nearest longhouse. He would need all of his warrior's skills to steal her from the Cayuga. He would have to tread on silent feet past many matrons, many warriors. His only weapons were his ability to fight and the knife tucked into his breechcloth.

Tales of the woman's powers had traveled far . . . to the village of his people, the Lenni Lenape, to a land that was as green as this region by the great lake but not nearly as cold. The braves of his village had to hunt far now for their furs, far into the land of the Iroquois. It was on the last trip into the enemy's territory that Night Wind had heard of the White Medicine Woman.

The woman had brought a dead child back to life. She possessed magical healing powers that could cure the most terrible of diseases. Night Wind's half brother, Red Fox, was sick, and no one in his village had been able to help him, not even the shaman. Night Wind was determined to bring back the woman healer to cure Red Fox.

A rustle in the treetops outside the stockade startled Night Wind, and he pulled his knife from his breechcloth, his muscles coiled in readiness. Flattening himself against the fence, he forced himself to breathe slowly. He would kill any man who interfered. But nothing moved in the yard.

His senses alert for danger, the Lenape brave padded across the yard to the first of the large Iroquois longhouses. He carefully lifted the deer hide that curtained the doorway and peered inside. Night Wind saw a storage room filled with furs, food, and tools. Beyond the room, family cubicles lined the main section of the longhouse. Glowing embers were all that remained of the Cayuga's cooking fires.

A dog suddenly appeared from the nearest cubicle, stretching and sniffing the air. Night Wind eased down the deer hide, moving away from the entrance quickly before the animal could detect his presence. The dog whined, but then became silent.

The woman healer would have a special house, Night Wind decided. Such magical powers would be revered and rewarded with private quarters in which to work her magic.

Night Wind spied a small thatched structure outside the circle of longhouses, and he thought she must be there, in a place of her own, a hut that could have been built for the shaman—or the village sachem.

He moved toward the hut, tensing when a dog inside the nearest longhouse whimpered, and a second mongrel growled low in answer. To Night Wind's relief, the animals soon quieted.

With his knife in hand, Night Wind continued toward the hut's entrance. Raising the fur flap, he slipped inside and paused just inside the door until his gaze adjusted to the dark interior.

The Lenape warrior smiled. The figure lying on the sleeping mat was covered by furs, but he could tell it was a woman. *The White Medicine Woman,* he thought. He could see the outline of her form, the sweep of long hair across the animal hide covering.

Night Wind moved in to take her until he saw the dog lying at her feet. He froze, his mind gauging the size and danger of the animal. His left hand went to the pouch strapped to his legging and extracted a piece of dried venison.

The dog woke and rose, instantly detecting his presence. With his left hand extended with the offering of meat and his right hand firm about his knife handle, Night Wind called to the animal softly. As he lured the dog away from his master, the brave silently offered a prayer to the Great Spirit that the woman wouldn't awaken and bring the entire Iroquois tribe down on him. The dog growled low, but inched closer, pausing to sniff the air, before edging toward the man.

The woman murmured and shifted in her sleep. The dog arched its back, baring its teeth. Night Wind's heart raced until the woman settled down again.

"Mah! Take it." The Indian held out the meat, waving it temptingly before the dog. The animal stared at the meat and then eyed the man, edging nearer, whining in recognition of food, before moving back as if unsure whether to take Night Wind's offering.

The animal followed Night Wind as the Indian lured it outside the hut. The man stopped, crouched low, and waited until the animal started to eat the meat. Then, with a swift swipe of his knife, Night Wind took the dog's life. He killed it cleanly, instantly, before carrying the bleeding animal to the rear of the hut. The brave was sorry to have to kill it, but there was nothing else he could have done. The mongrel would have alerted the Cayuga of his presence.

Night Wind set down the animal and returned to the hut. Once inside, he put away his knife. Then, he crept toward the woman on the sleeping mat.

* * *

A hand clamped over Rebecca Morton's mouth, startling her awake. She screamed, but the only sound that escaped her was a muffled squeak which was effectively stifled when the man changed his hold. *An Indian brave,* she thought, her blood cold with fear. He was strong and smelled of bear grease. She struggled.

His grip tightened and was painful. She was on her stomach, pressed into the sleeping mat, her face turned to the side away from her assailant. Her teeth had cut the inside of her mouth, and she tasted blood.

Panic seized her, and Rebecca fought him to rise, but he was too powerful. Still, she continued to fight him.

"Ku-les'ta! Chitkwe'se," a deep, guttural voice hissed in her ear. *"Ala'pi!"*

At the strange Indian tongue, Rebecca renewed her struggles. The brave grabbed a handful of her hair and jerked her head back. She inhaled sharply at the pain; tears filled her eyes as he continued to hold her.

"Ku-les'ta! Do not fight, and I will not harm you."

Shocked by his English, she froze.

His voice softened, but was no less menacing. "I will let you go, but if you cry out, I will kill you with my *K'-sheeg-an.*"

The Indian shifted, and a knife was suddenly there for her to see. He held it before her gaze, allowing her a moment to comprehend his message.

"You will be silent?" he asked.

Rebecca tried to nod, but couldn't. After a few seconds, the Indian shifted his hands, releasing his hold on her hair and across her mouth, and she was able to move her head.

"Kihalaalit," he said. "Good."

She wanted to turn around, to see exactly who held her, but although he'd released her hair and mouth, he continued to press her firmly against the mat, belly down, face turned away.

"Who are you?" she asked softly; she didn't want to anger him. "What do you want?"

He gave a muffled exclamation of displeasure, and Rebecca's heart raced with new fear.

"I am *Tipaakke Shaakha*. In your language, my name is Night Wind."

Rebecca stiffened as he leaned in close until she could feel his warm breath on her neck. She had the impression that he was a large man, taller and more muscular than any of the Cayuga. Her blood froze with fear.

"You are not Cayuga," she said in a shaky whisper.

He hesitated. "I am Lenni Lenape. The Cayuga are Iroquois. They are our enemy."

Her mind raced with what he'd told her. How did the Indian get into the village? she wondered. What had happened to the Iroquois guards? And where was her dog? A frisson of apprehension ran down her spine as she remembered the animal who had lain beside her. "The dog—what have you done to it?"

"Chitkwe'se." His angry tone told her that he'd lost patience with her questions.

Rebecca felt her breath slam painfully within her chest, for she could guess what had happened to the Iroquois guards . . . and her dog . . .

"You killed it, didn't you? *You killed a helpless animal!*"

"You would have me die instead?" The English language fell easily but uncomfortably from his lips.

"Yes!" she gasped, feeling chilled. "The dog was one of God's poor creatures. You didn't have to murder it!"

What kind of man would do such a thing? she wondered.

A blood-thirsty, half-crazed savage!

Rebecca swallowed hard. She had seen much since her capture by the Cayuga. She'd seen men killed for simply being English. She'd seen white women tortured for refusing to obey. But she'd finally come to understand the Iroquois tribe. The Cayuga protected what they owned and killed only if they felt threatened. She knew nothing of the Lenape, but what she'd learned from the Iroquois. What she'd heard hadn't been pleasant.

Poor dog, she thought. The creature had been guarding her while she'd slept and had paid dearly for doing so.

Tears filled Rebecca's eyes as she remembered the dog's big eyes and wagging tail. Anger welled up inside, making her reckless.

"Murdering savage!" She started to struggle in earnest, bucking off the mat, kicking her feet. "Killing a helpless animal!" she cried, not bothering to soften her voice. "Are you going to kill me, too? Is that why you've come here?"

"Chitkwe'se." Night Wind clamped his hand back over her mouth, hissing with fury when she nipped his finger as he struggled to get a good hold.

When she continued to fight him, the Indian grabbed hold of her hair again, jerking her head up from the sleeping mat. "Do you wish to die, white woman?" He held his knife to her throat.

She gasped and was immediately still.

"Do you?" he growled.

She couldn't answer. The blade of his knife had pricked her skin, and she felt a drop of her own blood trickle down her neck. Never had she felt so terrified, not even when she'd first been taken by the Iroquois.

Night Wind was exasperated. Why wouldn't the woman stay quiet? Why did she go on so about a dead dog?

She whimpered deep in her throat and he pulled on her hair to silence her. The medicine woman was a continued threat to Night Wind. "You must be quiet!" he commanded harshly.

He removed his knife from her throat and shifted to sit on her back. Without conscious thought, he lowered his weight onto her back to hold her while he tied her hands. He heard the sudden whoosh of air as her breath left her lungs, and was startled when her body slumped, lifeless, onto the mat.

He touched her neck, felt the throbbing there, and sighed with relief. The White Medicine Woman wasn't dead; she was out cold.

Night Wind slung her unconscious form over his shoulder and quickly exited the hut. He hurried toward the gate, anxious to escape now that he had his captive.

He understood her anger about the dog, but he'd killed the animal because it had been necessary. A barking dog would have meant his death.

The woman was foolish. She must understand why he did this; she must know what the Iroquois did to their captured enemy.

Deer-That-Runs and Raven Feather waited for him outside the gate. Night Wind nodded at the two men, raising his burden to show their success, and the braves grinned.

The three fled into the forest. Deer-That-Runs went first, Night Wind followed next, with Raven Feather in the rear to watch for Iroquois.

They traveled far without stopping. Night Wind easily kept pace with his two friends, never faltering with his burden, for he was used to hunting and carrying big deer the same way.

The woman woke up after a time and started to fight him. Night Wind stopped, warned her to be still, and threatened to drop her if she didn't. Within seconds, she was dead weight again.

The Lenape braves ran through the forest. Night Wind would call a halt when it was time to stop. He would go as far as his strength allowed him, far enough away from the Iroquois to rest without worry.

The time came two hours later. The brave stopped, signaling to Deer-That-Runs that they would rest briefly. Night Wind set his burden on the ground and asked Deer-That-Runs to blindfold and tie her up. While Deer-That-Runs did this, Night Wind and Raven Feather scouted the area for a more secluded spot.

Raven Feather called out. He'd found a clearing, sheltered by fallen trees, rocks, and tall brush. Deer-That-Runs carried the woman to the sheltered forest clearing and then the braves took turns sleeping for a time.

Rebecca woke up to find herself seated on the damp ground, blindfolded, her wrists and ankles tied. She was even more frightened by the fact that she couldn't see to judge the extent of danger she was in. She had no idea where she was or how far from the Iroquois village they'd traveled, but she guessed they had come a long way.

I must have fainted. She was freezing although she'd worn her Cayuga clothing to sleep in, because the nights were getting colder. Her cape-like garment adequately covered her from neck to waist, including her arms, and her deerskin skirt was long, reaching nearly to her ankles. But, she had no leggings beneath the skirt, no moccasins on her feet, and her toes and legs felt frozen in the chill of the bitter night.

Rebecca tried to move her feet up under her for warmth, but her ankle bonds were too tight. She was sure she was going to freeze to death.

"I'm cold!" she exclaimed. "Can anyone hear me? I'm cold!"

She heard a movement directly behind her, and she spun toward the sound. "Who's there?" No one spoke, and she felt a trickle of alarm that grew rapidly toward hysteria. "Night Wind?"

There was no answer.

"Talk to me!" she cried. She could barely hear for the thundering of her heart beat. "I know you're there. If you're not Night Wind, then who are you?"

A long spat of unintelligible babble rent the quiet, and Rebecca shielded herself with her arms. It wasn't Night Wind. Whoever it was; he sounded fierce—and furious. She tensed as she heard him approach. Something fell across her legs, and she cried out with fright, until she realized that the brave had draped a fur over her. The Indian had understood that she was cold.

"Thank you." The tension left her at the man's kindness. Dare she try to communicate with him? "Do you speak English?" she said. If only her hands were free! She wanted to see her captors. How else would she find out how many Indians she'd have to escape? Her skin prickled.

A crunching noise signaled another's approach. "Deer-That-Runs speaks no English, Medicine Woman. He sees you are cold; he gives you bear skin."

"Night Wind?" she asked. She felt strange. She'd guessed who it was before he'd spoken.

"Kihiila. It is Night Wind." He was silent for a moment. "You are warmer?"

"Yes, yes, I am," she said, but she couldn't stop her body's trembling.

She heard him squat down beside her and felt him adjust the fur, tucking the animal hide about her legs. The scent of him was strong and pleasant, a strange combination of odors, of pine and the forest and the wind.

"You will be warm soon," he said, and she heard him start to rise.

She reached out and grabbed his arm, afraid he would leave. "Why did you kidnap me?" Her bound wrists burned.

He didn't answer.

"Please . . . won't you take off my blindfold so that I can see you?"

"No," the brave said, breaking away from her hold. He rose to his feet. "We leave soon. If you see, you will run."

"I won't run," she said, her voice rising on a note of desperation. "Where would I go? I don't know where I am!" Rebecca strained forward and tried to stand, but failed. "Please—it's so dark. Will you take off the blindfold if I promise not to run away?"

"I do not trust a white man's word."

"But I'm a woman."

The silence that followed was charged with a strange tension. "I know this," he said, "but I will not take off blindfold. Not yet. Soon, when we near Lenape village."

"Why did you capture me?" she cried. "I deserve to know!"

"You are the White Medicine Woman."

Rebecca sighed with impatience. "I'm no medicine woman."

"You saved Cayuga boy-child. Now you must save Lenape brave—Red Fox. My brother."

Oh dear Lord! Rebecca thought. *The man believes I'm a healer!*

"What's wrong with your brother?"

"He is sick. The shaman can't heal him. You will know what is wrong, and you will save him."

I'm going to die, she thought. *They'll find out I have no powers, and they'll kill me as surely as my toes get numb when it's cold.*

She'd have to escape at the first opportunity. Somehow she would convince them to take off her blindfold and the leather straps binding her hands and feet, and she would sneak away . . . or die trying.

Rebecca shivered. *Death.* Was that to be her fate? To die at the hands of the Lenape?

She'd been so close to freedom! What cruel trick of fate had snatched her out of the hands of the Iroquois to place her here? Tomorrow she was to have been adopted into the Cayuga tribe. As a new daughter of the Iroquois, she would have been free to leave the village, to come or go as she wished. Then she could have continued her journey to the Delaware Colony!

She had waited weeks, *months,* for the opportunity to escape the Cayuga. She'd been journeying to her aunt's in the Delaware Colony when the Iroquois had abducted her, her and the family of four who had been with her.

It was important that she leave soon. She'd been summoned by her sick aunt months ago. Her mother's sister had a child who needed to be looked after. Aunt Veronica was dying, and Rebecca was to see that the child was well cared for. What if Aunt Veronica was already dead? Where was cousin Elizabeth? Rebecca hated to think of the child helpless and all alone.

Curse Night Wind, Rebecca thought. *Curse the savage for ruining all of her plans!* She had been so close to being free, and now she was a captive of the Lenni Lenape.

Two

They continued on their journey after only a brief period of rest. Night Wind had removed Rebecca's blindfold and ankle bonds. Yet he still watched her like a hawk as if he expected her to run at any moment. He'd given her moccasins for her feet and allowed her to keep Deer-That-Runs' fur for warmth. Her words of gratitude died on her lips when she realized that his actions weren't out of kindness. He simply didn't want to carry her again.

Now, as her feet became sore and her body tired, Rebecca regretted asking to be untied. She'd been nauseous being carried over the Indian's shoulder, but at least her limbs and feet had been spared this torture.

Night Wind was in a hurry to get to his village. Rebecca knew it was concern for his brother that kept the Lenape warrior to a grueling pace. She, on the other hand, was far from anxious to get to the Lenape compound. Once there, she'd be expected to cure a dying brave . . . without medical skills or knowledge. If she failed, she was sure she would be put to death. Rebecca prayed that the opportunity presented itself for her to escape . . . or be rescued by the Cayuga. At least with the Cayuga, she had a chance for freedom.

They traveled single file. Deer-That-Runs was in the lead, before Rebecca, while Night Wind came next with Raven Feather in the rear.

As she walked carefully through the forest brush, Rebecca experienced a prickle of awareness of the man directly behind her. The savage who'd held his knife to her throat and threatened to kill her if she didn't cooperate.

She'd had little chance to study him since he'd removed her blindfold. She'd noted the obvious differences in appearance between the Lenape and the Cayuga. These Lenape braves wore their hair long, unlike some of the Cayuga, whose heads were plucked of hair except for little tufts that adorned their crowns. Others of the Iroquois tribe wore their hair in war crests that reminded Rebecca of the comb on a rooster's head.

The two things that had immediately struck Rebecca about Night Wind was his dark, glistening gaze and his build. Each time their eyes met, little bumps rose along her arms and neck. She could feel that piercing gaze on her back as she tried to keep pace with Deer-That-Runs.

She was wrong about his size. He wasn't as overwhelming as she'd thought. His form cut a powerful figure, a figure that was no less impressive for his lack of height. She hoped that Night Wind had no idea how he affected her.

"Yun," Night Wind said. "We stop here."

Rebecca halted and sunk gratefully to the ground. Night Wind and Raven Feather approached from behind and joined Deer-That-Runs where the brave stood waiting for his leader's command. The three Indians conversed rapidly in their tongue. Rebecca glanced up, saw the intensity of their expressions, and wondered what they were talking about.

There was a hint of soft brightening in the November sky. Dawn would soon be upon them. Would they continue to travel by the light of day? Was that what they were trying to decide?

Night Wind came to Rebecca's side and untied her wrists. He offered her a hand. "Come."

She studied his long fingers before her gaze traveled the length of his fringed leggings, moving upward over his covered thighs to his breechcloth and the knife tucked into the leather ties at his waist. He wore a cape made of deerskin, which covered his chest and draped one shoulder. His right shoulder was bare, but he seemed oblivious to the cold.

His friends wore fringed hunting jackets made of animal skin, which Rebecca thought might be otter. Instead of leggings, they had tall moccasins that covered their legs to mid-thigh. All three wore earrings of beaded shells threaded on strings of leather. Savages, she thought.

"Come," Night Wind repeated, sounding impatient. Her gaze encountered his ebony stare. Something in his eyes frightened her. "We move to a clearing behind those trees," he said. "There." He gestured off the trail toward a dense thicket of evergreens. "It will be safe for healer *kou een*. To sleep. Tomorrow we go quickly. Red Fox is waiting."

Without a word, Rebecca grabbed the Indian's hand and he assisted her to her feet. Her heart thumped hard as she stood upright, within inches of his lean, lithe form. She saw his eyes flame as he gazed at her. Her body flushed with heat in sudden physical awareness of him.

"Thank you," she said in a shaky voice. Rebecca backed away from his disturbing presence. Her breathing became constricted as she walked away and sensed his continued study of her.

"You are warm?" he asked from directly behind her.

She gasped, for she hadn't heard him follow. Rebecca swallowed and faced him, silently willing the cadence of both her heart and her breathing to resume a steady pace.

"I'm fine, thank you," she said. *Hot,* she thought. *Why do I feel so hot?*

She gestured toward her feet. "Thank you for giving me the moccasins."

He gave her a slight smile. "Deer-That-Runs makes fine moccasins. Making moccasins is women's work, but he likes it. You must thank *him.*" He paused, and his expression was serious again. The slight sign of good humor was gone. "We did not think you would sleep in your *lenhoksi'na.*"

"No," she said. She didn't usually sleep with her moccasins. Her gaze went to the Indian who had made her footwear. He had gathered sticks and twigs for a fire and was carrying them to the hidden clearing. Night Wind was right; the embroidered moccasins were finer than any she'd ever seen among the Cayuga.

"Deer-That-Runs," she said, "is he a relative of yours?" Neither of the two braves had spoken to her. Had Night Wind forbidden them to make conversation with her?

Night Wind frowned. "Relative?"

She nodded. "Is he your brother? Your cousin?"

His brow cleared. "Deer-That-Runs is of the Wolf Clan. I am of the Wolf Clan. In that way, we are brothers. We do not have the same mother. In that way, you English would believe we are not brothers."

Rebecca inclined her head. She understood about clan ties from her life with the Iroquois. Deer-That-Runs was considered family to Night Wind because they were of the same clan. Was the line of clan descent determined by the mother as it was with the Cayuga? She asked Night Wind and was told that the descent in the Lenape tribe was like the Iroquois, determined by the women. She wondered what else about the two tribes might be the same?

She searched for Raven Feather and found the brave several yards away with his bow drawn, his alert gaze sweeping the forest. The Indian was hunting for something for them to eat. "Raven Feather—is he also of the Wolf clan?"

Night Wind studied Raven Feather. "Raven Feather is of the *Pele'*. The Turkey Clan. He is of different clan, but he is *Nee-tees.*"

"He is your friend."

"Kihiila," he said with a nod.

Rebecca thought quickly about what she'd learned. The bond between the three braves would make her chances of escape more difficult. Each Indian was committed to bringing her to their village. Red Fox as Night Wind's brother would be of the same clan as Deer-That-Runs, therefore, Deer-That-Runs would consider the ill brave his brother. As a good friend of Night Wind, Raven Feather's loyalty would be unquestionable. *Or would it?*

"How much farther to your village?" she asked. *Could she get Raven Feather to help her?* She watched the young brave, wondering how she would communicate with him. She knew some of the Cayuga language, but she knew nothing of the Lenape tongue. Her spirits plummeted at the realization that she would find no help from Night Wind's friend.

The heat of Night Wind's gaze drew her attention back to the leader. She flushed. Had he read her thoughts of escape?

"Many woods yet," Night Wind said. "Tomorrow. Perhaps not."

Rebecca's mind went blank. "Pardon me?"

His dark eyes narrowed. "You ask how far is my village. We travel many woods yet."

She nodded. "I see."

"You are not thinking of running away?"

"How could I?" she burst out angrily. "I don't know where I am!"

"Good. There are many evils in the forest. Big bears. Hungry *Tum-ma.*"

"Tum-ma?"

"Wolf." He grinned, and she stared, caught by the way humor had transformed his features. His face was startlingly handsome, his skin a golden copper color. His jaw was angular, his nose ruggedly formed. Studying him, Rebecca felt her skin tingle while her blood rushed to warm her entire body.

Deer-That-Runs came out from behind the thicket, gesturing for Night Wind and Rebecca to come. Relieved at the distraction, Rebecca started forward. Night Wind caught her arm. She froze, her pulse racing, as she turned to face him. Her arm burned where he held it.

"You will not leave us, White Medicine Woman," he warned her. His fingers tightened about her arm. The Indian's expression was fierce. "If you escape, we will find you."

His tone chilled Rebecca to the bone.

She raised her chin defiantly. "If I escape, no one will be able to find me!" She said it with more confidence then she felt. But she knew it would be true, because if she did escape then it would be because of a miracle. With God on her side, how could she not be successful?

"You must stop calling me the 'White Medicine Woman'!" she exclaimed irritably. "My name is Rebecca. Rebecca Morton."

How could she not be annoyed each time he referred to her as a medicine woman? She wasn't a doctor; she wasn't a healer. How had the story traveled so far? She was sure with each telling her power became more grand. What would he do if he learned the truth?

"The Cayuga will come for me," she told him, "and then I'll be free of you. They'll rescue me, and there will be nothing you can do about it!"

He raised one eyebrow, but didn't say a word. He didn't have to; his face said it all for him. Harsh. Forbidding. With tight lips, he gestured for Rebecca to proceed him. Then he fell into step behind her.

Rebecca clutched the ends of her fur wrap until her knuckles ached from squeezing so hard. *Savage!* She was so furious she could scream. How dare he kidnap her and keep her a prisoner? *Damn him!* Night Wind was like a jailer guarding his condemned charge.

Dealing with him was like playing a game of chance. As a skilled partner, he might think he's winning, she vowed, but in the end, I will best him!

Pine needles carpeted the clearing. The pungent, earthy smell of dried evergreen permeated the air, filling her senses. Rebecca readjusted the animal skin about her shoulders as she searched for a comfortable spot to rest.

"Meshake." Deer-That-Runs had formed a bed of pine needles and was signing for her to sit down. *"Meshake."*

She forced a smile. "Thank you." She wished she knew the Lenape translation, so that she could properly thank Deer-That-Runs for his kindness. He wasn't responsible for her captivity. His friend—the dark brute—was.

Aware of Night Wind's disturbing gaze, she sat down on the bed of pine needles. A quick glance in Night Wind's direction made her inwardly smile with satisfaction. The leader was alternately scowling at her and Deer-That-Runs. She gave Deer-That-Runs a genuine smile.

Raven Feather entered the clearing moments later, carrying a freshly killed rabbit. Rebecca took one look at the furry creature and turned away. Her stomach felt queasy. Her head hurt, her muscles ached. The only thing she cared to do was sleep.

Dare she believe she'd be safe while she slept? As long as they believed she could cure Red Fox, she'd be safe, she decided. They wouldn't harm her. The Indians wanted—needed—her alive.

She repositioned the fur around her and lay down to rest, cloaked with warmth. Soon, she relaxed. The braves talked in low voices and the scent of wood smoke drifted to her nose. The savages were preparing their food, so she wouldn't have to worry about them bothering her for a while.

Moments later, Rebecca fell asleep.

Night Wind stared at the sleeping woman and was troubled. Why did the healer want to escape? He knew she thought of leaving them; he had seen it in her eyes . . . eyes the color of a clear summer sky. He could see the discontent in the downward turn of her pink lips.

He'd been surprised to find out that the healer was young. She looked good to him, and that surprised him, too. She was, after all, a white woman, and normally white women held little appeal for him.

Was it because she had the powers of magic? He had felt his body burn when he'd touched her arm. He had felt his manhood harden when she'd gazed into his eyes.

She didn't look like someone who had special pow-

ers, but she must, for she had brought a child back
to life.

Night Wind decided that she must have cast a spell
on him. Why else would he be drawn to her? He
would have to be careful. She could cure the sick, and
that was good. But what if she used her magic for
evil? To control him and make him forget about Red
Fox?

Deer-That-Runs was to stand guard first, so Night
Wind settled himself on the ground several feet from
where the white woman slept. He closed his eyes to
get some sleep, but he could see her still. Haunted by
her image, he was unable to relax.

Her hair was brown like the pelt of a *Nakuee,* mixed
with the red of an *Oopus.* Unusual, this hair of two
colors like the beaver and the fox.

Rebecca's skin was smooth and white. Her eyes
shone with the brightness of the sun, and she had
spirit.

He was physically moved by the healer, but he had
to remember that she had been with the Iroquois, the
enemy of his people. The woman must be watched.
He wouldn't allow her to escape or trick him. He
wouldn't allow her to overpower him with her magic.

They would travel by day, Rebecca learned shortly
upon awakening after a few hours' rest. Night Wind
wasn't about to sleep the whole day away, not with
Red Fox lying sick, perhaps dying, and waiting for
the one who would heal him.

She was hungry when they again resumed their
trek. She wished now that she had eaten some of the
cooked rabbit. It had been cold, but at least it had
been roasted over the fire. She had no idea when
they'd stop next or what they would eat once they had

done so. The thought of the charred rabbit made her mouth water and her stomach burn with hunger.

Night Wind had taken the lead. Rebecca studied his back as she stumbled in his wake. They were no longer traveling along the cleared trail. They used the cover of the brush. A number of times Rebecca became snagged by briars. Her legs were scratched, and her fur wrap carried pieces of broken barbs.

By the time they stopped again, a few hours after they had begun, Rebecca's hunger and thus her temper had gotten the better of her. She was tired of the exhausting pace.

Night Wind handed her a corn cake. *"Yun. Miitshe."*

Rebecca stared at the cake before she grabbed it and began to eat. "Why didn't you give me some of this before?"

He gazed at her from beneath lowered lids. "You eat what we eat, or you not eat."

"I'm tired of doing what you say," she argued. "You need my help, yet you treat me like a slave!"

"Kwe!" He shook his head. "You wish not to be here. You wish to run away. You think I should treat you like revered matron?" He made a sound of disgust. "You are *Kipitsheoote.* Fool-ish, Reb-bec-ca."

It was the first time he had called her by her name, and the effect on her senses was strong and immediate. Her heart raced within her breast. Her head swam as she took a bite of the dry corn cake. *I'm dizzy because I walked for miles and haven't eaten.* But deep down, she knew that the fluttering in her stomach wasn't because of hunger. She had gone past the point when her belly had painfully demanded food.

To her dismay, Night Wind sat down right beside her and began to eat a corn cake.

"You obviously don't trust me," she said, hoping

to make him see reason. "Why then won't you let me go? Why trust me to cure your sick brother?"

He turned to stare at her, his expression fierce, something in his eyes warning her that she was treading on dangerous territory with this line of conversation. "You will cure Red Fox or you will suffer."

The calm, soft way he'd delivered his answer was more frightening than if he'd pulled his knife and held it to her throat. Rebecca had trouble swallowing the dry corn cake.

She decided to court danger. She needed to know how he reacted to her challenging him. "You had no right to take me from the Cayuga. I demand to be let go. I would have been free now if it weren't for you! I was to have been adopted into the tribe. Damn you! I could have left after that—any time I wanted!"

"You would become daughter of the Iroquois?" Night Wind had grown very still, his body tense, as he held her gaze.

She averted her glance. "Yes."

"The Iroquois are our enemy."

Rebecca bristled at his accusing tone. "Well, I'm not your enemy, but then neither am I your friend!"

He grunted and went back to eating. "And you ask why we treat you like slave."

"I'm not a slave!"

Night Wind paused in taking a bite. "You should be treated like enemy, but you are healer so we are good to you." He bit down on the cake, chewed, and then swallowed it. "You are medicine woman, but you have to show us." He hesitated, and it seemed that his mind was actively considering something. "You must show us your healing powers . . . or we will remember you are Iroquois. We will remember you are our enemy."

Rebecca was terrified by the Indian's words. "You will kill me if I don't heal your brother?"

He nodded, his face solemn. "This is so. But if you make Red Fox well, we will reward you."

"You'll let me go?" She became so excited at the prospect of being released that she never realized that he hadn't actually promised this.

Rebecca refused to think of the consequences should she fail. "I'll go with you to your village, and I will see what I can do for Red Fox."

Night Wind inclined his head. "You will heal him," he said.

"I will . . . try." Rebecca glanced across the clearing toward the other two Indians, who were watching her closely. They mustn't doubt her ability to heal. "I will cure your brother," she said with feigned confidence.

Rebecca knew that she'd better pray long and hard; she was going to need all of the Heavenly Father's divine assistance. *Good Lord,* she thought. *I just promised to do the impossible!*

Night Wind was satisfied. The woman had said that she would heal Red Fox, and he believed her. He had allowed her to believe he'd let her go, and she had seemed pleased.

He didn't understand the white woman's anger, for he had explained about his brother. She was a gifted one; she should understand. Why had she become angry when all he wanted was for her to use her healing powers and make Red Fox well?

He had taken her from the Iroquois, but soon she would see that the Lenape were good people, kind people. She would like them much better than the enemy—the Cayuga.

Soon they would be at his village near the river. Was Red Fox already dead? No! Night Wind thought. His brother was alive, alive and waiting for the one who would help him.

Hadn't Night Wind prayed to *Kitanito'wet* for guidance? And hadn't the Great Spirit sent him a message? A message that would send him into his enemy's village to steal away the White Medicine Woman?

Red Fox was alive. He had to be. Night Wind turned to briefly eye the one who could save Red Fox, noting the softness of her long hair, which she wore unbound.

Yes, the healer can make my brother well, he thought, facing ahead. He himself had felt her magic. He could feel her power whenever she was near him. Was she a witch? Many of his people feared the powers of a witch, but not Night Wind. Still, he must be careful.

She was *uitiissa* for a white woman. *For any woman,* he decided. He studied her out of the corner of his eye. He wondered how it would be to lie with her, to touch her pale skin, to taste the honey of her mouth. Were her white breasts full and firm? Would she cry out and surround his waist with her legs as he thrust his staff into her woman's form?

A tremor of desire coursed through him, making his loins harden and his penis stiffen. He fought it, but the ache wouldn't leave him. It taunted him with the woman's charms; it lured him toward the forbidden.

He must not think about Reb-bec-ca Mor-ton. He must remember Red Fox and forget the haunting beauty of the one who would save his brother's life.

She sighed in her sleep, and as if drawn, he scrambled to her side. His hand hovered over the silken strands of her dark hair. He wondered if it would feel as soft as it looked, and his fingers lowered as if to touch it.

"Kayah! K'pet'ching'weXi."

Night Wind jerked back his hand as if burnt as Raven Feather approached, a grin on his face, his hand displaying his recently acquired game—a gray squirrel.

The brave jumped to his feet and slapped Raven Feather on the back. *"Kwe,* Raven Feather. You have done well with the hunt again."

Although Raven Feather would have cleaned the squirrel, Night Wind offered to do it for him. He needed something to keep him occupied.

Something to keep his mind off Reb-bec-ca Morton.

Three

Rebecca stumbled behind Night Wind, her anxiety increasing with each step she took. They were near the Lenape village; she could feel it. It was nothing that Night Wind had said or done, but she knew it just the same.

The air had become colder. Dusk was upon them, and the wind teased the treetops above, rubbing branches together to create eerie sounds. A crackle in the forest brush alerted them to the presence of animals, but it wasn't raccoon or bear she feared. It was the prospect of meeting Night Wind's people.

Rebecca stared at Night Wind's back and thought of escaping. Wouldn't she have a better chance for survival if she ran? Yet, how could she flee when Night Wind was ahead and his two friends behind her? She'd not get five feet without their knowledge. She should have escaped during the night when only one of them was awake.

She shifted her fur wrap, grateful for its presence as well as her new deerskin moccasins. Rebecca's feet were blistered and sore, but she considered herself lucky. Without the moccasins, her soles would have been in worse condition.

For a moment, she allowed herself to soften toward the Indian who had given her the footwear. Then she remembered that she wouldn't have needed the moccasins if they hadn't taken her from the Cayuga. She would have been wearing her own moccasins. She would have been an adopted daughter of the Iroquois by now if not for Night Wind and his two friends. And she would have been free and on her way to her Aunt Veronica's in the Delaware Colony.

Her teeth grated until her jaw ached. Rebecca stared at the back of Night Wind's head and pondered all the horrid things she would do to him if their positions were reversed, and she was the one in control.

The first thing I'd do would be to take his knife away, hold it to his throat to frighten him, and then scratch my name into his bare shoulder. Rebecca was surprised at her own merciless thoughts, yet she experienced a sense of gleeful satisfaction as she allowed her imagination free reign.

She would tie him between two trees, taunt him with threats, and then she would go to her aunt's, leaving him there to wonder if he'd ever get himself loose.

Her gaze fastened on Night Wind's shoulder, the one that rose tantalizingly above his fur wrap. Rebecca's heart thumped hard. How could she mar that golden copper skin? Did it feel as smooth and as supple as it looked? And how could she tie him to two trees when his strength was such that she'd never overpower him?

Rebecca could picture him without the fur. His chest would be broad and muscular, but not overly so. His skin would be smooth and his nipples dark.

She recalled how he'd carried her over his shoulder and wondered at the power of his legs. His thighs, she supposed, were taut and sinewy, his calves thick. She had a clear image of him riding a woman, like when she'd accidentally seen Joseph Worly riding Kate Hampshire when she was child and had stumbled upon the couple in the woods.

Rebecca gasped, shocked by such thoughts about the Indian. The man had kidnapped her, blindfolded and tied her up. How could she think such sensual— private—things about him?

She tried to concentrate on other methods of torture that would give her a sense of satisfaction and make the heathen pay for his capture of her. Anything to take her mind off the intimate act between a man and a woman . . . between him and her. But her imagination betrayed her, bringing forth startlingly frank pictures, and Rebecca felt her face flush with embarrassment. Dear Lord, don't ever let the savage know what she'd been thinking!

The day went on, and darkness cloaked the land. Rebecca's muscles were screaming for relief when Night Wind called a halt. Rebecca nearly fell in her haste to sit down on the ground; she was so grateful to be able to rest her sore calves and feet. She closed her eyes, ignoring the three Indians who conversed quietly nearby until Night Wind spoke her name from directly above her.

"You are hungry?" he asked.

She glanced up, caught by the glitter in his dark gaze. "How do you know English so well?" she asked.

"Come," he said, ignoring her question. He held out his hand to her.

Ignoring his outstretched arm, she tried to get up on her own. Her muscles refused to cooperate. Disgusted that she was forced to accept his assistance, Rebecca painfully rose. The warmth of his copperskinned hand engulfed hers as her body came into close contact with his. Her heart started beating a rapid tattoo at his nearness. He released her abruptly, stepping away, and her heartbeat and breathing returned to normal.

"You will pick berries," he said.

She stared at him in astonishment. "It's November. There are no berries! I'm tired and sore. Can't you understand that?"

Night Wind scowled at her for a moment, and then his lips curved with amusement. "Come, Medicine Woman. Didn't the Cayuga teach you anything? Woman prepares the food in my village. You will gather berries for us to eat!" He spun from her abruptly and moved to a patch of what appeared to be dead briars.

"Here," he said. Among a patch of leafless briars hung a couple of dried dark berries.

"No."

His eyes flashed with anger. "You will pick berries!"

Rebecca swallowed hard. "They're safe to eat?" She studied the bush doubtfully. Then, she turned as she felt the intensity of Night Wind's gaze. There was a twinkle in his ebony eyes. "You're laughing at me! Why?" She glared at him. "Are you playing some sort of game?"

He raised his eyebrows. "Game?" He frowned. "To eat is no game. It must be done. It is shameful that you not know about a woman's work, but you will learn. You must find more of these berries while I hunt for meat." He reached for his knife, slipping it easily from his legging strings. He held the weapon out to her, handle first. "Or you can kill squirrel while I pick berries. It matters not to me." His tone challenged her, ridiculed her for not knowing a woman's place.

Rebecca shuddered with revulsion as she stared at the knife. Their gazes locked for several seconds. Her heart raced within her breast at the tension she felt when she was the focus of this man's attention. She averted her glance. "I'll pick berries," she said in a low voice.

"Good."

As she rounded the bush, preparing to pick the tiny fruit, Rebecca watched Night Wind return to his friends. He spoke with them briefly, before he disappeared past evergreens into the forest. She silently cursed all three of them.

There were more berries than Rebecca had thought, and soon her left hand was full and a small pile of the dried fruit lay on the ground next to where she knelt. She rose, carefully cradling her handful, and approached Deer-That-Runs where he crouched to start a fire. He held a stick upright between his palms and rotated it back and forth in a spinning motion, the tip against a fallen tree log. Rebecca stood a moment, observing him in silence, amazed when the friction caused a spark, which ignited when the Indian added dead leaves and dried grass.

Always before, Rebecca had been sleeping when the Indians had started a fire; she had never seen a fire started in this way. There was no need to do it in the Cayuga village, for the Iroquois used the hot embers from the previous day's cooking fires to begin the fire for the new day. This method of fire-starting, Rebecca knew, was difficult without the flint used by the English, but Deer-That-Runs had accomplished the task quickly and efficiently, making the chore look easy.

Having successfully started his fire, Deer-That-Runs looked up at her in question.

"You do that well," she said.

He frowned.

"The fire." Rebecca gestured toward the rapidly building flames. She moved closer, unafraid of the brave, and set down her handful of berries. "You are skilled in fire-making. *O-jis-ta.*" She used the Cayuga word for "fire," hoping that there were similarities between the Lenape language and the dialect spoken by the Iroquois Cayuga, but she could tell by the brave's puzzled expression that there were none.

She picked up the stick Deer-That-Runs had used and rolled it between her palms, mimicking his earlier actions. "You make a good fire." She nodded and smiled as she continued the motions.

The brave's expression brightened. *"Taande."* He grinned, repeating the word, as he added fuel to the fire.

"Taande," Rebecca said. "Fire."

Deer-That-Runs spoke quickly in his own tongue, and while his words were unintelligible to her, she knew he'd understood that she'd given him a compliment. He'd understood and was pleased.

Raven Feather approached from outside the clearing of their camp, and Deer-That-Runs said something to his friend. Raven Feather looked at Rebecca and grinned. Suddenly, she felt like grinning back at them.

"Okottimaang," Deer-That-Runs said, studying Rebecca's pile of berries. *"Hit kung."* He rose from the fire and searched the forest floor, returning to them after some time when he'd found a rock that was flat and wide. Next, he scooped up her berries and set them on the rock, which he then held up for her to see. *"Lo'kas."*

"Dish?" she guessed. *"Lo'kas."*

"Lo'kas," he repeated, nodding. He emptied off the make-shift dish and handed it to her empty.

She nodded. "Thank you. I was looking for something to carry them." Rebecca returned to the bush to retrieve the pile of berries and pick some more.

It seemed like a long time passed since Night Wind had left them. With no berries left to pick, Rebecca

decided to try to converse with his two Indian friends.
She used hand signals to ask questions.

"How far to your village?" she asked, wondering
if they were close; she had a feeling that they were.
Why, if it was true, had they stopped to rest?

The three people were seated around the fire, enjoying the warmth on a rapidly cooling night. Rebecca
stood and gestured with her hands to form squares
signifying houses. "How far?" she said. She walked
a few feet and stretched out her arms to show distance.

The braves chuckled, amused by her antics.

"Your people," she said, her gaze straying for a second in the direction Night Wind had gone. Rebecca
quickly searched her brain. "Lenni Lenape." She
pointed toward Raven Feather. "Your people. Village.
How far?" She lifted her feet, pretending to be walking.

Deer-That-Runs had risen to his feet and was dancing about, joining in Rebecca's game. Rebecca
laughed, enjoying his silliness, until Raven Feather
cried out and spoke excitedly to his friend. Deer-That-
Runs listened with rapt attention, and then he smiled,
nodding. He transferred his gaze to Rebecca.

"Week wam." The brave grinned, his eyes twin-
kling. He made hand motions, that Rebecca realized
depicted a house.

"Week wam," she murmured and then brightened.
"Wigwam!" she exclaimed, and Deer-That-Runs nodded happily and then danced about, acting silly.
"Many wigwams," she said. "Vil-lage." But the brave
ignored her, caught up in his dance.

Affected by the Indian's lighthearted mood, Rebecca watched and giggled as Raven Feather joined
in. Once they settled down and she had their attention
again, she used exaggerated hand signals to ask more
questions. She enjoyed their attempts at conversation;
she was both surprised and charmed by this playful

side of the Lenape. For the first time since her capture by Night Wind and his friends, she was feeling hopeful that everything would be all right.

It was Raven Feather's turn to ask questions. He waved his arms and danced about, but Rebecca couldn't understand what he wanted to know. They were chuckling, amused by the brave's efforts to make himself understood, when Night Wind returned, coming upon them silently, startling them from their laughter.

"Night Wind!" Rebecca exclaimed, rising to her feet.

He glowered at her, and she drew back, surprised. "You will not speak with Deer-That-Runs and Raven Feather. You will not charm them from their mission." His tone was clipped, his expression angry.

Rebecca recoiled from his verbal attack, hurt. "I was merely talking—"

"Enough!" he said, promptly dismissing her. His gaze sought his two friends. "Do not be taken in by her," he told them in their own language. "She wants only to escape, and she will use any methods to do this. We cannot allow this. Red Fox needs her."

"This is true?" Deer-That-Runs said, eyeing the woman suspiciously. "She has said this?"

Night Wind nodded.

Tension filled the air as the braves studied the Medicine Woman.

"We will watch her," Raven Feather. "She will not escape."

"What did you tell them?" Rebecca cried, her expression anxious.

"That you will try to escape, and we must not let you."

She shook her head. "I promised to help Red Fox, didn't I?"

"Because I promised you will die if you don't. How

can I trust such words if they are forced?" Night Wind spun from her abruptly and moved away to prepare the squirrel that Rebecca had just realized he'd been carrying. He knelt on the ground, set down the animal, and slide his knife down the squirrel's belly.

Rebecca glared at him.

He looked up from the animal. "You have something to say to me, Reb-bec-ca?"

"How do you know English so well? You've never answered me." Rebecca stood with her hands on her hips.

Night Wind looked at the ground before he answered. "I am my father's eldest son. Our village was once many suns east of this place. I was sent to the nearby trading post for goods. The Englishman there was a teacher and liked to teach this Lenni Lenape boy." He gave a twisted smile. "I know your language very well, white woman."

Rebecca turned away from his dark stare, silently relieved that she could speak with him in her own language. That would help her more than he realized.

Annoyed, hurt, and more than a little angry, Rebecca stayed to herself until it was time to eat. She debated whether to refuse food, but then she quickly remembered the last time she'd done so. The only one she'd be hurting by doing this was herself. Besides, if she did have a chance to escape—and she was seriously considering running tonight—she would need all the energy she could garner. She would need a clear head and full stomach if she were to be successful.

The crude meal the Indians prepared wasn't bad. Raven Feather had soaked the berries Rebecca had gathered in the water he'd carried in a skin sack. The berries weren't plump and juicy like they would have been when they were fresh, but the moisture made them easier to chew and swallow.

The squirrel had been roasted over the fire and had

a pleasant smoky flavor, which Rebecca attributed to the addition of leaves to the fire. There was just a little share of meat for each of them, but along with the berries, it was a satisfying meal.

Soon, the Indians and their captive were on the trail again. Rebecca studied her surroundings carefully as she walked. Tomorrow, she thought. If she had understood Deer-That-Runs correctly, they would be reaching the Indian village sometime tomorrow. If she were going to escape, it would have to be soon.

Four

"He!"

Rebecca froze as the strange sound came again from the dense forest directly ahead. She felt the sudden tension within Night Wind's body, and chills of fear ran down her back.

"He, Tipaakke Shaakha!"

She gaped in astonishment when suddenly Night Wind laughed. He flashed her and his two friends a slow smile over his left shoulder. Then, he cupped his hands to his mouth and shouted back. *"O-ho!"* His cry was jubilant. "Is that you, Thunder Arrow?" He called in his language.

He waved Rebecca and his two traveling companions forward as several figures emerged from behind trees. The small traveling party was soon surrounded by a large band of heavily painted savages.

Rebecca gasped and moved closer to Night Wind, unconsciously seeking a grip on his muscled arm. The tattooed and painted faces of the men made them look fierce and blood-thirsty, nothing like the three braves who had kidnapped her. These Indians appeared bent on making war.

Soon though, Rebecca relaxed. The way Night Wind was conversing with these men meant that he knew them. These must be friends from his village. They had finally arrived at their destination. Her mouth went dry. The moment Rebecca most feared was here.

The Indians spoke rapidly, and Rebecca studied them, eyeing the group apprehensively. They were such a fierce looking band of men. She saw their obvious pleasure at seeing Night Wind, and briefly she wondered at the relationship of one man in particular, the one who was doing the most talking. The brave had a tattooed face and a bulky body covered with bear fur.

She'd been wrong to assume that all Lenape braves wear their hair long, Rebecca thought. Some of the men were bald but for their scalp locks much like the Iroquois. A few wore their ears slit along the upper rim, and the flesh hung down forming a ring, some of which were torn.

Their dress varied. They all wore breechcloths or loincloths with leggings or high moccasins that covered their calves. Some of the braves wore hunting jackets like Deer-That-Runs and Raven Feather, while others wore fur mantles like Night Wind's. But unlike her kidnapper who wore nothing over his one shoulder, allowing the cold to caress his bare skin, the braves, who wore furs over one arm, had fabric sleeves to cover the other arm. Sleeves of white man's cloth. Rebecca chose not to dwell on how they might have acquired the muslin.

The mood among the Indians suddenly changed. She studied Night Wind and wondered whether the men were discussing Red Fox, the ill brave.

"What's wrong?" she asked, tugging on his arm. "Is it Red Fox?"

He nodded as he shot her a glance, his expression worried. "Red Fox is alive, but he is not good."

Night Wind spoke to his friends. Rebecca had difficulty breathing when she became the focus of the Indians' stares.

"I have brought the White Medicine Woman," Night Wind said in his native tongue. "She will heal Red Fox. She will cure our sick brother."

"What are you telling them?" Rebecca asked, her voice sounding anxious.

Night Wind fixed her with his narrowed gaze. She squeezed his arm as he studied her. "I tell them the truth," he said after a long pause. "I tell them that I have brought the White Medicine Woman and that you have promised to heal Red Fox."

"What if I can't help him?" she said. "What if Red Fox dies?"

A flash of anger lit up Night Wind's eyes, making him appear fierce, frightening. "You will heal him, or *you* will die."

She gasped, blanching.

"Come," he said, his tone softening. "We are near my village—*Tulpeuta-nai*. Do not fear until you see Red Fox. Do not be afraid of what might not be."

Rebecca allowed herself to be led toward the Lenape village, wondering if this short journey could be a walk to her death.

The Indian compound was a cluster of domed wig-wams and small cabins, each big enough to house one family. The scattering of homes formed three sides to the village's public yard and the Indians' source of water—a small river—closed the fourth side of the square. There was no stockade fence about the Lenape village to protect the inhabitants or their homes from enemies.

There was a great commotion as the Indians and Rebecca entered the village. Cooking fires glowed in the darkening autumn sky, and the scent of roasting meat filled the air, making Rebecca's stomach rumble with hunger. Women and children came out of their wigwams to greet the returning braves. Dogs yapped and howled, and a little Indian boy ran to greet Night Wind, hugging him and laughing when the warrior lifted the child high and shook him playfully, before putting him down again.

The residents of Night Wind's village surrounded the newcomers. Rebecca was thrust into the center of curious women and children, who pulled on her hair, touched her white skin, and tugged hard on her clothing. She was overwhelmed by the crowd, and as the villagers pushed and grabbed at her, she felt herself stumble and go down. She panicked, wondering if she was to be trampled to death.

Suddenly, Night Wind was there, ordering his people away, pulling Rebecca to her feet. He tucked her against his side as he spoke rapidly to his people. Relieved, her heart racing from the ordeal, Rebecca was curious to know what he was saying.

"Come," he said to her as some of the Indians dispersed, returning to their homes. "I take you to Red Fox."

Rebecca's heart thundered within her breast. She was afraid to see Red Fox, the brave she was supposed to heal.

A small gathering of Lenape followed Night Wind and Rebecca as they crossed the public square and headed toward a small wigwam secluded from the others. They passed the largest building in the village, constructed close to the middle of the square. The Indians' ceremonial house, Rebecca thought. Smoke rose from a hole in the dome-shaped roof. There were cabins made of bark and domed wigwams of thatch. The small sheds by many of these wigwams were too small for living; Rebecca decided that they had been built for storage.

The structure they went toward was built of bent wooden poles and covered not with tree bark, but with animal hides and dried thatch. Night Wind raised the deer skin that shielded the door opening and gestured for Rebecca to precede him. She went inside. As her eyes adjusted to the interior of the wigwam, she saw a fire burning in a pit dug in the center of the dirt floor. Rebecca wondered if the fire was for heat, for cooking, or for both.

Her gaze went immediately to the figure lying on the raised sleeping platform. The golden glow cast by the fire highlighted the ill brave, and Rebecca was surprised to note that the Indian looked small, almost lost upon his bed. With a rapidly beating pulse, she saw that the wigwam was full. Family members, crouched near the bed, stared at her, waiting in expectation.

A strange odor permeated the wigwam. Rebecca hesitated by the door flap, studying the many faces through the smoky haze that filled the room. The various expressions on people's faces told her they were obviously loving family members of the sick brave. The sight of them made her stomach wrench with compassion . . . and fear.

A woman rose from kneeling near the head of the patient's bed. She said something to Rebecca in her native tongue, and Rebecca looked to Night Wind for the translation.

Night Wind's glittering gaze met Rebecca's. "This is Red Fox's mother, Ice from Sky. In our language, she is called *M' hoo kum a."*

"What an unusual name," Rebecca murmured, nodding at the woman and attempting to smile. *This woman is Red Fox's mother. How will she feel if I fail to help her son?* The magnitude of what she was expected to do hit her once again. Her stomach hurt, and her pulse was erratic and so loud that she could barely hear the woman and Night Wind as he continued to translate Ice From Sky's words.

"M' hoo kum a is glad to see the one who can help her ailing son," Night Wind said. "She says her son is not well. He has been sick for many days. For a time, it seemed as if the Great Healing Spirit would make him better, but then he grew worse again." His gaze seemed to search Rebecca's soul.

"What is wrong with her son?" she asked without thinking. "Ah—what are his pains?"

Night Wind looked impatient as he stared at her a long moment. Rebecca wanted to hug herself with her arms to ward off the sudden chill, but she was afraid that the Indians might take it as a bad sign. They must not guess that she didn't know what to do. She must have their confidence. She had to earn their trust so that they would leave her alone with Red Fox. How else would she be able to think clearly and decide what to do?

The fire crackled and spit sparks, one of which landed close to one family member and was quickly smothered by the woman's hand.

"Medicine Woman," her kidnapper said, "why don't you move to see Red Fox?"

Rebecca took a step and stopped. "I must be alone with him."

She felt Night Wind stiffen behind her. She spun to face him, bolstered by a sudden determination to do what she could for the young brave.

"There are too many people in here," she said. "How can I examine him with everyone looking on? You stay if you like; the rest must go."

Night Wind held her gaze steady for several seconds before he murmured rapidly to Red Fox's family.

They rose without complaint and exited the wigwam. The tribe's shaman wanted to stay, it seemed, but Red Fox's mother spoke sharply to him. The man glared at Rebecca as he was leaving.

Ice From Sky touched Rebecca's arm as she passed her, murmuring something to Rebecca as she went.

Night Wind's gaze softened. *"M' hoo kum a* thanks you for coming to save her son. She says that the Great Spirit must look upon her kindly to send us such a wonderful gift." He stared at the door flap where the woman had departed. Then he turned back to Rebecca. "The Great Spirit—it is what you English call God."

Rebecca blinked. "You believe in God?"

"We believe in many gods, but—yes—we pray to a great one. Our Creator."

When everyone but Night Wind, Rebecca, and the ill brave had left the wigwam, the dwelling was quiet but for the soft sound of their breathing. Rebecca moved toward Red Fox's bedside and gazed down at her patient. "Why, he's just a boy!" she exclaimed.

Rebecca guessed Red Fox was about ten years old from his smooth skin and baby-like features. She felt a stirring of sympathy for the family. He was only a child.

"How long has he been ill?" Rebecca turned toward Night Wind as he joined her at Red Fox's sleeping platform.

"By your white man's terms, he has been sick a fortnight." His dark gaze settled with concern on the boy's flushed face. Red Fox looked amazingly tranquil for one who was so ill; only his pale coloring and the occasional rasp of his breath gave testament to his poor condition.

"He's been this way the entire time?" Rebecca asked with surprise. "He hasn't eaten and yet he still lives?"

Night Wind shook his head and reached out to stroke the hair from the boy's forehead, frowning as he did so. Rebecca saw his scowl, but was so moved by his affectionate gesture toward the boy that she didn't think much of it. She felt a queer little feeling inside at his display of gentleness.

"For a time it seemed as if Red Fox would get well," Night Wind told her, confirming that the boy had indeed eaten during the time he'd been sick. "He woke and ate food prepared by members of his clan. He drank special healing drink fixed by our shaman." He continued to stroke the child as he spoke. "For two days he sat up and he was weak but he was happy, happy to see his *Onna* and *Nukuaa,* happy to see his *Niimut*—brother."

He paused and raised his eyes to stare blankly ahead at the wall of the wigwam. "Then, after the sun had risen three times, Red Fox became sick again." There was pain in his voice as he continued. "He became worse until he fell into a sleep of bad dreams." Night Wind blinked and then faced Rebecca. "Now he sleeps without sound, but it is a sleep of near death. My brother dreams of the Afterworld.

"You are his only hope. Tales of your healing powers have traveled a great distance from the Cayuga to our village. I was hunting when I heard this. I knew that you were the one—the only one—who could save him."

The boy moaned and shifted restlessly.

"See," Night Wind said. "Red Fox is agreeing."

Concerned by the boy's coloring, Rebecca placed her hand against his flushed cheek. "He's feverish. Has he been this way before?"

"Kihiila." He nodded, his expression grave. "But he became well again. We thought the Great Spirit had answered our prayer, but this may not be true. Red Fox is not well."

Rebecca studied the man at her side. The glow of the fire softened his features, making him appear gentle. Her heart thudded within her chest as she realized how attractive he was.

Strange, she thought, *it must be because I've lived too long with the Indians that I could find one to be good looking.* Before her taste had run to fair-haired Englishmen with smooth, handsome features and fine gentlemanly manners. Now to find this man so appealing . . .

"You waste time, Rebecca. Red Fox lies waiting."

She glanced down again at the child, grasping for something she could do to help him. She tried desperately to think of anything she might have learned about healing from the Cayuga, any knowledge she'd acquired from the women who had raised her—her beloved mother and her aunt.

A coarse woolen blanket covered the patient up to his shoulders. The back of Rebecca's neck prickled with alarm. Where had the Indians gotten the blanket? *A white man's blanket.* Could the blanket be a carrier for disease? Had the boy contracted a white man's sickness? She'd heard of whole Indian tribes being wiped out by illness carried to them by the English.

Rebecca grabbed the edge of the blanket and raised it up to inspect the boy's chest. She expelled her breath with relief. There was no sign of any pustules or pox. His skin was hot to the touch, but smooth and unmarred. *Thank God. It's not smallpox,* she thought. *But what then?*

"Has anyone else been ill like this?" she asked, meeting Night Wind's gaze.

The Indian shook his head. *"Maata*—no." He

stared at her hard. "Why you do nothing? Why are
you not healing him?"

Dropping the blanket, she faced the brave with her
chin raised. She'd not be intimidated by the man's impatience. *Heal him of what?* she wanted to say.

"It will take time," she said, daring him to argue.
"You must be patient. I could think easier if you
waited outside."

To her dismay, he refused and sat down near the
door of the wigwam. *"Maata.* You will heal Red Fox."
He folded his arms and stared straight ahead without
emotion on his face.

It must be difficult for this man to be dependent
on another for assistance, Rebecca mused, especially
when that person was a woman. A white woman.

His silent presence unnerved her. How could she
do anything with him sitting there like that, ready to
pounce on her if she did anything he thought wrong?

"Must you wait there like that?" she said.

He had continued to sit unmoving, staring ahead.
He turned his head a fraction and looked at her. "You
want me to go?"

She nodded, feeling relieved.

"Maata."

No, he'd said. Rebecca's mouth tightened. "Why
not?"

"I am to stay in wigwam. I will see that you make
Red Fox well. You will not harm him . . . and *you
will not escape."*

Her stomach twisted. "I will not try to escape. I
already told you—"

"You will heal him," he said. "Or my people will
remember that you are Daughter of the Iroquois. You
are our enemy."

With constricted breath, Rebecca spun back toward
Red Fox. She felt her hand tremble as she touched

the boy's cheek. "I'll need water," she choked out. "Cold water," she said with more strength. She glared at Night Wind over her shoulder. The brave still hadn't moved.

"Can you bring it to me," she asked, "or are you afraid to trust me alone with the poor boy for the little time it will take you to get it?" She shook her head in incomprehension of the man's reasoning. The man trusted her to save Red Fox, to give him cures, but not enough to be alone with him.

It just didn't make sense to her. What did Night Wind think she'd do to the child while he was gone? Murder the boy and run? She'd not get across the yard, before someone would recapture her. She knew it, and he must know it. Why then was he being so stubborn?

Something flickered across his features. Apparently, he'd just realized how little were her chances of escape, even in his absence. He came to his feet in one fluid motion and lifted the door flap. "I will get water," he said and then he was gone, the animal hide covering swaying after it fell.

Rebecca could hear his voice through the walls of the wigwam, and then Night Wind was back, sitting as he was before.

"Sleeping Turtle will bring water."

She experienced exasperation and a growing desire to hit the man for his unwillingness to trust her. "Good!" she said, abruptly turning away.

Rebecca studied her surroundings while she waited. Dried corn, fruit, and other vegetables hung from the bent roof poles. Red Fox's bed was a raised platform, covered with dried corn husks and animal furs. A folded woolen blanket had been put behind his head, serving as his pillow. The fire in the center of the wigwam crackled and gave off a pleasant warmth. Its golden glow cast shadows against the outer walls.

Within moments after Night Wind had ordered the requested water, the flap lifted and an Indian maiden entered the wigwam. She carried a skin sack filled with water.

Rebecca stared. Sleeping Turtle appeared to be about fourteen years old. She had smooth, copper skin, and large doe-like eyes which were dark and glistening . . . and beautiful. Her hair, which was secured at her nape, was sleek, black, and shiny under the firelight.

Night Wind immediately rose and smiled as he accepted the water skin. Rebecca's belly flipflopped at the warm look on his face and the reciprocating warmth of Sleeping Turtle's expression.

The girl smiled at Night Wind, and her beauty intensified with the gentle curve of her lips. Her whole face lit up with pleasure until her gaze alighted on the boy on the bed, and her expression grew sad, poignant. Night Wind spoke softly to the young maiden, and then the girl left as quickly as she had come.

Night Wind offered Rebecca the water bag. She saw the way his arm muscles flexed as he gave her the skin.

"Here is the water," he said, following a lengthy silence.

Something odd in his voice struck a nerve within Rebecca. She tore her gaze from his body, averting her glance. "Thank you," she murmured, and set the skin down at the foot of Red Fox's bed. She was afraid to look into Night Wind's eyes, afraid that she'd recognize the same physical awareness in them that she was experiencing.

Dear Lord, what had possessed her to have such indecent thoughts!

Forcing her mind back to Red Fox, Rebecca searched the wigwam for a vessel in which to pour the water. There was a small pile of assorted personal articles beneath the raised platform bed. There, she found a clay pot, which she guessed was normally used for cooking, her assumption based on the point-shaped bottom.

She examined the pot, determined that it was clean enough, and then she bent and wedged the vessel into the dirt floor by pressing and twisting the clay pot against the ground, creating a small hole. The hole did little to cradle the vessel snugly, and the pot tipped to one side. Rebecca wondered how she was going to better support it so that it wouldn't topple after she poured water into it.

Suddenly, Night Wind was crouched down beside her, his hand encompassing hers as he helped to steady the earthen vessel. Rebecca had difficulty breathing as Night Wind worked closely to help her. Her body buzzed with sensation. Her scalp tingled as did her spine. She could smell the clean, woodsy scent of Night Wind; she could feel the radiating warmth of his lean form.

When the pot had been secured and filled with water, Rebecca rose to her feet, shaken by her reaction to Night Wind's nearness. His alluring scent rose again to her nostrils as he too stood. She gasped and took a step backward, but came up against Red Fox's bed.

Their eyes locked. Night Wind's gaze glittered, and Rebecca's heart leapt into her throat as she looked away, breathless and lightheaded. She was appalled at the way her body was betraying her. The man was a savage! And she was here to heal his brother . . .

Or die if she failed.

"Red Fox's fever is growing worse," she said. "We must bring it down. We must bathe him with the cool water." It was a method she'd learned from her mother and her Aunt Veronica, when they had once tended a neighbor woman when Rebecca was ten years old. When life had been simpler, safer . . . before Aunt Veronica moved to Delaware.

Night Wind didn't argue as Rebecca had half expected he would. He nodded and then to her stark amazement stepped outside the wigwam, returning moments later with a small piece of tanned doeskin, soft as goose down and as white as snow. He dropped the cloth into the pot of water.

"That will work well," she said in a gentle voice. "Thank you."

Night Wind didn't return to his seat on the floor, but stood at the foot of Red Fox's bed, watching Rebecca as she bathed Red Fox's forehead. Rebecca tried to control the trembling of her hands as she bent to wet the cloth and then rose to wipe the boy's flushed face. She could feel the piercing intensity of Night Wind's dark gaze. His presence made her edgy, nervous. He was a constant reminder of the posed threat to her well being should she fail.

She continued to use the cool, wet doeskin on Red Fox's face and neck. She refilled the clay pot from the water skin three times. It seemed that hours passed with no apparent change. Now, she was out of water and running out of time. Red Fox's fever still raged, and he began to mumble.

Rebecca bent her head, closed her eyes, and began to pray. "Our Father, Who art in heaven . . ."

What more could she do?

Five

"You are not helping him!" Night Wind exclaimed. He had barely left the bedside.

"What do you want me to do?" she said angrily. "I can't think; I'm so tired!"

"You are a great healer!" he replied. "Make him well!"

"Am I? I am no magician. I know nothing of—" Rebecca stopped, realizing her mistake. As long as he believed she could help Red Fox, she was safe, and there was hope of escape.

"You know nothing of what?" Night Wind said in an unusually soft voice.

Rebecca trembled. She swallowed hard before answering. "Of how long this healing will take." Her life hung in the balance with the young boy on the bed. She found the courage and confidence to continue what she started. "You must be patient." She grabbed the skin sack from the edge of the bed and thrust it in Night Wind's direction. "I need more water."

Night Wind glared at her and then stared at the water bag, before taking it from her hand. He spun from her in silence and left the wigwam, returning moments later with the water. He ignored her when she would have reached for the sack, bending to fill up the pot himself, rising to give her a hard glance, designed—Rebecca supposed—to intimidate. Only she didn't feel intimidated. She was determined to dismiss Night Wind's presence and continue this doctoring with a clear mind.

Rebecca wet the doeskin and squeezed out the excess water. Next, she lowered the blanket, prepared to extend her ministrations to Red Fox's chest and stomach. She sensed Night Wind's surprise as she placed the damp cloth onto the boy's breast. She shot him a glance.

"Would you like to do this?" she asked.

He waited a few seconds before answering. There was a strange glitter in his obsidian eyes, and Rebecca caught her breath as he continued to study her. "I will do this for Red Fox," he said, moving closer and then reaching for the cloth.

Their fingers brushed as the doeskin exchanged hands. Rebecca's skin burned at Night Wind's touch. She stood back, her thoughts and heart racing as she contemplated what to do next if the child didn't respond to treatment.

Night Wind and the Lenape people expected a miracle cure. Dear Lord, she knew so little of medicine, but she dare not let them know. They would be upset to learn that all she knew were some remedies taught to her by her mother and her aunt, and some herbal medicines she'd learned from the Cayuga. She didn't think bleeding the boy would help. Somehow she would find a way to make young Red Fox well.

The strange odor she'd detected earlier when she'd first entered the wigwam had disappeared. Curious, Rebecca asked Night Wind about the smell. The brave paused from bathing the boy's stomach, and flushing, Rebecca looked away from his fine-boned hand.

"The shaman offered the spirits a gift. It is what your white man calls to-bac-co." He dipped the doeskin into the pot of water. "He takes the to-bac-co and puts them with the leaves from a plant used to heal sickness of the—" He placed his beautiful male hand on the fur covering his mid-section. *"—uoote."*

"Stomach," she said.

He nodded. "The shaman places the leaves onto the fire. The leaves burn and smoke rises through the roof of my little brother's *week-wam*. The spirits see and smell this. We pray to our *Manit'towuk*. They hear our prayers and answer."

Night Wind hoped his own special spirit would choose to heal Red Fox. He believed the spirit had sent the Medicine Woman. He thought that she was the answer to the shaman's prayers.

Night Wind felt water run past his fingers onto Red Fox's bed. He glanced down at his dripping hand. "How much longer must Red Fox be washed?"

Rebecca smiled. Night Wind sounded impatient. "You're not washing to clean him, but to lower his temperature."

He scowled at her. "I know this. Night Wind is no fool."

"I didn't say you were."

"Enough," he said, dropping the cloth into the pot. "These things do not make Red Fox well!" His eyes glowed with fury. "You are not helping Red Fox! Why?"

"I'm trying to help him, but you're making it difficult!" she exclaimed. "You're scaring me. How can I think when all I can remember is that if I fail, I'll die!"

The Indian's face did not soften. "You are the White Medicine Woman. You will heal Red Fox."

"Then kill me now and be done with it!" she cried. "I'm so tired. I can hardly see. We've traveled so far . . ." She was exhausted, she realized. Perhaps that was why she couldn't remember many of the things her mother had taught her. What special medicines did her mother use? How did her mother finally bring down Martha Ross's fever the day after her own husband had become ill? Perhaps if she rested, she'd be better able to help Red Fox.

Something flickered across Night Wind's expression. "Come then." He fumbled among the belongings stored under Red Fox's bed and came up with a soft fur. "Sleep. I will watch Red Fox."

Rebecca studied the Lenape brave as he spread out the fur on the floor on the opposite side of the fire, but away from the door. She was concerned for the boy, but the thought of sleep was just too inviting. And she knew she'd be better able to care for the child after a short nap. "You will wake me if he grows worse?"

Night Wind nodded. His gaze was on Red Fox and he touched the boy's cheek with a gentleness that was in contrast to the way he treated Rebecca. *"Taau.* My brother's fever has broken." His eyes gleamed and his countenance wasn't as fierce as he faced Rebecca. "You have helped him with your water."

Rebecca experienced a frisson of warmth. Was that his way of apologizing to her? She steadily held his gaze. No. She was sure that it wasn't in the man's nature to apologize. He was conceding that she'd brought down Red Fox's fever, and that was all. But Red Fox had suffered from fever before. Lowering his temperature was a long way from curing the child.

Images of her Aunt Veronica came to mind, and the woman's daughter, Elizabeth, who was supposed to be in Rebecca's care. How was Aunt Veronica? Had her illness become worse? Was she dead? And where was poor Elizabeth? Who was there to care for the little girl?

I have to get away from here, Rebecca thought, staring at Red Fox. She had to leave. But how? How could she escape from under the eagle eye of Night Wind? And would her conscience let her go without helping the sick boy?

"Go," Night Wind said, drawing her attention. He pointed toward the sleeping mat. "Sleep. I will wake you if he worsens."

Conscious of Night Wind's disturbing presence, Rebecca did as she was told and stretched out on the bed that the brave had prepared for her. She turned onto her side, facing the wall of the wigwam, and curled up, trying to get warm. She felt something cloak her, and startled, she glanced back, meeting Night Wind's dark, glistening gaze. The Indian had covered her with his fur garment. His chest was bare. Her gaze fell on the sleek musculature of his upper torso, and she swallowed against a suddenly dry throat.

"You must stay warm, Medicine Woman. You must not get sick."

"Thank you," she said, her heart racing. Then a Lenape word came to her. *"Wa-nee'shih."* She wasn't sure where she'd heard it, but instinctively she knew she had spoken her thanks in the Lenape tongue.

Night Wind nodded, but his face was unreadable as he went back to Red Fox's side.

Although she was exhausted, Rebecca found that she couldn't sleep. Her situation, strange surroundings, and the dark forbidding presence of the Indian who had kidnapped her made sleep impossible. There was a scent about the fur blanketing her that made her extremely conscious of the knowledge that it belonged to Night Wind. A pleasant, masculine odor filled her senses, and she was unable to banish the mental image of the brave's bare chest and thick arm muscles.

She studied the wall, at the way the golden firelight played against the intricate pattern of the bent willow branches that comprised the crude dwelling's frame. Rebecca fought to get rid of the curling sensation in her abdomen.

The fire crackled, and she felt increased heat. Night Wind had added wood to the flame. The light, the enveloping warmth of her fur covering, and the soft sounds of the fire lured her into a dream-like state. Her mind dulled and her limbs grew heavy. She heard movement behind her, but she no longer cared where she was or who was with her. For now, no one would hurt her. It was safe to rest.

That strange yet familiar scent that she'd detected earlier filtered into her consciousness, but she didn't look; she didn't move. Soon, she fell asleep.

Rebecca woke up later, feeling rested. The familiar feel of furs beneath her cheek made her believe she was back with the Cayuga, in the hut. A noise nearby brought her fully awake, and she opened her eyes to see the strange wigwam. She was disoriented for a few seconds. She sat up, her gaze moving anxiously toward the platform bed where Red Fox lay with his eyes closed. No one else was in the wigwam. Night Wind had gone.

She threw off the fur, rose from her sleeping mat, and approached Red Fox. Was he dead? Dear Lord, had he died while she slept?

Common sense told her to relax. Night Wind would have woken her if something had happened to Red Fox. *But Night Wind left you alone with his brother,* she silently told herself. *Because you were sleeping, and he didn't have to be concerned with trusting you.*

Rebecca's stomach grumbled, and her thoughts

turned to food. She was ravenous. It had been hours since she'd eaten the small supper of squirrel and dried berries.

Her belly rumbled again as she recalled many of the delicious meals she'd eaten among the Cayuga. She thought longingly of *Oh-no'-kwa,* a delicious Iroquoian corn dish. Made of hard blue corn that had been cracked and ground in a mortar, the meal was sifted through a basket sieve and then boiled with meat and grease.

At first, Indian food had seemed strange to her, but she'd grown to like the Cayuga style of cooking. And she'd improved on their recipes, earning praise from White Flower, while drawing scathing remarks from some of the other matrons who were not willing to try Rebecca's cooking.

How were White Flower and her little son, the same son whom she had supposedly *saved?* She'd been shocked when the babe had begun to cry. Dropping the child into the cold water of the lake had been by accident. She didn't know why tiny *On-he* had lived. *On-he Ket-ge-a* was the child's full name, meaning "life from above" in English.

Life from Above. The title was a testament to the wonderful gift that *Ni yoh,* the Great Spirit, had given to the village with the saving of the babe's life.

Her life had changed after that eventful day. She'd been a slave since the Cayuga had captured her and the family of four whom she'd been traveling with from her home in New York to her aunt's cottage in Delaware. Her captors had suddenly become her friends. She was raised from slave to healer. Soon, she was to have been made an adopted daughter to the tribe.

Were they upset by her disappearance? White Flower and her sister Doe Eyes? Little *On-he,* White

Flower's son, was too young to remember her. But what of the village sachem, Killing Bird? *On-he* was his son, and there had been no doubting his gratitude when Rebecca had saved the child's life. Killing Bird had immediately changed Rebecca's status within the tribe.

Had the sachem ordered a search for her? Or in his joy of his living son had he forgotten all about her?

White Flower, if no one else, would be greatly concerned for Rebecca. By his wife's desire alone, the sachem would order his people to find the woman who had saved his child. Rebecca brightened with hope. Perhaps a party of Cayuga was on its way to rescue her! She imagined herself back among the Iroquois and preparing for the adoption ceremony that would give her the freedom she so craved. Rebecca hoped that they came for her quickly.

The flap lifted, and Rebecca gave a start as Night Wind entered the wigwam. He wore only his breechcloth and leggings; his chest was bare. She gave a silent gasp at the feeling that surged down her spine and through her limbs as she looked at him.

"You are awake." His accented voice rumbled deeply.

She swallowed hard. "Yes."

He came to the side of Red Fox's bed, where Rebecca stood. She felt her body's nerve endings hum to life as he moved to stand within inches of her.

"Your brother is fine," she said, avoiding his piercing onyx gaze. "You didn't wake me."

He shook his head, drawing attention to himself once again, to the fall of his shiny black hair that he wore loose and long to below his shoulders. He moved, and she caught sight of his earring—a strip of beaded sinew.

A movement at the doorway drew Rebecca's glance.

A woman entered, cradling a bowl with steaming contents.

"This is Angry Woman," Night Wind said. "She is *Donniina* to Ice From Sky, Red Fox's mother."

"She is Red Fox's aunt?" Rebecca asked.

He nodded. The woman said something to Night Wind, and the brave translated. "Angry Woman brings broth for Red Fox. Special medicine to help him grow strong. He will drink it if he wakes soon."

Red Fox's aunt held out the clay bowl with the hot broth, and Rebecca accepted it, eyeing the contents curiously.

"What's in it?" Rebecca asked. She looked up from the bowl to study Angry Woman. The matron was thin and dirty. *Strange,* she thought, since all of the other Indians, including the woman's sister, seemed to bathe more frequently than any English lady.

Ice From Sky's sister smelled strongly of bear's grease, for she had used it well to oil her hair, which was bound with a piece of sinew at her nape. Her cheeks had been reddened heavily with vermilion, and while it was the practice of the women to do so, Angry Woman's face seemed overdone with the paint.

The matron spoke again, and Rebecca noticed gaping holes in her mouth. Angry Woman was missing several front teeth.

"Angry Woman says it has magic plants," Night Wind said. "It will make Red Fox strong."

"But what if he remains unconscious?"

Night Wind's gaze narrowed. "She will continue to bring medicine until Red Fox is well enough to sit and drink." He then murmured something to Red Fox's aunt, and the woman nodded and left.

Rebecca turned away as soon as the woman departed. She set the bowl on the dirt floor near the end of the bed and then rose and felt Red Fox's forehead.

"His skin has gotten cooler. Good." She felt tremendous relief.

"It has done so before," Night Wind said, causing her to worry again. He glared at her accusingly. "You have done nothing for him."

"What do you expect me to do?" she cried. "It will take time! I cannot give him medicine until he's awake and able to eat. I've brought down his fever some and now I'll—" She thought quickly. "Make him a special medicine, one that will ensure that he breathes easier." *What medicine?* she wondered. *I know nothing of medicines. What am I going to do?*

Something moved in Night Wind's features. "You are Medicine Woman." He paused. "You know what is best, but you must heal him quickly."

Rebecca was stunned. Concern for the boy was slowly eating away at the poor savage. His trust encouraged her to think harder for a remedy.

"I appreciate your trust," she said gently. "I'll not hurt him. You brought me here to cure your brother, but you must allow me time to do this in my own way."

She suddenly felt as if she did, in fact, possess the power to cure Red Fox, as if by determination alone she'd been granted a special gift.

"What is this medicine?" Night Wind asked.

Rebecca looked away. "You will see. It's a special preparation we English use when our patient is sick. It won't hurt him," she quickly assured him.

Rebecca grew thoughtful as she looked about the wigwam.

Let me think . . . Grease from a goose spread on the breast cures a cold. . . . For a sore throat, I could use a dirty stocking about his neck . . . if I owned one. I haven't worn stockings since the day I was captured and Doe Eyes, White Flower's sister, took a lik-

*ing to mine. . . . To heal the mumps, Mother said she
rubbed Auntie's neck on a hog trough—a hog itself
would do, too, she said, if one didn't have a trough.*

She closed her eyes. *Dear God, I don't know what
is wrong with this child? What am I going to do?*

"Medicine Woman—"

Startled, she opened her eyes. "Yes?" Her pulse
raced as she met his gaze.

He narrowed his eyes. "You are not healing—"

"I'm thinking! I told you it would be easier if you
waited outside!"

Night Wind backed up, and to her astonishment,
went outside to wait.

Rebecca hurriedly searched the wigwam for something she could use to make this "special medicine."
She only hoped that he believed it would work, that
he didn't suspect that she hadn't the slightest idea
what she was doing.

The Cayuga believed in their shaman's magic. The
only thing that the medicine man had done that Rebecca had seen was to chant and dance and sprinkle
a powder made of ground plants about the sick person's wigwam.

She didn't know any Indian dances. She could
chant—or pretend to. Night Wind wouldn't know if
she was faking. As for the plant powder, she could
grind some corn, she supposed, or burn some tobacco,
and no one would know that she wasn't making magic.

Rebecca paced nervously about the wigwam. *But
what happens when the child doesn't respond to treatment?*

She paused and clenched her fists. Damn, but she
had to remember! What would her mother do if she
were in this position? What remedy would Aunt Veronica claim was the best choice for this sick child?

"Medicine Woman." Night Wind entered the wigwam, his powerful form filling the room with tension.

"I will need some tobacco." Rebecca came forward. "And . . . some—"

He scowled. "A medicine of tob-bac-co?" he interrupted.

"You said you would trust me," she reminded him.

Night Wind grunted and then asked her again what she needed. She told him about the tobacco and, thinking quickly, she requested camomile. The plant had been a favorite remedy of Aunt Veronica's, brought over to the Colonies by Rebecca's grandmother, Mary Smythe.

The brave shook his head, apparently not having heard of the herb, which she'd known, immediately after asking, that he wouldn't. She searched her brain for another of Aunt Veronica's plants.

What was she doing? These Indians knew more about plants and herbs than any English doctor. How could she fool them when they knew so much?

Chant, she thought. *No, pray. You'll be praying to Almighty God. Let them think you are calling to the great spirits.*

In the end, she asked for Mugwort, a plant that she knew the Indians used to make healing charms. Night Wind left to get what she requested and returned moments later with a tobacco pouch and a small bag of dried Mugwort leaves and roots.

Rebecca thanked him as she took the small skin satchels. Her hands trembled as she withdrew some tobacco and lay the dried leaves on the fire. Next, she ground up the Mugwort root and sprinkled some of the resulting powder beside the boy on his sleeping platform. The rest remained in the stone mortar.

In a great display of ceremony, she stood and began to chant. She created strange, foreign words as she sang, hoping that Night Wind wouldn't guess that the musical words were fake, that she—the White Medicine Woman—was a fake. As she chanted her eerie song, she prayed to God that He would help the child get well and free her from the Indians.

The scent of burning tobacco filled the wigwam. She closed her eyes, inhaling the odor, swaying as she held her hands over the boy. Night Wind watched silently; throughout the ceremony, she could feel his presence. She must be convincing, for he didn't stop her as she carried on.

Red Fox woke just as Rebecca was adding tobacco to the fire. The boy's soft murmurs drew her attention. The child gazed searchingly about the wigwam, before calling to Night Wind.

"Kweh!" Night Wind exclaimed, coming forward.

With a cry of joy, Rebecca left the cooking fire in the center of the wigwam and joined Night Wind at the boy's side. Red Fox's eyes were open, but he looked groggy and disoriented. His brother spoke softly to him in Algonquin, and Rebecca watched the boy's eyes brighten.

"This is Medicine Woman," Night Wind said. "She has been helping you."

Red Fox looked at her. *"Wa-nee'shih."*

Rebecca smiled at the boy's thanks. She met Night Wind's gaze. "Tell Red Fox that he is welcome. It is my pleasure to help him."

Night Wind held her gaze, something unfathomable shimmering in the depths of his dark eyes, before he translated her message to his young brother. Red Fox managed a weak grin.

"He needs to eat," Rebecca said softly. "Ask him if he is hungry."

"Are you hungry, little warrior?"

Red Fox nodded while he answered. The child

spoke slowly as if he had difficulty finding the strength to speak.

"Red Fox says that he is hungry a little. His *uoote*—" Night Wind patted his hard, flat belly. "—it gives him pain."

Rebecca's breath had caught when he'd touched his stomach. A sudden shaft of feeling invaded her body, filling it with warmth as she envisioned how he must look beneath his clothing.

"Shall I make him some broth?" she asked.

"Angry Woman will prepare—"

"There is no need to disturb Angry Woman," Rebecca said. For some reason, she didn't want Red Fox to eat his aunt's cooking. She wanted to prepare the child's first meal of broth. Night Wind looked wary, and she was annoyed.

"You may watch me make it if you'd like," she said tightly. "I told you to trust me," she added in a sharper tone. She asked God's forgiveness when she said, "Did I not make special magic for Red Fox? Is he not awake?"

The brave appeared uncomfortable. "You are right," he said, surprising her once again. "Red Fox is awake because of you. I will trust you."

Despite her earlier irritation, she felt something inside melt with pleasure at the Indian's words.

"Thank you." Rebecca thought hard to recall the ingredients of a tonic that White Flower of the Cayuga tribe had once made for her husband when he'd been weak and recovering from an illness. Rebecca had helped White Flower prepare the broth.

She settled for a simple broth made from venison and rabbit meat, flavored with the sweet taste of tree sugar.

While she cooked the broth over the fire, Night Wind helped Red Fox into the position for eating. He used several folded blankets and beaver pelts to prop up the child so he could sit.

The boy watched through heavy-lidded eyes as Rebecca poured some broth from the pot into a small drinking bowl. She rose from the fire pit and approached him with a smile. When the boy reached out to accept her offering, she noted how frail and thin-skinned his arms appeared.

"You must drink and eat so that you can grow healthy and strong again."

Night Wind translated Rebecca's words. The boy nodded his head and murmured a reply.

"Red Fox says he will do as you say." Night Wind's expression softened. "He wants to be strong, to be able to hunt like a true warrior of the Lenni-Lenape." He said something else in Algonquin to the child, before addressing Rebecca in English. "Come, Medicine Woman. My brother will drink your broth, but now you must eat and rest. There are others who will care for Red Fox. People of his clan who will love and watch over him."

"I'd like to stay." She didn't want to leave now that the boy was awake and improving. Something inside her had softened and warmed toward the Indian child as she'd nursed him. Once before the boy had seemed to recover and then had become worse. A warning light lit up in her brain. She wanted to care for him until she was sure he was eating properly and well on the mend.

Night Wind had grown silent. He wore a strange look as he studied her. "You may stay," he said after several moments, "but only if you eat."

"I am hungry." She smiled at Red Fox. "The little warrior and I can keep each other company while we eat."

Night Wind translated Rebecca's words for the boy, who grinned.

"I will have food brought to this lodge," Night Wind said. "Now that my brother is awake, I must tell our father."

Rebecca was startled that she could have so quickly forgotten the child's family. "Yes, please tell him," she said. "The boy and I will be fine. Won't we, Red Fox?"

The child must have guessed what she was saying, for he nodded and smiled as if he understood.

"Now you must finish this, Red Fox," she said after Night Wind had left. She raised the cup to the boy's mouth while she lifted the boy's head. He sipped the broth, grimaced, but then he smiled at Rebecca and sipped again.

"I suppose your medicine brews taste terrible, too," she said, returning his smile. Rebecca liked the boy. Red Fox trusted her, and it made her feel good. She wanted to see him run and play among the other children. She wanted to see his expression when he returned from his first hunt.

But that is nonsense, she thought. She would not be here long enough to see such a thing. She had to get free and find her cousin; little Elizabeth needed her. Rebecca thought of the girl's mother, her Aunt Veronica, and she recalled the happy times she'd spent with her relative when she was a small child and her aunt had lived with her and her mother. They had been poor, but happy, and although Rebecca had wondered how it would have been if her father had lived, the two sisters had done their best to make her feel privileged.

Oh, Aunt Veronica, if you're gone, I hope you didn't suffer much.

Thoughts of her aunt's death filled her with fear. It

had been difficult when her aunt had married Jack Webster and moved away. Both her mother and she had missed Veronica terribly. To think that she might now be dead. . . . She closed her eyes to hold back tears.

What was happening to her child, Elizabeth?

A hand touched her arm, and Rebecca tried to smile at the child, who gazed at her worriedly. "You're a dear boy, Red Fox," she said with affection. His concern comforted her. "I'm fine. Honestly."

Rebecca sat with him until the boy's mother arrived awhile later.

The woman spoke rapidly in the Algonquin tongue, and Rebecca was at a loss to what she was saying. ". . . *Meech wah kun.*"

Rebecca shook her head. "I'm sorry, but I don't understand."

Red Fox's mother was a lovely woman with pretty dark eyes and unlined skin. The radiance of her smile when she'd seen her son awake lit up the wigwam. She looked at her child with such love that Rebecca was emotionally moved.

Ice From Sky held up her hand and then began searching the supplies within the wigwam. She seemed frustrated that she couldn't find what she was looking for, until she glanced at her son. She gave a wild cry of satisfaction as she took the bowl from her son's hand. She waved the vessel before Rebecca. ". . . *Meech wah kun.*"

"Night Wind couldn't return. She is saying that you must eat," a male voice announced from the wigwam door.

Rebecca experienced a shiver of apprehension as she observed the village shaman step inside and release the door flap. His countenance was dark, forbidding, as his black eyes regarded her with distrust.

"You speak English," she said. He'd never before given her a sign of this knowledge.

The shaman inclined his head slowly. "I have learned your language. I have spoken with the white man." His gaze hardened. "I trust not *Shu wun uk.*"

"Uncle." The boy's voice called in Algonquin from his bed.

Iron Bear looked at the boy on the bed, and his features softened. "Ah, Red Fox," he said in Algonquin, their native tongue. "You are awake! I am glad to see you are getting well, little warrior."

He ignored Rebecca as he approached the bed. Ice From Sky greeted the shaman from her son's side. "See," she said. "The Medicine Woman has helped my son. She is the one that Night Wind saw in his dream. She is the great one."

"Pah!" The medicine man's lips tightened briefly. "We shall see how great her powers are. I will believe them only when I see Red Fox is up and hunting with the others. He has lost this sickness before, only to have it return. Perhaps Medicine Woman has done nothing."

"I feel well, Uncle," the child said, struggling to rise to his elbows, but falling back weakly.

"No, Red Fox!" Rebecca rushed to the boy's bedside. She pushed him back against the fur. "You're still weak." She didn't know the subject of their discussion, but she guessed by the shaman's unpleasant expression that they had been talking about her.

"What are you telling them?" she asked Iron Bear. "The boy's still recovering. It will take time for him to regain his strength."

"Do not tell me of time, Medicine Woman," he said with scorn. "Iron Bear knows of time; he knows of this young brave's illness. I have watched over Red Fox myself. If anyone can help him, it will be the

Gods, not you! Beware of the great spirits, for they
punish those who deceive!"

Iron Bear spoke to the mother and son, before angrily exiting the wigwam. Rebecca felt the tiny hairs
rise at the back of her neck. Did he know that she'd
been faking? she wondered with alarm. Or had he
only guessed? She could imagine what they would do
if they learned that she knew practically nothing of
medicine, nothing but the small bit of knowledge
taught to her by her mother and aunt.

And the image frightened her.

Six

Red Fox was up and moving slowly about the village, and Rebecca was relieved to see the child recovering. It had been two days since he'd awakened and begun eating again. He was still weak, but considering the length of his illness, his activity out of bed seemed a miracle to Rebecca. The reason for his sickness remained unknown, a fact that disturbed her. With her freedom looming in the wake of his recovery, she could only pray that the boy's mysterious illness didn't return.

For the time being, Rebecca lived with the village matron, She Who Sees Much, and her daughter, a young beautiful Lenape maiden with the even lovelier name of Sun Blossom. When Red Fox had begun eating solid foods, Night Wind had come for Rebecca and escorted her to her new home.

"You will be free," he'd said, "if my brother is well at the end of seven suns."

She'd seen little of Night Wind since Red Fox had opened his eyes. To her surprise, she missed his disturbing presence . . . missed being the focus of his glistening onyx eyes.

Her stomach filled with burning heat as she recalled the strange tension she'd sensed when he and Sun Blossom were together. Rebecca told herself that the burning she'd felt was not jealousy; she wasn't bothered by the undercurrents of physical awareness between Sun Blossom and Night Wind, by the sparks of fire in the young woman's eyes as she'd spoken to the handsome brave.

But when she couldn't stop wondering if the two were in love, Rebecca began to worry about her many thoughts of Night Wind. Was it because she herself was attracted to him? *Dear Lord, he is my captor. I must be mad to even think of such a thing!*

Rebecca sat outside She Who Sees Much's wigwam on a rush mat, shelling beans. It was a beautiful autumn day. The temperature was cool, the air crisp, and the strong scent of evergreens was particularly noticeable. The women of the village had harvested their fields long ago, and many matrons worked outside their lodges, weaving baskets or shucking corn while others made clay bowls or pots, a tedious process that would render the finished product extremely valuable.

Earlier, Rebecca had swept out She Who See Much's wigwam and she was enjoying the light chore before moving on to other heavier tasks. As she worked, she raised her glance from her bean pot and saw Sun Blossom cross the compound. The maiden stopped to speak with Night Wind, who had his bow slung over his shoulder and his quiver of arrows at his back. He was speaking with several braves, who were similarly armed. The men, Rebecca thought, were going hunting.

What was Sun Blossom saying to Night Wind? Rebecca wondered irritably. What could she possibly want with him now?

The familiar burning plagued her stomach as she watched the Indian maiden hand Night Wind a satchel. She saw the brave smile at the woman, and Rebecca's belly hurt worse.

When Sun Blossom left the group of men, Rebecca saw the way Night Wind followed the woman with his eyes. She saw a red haze. Tension and jealousy made her jaw ache.

Suddenly, Night Wind's gaze fastened on Rebecca. She blushed, embarrassed to be caught staring at him. She looked down at her beans, working faster, but she could feel him watching her. She rose and went into the wigwam, busying herself until she could regain her composure, searching for the things she'd need to grind corn. When she came outside again, she saw, to her disappointment, that Night Wind had gone.

Seconds later, Night Wind came out of the Lenape ceremonial lodge. Her face flamed as he approached. She'd sat down on the ground to work, and she put aside her beans to grind corn. He stood above her. She could see the fancy quillwork of his moccasins and feel his imposing presence as a threat. Her fingers trembled as she ground corn.

"When can I leave?" she blurted out. She hadn't meant to ask the question, for she knew his answer. They'd had a similar discussion about her freedom before.

Night Wind's brow darkened. "You must wait, Medicine Woman, until the moon rises five more times in the night sky." His eyes narrowed. "I told you this."

Yes, he had, she thought. But didn't he know that she was scared of her growing feelings for him? That she needed most desperately to get away? She stared down at her mortar and pestle as the tension between them grew. She was silent, because she didn't know what to say. Finally, she looked up.

The Indian studied her with a knowing look that disturbed her. "I leave for the hunt," he said. "I will return in one day. If Red Fox is well, we will thank the gods who helped save him . . . and the Medicine

Woman that *Manit'towuk* sent us," he added with a intonation that sent ripples of pleasure along Rebecca's spine.

Rebecca avoided looking at the bared shoulder of his right arm and found her gaze caught by the masculine line of his throat . . . his well formed jaw . . . and his sensual lips. She swallowed hard. What was it about this man that fascinated her?

"Then I'll be free to go?"

His mouth firmed, but he nodded. "Soon."

"Thank you."

He looked startled. "You are thanking me? Why?"

"For allowing me the chance to return to my people."

He was angry. "The Cayuga," he spat.

She shook her head. "My aunt—a white woman." *If she's still alive,* Rebecca thought. "She lives in the Delaware Colony."

Night Wind glanced at his friends. "I must go." He moved away, and Rebecca's gaze fastened on his broad-shouldered back.

"Good luck," she said. He turned, his eyebrows raised in question. "With your hunt."

This time he arched only one eyebrow. "It is not luck that puts meat on our fire and food in our bellies. It is skill taught to us by our fathers." Then he gave her a look that melted her insides and left. There had been amusement shimmering in those onyx Indian eyes . . . and something else too.

The next twenty-four hours seemed empty to Rebecca. She spent the remainder of the day finishing a basket and doing chores. The two women she lived with were friendly and taught her a lot about the Lenape way of life, the similarities as well as the differences between the Lenape and the Iroquois.

Sun Blossom spoke a smattering of English, which

both surprised and pleased Rebecca. Up until then, Rebecca had thought the only Indians who could speak her language were Night Wind and the shaman, Iron Bear. Sun Blossom's English was more fractured and difficult to understand than the two men, but with patience, Rebecca was able to communicate with the maiden. She questioned Sun Blossom about the women's position within the tribe. She asked about other aspects of Lenape life, and Sun Blossom was happy to provide answers.

"Women own *week-wam*," the young woman told her. "She digs in fields . . . grow corn. Grow beans and squash."

"While the men hunt and protect the village," Rebecca said, and Sun Blossom nodded, smiling. It was the same with the Cayuga. At first, Rebecca had thought the women do all the hard work, but then she learned differently. The women worked in the fields, for the Lenape believed the women held special powers of fertility over the earth.

The hunters came back during the night when Rebecca was sleeping. At the men's joyous cry, the villagers awoke and went out to greet their loved ones and to see what the braves had brought back with them. Rebecca stumbled outside in Sun Blossom's wake, rubbing the sleep from her eyes. She was immediately aware of Night Wind among the hunters. She became instantly alert, her senses tuned in to his powerful masculinity, his beautifully sculptured features and dark eyes.

The hunt had been successful. The warriors including Night Wind were laughing and being congratulated by their families and friends. There were deer and bear as well as smaller game like rabbit, opossum, otter, and squirrel. Each brave had brought back all he could carry. The meat would be dried to last the cold winter months; the hides would be tanned and used for clothing or skin satchels.

When Night Wind found her gaze above those who had gathered in the square, Rebecca's heart began to beat faster. She felt a tingling at her neck and a strange weakness in her legs while his eyes steadily held her transfixed. Then Sun Blossom was there, touching the brave's shoulder, drawing away his attention, and Rebecca felt a sharp stab of jealousy.

The gathering split up, each family returning with their loved ones. Night Wind disengaged himself from Sun Blossom's grasp and came to where Rebecca stood, away from the center of the compound. She thought Sun Blossom looked angry.

"You were successful," she said, sounding breathless.

He nodded solemnly, his dark eyes glowing as he studied her. "Skill, not luck," he said. His grin brought her a feeling of warmth. "How is Red Fox?" he asked, his voice low.

"He is well. His family have been caring for him. He has begun to join the other children."

They stared at each other silently for a long moment. The physical tension between them hung in the air. The question of when she could leave was there in Rebecca's blue eyes. Something flickered in Night Wind's expression.

"Re-bec-ca," he said when she looked away. He touched her cheek, demanding that she gaze at him. "Your time here has been terrible?"

His voice was a loving caress; his gaze was like fire that warmed and then seared her, jolting her senses to life. "Has it?" he asked again when she didn't immediately respond.

Overwhelmed by his effect on her, Rebecca shook

her head. "She Who Sees Much and Sun Blossom have been good to me."

"And Night Wind?" he said.

She averted her gaze. "What about Night Wind?" she said, as if the man before her wasn't the one they were discussing.

He cupped her jaw, playing his fingers against her skin. She closed her eyes, enjoying his touch, seduced by his tenderness, this surprisingly different side to this complex man.

"Night Wind has been . . . kind," she whispered, opening her eyes.

"Then why do you wish to leave?"

Surely, he didn't want her to stay. Or did he? "I must go," she said. "There's a child—my cousin. My aunt is dying; she might well be dead, and her daughter needs someone to care for her."

Night Wind frowned. "But you were in village of Cayuga."

"I was captured by the Iroquois," she said. She paused and then continued, "Like you captured me. I was a slave until I saved the son of their sachem."

"This is true?" The brave had tensed.

Rebecca nodded, her heart rhythm accelerating, as she wondered if she'd been wise to admit her past to Night Wind. What must he think of her to know she was kidnapped and made a slave before she'd become Medicine Woman?

Night Wind stared at the woman before him, his mind assembling all that she'd told him. He didn't want her to go. He was sure if she stayed she would be happy among his people. But he understood the ties of kinship; he couldn't find fault with her wanting to find this child. Elizabeth.

The villagers had gone back to their beds, but Night Wind sensed someone staring at them. He turned and saw Sun Blossom approach. He found himself comparing the two women. Sun Blossom was beautiful by Lenape standards, but it was Rebecca that made his blood heat whenever he was within distance of her.

Rebecca's hair was long and dark, much like the women of his village, but in the sunlight, it lit up with fire. Its shiny strands glistened with a burnished copper fire under the brightness of the sun.

Sun Blossom spoke, but Night Wind didn't hear what she was saying, for he was studying Rebecca's mouth. He wondered how her lips would feel pressed hard beneath his own.

". . . Red Fox."

It was his young brother's name that alerted Night Wind that something was wrong.

"I have just spoken to Ice From Sky," Sun Blossom said in Algonquian. "Red Fox has taken ill again. He is worse than before."

Night Wind's gaze narrowed upon Rebecca. "You lied," he accused.

Rebecca froze, experiencing an impending doom. "I didn't! What is it?"

"Where is he?" he asked Sun Blossom, his gaze never leaving Rebecca.

"In the wigwam of the shaman. Ice From Sky and Iron Bear are with him."

Angered, Night Wind grabbed Rebecca's arm. "Come!" he demanded. "You have not healed him! You must do this now!"

Rebecca's breath rasped in her throat as Night Wind dragged her across the compound toward the shaman's wigwam. Frightened, she saw all chances for freedom leaving her, for she had already done all that she could.

The occupants of the wigwam were somber when

Night Wind pushed Rebecca into the shelter before him.

"Why didn't they come for me?" Rebecca asked, her gaze fastening on Red Fox's pale figure on the sleeping platform.

Night Wind asked the boy's mother. Ice From Sky spoke rapidly, and Rebecca saw his face change.

"It has only just happened," he told Rebecca. "Until then, he was well."

Ice From Sky spoke again as Rebecca moved to the boy's side.

"What did she say?" Rebecca asked as she felt Red Fox's forehead. Night Wind didn't answer, and she glanced to find him scowling.

"Come with me." The brave gestured for Rebecca to leave the wigwam.

Rebecca paled as she obeyed him. "Where are we going?" Her heart raced with renewed fear. But Night Wind wouldn't tell her. He waited for her to leave the wigwam and then he took her to a similar structure on the other side of the village.

Night Wind opened the fur door flap of the wigwam. "Wait here until I return," he said without expression.

"Night Wind . . ." She touched his arm and saw him flinch. Swallowing hard, she let go of him.

He stood there, tense, his gaze meeting her with a hardness that gave her chills.

"Why am I here? Why can't I care for Red Fox?"

"Onna and *Nakuaa* forbid it." His voice was cold. "You will stay here until the council decides your fate." He ordered her into the wigwam.

Inside, Rebecca glanced about the wigwam. It was smaller than Red Fox's and the one she had shared with She Who Sees Much and Sun Blossom. A single sleeping mat was situated against the far wall. The fire in the center of the wigwam had gone out; all that was left were warm ashes. There were cooking utensils and a few other supplies within the wigwam, scattered about the perimeter of the house.

"Whose wigwam is this?" she asked as he followed her inside.

"It is Night Wind's," he said, and then he left her alone and frightened, wondering if she were to be condemned to die.

Village of the Cayuga

"Are there no signs of Medicine Woman?" White Flower asked her husband. "I am worried. Who could have taken her? Who would do this?"

When the Cayuga village had awakened to find Rebecca gone, they'd been concerned. The discovery of her dead dog had made them fear for the woman's life. The white woman was to have become a revered daughter that day, and someone—an enemy—had taken her. They had begun immediately to search for the one who had saved White Flower's only child.

"I do not know. But we have not given up the search," White Flower's husband said. "We will find who kidnapped Medicine Woman and we will make them suffer for their deed."

"Do you think she's all right?" the Indian woman said anxiously.

"Who took her must have heard of her powers to heal. I do not think they will harm her."

But White Flower's fears were not calmed. Only someone who was the enemy would take Rebecca in such a manner. "We will find you, Daughter of the Cayuga. We will bring you back to your village, and we will kill the one who stole you from your home."

* * *

The Lenape Village of Night Wind

Hours passed and no one came. Rebecca lay on the sleeping pallet, covered with soft beaver skins, and she dozed for a while. Concern for her life gave her terrible dreams. She woke up, sweating and gasping for air.

She sat up, her head aching, her lungs on fire, and gazed about the wigwam, but saw no one. She relaxed and studied her surroundings. Her gaze sharpened as she realized that the belongings here were *his*. Night Wind's.

It was morning. Light filtered in through the smoke hole in the wigwam roof. Rebecca rubbed her bare arms. It was chilly, and she pulled Night Wind's fur up to cover her shoulders. She heard voices outside the wigwam and her heart thumped hard with anticipation. The door flap lifted. Night Wind entered the wigwam. Rebecca wondered where he'd spent the remainder of the night. This wigwam, after all, was his. It occurred to her that he had kept vigil at Red Fox's bedside.

Their gazes collided. Rebecca's breath caught; Night Wind's ebony eyes glistened with pain. He looked tired, worn, and sad.

"How is Red Fox?" she asked, her voice quivering. She dreaded his answer.

"Red Fox is dead."

"No!" she whispered, stricken.

Night Wind grabbed her arm and hauled her up from the pallet. A new element of danger surrounded him. He was angry, more angry than she'd ever seen him.

"I'm sorry!" she gasped as she was dragged from

the wigwam. "Night Wind!" she cried, "where are you taking me?" Was she going to die? Be punished for failing to heal the boy?

Night Wind pulled her behind him across the square to the large ceremonial building in the center of the village. He released her arm and ordered her to proceed him into the structure. Rebecca's heart pounded so loudly that she could barely hear what he was saying. Her palms were sweaty. Her blood roared through her veins as the Indian gave her a shove and she stumbled inside.

Frightened, she blinked to adjust to the light and crouched ready to defend herself.

Seven

The building, to Rebecca's relief, was empty. She could feel Night Wind's imposing presence as she moved farther into the structure. Hands raised in defense, her knees bent in a protective stance, she waited for him to kill her.

"You wish to fight?" he asked softly.

She rose to full height. "No," she said. She bit her lip. "Didn't you bring me here to kill me?"

He shook his head, his dark eyes glowing with sincerity, and she relaxed. With the immediate threat of death gone, Rebecca broke her gaze from Night Wind and looked at her surroundings.

Her attention caught on an oval face that had been carved and painted into the center support pole. Half black and half red, the sight drew her in for a closer look. She felt a chill and hugged herself with her arms. The image was simple, but eerie and fascinating. She reached out to touch the face, but withdrew quickly when she was overcome by a dark feeling of doom.

"This is the Big House," Night Wind's deep, hypnotic voice said over her shoulder. "It is the place where we speak to the spirits. We give thanks here; we celebrate life. We come here when a warrior has reached the end of the white path."

She shivered. Night Wind's breath caressed her

neck and scalp where the hairs prickled with sudden physical awareness of the man. The white path, she understood from his words, was life.

"What does this mean?" she said, boldly touching the carved face.

Night Wind explained. "It is the look of our creator." His hand gestured toward the poles supporting the outer walls. "See the faces there. There are twelve faces in the Big House. Two here." He touched the center pole, showing her another face on the opposite side. "Ten there," he said, referring to the outer poles. "One for all levels of the universe."

Fascinated with the concept, Rebecca stared at the brave as he spoke, watching his lips as they formed each word. He had lost his aura of anger and the effect on her senses was as intoxicating as a glass of mead. The danger she faced seemed distant, far away as if in a dream. She moved from Night Wind in an attempt to regain control. She wanted to ask more about Lenape beliefs, but she held back, wondering nervously about Night Wind's reason for bringing her here.

"See this house, Reb-bec-ca," he said. "See the place where we will dance the song of death. *The death of Red Fox.*" He grabbed her by the shoulders, spinning her to face him.

Rebecca stared at him, her heart in her throat. She could hear wild cries from outside. Cries of sorrow. She realized that the Indians had begun to mourn their loss.

"Hear, *Medicine Woman,*" he said, a scathing tone to her title. "Hear my people's sorrow for their lost son . . . their future sachem."

She closed her eyes and swayed on her feet, dizzy with fear. Red Fox would have been chief. Rebecca was stunned by this knowledge.

Her eyes filled with tears. She opened them to gaze

at Night Wind with sadness, with regret. Her arms burned where he held her. "I'm sorry. I tried to help him."

"You did not want to come!" he growled, squeezing her arms. "You did not want to heal him!"

"I cared for him!" she cried, jerking away from his bruising hold. "You should have left me with the Cayuga! I told you I would try to help him, and I did!"

"You healed the Cayuga child; you did not heal Red Fox!" He caught her to him. Groaning, he lowered his head and crushed her lips with his own in a savage kiss meant to punish.

Rebecca whimpered and fought him, shoving at his shoulders to be free. He released her abruptly, his eyes glowing hotly with anger . . . and desire.

"Why did you do that?" she gasped, stunned by his actions. She touched her lips which were sore from his attack. Her mouth tasted of copper; she must have cut the inside.

In a strangely gentle move, Night Wind reached out and touched her mouth, caressing her swollen bottom lip. His gentleness made Rebecca tremble, and burn, and wonder how she'd feel if he kissed her tenderly, in affection instead of in anger.

A hard look descended on his features. His hand fell away, and he stepped back. The mourning cries of Night Wind's people increased in volume, filtering inside the ceremonial house. A woman wailed in agony. A man shouted in sorrowful anger. Rebecca hugged herself with her arms and stared at Night Wind.

They are crying for Red Fox, she thought, but they could as well be crying for me, for I am going to die.

Tears pooled in her eyes as she recalled the innocent smile of the endearing child she'd briefly known and cared for. *Why, God, did You put me in this po-sition? You know I have no special powers and can't heal anyone!*

Night Wind watched her silently. She averted her gaze as she fought to banish the large lump in her throat. The last thing she needed was to indulge in self-pity. She had to think! Find a way to escape death!

Why did Red Fox die?

She moved away from Night Wind's disturbing presence. She couldn't think clearly when he was too near. The memory of his brutal kiss remained, but even more unnerving was the lingering effects of his tender touch.

"What are they going to do with me?" she asked.

His eyelids lowered over glistening dark orbs. "It is for the Council to decide this."

She swallowed hard. "When will I know?" She fought a rising tide of hysteria.

"Council will meet when the time of mourning is done. My people will cry for their lost son for many suns, many moons, yet."

She gasped. "I have to wait days to learn what's to become of me?"

He stepped closer, his face stern. "Are you anxious to die, white woman?"

She blanched and pulled back, but he grabbed her arm.

"I should not have brought you here, Reb-bec-ca," Night Wind said, glaring at her. "You promised to help us, but you lied, and now my brother is dead!"

How could she have ever thought him kind?

"Come," he ordered.

"Where are we going?" Rebecca cried out as the brave dragged her toward the door.

"Outside. You will see what death does to my people."

The man was a cruel savage, she thought. Didn't he see that she was sorry? That Red Fox's death wasn't her fault? She had tried to tell him that she was no healer, but he wouldn't listen to her. So, she had resorted to her aunt and mother's home remedies . . . little help for so sick a child. *But he had seemed to get better.*

She allowed him to pull her outside. The bright sunlight momentarily blinded her after being in the dark interior of the Big House. Unable to see, she felt vulnerable as the cries of the villagers resounded about her. Her eyes adjusted to the light, and she gasped at the sight before her. Men and women ran about the square, dressed in ragged garb, wailing and moaning. One woman beat her breast and screamed with sorrow. She pulled at her hair until the sinew tie holding the dark strands at her nape fell free. She tugged at handfuls of hairs as she sank to the ground, weeping. Then, she pounded the ground with her closed fists until her hands bled.

Rebecca stared, stunned and horrified. Who was the woman? It wasn't the dead boy's mother, Ice From Sky. Could this woman be a close relative?

She glanced at Night Wind, saw the way he was watching her, and she flushed. "That woman—she—"

"That is Angry Woman, sister to Ice From Sky."

And then Rebecca recognized the woman as one of many who had brought Red Fox broth to drink.

"She will hurt herself!"

Night Wind's eyes narrowed as he turned to regard the screaming woman. "She is mourning in the custom of my people. She is showing how sad she is that the child has died."

The woman stopped then and moved away from the village center, seating herself before a wigwam.

Suddenly, a little boy of about four years came out of the wigwam where Rebecca had ministered to Red Fox. He was naked; his face was smeared with a black substance and his cheeks were painted with red lines. He carried a small bow, perhaps crafted especially for him, and several arrows. The child began to sing in an angry tone as he ran about the village, his antics mirroring a mad man's.

Rebecca inhaled sharply. The boy's pain made her stomach clench in sympathy. She didn't have to ask to know who the child was. It could only be someone close to Red Fox. His younger brother. She looked away, unable to bear the sight.

Night Wind grabbed her head and forced her to watch the boy. "Feel his pain, *Meteinuwak X' quai.* Hear him cry for his older brother. Know that Gift From Forest will never again see his *Niimut.*"

Rebecca began to sob, for she could well feel the boy's pain. And she felt responsible. Her head told her it wasn't her fault, but her heart spoke otherwise.

When the young child, Gift From Forest, had appeared, others within the village stood, transfixed, watching, their faces showing their sympathy and grief. Rebecca expected that any moment they would glare accusingly at her, but they never once looked her way, their sole attention was with Gift From Forest. The proceedings continued. Ice From Sky came out of the wigwam, and Rebecca's throat tightened with her tears.

She heard a sound from Night Wind. She glanced at him, but she could read nothing in his expression as he stared at Ice From Sky. He tore his gaze from the woman and looked at Rebecca, his onyx eyes glittering. "You have seen enough," he said.

He took Rebecca back to his wigwam. "You will remain here until I come for you." He turned to leave.

She grabbed his arm. "Where are you going?" The heat of his skin burned her fingers. She was grateful to be inside again, but she was afraid for her life, afraid to be left alone.

Night Wind stared at her, his gaze devoid of emotion. "I must go. I must see to the burial of the one who has left this world."

Stung by his tone, Rebecca released him. "I can't stay here. You can't expect me to wait here without knowing!"

The brave glared at her. "Do not try to leave us, Medicine Woman. If you do this, you will be killed. Wherever you go, we will find you."

Her blood froze. "You would kill me?"

He didn't answer her, and she believed then that he was capable of her murder. *How could I have forgotten that he is a savage?*

"I will come for you when it is time."

Rebecca felt dizzy with fear as Night Wind left her.

The day passed slowly as Rebecca waited. The sounds outside the wigwam intensified with each hour, and tortured by the noise, Rebecca put her hands over her ears to shut out the horrendous cries. But the sounds continued, and soon the rhythm of drums joined the cacophony of wails, and she couldn't escape them. She lay, huddled on the sleeping mat, a fur over her head, her hands over her ears.

"Stop! Stop it!" she cried.

And the drums continued to pound and the mourning went on until Rebecca wanted to scream.

* * *

The Indian woman watched the mourners with a hidden smile. She herself had participated in the ritualistic display, but unlike the others she was glad Red Fox was dead, for it meant that her own son would move up in the line to be chief.

The matron sat on a mat outside her wigwam and studied Night Wind as he crossed the yard. The warrior had painted his face black in the tradition of a man mourning his brother. The woman scowled. Night Wind and Red Fox were not brothers! They had shared the same father; they were not of the same clan. Night Wind was of the Wolf clan while Red Fox was of the Turtle. Since kinship was determined by mothers, not fathers, it would be Dark Eagle who would be future sachem . . . that is, if anything happened to the next in line, Gift From Forest, Red Fox's younger brother.

The woman wasn't concerned about Dark Eagle's chances of being sachem. She could get rid of Gift From Forest as easily as she had his brother.

Night Wind approached, and the woman stiffened. He nodded and passed by her to enter the next wigwam. The matron relaxed. The brave suspected nothing of her involvement. The only one Night Wind thought responsible for the boy's death was the one who couldn't save him—the white woman.

She smirked. *Good.* She could continue with her plans with no one being the wiser.

Eight

"Come, Medicine Woman."

Rebecca glanced up. Sun Blossom stood in the doorway, motioning her to follow. The Lenape maiden looked at her without expression.

Where was Night Wind? Rebecca wondered, swallowing hard. He had specifically told her to wait for his return. Would he be angry if she went with Sun Blossom? Where was the young woman taking her? "Where is Night Wind?"

"Tipaakke Shaakha is preparing for the Big House. He cannot come for you."

Rebecca stood from where she'd been crouched beside the fire pit. For two days she'd been a prisoner within the wigwam. Each day she'd been brought food supplies by someone within the village. It was never the same person. No one looked at her. No one said a word.

"Where are we going?" she asked as she preceded Sun Blossom into the yard. She felt anxious. Night Wind was angry, but he was still her only ally within the camp. Now he was gone, and she was unprotected.

"We go to Big House. My people there speak to the Great Spirit."

As the women crossed the compound, Rebecca noticed that the village had visitors. There were many unfamiliar faces among the Indians. The number of

Lenape had increased. She stopped and stared as new arrivals came out of the forest and were greeted by the village residents. People from other villages, Rebecca guessed, had come to pay their respects to the deceased child and his grieving family.

The inside of the Big House was filled to overflowing. Woven mats and bundles of dried grass had been spread on the ground for people to sit on. Those attending were seated along the structure's walls in two rows, for there were so many of them. There were two fire pits within the house, one centrally located in each half of the building. A fire had been lit in each pit, and smoke unfurled upward, filtering through holes in the gabled roof.

The air smelled of bear grease, smoke, and burning tobacco. Indians conversed quietly, almost reverently, as they waited for the ceremonies to begin.

Rebecca experienced a jolt of terror as she wondered why she'd been brought here. Where they going to sacrifice her in atonement for Red Fox's death?

She was led to an empty spot along the wall, in the back row, next to a crinkle-faced matron she'd never before laid eyes on. Sun Blossom sat on her opposite side. Rebecca strained for a glimpse of Night Wind, but couldn't find him anywhere among the crowd.

Men and women were dressed in their finery. Their clothing was highly decorating with beads, quill work, and shells that must have been brought from a faraway place near the sea.

A brave began playing the drum, and several dancers went to the center of each half of the structure. They danced around the firepits while the Lenape chanted and sang a sorrowful song that made a lump rise to Rebecca's throat. The air was smoky, filled with the scent of burning herbs and ceremonial plants.

The drummer ceased, and a big masked man came

forward to speak to those seated on the Big House's south side. His identity hidden by the strange mask, he walked about as he spoke, addressing those seated in each section of the Big House. The people listened with rapt attention as the orator, whom Rebecca finally recognized as the shaman, Iron Bear, led the ceremony commemorating the passing of a young warrior.

A harsh cry resounded about the building, and all heads turned as a figure appeared from the west door. The Indian, his face smeared with charcoal, his cheeks lined with red paint, sprang into the center, his naked body glistening with grease and oil.

The brave cried out and shook a spear in one hand and a bow in the other. He began to dance, his motions mimicking a warrior engaged in battle.

"He is protecting the dead one from evil spirits," Sun Blossom explained in a hushed voice.

Rebecca nodded, watching as the man dipped and spun, the paint and his long flying hair hiding his features. "Who—"

Her words ceased abruptly when the warrior screamed, his bellowing voice seeming to shake the walls of the house. The man quieted and began to dance slowly, gracefully, his muscles and limbs fluid as he moved about the room. From the west side of the structure where the Turtle clan sat to the south and east where the Turkey and Wolf clans were seated, the brave danced a song of grief. In his dance, he fought off the demons that might come for the dead one's soul.

The drummer began to play, keeping time with the dancer's footsteps. As the warrior's actions hastened, so too did the beat of the drum. Soon, the brave's dance was a display of frenzied activity and energy, and the people within the Big House began to cheer as the man danced and moved faster about the room.

She was too fascinated with the dance to be embarrassed by the sight of his nakedness. The dance continued for a long while, the dancer's steps becoming more wild, more significant of a man's grief. The drums beat faster, louder, and Rebecca's heart raced in equal rhythm.

As if one, the Indian and the rhythm of the drum stopped at the same moment. The ensuing silence was deafening to Rebecca's ears, and she stared at the man, transfixed, wondering who he was. She was physically moved by his performance, her breathing erratic, her pulse racing.

Then the dancer looked up and met her gaze. Her heart stopped, and then began to beat rapidly as she recognized the Lenape brave.

The man was Night Wind.

The ceremony continued with dancers and chanters, and gifts from village residents to the deceased one's family. Rebecca felt like an intruder as she watched the proceedings. No one other than Night Wind had bothered to glance her way, and the brave's gaze seemed to scorch her whenever he looked her way. She had never before experienced such a startling physical reaction to another human being. Her whole body throbbed with heat, almost in rhythm with the Lenape drums. Her nipples tingled, and her breath grew alternately shallow and harsh.

Without Rebecca's awareness, Sun Blossom had disappeared, and Rebecca felt more alone, more awkward. Hours passed, and forced to remain there, Rebecca became hungry and tired, but these people seemed oblivious to the need for food and sleep.

Then, Night Wind appeared, crouched at her side. Rebecca gasped, for she had lost track of him. His face had been scrubbed clean, and he had put on his loincloth. His chest was bare, and she couldn't keep her gaze from dropping to his smooth, hard muscles.

The brave took her arm and pulled her to her feet. "Come," he mouthed to her.

"Night Wind," she breathed. Her stomach went into spasms as soon as he touched her. Her breathing grew rapid as he took her from the Big House to a large firepit outside in the yard.

He released her and she shivered. He gestured for her to sit on one of the rush mats that had been laid out in a circle around the fire. She sat down, leaning toward the flame for warmth.

Night Wind bent over the huge pot on the fire. "You are hungry," he said, without looking at her. She saw him scowl. "Come. There is nothing here for you to eat. Let us go to the *week wam.*"

Reluctantly, Rebecca left the fire to follow Night Wind. She took a seat on her sleeping pallet, while the brave worked to light a flame in the firepit. Soon, he had a fire, which he continued to feed until the structure filled with heat.

"I didn't mean to take you from your ceremony," Rebecca said when the silence had gone on for too long.

He looked at her then. "I have mourned my brother. I will continue to feel his loss until the day I reach the end of my white path."

"Yes, but—"

"I will go back to the Big House when it is time. The mourning time for my people lasts for twelve days. I am not done."

He stared at her, his onyx eyes glowing, and flushing, she looked away. The image of his oiled naked body was clear in Rebecca's mind. Suddenly, she was embarrassed that she had seen his genitals. Night

Wind was a magnificent figure fully clothed; without clothes, his beauty was more startling.

She thought of his smooth chest muscles and wondered what it would feel like to touch them. Rebecca mentally scolded herself for her shocking thoughts.

When she faced him again, he was busy preparing something for them to eat. Since coming to the village, she'd learned that Lenape men didn't cook. It was up to the women to fix the food, and they made two meals, leaving a pot over the fire for any other time their men might get hungry. Night Wind's cooking surprised her. Why didn't he demand that she make the meal? He probably decided that the White Medicine Woman couldn't cook or heal.

He fixed *sa pan,* a dish she'd learned to enjoy during her stay with the Indians. It was made of green corn that had been dried, roasted, and then ground and sifted. To this, Night Wind added water and then boiled the mixture until it made a tasty, sweet porridge.

Studying Night Wind, Rebecca couldn't help but remember his tender touch on her lips . . . and now he was here making sure she ate. She was puzzled by his kindness to the one he blamed for his brother's death.

When the *sa pan* was ready, Night Wind ladled the porridge from the clay pot where it had cooked over the fire into a *lo' kas,* a Lenape wooden bowl. Then he gave Rebecca her share with a spoon.

"Thank you," she murmured, cradling the bowl, enjoying its warmth.

His obsidian eyes burned as he gazed at her. She felt an answering flame in her abdomen. Her breasts tingled and felt full. Rebecca fought the urge to cover herself with her arms. She kept her hand about the wooden bowl instead, pretending an interest in the porridge's white wisps of rising steam.

Night Wind said nothing, but she sensed that he continued to watch her as she placed the tip of her spoon into the *sa pan* for her first mouthful. The spoon shook as she lifted it to her lips.

"Shi'kiXkwe."

Rebecca met his gaze. "What does that mean?"

He looked away and proceeded to fill his own bowl.

"Night Wind?"

He stilled, and an odd tension filled the ensuing silence. He regarded her over his shoulder, his gaze intense. "It means Woman of Beauty."

She was startled. Had he been referring to her? Rebecca inhaled sharply at his expression. He thought she was beautiful!

Night Wind's attention went to his food. He tasted his *sa pan* and seemed satisfied with his culinary efforts. He ate several mouthfuls and stopped to pour each of them a cup of water. Rebecca accepted a wooden cup, her fingers tingling as their hands brushed. Then, she watched him as he took a sip from his own, the way his throat convulsed as he swallowed, how he wet his lips when he was done.

Rebecca looked away, disturbed by her body's reaction to his simplest actions. She concentrated instead on her food and finished her *sa pan,* satisfying her hunger. The warmth of the fire and the heat generated from eating the hot porridge dispelled the chill from the November day. She sat back, replete, and observed Night Wind, who was too busy satisfying his own hunger to pay her any mind.

Rebecca felt her face heat as her thoughts went wild, returning to the image of Night Wind dancing naked in the Big House. She'd never before seen a fully unclothed male, and the Indian brave was beautiful in his dance, a specimen of pure male at his most vulnerable, grieving for someone he cared for dearly.

What would it be like to be the recipient of such love? It had been a long time since Rebecca had experienced tenderness and affection, nearly six months since she'd seen her mother, and her father had died when she was only a few months old . . . before she'd had the chance to know him.

She studied the brave as he stirred the *sa pan*. His black hair shone in the firelight. His features were shadowed in the glow by the rough plains of his face.

"Do you want more?" he asked, fixing her with his gaze.

Heart racing at being caught staring, she shook her head, and he proceeded to fix himself another bowl. Rebecca recalled the energy he'd exerted during the dance. She understood why he was so hungry. Since her capture, she'd never seen him eat so much.

He looked at her and frowned. "You not thirsty?"

She nodded hurriedly and placed the cup to her mouth. The water was cold, but she was warm enough now to enjoy it.

"I appreciate the food," she said after a long moment of silence.

He grunted his reply and continued eating. Stung by his reluctance to make conversation, Rebecca didn't say another word.

When he was done, Night Wind collected their bowls and went outside. Rebecca could picture him scouring the wooden vessels with sand; the Indians rarely used water for cleaning their utensils, but she thought the sand worked quite well.

He returned within seconds, it seemed, and put away the bowls and cup. "I must go back to the Big House," he said, only then facing her, his features stern.

She started to rise.

"No." He held up his hand. "You will stay here."

"But I want to go back."

He shook his head. "You will stay here," he said, his tone commanding no argument. "I will come back."

Night Wind left, and Rebecca lay upon the sleeping mat, listening to the strange music coming from the Big House. She fell asleep to the continuing sound hours later. Night Wind had never returned.

She felt warmth. Something within the wigwam moved, and she realized that she was no longer alone. She didn't move, but lay, listening. She could hear the mourning songs from the Big House. Rebecca's breath stilled as she struggled to hear whoever was inside the wigwam, but could hear nothing. The thought of danger brought her fully awake, and she bolted to her feet, searching wildly for the intruder.

"Night Wind?" she gasped. It was too dark to see.

"Kihiila. Reb-bec-ca. It is Night Wind." He moved into a small shaft of moonlight filtering in through the smoke hole in the wigwam's roof.

Rebecca inhaled sharply. Naked, but for his breechcloth, he made her heart palpitate with desire, her mind racing with wanton thoughts. He didn't stop to stare; he bent to rummage through his supplies, gathering furs. He prepared a sleeping mat only a few feet from where she'd slept. A lump rose to her throat as she watched him. The thought of sleeping so close to the attractive warrior made her stomach flutter with anticipation.

He looked at her. "I must sleep here. There is no other place."

She was infused with heat. "The village has many guests," she said.

He nodded. Night Wind reached for the ties of his breechcloth. Rebecca gasped, and he smiled, a flash of white teeth in the darkness, and dropped his hands.

"But you have already seen me without *sahk-koo-ta'kun*," he said.

"Yes," she breathed, her heart thumping. She had seen him without his breechcloth before. *But never when we were alone together.*

The brave yawned, and she saw how tired he was. Had he danced again before the others? She could detect no odor of bear's grease and the charcoal and red paint was gone from his face. Then, she noticed his hair was damp. He must have bathed in the river, she thought, as she settled herself back onto her sleeping mat.

The one thing that had most struck her about the Indians was how faithful they were to bathing daily. She had grown to like the practice as well, and wondered how her mother and aunt could have thought that a person could become ill simply by taking frequent baths.

As Night Wind positioned himself on the sleeping mat, the scent of him came to her.

"Sleep well, Night Wind," she whispered.

His reply was a sleepy-sounding murmur in Algonquin, the words musical and pleasurable to her.

Rebecca fell asleep, Night Wind's presence making her feel safer and more secure from the uncertainty of her fate.

The drums had grown silent; the Lenape had gone to their beds for the night.

She awoke to light filtering in through the wigwam's smoke hole. She opened her eyes and then sat up quickly, her gaze darting to Night Wind's pallet, but to her disappointment, he had gone. Rebecca rose to her feet, longing to go outside and walk about, but when she opened the door flap, there was a fierce Indian warrior standing guard before the wigwam. Any hopes she might have had for freedom died.

She allowed the fur flap to fall and paced about the shelter. *I'll go mad if I don't get out of here!*

Rebecca recalled Night Wind's wet hair. He had taken a bath. How she longed to do the same, to feel clean again!

You're mad to be thinking of cleanliness while your life hangs in the balance, she mentally scolded herself.

Her stomach rumbled and she began to think of food instead. If she didn't keep up her strength, she'd lose her reasoning powers. She'd need all her wits about her if she were to think of a plan to escape.

Rebecca searched the wigwam for something to eat and found some ground corn and a skin of water. She mixed the two to a consistency that would form corn cakes. What she wouldn't give right now for one of her mother's flour cakes!

Placing the corn cakes in a clay pot, she stoked up the fire with kindling that Night Wind must have brought in during the night, and then she carefully set the pot in the flames. She handled the pot reverently for she knew how many hours it took to make it.

She left the pot on the fire until the smell of corn cakes filled the air, and she knew they were done. Smiling with satisfaction, Rebecca found a spoon and flipped over the two cakes to quickly toast the other sides. Next, she removed one cake, struggling as it kept slipping from the spoon. Finally, using a piece of buckskin, she held onto the hot pot and dumped the cake into a bowl.

She was enjoying the smell while she allowed it to

cool when the fur door flap lifted, and she saw Night
Wind looking at her with a surprise in his onyx eyes.

"You know how to cook," he said, sounding
amazed.

"I learned to cook your way during my stay with
the Cayuga."

His face darkened. "Our way is not the way of the
Cayuga."

"No," she mumbled, "of course not."

Night Wind came to her and handed her some dried
venison. "Eat. We must go into the forest."

Rebecca, who had already begun to eat her corn
cake, paused in the act of taking another bite. "Why?"
she said, taking the venison from his hand. "Why
must we go into the woods?"

"You will see." His mysterious answer gave her a
prickling of unease.

Nine

The Big House remained empty when Night Wind and Rebecca slipped from the wigwam into the dawn-ridden sky.

"Is the ceremony *over?*" she asked in a hushed voice. The villagers and their guests had danced and sung well into the night. Usually, the Lenape were up and about by now, doing their daily chores. Their exhaustion was exhibited by their absence in the center square.

"No, my people will rise soon to continue the dance of mourning." Night Wind shifted a satchel from one hand to the next and then checked on the arrows in his quiver.

Rebecca noted with surprise the stock of provisions he carried. How far were they journeying? She became puzzled when he stopped at another wigwam, went inside, and came out within seconds with a puppy in his arms.

He handed Rebecca the dog. "You carry."

"Why are we taking the dog?"

"It belonged to the little one. We go to pray over the boy's resting place."

The dog had been Red Fox's, Rebecca realized. They were going to visit the boy's grave. Her eyes drifted to study the sack of provisions and the bow slung over Night Wind's shoulder. How far was this place that they would need food enough for two days? Unless Night Wind planned to leave her in the woods. Alone . . . and cold.

Rebecca kept her fears to herself as she took the sleeping puppy and fell into step behind the dark, disturbing warrior. Night Wind said nothing more as they began their trek into the woods.

The route they took was a small path which had been recently cleared away. Rebecca could tell this by the appearance of the cut brush. No doubt Night Wind had come this way when he'd first gone to Red Fox's burial site.

She watched her step as she negotiated the terrain beneath her feet. The path was uneven. An unseen rock could easily make her stumble and fall.

Before they had left, Night Wind had ensured that she was amply provided with furs and leggings, but even so, the bite of the mid-November wind chilled her, stinging her face and neck, creeping inside the tiniest opening in her fur mantle to freeze her skin. The puppy awoke and squirmed within her arms, until she was forced to stop and set him down. After he relieved himself, he was only too happy to be carried again.

Night Wind and she walked for what seemed like hours to Rebecca. Indeed, it must have been quite a long while, for by the time they reached a small clearing, the sun was high in the November sky. There, Night Wind set down his pack of provisions and took the puppy from Rebecca's arms. He placed the puppy tenderly on a beaver pelt and then made a seat nearby for Rebecca. He then took out food and handed it to her, his fingers brushing hers lightly.

"Eat," he said.

She took a bite, recognizing it as a meal she'd learned to make since her stay in the village. *Ka-ha-*

ma'kun was a favorite of the Lenape men, who carried it on their hunting expeditions.

"Why have we stopped?" she said. Rebecca glanced about the clearing and saw nothing unusual about the place.

Night Wind withdrew his knife from his legging strap. He fingered the blade of the weapon, running his thumb carefully along the sharp flint.

He didn't look at her. "We are here to pray to the spirits to ensure that the little one gets to the Afterworld safely."

"Why here?"

The way he studied the knife made her nervous. He glanced up to gaze at her over the blade, and she shuddered and raised her hand to her throat.

Was he going to murder her in cold blood?

"Here is the resting place." In a sudden move, he jabbed his knife in a direction to the right. Rebecca gasped as if the blade had been aimed directly at her.

And then she saw the fresh mound of dirt between two trees. A small painted totem pole marked the grave site.

"Red Fox's grave," she whispered in dawning comprehension.

"We do not speak of the name of our dead, Rebbec-ca. It is wrong to do this. More wrong here because it will be holy ground."

The puppy woke then and howled, sensing the food. Rebecca smiled as Night Wind hand-fed the dog while rubbing the puppy's head, his fingers entwined in the animal's soft fur. When the dog was finished eating, the animal licked Night Wind's fingers in appreciation.

Rebecca frowned when Night Wind withdrew. He showed no appreciation for the puppy's loving warmth. The brave rose abruptly and moved to the boy's grave. He stared at the recently disturbed earth.

"It was here that I came a day ago to prepare this grave," he said quietly after a long moment of silence. "I searched for miles until I found this spot. It is a good resting place. A peaceful place." He turned to her, pinning her with his gaze. "When I am done, the spirits will be satisfied and make this ground holy."

Puzzled by his words, Rebecca approached as he swung back to the grave. "He was an endearing child," she said softly as she came up beside him.

Night Wind said nothing. His face looked as if it were carved from stone.

Tears filled her eyes, blurring her sight of the small grave. "I'm sorry," she whispered, her throat tightening. "I'm so sorry."

He spun and grabbed her shoulders. "Why didn't you use your powers! You could have healed him!"

Stunned by the violence of his tone, she couldn't answer him. She broke down then, crying in earnest. Huge gulping sobs tore from her chest. She cried and shook so hard while he held her that her stomach hurt.

He released her and turned away. "Go and sit, Medicine Woman. We do not need your tears. There is work to be done."

Rebecca choked back her tears. "Can I help?"

He scowled. "You are to watch, nothing more. There must be a witness and no one else within the village could leave the mourning ceremony."

She sat as she was told, back where they had first set down the provision. The puppy slept on the beaver fur, oblivious to the tension between the two people. Rebecca watched curiously as Night Wind knelt before Red Fox's grave. He raised his head and began to chant. His deep voice was musical as it rose and fell with the sweet soulful sound of the Lenape song.

Rebecca wondered what he was singing, the meaning of his words, but didn't dare ask. She knew it was a special moment for him, and she must not interrupt or interfere in the ceremony.

Why must he have a witness? she wondered. A witness to what?

He became silent. Night Wind rose and came to where his satchel lay on the ground beside her. He rummaged inside and withdrew a small bow and a quiver of arrows. *Red Fox's bow,* she thought. He took them to the grave and set the weapon upon the mound with reverence. He returned, took some food and then set it on the grave next to the small bow. When he was done, he stood at the foot of the grave and prayed in his native tongue, his volume intensifying as he looked up with his arms extended toward the darkening sky.

He continued to pray and chant for a long time, and Rebecca watched, fascinated. Then, he faced her with a frighteningly blank look in his dark eyes. He approached and crouched where she sat. Rebecca shrank back in reaction to his expression, her heart beating a rapid tattoo.

But it wasn't her he sought. He picked up the sleeping puppy beside her, and the animal woke up and squirmed in his arms. Rebecca experienced a strange ill feeling as Night Wind carried the animal to the dead boy's grave. Her fears calmed slightly when he set down the dog and spoke soothingly until the animal lay down, his tongue trustingly licking Night Wind's hand. Then, Night Wind pulled out his knife.

Rebecca stood up, seeing his intention. "No!" she cried out, but it was too late. Night Wind had slit the puppy's throat. The dog lay, his life blood draining onto Red Fox's grave. The animal was dead.

She stared in gaping horror as Night Wind rose as if in a trance. Rebecca saw his expression. His face was hard, cold. She looked down and saw the dog's blood on his hands, and something within her snapped.

"Monster!" she screamed. She threw herself at him, beating his chest, his shoulders, with her fists. "You barbaric, murdering savage!"

The shock of witnessing the death of an innocent puppy made her hysterical. She pounded his chest, sobbing. "Savage. A puppy!" she cried. "A poor defenseless puppy!"

Night Wind endured her blows, standing stoically for a time, until she began to curse and pummel his stomach. With a growl of anger, he grabbed her arms. She hollered and squirmed against his grip, but she was no match for his strength.

He didn't say a word as he fought for control. When she finally slumped against him, exhausted, he was silent a few seconds before he spoke. "It was necessary."

She looked up, meeting his gaze, her horror mirrored in her wide-eyed gaze. "Necessary! To kill an innocent animal?" Rage and fear warred with her horror. "Is that how you did it? Is that how you killed my dog?"

A muscle moved along his jaw. "This is not the same."

"You told me why you killed my dog. You feared for your life. But this puppy posed no danger to you! Why did you have to kill it!"

"It is the Lenape way. The way of the Spirits. If a sacrifice is not made, then Red Fox's spirit would not make its way to the sacred Afterworld. He would roam the earth, forgotten. The gods must be appeased."

"Why that's barbaric! It's sav—"

"Savage," he interrupted, his visage as frightening as a sudden burst of thunder. "According to the white man, I am a savage, Reb-bec-ca. I kill and hurt for no reason."

Rebecca blinked then looked away. She could understand why he'd killed her dog. The dog had been a threat to him. The animal might have caused his capture and his death. But the puppy?

"Wasn't your brother a good boy?"

Night Wind appeared offended by her question. "He was."

"Then why must you appease the gods so that he might get to heaven? The Bible says—"

"Who is this Bible?"

"The Bible isn't a who, it's a book. The written word of God."

"Your God has written for you a book?" Night Wind was thoughtful. "I have seen your white man's books." He knew of books through his dealings with the English. They were marks on what the white man called parchment. The man who had showed it to him had told him that it was words that all English people who could read could understand. Night Wind had asked the man what this "read" meant, and was told it was to know what the marks meant, that the marks actually represented the things man said.

Now here was Rebecca telling him that the Great Spirit had made marks for her. "You have seen the Great Spirit?" She was a healer, and this, he thought, could be possible.

Rebecca narrowed her gaze and then realized that he was serious with his question. "Of course not! The

Bible was written by great men. God spoke through them."

"And you believe this to be true?"

She nodded.

"Then these men have seen and talked to the Great Spirit," he reasoned.

"Well . . ." she said with the realization that he would never believe the truth.

He grunted. "And you say our ways are strange." He dismissed the conversation as if he'd lost interest. "Come. We must return to the village."

"What about the dog?" She looked at the animal, saw the blood, and felt sick.

"We must leave it. The spirits will take it."

"But shouldn't you bury it?" Her stomach roiled in angry protest.

The brave shook his head.

"I'll do it then," she said. The dog would be eaten by the animals of the forest, not taken by the spirits as Night Wind believed. She started to move closer, but he grabbed her shoulders hard. "Dog is dead. He will not know he is left for the gods."

"The gods aren't going to take him, but a wolf might!" The mental image of her own words made her jerk from his hold and run to the bushes where she lost her last meal.

She vomited until her belly was empty while Night Wind stood by silently watching. When she was done, she straightened, her face pale, her blue eyes luminous with tears. "I'll leave the puppy," she said. *Damn him! Damn him for his barbaric, insensitive ways!*

"For the spirits," Night Wind said, nodding with satisfaction.

"For the animals!" she spat back, her anger with him renewing her spirit, and she stomped toward the trail that led back to Night Wind's village.

Night Wind didn't say another word, but sometime later when she looked back over his shoulder, she saw that he had fallen into step behind her. She refused to look back again after that, but trudged on, her chin raised in defiant anger. Her stomach felt queasy, and the feeling of nausea lingered long after she'd gotten sick, but she didn't let him know that. She didn't want him to think she was weak.

The forest spread out before her. She continued, and the horror of the sacrifice subsided. She felt less nauseous. Her interest in her surroundings grew. *Where are we?* Were they east or west of the village? North or south?

She studied the woods. If she tried to escape, would she survive the night? Could she survive the journey to Delaware?

If only she had food enough to last her a few days. She would be warm enough in the furs and leggings. The air was cold, and her cheeks stung, but she could endure that.

The trail ended, and Rebecca stopped. "I can't find the path!" she exclaimed. While she was contemplating escape, she must have strayed from the original trail. She turned to Night Wind. "Can you lead the way?"

Night Wind nodded. He took out his knife as he passed her, and began hacking a fresh path through the underbrush of the woods.

Rebecca hesitated before following. She studied her surroundings, and was wondering if this were a good time to flee, when Night Wind called to her, and she suddenly realized that he had stopped and was waiting for her to join him.

"Come, Medicine Woman. We must get back to the village before the moon rises in the night sky."

He stared at her as if daring her to escape. He

turned back to cutting brush only after she had started to obey. It had been weeks since the leaves had fallen from their branches, but briars and evergreens had taken growth over most of the woods, and tall dried grass filled in the ground cover.

Rebecca knew she had to escape and that this might be her only chance. She studied her captor's back, saw his concentration on clearing the path, and she bolted in the opposite direction. She ran, heedless of the obstacles in her path. Branches slapped her face as she brushed past them; thorns caught her clothing as she stumbled through briars in a desperate bid to be free.

She never heard him behind her. She was running, getting away, and then suddenly, she was flying through the air and falling as Night Wind threw himself onto her. Rebecca hit the ground hard. Her head reeled as she lay, winded from the impact. Night Wind lay beside her. He recovered more quickly than she, rolling to the side, flipping her onto her back, and pinning her by the shoulders.

She gasped for air, and as her breath slowly returned to her, she became conscious of his anger. He was frightening. "I told you what would happen if you tried to escape!" he growled, glaring.

She could feel his weight pressed into her as if his lower body had been specially molded to fit her own. Her abdomen was cradled between his legs, and his thigh muscles burned her through layers of buckskin and fur. His chest was solid, an immovable wall of rock rising above her. He released her one shoulder, slipping his hand toward his leg. She squirmed, afraid for her life, when he drew his knife.

"Are you going to kill me?" she asked. Her voice quivered. She held her breath when he held up the blade. He eyed the weapon as if he were contemplating its sharpness. He would enjoy using it on her, she thought.

He lowered the blade to her face. She inhaled sharply. He fixed her with his gleaming gaze. Her blood turned to ice crystals.

"You should not have run, Medicine Woman." He made as if he would cut her, but he only caressed her with the blade. Her heart thundered as she held her breath.

Staring at him in fear, Rebecca flattened herself against the ground. She swallowed hard as he stared at her with onyx eyes glittering. The image of his wild dance returned to her. This man was grieving, she thought. Half crazed. Dear God, why had she tried to escape! What could she have been thinking to believe she could out distance him?

"If you're going to kill me, do it and be done," she said.

"Perhaps I will only cut you instead," he said menacingly. He raised his knife and shifted his hold on her. In a bid for life, she began to struggle, but she couldn't budge his weight.

"Chitkwe'se!"

She froze, sensing the urgency of his tone.

"Do you want to die?"

"No! But I don't want to be maimed either!"

He dropped his knife, and mesmerized by his look, Rebecca heard it thud onto the ground beside her. Staring at her mouth, he cupped her jaw.

"I cannot," he growled, then he slowly kissed her. Then as passion overtook him, his mouth ground against her lips, and she whimpered in protest. His assault softened, enticed . . . seduced, and she moaned and surrendered.

Night Wind raised his head. She was gasping; her whole body awakened with renewed life. This close

she noted little things about him that she'd never noticed before . . . the tiny lines at the corners of his
eyes . . . the small star-shaped scar on his cheek that
was invisible at a quick glance.

She stared at his mouth, recalling the fire of his
kiss. Such an interesting mouth with thin sensual lips.
Such a beautifully created male mouth . . .

His expression changed. He scowled at her and
rose, jerking her to her feet.

"You are not to escape," he commanded. The man
who had tenderly kissed her, showed her what it was
to desire someone, had vanished. In his place was the
angry savage who had kidnapped and threatened her
more than once.

"I do not tell untruths, Reb-bec-ca. I mean what I
say. If you try to leave again, I will use this." He held
up the knife. "I will be forced to punish you."

She didn't doubt that he meant it.

The return journey to the village seemed shorter to
Rebecca, despite their straying from the original path.
Night Wind had forced her to take the lead, so he
could keep his eye on her, and she was conscious of
his gaze boring into her back as she followed his directions for the journey.

It was dusk when they arrived at the village. Rebecca heard the mourning ceremony in the Big House.
The villagers and their guests were still beseeching
the spirits to bring Red Fox safely into the Afterworld.
Their prayers, she knew, would be accompanied by
the rhythmic beat of the drums, the shaking of the
Lenape gourd and turtle-shell rattles, and the graceful
footsteps of the warrior-dancers.

Night Wind was solemn as he entered the village.
He left her at his wigwam with a warning. "Escape
and suffer," he said. The door flap remained open,
and she saw him wave to another Indian. She got a

glimpse of the guard's tattooed face before the deer-skin fell to close her inside.

And then her captor left her.

Ten

She was called to appear before the tribal council on the fourth day after Red Fox's death. Ice From Sky, the boy's mother, was present along with other respected matrons of the village. Rebecca saw Night Wind and Iron Bear among the male members, and her eyes met Night Wind's as Sun Blossom brought her before them into the circle in the yard.

Iron Bear looked formidable in his full feathered headdress and medicine man's garb. He carried one of the tools of his position, a turtle shell rattle mounted on a long whittled stick. His face was painted beyond recognition, but Rebecca recognized the man's familiar glare and his bulky form.

Night Wind looked away after one quick glance. Rebecca silently begged him to look at her again. She sought support from the man who was responsible for bringing her to the village, but he refused to meet her gaze. The brave stared at the ground near his feet. The village chief addressed members of council, and Night Wind switched his attention to Beaver Hawk, still refusing to glance Rebecca's way.

"We are here to discuss the White Medicine Woman," the sachem addressed the people of his village. "She was brought here to heal our little one, but she has failed her duty."

Night Wind tensed as Beaver Hawk began his

speech. He considered himself responsible for Red Fox's death, for he had brought the White Medicine Woman to his village to cure the boy, but she had failed him . . . and she must be punished.

He had been angry at her for not healing Red Fox, but his anger had since passed. Perhaps he'd been wrong to take her from the Cayuga. She would die, and it was because of him. The knowledge hurt him, and it surprised him. Why should he care what happened to the white woman?

The tribal elders discussed the woman's fate, and Night Wind's jaw tightened. Had it been unfair of him to expect Rebecca to heal his brother? Red Fox had gotten well after being in her care, but then he'd died afterward despite Rebecca's powers. Were her magical powers not strong enough? Would her magic save her own life?

". . . For her failure to heal, the white woman must be punished. She will be banished from *Tulpeuta'nai*. If she survives nine risings of the morning sun, then we will know that the gods look kindly upon her and that the end of the little warrior's path was meant to be." Beaver Hawk paused to take a breath. "If this happens, the woman healer will be allowed to return to our village. She will be forgiven and accepted again as the White Medicine Woman. But, if the woman dies, we will know that she held back her powers to help our enemy, the Iroquois."

"What are you doing?" Rebecca gasped to Sun Blossom. "Where are you taking me?"

The council had concluded its meeting, but she had yet to be told of their decision. She was to be punished, but the Indians apparently thought it unnecessary to tell her what form her punishment would take.

Despite Rebecca's entreaty, Sun Blossom was close-mouthed as she escorted Rebecca back to the wigwam. "Someone will come for you," was all the Indian maiden said before disappearing.

Who was coming for her? Was she going to die?

Rebecca's stomach churned and hurt until she thought she'd vomit. She stood in the center of the wigwam with her eyes closed, clenching her sweaty palms. *Dear Lord, help me escape and find Elizabeth. The girl needs me. I want to live.*

The fur flap curtaining the door lifted, and Night Wind entered the wigwam. Rebecca froze and stared at him. Was Night Wind to be her executioner?

"What have they decided?" she asked. She was amazed by how calm she sounded.

"The council had said that you will be banished from Turtle-Town."

Rebecca started. "They are going to let me go?" Her head swam with the rush of joy.

Night Wind looked stern. "This is not something to be happy about, Reb-bec-ca. You will be sent out into the forest without food, without water. The nights are cold, so too the days as great. You will have no blankets or furs to keep you warm, no sleeping mat or fur-lined moccasins."

She shuddered at the imagined chill of his revealing words. "And my clothes?" she said. "Will they strip me naked before they send me away?"

The brave shook his head. "You will keep your tunic and your moccasins, but they will do little to keep away the cold." He grabbed her arm and forced her to the doorway. With an angry sweep of his arm, he gestured to the sky. "See how the clouds fill the sky? Soon it will rain, and the rain will become snow." He paused to allow his message to sink in. His dark eyes glittered. "You will die, Medicine Woman . . . as my young brother, who reached the end of his white path."

"No," she said. "No, I won't."

He forced her to look at him. "Where will you go? How will you find the way?"

"I'll go to my aunt's in the Delaware Colony."

"How far is this aunt's? One rising of the sun to the moon? Two?" He shook his head, his expression mirroring his regret. "I should not have brought you here."

"I'll survive," she insisted.

"You will die in the cold," he said without feeling, and his lack of emotion frightened her as nothing before could.

Night Wind released her arm and stepped out into the yard. "Come."

"Now?" she whispered "I'm to leave now?" She anxiously studied the darkening sky. Soon it would be night with freezing temperatures. He was right; she would die. How could she possibly survive?

"If you live for nine risings of the sun, you may return to our village, and all will be forgotten."

"Nine days," she murmured with horror, and he inclined his bead. "Why nine days?"

"The Great Spirit waits twelve days before accepting a warrior into the Afterworld. Three of them have passed; there are nine left. If you live past this time, then you will be innocent of any wrong to my people. We will know that it was the decision of the gods for our brother to die. We will know that his death was not by your hand."

"But I had nothing to do with Red Fox's death!"

"You are the White Medicine Woman. You healed a Cayuga child, but you allowed a young Lenape warrior to die."

Without further discussion, Night Wind took her

into the forest. He led her down a trail farther, and deeper, into the woods. After they had traveled for a time, he stopped, faced her, and withdrew his knife from his legging. Rebecca's heart thumped as she saw the weapon.

He extended the knife to her, handle first. Rebecca looked at the carved handle and at the man who must have spent many hours crafting the weapon.

"Why are you giving me this?"

"If you are to survive, you must have a weapon. Every warrior has something to defend himself. Even those who have reached the end of the white path. It is only right that you have one to fight off the bad spirits in this world . . . and in the next."

Her hand shook as she accepted the knife. "Thank you." She looked down, stunned by his kindness. When she raised her head to meet his gaze, his eyes flamed with emotion, and she trembled in response.

"I will leave you now."

Her blood froze as she held his gaze. "You're leaving me already?"

"I cannot stay. It is not right." He pointed to his right. "Your Delaware Colony is in that direction. You will have to travel many days." A muscle twitched along his jaw. "Farewell, Medicine Woman."

And he headed back toward the village.

Watching him leave her, Rebecca felt an overwhelming surge of panic. She wanted to call after him, to beg him to stay, but she knew he wouldn't, and she'd only humiliate herself for asking him.

"Tipaakke Shaakha!" she cried.

She saw him freeze, before he turned slowly around. His face was hard, like it'd been carved from stone. His features bore no softening or offer of sympathy for her plight.

."I'm sorry," she said. "For failing Red Fox." *For failing you.*

He stared at her for a long moment before he gave her a nod. Then, he turned and, without a backward glance, continued toward his village.

It wasn't long before Rebecca understood the full meaning of Night Wind's words to her. With his departure, she was suddenly afraid as she realized how alone she was . . . how vulnerable to the dangers of the woods and night.

She forced herself to keep walking, while silently praying that she came to no harm. Were there other Indian tribes out there, waiting to capture her? What about animals? Could there be bears and snakes and wolves just waiting to pounce?

She shuddered as she negotiated the uneven path. She couldn't walk forever, she thought, but she couldn't stop now. Already, the cold was slowly filtering through her fur mantle and past her tunic. Her calf-high moccasins did little to protect her feet. If she paused to rest, Rebecca realized, she'd freeze.

Rebecca gripped firm to Night Wind's knife as she considered her options. She had taken the direction he'd said led to Delaware; and she was scared, for she knew that if Night Wind was right and her destination was days away, she'd die long before reaching it. She couldn't continue for days and days. She had to sleep and eat sometime.

She kept her chin high, and her thoughts on Elizabeth, her young cousin who needed her. She was hungry and thirsty, and she wanted only to sleep. *I'll keep going until I can't walk anymore.* Or until she found food or a sheltered area where she could rest for a little while.

Rebecca kept to the trail until the path narrowed and then disappeared. The sounds of the forest night were frightening, and she tried to ignore them. But she couldn't ignore the dangers of their warning.

She used Night Wind's knife to cut a clean path, but the process was slow and tedious, and she knew she couldn't continue for much longer without food and rest.

Finally, after what seemed to her miles of endless walking and hacking at overgrown brush, Rebecca decided to find shelter for the night. Her journey would be easier by daylight, she decided. *But where shall I sleep? And will I keep warm?* As Night Wind had said, she had no furs or blankets to keep her warm.

The breeze was brisk, and her cheeks stung. She shivered as the cold slipped down her neck to nip at her back. An owl hooted in a nearby tree, and she froze in terror, recalling the bird calls made by the Indians. A twig snapped from somewhere in the near distance, and Rebecca raised her knife, her heart racing and her mouth dry with fear.

Don't panic, she told herself. *If someone or something is out there, you'll need all of your wits about you.*

She tried to relax, to free her breathing, and calm herself down so she could rationally plan her next move. She stood immobile for a time, trying to think. She continued her search for a place to bed down, ignoring her fears and the sounds of the night. She found a spot in a copse of pines and prickly bushes. The entrance to her resting place was small, the area inside cramped, but there was enough room for Rebecca to curl up on her side and close her eyes.

The ground was cold, but covered in pine needles. She lay down, got up again, and rearranged the pine needles so that a small pile cushioned her head. *An adequate bed,* she thought, settling herself down.

She lay, shivering, with the scent of dried pine thick

in her nose and the cold hard ground beneath her weary body. An hour of shivering drove her closer to exhaustion and the point of sleep. Comforted somewhat by the seclusion of the spot and the hidden thorns that surrounded the small stand of evergreens, Rebecca was able to ignore the rustle of the wind in the treetops and the cries of the forest night creatures. She slept until the dull light of the new day woke her, and the need for food became her next concern. She needed to keep up her strength and go on with her journey.

The wind whipped up in a frenzy at Red Fox's grave site. Night Wind stood over the small dirt mound, his arms raised, his eyes closed, and his head thrown back. His dark hair flapped about his face and shoulders as he chanted to the gods and sought solace in his heart.

He was naked but for a small strip of cloth protecting his genitals. He endured the cold, reveling in it as he tried to forget the white woman and the dangers she faced in her banishment.

He shouldn't have given her his knife, but he couldn't have left if he hadn't helped her. It was his fault she was facing death.

Aye! If the woman had magical powers, why hadn't she saved Red Fox? Why wouldn't she save herself?

The fear in her blue eyes had eaten at his soul, made his stomach wrench with sympathy. *I must not think of the woman. She did wrong. She failed Red Fox.*

Then why couldn't he get her out of his mind?

"Oh, great spirits, guide me to do what is right. Forgive my helping her. Help me to stay strong for my people."

Night Wind lowered his arms and bowed his head. He stared at the grave and saw that the dog was gone, taken by the gods in his offering. The woman's reaction to the sacrifice returned to him. "She does not understand, little one," he murmured to his brother's spirit. "She does not understand our ways. It was necessary to kill the dog to ensure your safe journey to the Afterworld."

Night Wind had been at the grave site for two days; having left the woman, he'd come directly here to pray.

Was she dead? he wondered.

Forget her! an inner voice commanded. *Go back to your people. Even now Ice From Sky is mourning her dead son. Think of her and her loss.*

He spun from the grave and retrieved his moccasins from the edge of the clearing. He put them on after donning his leggings and fur wrap. When he left the clearing and headed into the forest, only his right shoulder was bare.

He didn't return to his village. He could not rest until he knew that the woman had survived the two days since he'd left her. He could not forget the White Medicine Woman's eyes . . . her face . . . her haunting beauty. He remembered every little thing about her.

He would find her, and if she were dead, he would bury and pray to the spirits for her. There would be no one to mourn her death . . . but him.

In the Lenape village, a woman watched Ice From Sky leave the compound and head for the forest. She followed her, observing from a distance, a malicious smile curving her lips as Ice From Sky found a spot beneath a tree and knelt. Ice From Sky began to cut her arms, lashing herself with a knife, keening to the heavens in pain of her loss.

The woman watched the mourning mother for a

while and then returned to the village, pleased. There was work to be done. Gift From Forest still stood between Dark Eagle and the chiefdom. She went to her wigwam and got out her satchel of roots and herbs. She had a potion to fix and a child to drink it. She cackled softly. Soon Gift From Forest would join his brother Red Fox in the great Afterworld. Soon, Dark Eagle—her only son—would be the next in line to be the sachem of the Lenape tribe.

On her third day in the wilderness, Rebecca found a handful of berries, but no water to quench her thirst, and she was scared. Had the air gotten cooler? She was so cold she was numb and she silently prayed for the wind to stop. She wouldn't feel so frozen if not for the frigid wind.

She had slept for a few hours huddled within the pine and brush shelter and had risen, rested but extremely cold. Her search for food had sent her moving again, but she was having little luck finding nourishment, and now it was thirst more than hunger that drove her on.

The sky above was cloudy. Rebecca had been walking for over two hours she'd guessed, and there was no sign of life anywhere, not even a bird in a tree top.

Where am I? She glanced about uneasily. Had she come this way before? Had she traveled in a circle? *Dear God, I'm lost. I'm hungry, and thirsty, and cold. Am I going to die?*

A branch snapped in the near distance. Rebecca froze and searched for the source of the sound. Perhaps she'd been hasty in her assumption that no man or beast roamed this area. She could see nothing.

Surely, if it were human, then whoever it was would have shown themselves. She was getting jumpy. She must not panic and allow fear to steal her reason. She was on her own in the forest; she had only herself to rely on to keep alive.

On the other side of Rebecca, in the opposite direction of the sound she'd heard, the Indian watched the white woman struggle with indecision before continuing her trek. He'd been glad to find her alive. He was glad of her spirit and her ability to survive. Night Wind felt a warmth of satisfaction as he saw her change her direction in a course that would take her to water.

Six days left before she would be forgiven. Would she make it? He would follow her till the end if he must. He would know the final outcome, even if he could not help her . . . even if he had to see her die.

Back at the Lenape village, a little boy began to sicken, and the Indians grew concerned that soon they would lose another child . . . another son of the clan of the sachem.

Eleven

Tears came to Rebecca's eyes when she saw the stream. Never had she realized the full beauty of water and her dependence on it. She stumbled to the water's edge and bent to take a drink. Cupping her hands, She scooped up the sparkling, clean water and brought it to her lips, sipping and enjoying the cold moisture on her tongue. The temperature made her shiver, but she didn't care.

Where there was water there must be food, she thought, rising to her feet. She pulled out her knife and eyed the blade thoughtfully. She had a mental image of the man who gave her the weapon. Rebecca longed to see him again. Did he think of her at all? Or had he already forgotten her? She'd cursed him and his people many times in the last three days. Why did she want to see him?

She swallowed against a tight throat and fought to dispel the image. Rebecca focused on the task before her. The knife blade looked sharp. She felt it with her finger, and a small streak of blood rose to the surface of her skin. Yes, it was sharp; it would do the job. But could she kill an animal for food?

Yes, yes, I can! She was hungry, and if it came down to it, she wanted to live badly enough. And hadn't God made animals for man's use?

The days had grown cooler, and the nights were

worse. Rebecca searched for a place to stay and decided to build herself a shelter of sticks and grass and whatever else she could find that might shield her from the elements.

A lightning strike had left a good-sized tree splintered a few feet up from its base. The part that was still standing would make a good support for one side of her lean-to, she decided. What could she use for the other side and back? And what about the roof?

She scouted for over an hour before she found something suitable. She had strayed a distance from her original spot, but she found her way back, dragging the log behind her. Her hands were cold, and her fingers hurt each time the log bumped over the uneven ground. She felt lightheaded and out of breath when she finally reached the splintered tree. Hunger and the need for sleep had left her weak. But she was determined to build a lean-to and stay until she regained her strength.

Rebecca rested for a while until her dizziness passed. She drank from the stream and worked on her shelter. When she was done, she lined the shelter and turned her attention to finding food.

He spied her not long after he'd left his brother's grave, about a half-day's run away. He had taken the direction he'd told her, his feet familiar with the area's terrain. His speed was notable in his tribe. Night Wind had run fast even as a small boy, and although the elders of the village had named him after the conditions of the time of his birth, the children of the village claimed it was because of his running ability. He could outrun, they said, the night wind, which could be swift and vicious.

She was at the stream, bending to take a drink,

when he reached her. He could tell that she was thirsty, that she'd not found water before this. Forbidden to interfere, Night Wind watched her from a distance. His joy at seeing her alive matched any he'd ever felt before.

He knew he should return to his village. If danger should come to Rebecca before the final morning of her banishment, he could do nothing but watch helplessly.

He observed with amusement her attempts to build a shelter. Later, he felt a stirring of pride as the structure was complete. It looked poor by Lenape standards, but for an unexperienced white woman, it was a good attempt. If the wind didn't strengthen, then he knew it would serve her well.

He watched now as she searched for food. He experienced a burst of admiration for her courage. Knife drawn, her gaze alert, she stalked about the forest, looking for game. A rabbit scurried within yards of her, and she spun and then froze, staring at the creature as it nibbled on some dried grass.

You must kill it, Shi'ki, he thought. He saw her crouch and pick up a rock. The rabbit stilled, stared back at her and then went back to eating when Rebecca didn't move.

Night Wind could sense the woman's inner struggle as she inched closer to the animal.

You cannot kill him that way, Rebecca. As a small child, Night Wind and his friends had spent many hours trying to hunt with rocks, and he had finally mastered the skill. But he didn't think a white woman had the skill to kill this way.

He observed with fascination as the rabbit nuzzled the ground in his quest for food and Rebecca's reaction as she crept closer.

At that moment, Night Wind wanted to show himself, to kill the rabbit for her, to cook it over a fire and watch happily as Rebecca satisfied her hunger. The desire to do things for her was strong. *Too strong.*

Go back to the village, he told himself. *Go back before you do something that is forbidden.*

A nearby crash in the forest brush scared both the animal and Rebecca. The small animal darted off. Night Wind saw a huge eight-point buck step from the bushes. Even from his distance, Night Wind detected the fear in Rebecca's eyes.

No, Rebecca! Do not panic! He will not hurt you. He is more frightened of you.

But she stood, her knife poised in readiness to defend.

The brave held his breath. Rebecca's arms shook as she held the blade high. Night Wind admired her beauty and spirit, her determination to survive.

The large buck saw the woman and froze. Night Wind recognized the tension in the deer's coiled muscles. Expecting the animal to turn and run away, he was alarmed when the deer in its fear ran toward her.

Night Wind reached for his bow and arrow. He notched the feathered arrow in readiness as Rebecca fled from the charging deer.

Night Wind pulled back on the bow string. His pulse pounded in his brain. An inner voice scolded him, warned him that he must only watch. *You cannot help her. She must live by her own design for nine days. If you break the law of banishment, Red Fox will not enter the Afterworld. His spirit will forever roam the earth, restless . . . crying . . . wandering unhappily . . . in pain.*

He eased back the bow string, and the arrow fell to the ground at his feet.

* * *

Rebecca screamed and ran from the angry animal to the safety of her lean-to. Her breath slammed within her throat as she reached the entrance, fell to the ground, and scrambled inside on her hands and knees.

"You'll find out now how well you can build, Rebecca," she whispered.

The deer jarred the side of the shelter as it sailed over the roof. The wall, that was constructed of loose sticks wedged into the ground, started to give. *Please, God, don't let it fall!* Rebecca prayed.

Suddenly the noise stopped.

Rebecca listened carefully, her breath rasping loud in the quiet. Where she heard nothing for several minutes, she slipped from her shelter and looked around. The deer had jumped over her lean-to! He hadn't been charging her; he'd been running to escape!

The woman eyed her shelter and grinned. Then, she laughed. The unstable side of the lean-to moved, and the roof fell in, collapsing the structure. Only the one side still stood. Rebecca's laughter died.

"Damn, now I'll have to build it over!" she exclaimed with frustration. She started to reassemble the side and roof. Night was approaching fast; the forest would soon be cloaked in darkness, and the air temperature would drop further.

Food would have to wait, she thought as her stomach rumbled. Shelter was her main concern. Once she had successfully rebuilt her lean-to, she could think again of food.

Rebecca noticed moisture on her head and hands while she was fixing the roof. She looked up and felt the wetness on her face. *Snow!* The flakes fell, one by one, huge white stars drifting to kiss the ground.

Dear God, how would she survive a snowstorm!

The wind picked up and she hugged herself with

her arms. Shivering, she stared at her surroundings, praying for another miracle. "Please, God, make the snow stop and find me food."

Think! Don't panic! she told herself. She'd lived for four months with the Cayuga and then weeks with the Lenape, she must remember something about hunting and trapping. Tears blurred her vision when she drew a blank. *I'm going to die! I'm going to freeze or starve to death!*

She shivered and hugged herself harder. The snow had increased and soon she'd be wet if she didn't get into her shelter. Rebecca crawled into her lean-to, praying for the snow and the wind to stop, and curled into a ball to sleep the night.

Night Wind frowned as he gazed up at the darkening sky. He could survive in such weather; he was used to hunting under these conditions. But could a white woman live without help? Could Rebecca make it for the full nine days?

He knew she was hungry. The warrior had never before felt fear as when the buck had run toward the lean-to, knowing that Rebecca was huddled inside.

He studied her lean-to. The shelter had been sturdier than he'd thought to withstand the jolt of the deer's hind legs. He smiled, but his grin vanished as he thought of the dangers ahead of her.

He thought of the dried venison in his satchel and debated whether to leave some where Rebecca could find it. *I must not,* he decided. *I am forbidden to help her.*

But what of the dried corn in his bag? She would have to find it and fix it herself. It wouldn't be the same as giving her the dried venison. The venison was already prepared, while the corn could not be eaten without cooking. It was his fault that she was roaming the forest alone, that she'd come to his village in the first place.

Sometime later when Rebecca had settled in her lean-to for the night, Night Wind crept near her shelter and scattered a handful of dried corn on the ground. He put them in a place that wasn't too conspicuous, otherwise she would wonder why she hadn't seen them earlier.

Night Wind bedded down for the night not far from Rebecca's campsite in a spot where she would not find him. He lay, wrapped within his fur. He was used to the cold and had endured much worse during the long winter months.

He woke long before she did and crouched, staring at her shelter, waiting for her to emerge. *I should go back to my village. My people will be wondering where I am.* But he didn't move. He couldn't; his concern for her safety kept him from leaving. Concern . . . and something more.

Rebecca had days left to survive on her own. He should leave now, before he was forced to help her if she came up against danger.

She came out of her make-shift shelter, stretched, and looked around. She appeared well rested, as if she'd slept in a cozy cabin on an English featherbed instead of in the forest on the cold, damp ground.

Night Wind devoured her with his eyes. She was beautiful with her tousled hair. He was close enough to notice the tiniest things about her, but not enough to touch, which he longed to do. Her breath misted in the cold air, and her cheeks were pink from the day's chill.

The brave felt like he'd been kicked in the stomach as he studied her and realized how much he enjoyed looking at her, how much he'd enjoyed kissing her. He saw her walk over the corn, unaware of its existence, and he wanted to call her attention to the presence of the food.

But he couldn't.

It was forbidden.

Why did he want so much to help her?

Rebecca went to the stream and splashed her face with water, exclaiming at the cold. He saw something catch her attention, as she stared, transfixed, at the running water of the stream. He saw her hand move like lightning into the water. She pulled out a tiny fish, laughing with delight, and threw it where it couldn't return to water. The sound of Rebecca's laughter warmed him. He itched to hold her in his arms.

What are you going to do with the *Num ai tut, Shi'ki?* he thought.

He saw her hand dip again, and another fish flipped from her fingers onto the stream bank. The fish wiggled and jumped and she spent several seconds trying to pick it up. Clutching her catch, she went into her shelter and came out with some sticks. She took a stick and held it between her palms, spinning the end against a rock.

Night Wind was startled. She's trying to make a fire! He knew that what she was doing would usually create sparks, but the damp air made it difficult. Rebecca worked a long time, before she had her fire. She quickly fueled it with pine needles and dead leaves, and then the dry sticks she'd retrieved from her lean-to.

Night Wind watched with admiration and a great deal of amusement as Rebecca skewered the tiny fish to cook over the fire. He would have eaten them raw so small as they were, but he was proud of her spirit and her ingenuity. The white woman was an unusual English one.

It was only after she had finished eating the fish and was looking for more to eat that Night Wind knew he could leave her. She would make it, he thought, pleased. She had proved it. It was time for him to return to Turtle-Town.

"Mama, I want to stay!"

The little girl held onto the coverlet of her mother's bed, but the other woman in the room grabbed the child's hand and disengaged it from the quilt.

"Come, Elizabeth. Your mother must rest."

"I don't want to leave her."

"Girl, please!"

"It's all right," Veronica Webster said weakly. "She can stay."

"But Veronica—"

"Come, baby," Elizabeth's mother said, and the little girl cried out with joy and bolted to the sick woman's side.

"Oh, Mama, I thought you were dead."

Veronica gave her daughter a sad smile. "No, no, my love," she whispered. "I'm fine. I was just resting."

"Mama, you won't leave me, will you?" Elizabeth glanced over at Agnes Martin, the neighbor who had come to help nurse the ailing Veronica. "I don't want her to stay, mama. Please make her go away."

"Come closer, Bethie," her mother said. "I will send her away as soon as Rebecca comes."

The girl stared at her parent with wide eyes. "Where is Rebecca?" She had heard all about her cousin Rebecca and had been anxiously waiting to meet her mother's precious niece.

"She'll be here soon," Veronica assured her. But the woman was troubled. *Where is the child? She should have been here months ago.* Something terrible must have happened to keep her away without word.

Rebecca had eaten the fish. She was debating if she should continue her journey when it began to snow again. It started as huge white flakes drifting slowly down to earth, and then the snow intensified until it was fine and so dense she could hardly see. The beauty of the scene touched her until the dangers of being caught unprotected in a snowstorm hit her hard. Heavy snow meant poor visibility and cold and wet conditions. At best, she could lose her way; at worst, she could freeze to death. And if she survived the storm, then anyone would be able to find her tracks in the fresh blanket of newly fallen snow. There were other Indians in these woods. She'd been fortunate so far not to have met up with any, but how long could that luck last?

Rebecca felt a prickle of alarm and wondered what to do. She was miles, days, from Delaware. She wasn't even sure she'd taken the right trail. Night Wind had shown her in what direction to travel, but she could have easily made a wrong turn. She'd been forced a number of times to make her way through thick, dense woods.

Dear Lord, what should I do?

She stared at her lean-to, watching her fire hiss and steam as the snowflakes fell on it, and she prayed to God for guidance.

Should she stay here until the snow stopped? What if the snow lasted for days? For weeks? For months?

She had to think of her survival. The two tiny fish and the handful of dried corn she'd found afterwards wouldn't sustain her for long.

Strange that corn, she thought. She'd found it after

she'd eaten the fish; she had thought she'd been seeing things when she spied the kernels on the ground. But when she'd picked them up, she'd realized that they were real enough. She soaked them in the stream and then cooked them over the fire, using a flat rock as a frying pan. When she'd tasted the results, she had known she wasn't imagining it and she ate the corn, wondering how it got there, but unwilling to dwell too long on the matter. God was answering her prayers, she'd decided, as she enjoyed the corn and felt better for it.

But what now? If it snowed for too long, then the stream would freeze, not that she could exist on a diet of tiny fish and stream water.

What was she to do?

Twelve

Rebecca decided to stay put for awhile. She gathered what firewood she could find and stoked up the fire, so that it would continue to burn despite the wet snow. She stored the rest of the wood inside her lean-to in the hopes that it would stay dry.

Huddled close to the fire, her hair damp and her body chilled, she held out her hands to warm near the flame. Night Wind's words came back to her.

"The Great Spirit waits twelve days before accepting a warrior into the Afterworld. Three of them have passed; there are nine suns left. If you live past this time, then you will be innocent of any wrong. We will know that it was the decision of the gods for our brother to die. We will know that his death was not by your hand."

Would she make it? And if she did, would she return to the Lenape village until winter turned to spring? Would she be forgiven if she did and would Night Wind help her to get to Delaware?

She longed for the comfort of Night Wind's wigwam. She missed his disturbing presence. He had been her captor, but for some reason, she'd felt secure with him. He'd been her protector against the natural elements . . . and the anger of his people.

She recalled Ice From Sky, Red Fox's mother. Did

the matron hate Medicine Woman for failing to save her sick child?

I did all I could and Red Fox improved. What had happened afterward to change things so suddenly? Had he been exposed to something else? Had he eaten something harmful to his young life?

The boy's death saddened her. She felt an ache deep inside that made her sorry she'd ever come to the Lenape village, sorry she'd ever met Night Wind.

Her captor.

Her savior.

The one man who affected her like no other man before him.

That night she sat by the fire and contemplated her next move. By the time the sun came up, signaling dawn, Rebecca had made her decision. She felt she had to move on. She'd gone through her meager supply of dry wood, and although it had stopped snowing, the sky looked ominous. A new storm was on the way.

Rebecca hated to leave the security of her shelter and the warmth of her fire, but she knew that if she didn't go, she could be trapped here for the remainder of the winter. She left in what she hoped was the right direction as the clouds darkened and the air grew colder.

The Cayuga warriors returned to their village and reported to their sachem.

"Great chief," one said. "We have found the trail of our enemy. Word has come to us of a child's death and a woman's banishment from *Tulpeuta'nai.*"

"Tulpeuta'nai," Killing Bird said. "Stutterers?"

The brave nodded. "We are prepared to leave and see if the woman is Medicine Woman. We believe it is."

The sachem shook his head. "Why would the woman not heal the child?"

"He is the child of our enemy. Medicine Woman is a true daughter of the Cayuga, not the Lenape." It was White Flower who had spoken. Her husband looked at her thoughtfully and then nodded, agreeing.

He addressed his band of braves. "Go then. Find Medicine Woman and bring her back to her people. The Cayuga miss her. Her lodge awaits her. The clan of the Deer is waiting to welcome a new daughter."

The leader of the band nodded, and the Indians gathered supplies for their journey to find the White Medicine Woman of the Cayuga.

Rebecca was feverish by the seventh night. It had stopped snowing days ago, but she was wet, chilled to the bone, and unable to find anything to eat. She ate the snow to quench her thirst, but its temperature only made her feel colder. Weak with hunger, she'd fallen asleep two nights past and the fire had gone out while she'd slept. There had been no wood or kindling available to start a new fire.

The chills set in shortly afterward. Now she shook so badly, she knew it was because she was ill and not just due to the cold air. She sat, huddled in a tiny clearing, which she'd done her best to rid of snow. A huge boulder sheltered her back, but other than that there was no real protection from the elements. She had cursed herself daily since leaving her crudely constructed lean-to. At least, it had been shelter. She had to remind herself that there was nothing left of the lean-to anyway, for she'd had to burn the sticks and branches that had formed the roof. She would have been no better off if she'd still been there.

I am going to die.

It was twilight. The night was encompassed by an eerie glow. *Dear God it's going to snow again!*

And then she heard it, the one sound that brought terror to her bones and made her blood freeze with fear. She'd heard the call of a wolf and the answering cries of several others. She hugged herself with arms stiffened by the cold, and tears slid down her cheeks. A pack of the beasts were on the prowl, and here she was vulnerable, unprotected, and ill with no hope of successfully warding off attack.

She rocked as she sat, trying to get warm, as low sobs tore from her throat. *Night Wind, where are you?*

Did he really want her to die?

Thirteen

He dreamt of her death . . . a vicious wolf attack. Night Wind woke up, gasping, filled with a sense of urgency to find Rebecca. He had dreamed of the white woman every night since leaving her in the forest, but this was the first dream that foretold of her death.

He rose from his sleeping pallet and dressed in the night silence of the village. She'd been out there for seven days. How far could she have gone? Would he be able to find her?

And if she were in danger, how could he help her when the council had expressly forbidden it?

Arming himself with weapons, Night Wind left Turtle-Town. His heart cried out to Rebecca, reaching over the distance, encouraging her to have courage and strength—and the will to live. He headed in the direction he'd last seen her, and hoped that the snow was still intact enough for him to find her tracks. If not, there were other ways to trail her.

He hoped that he found her quickly and that no man or beast had found her first.

She could see them now. Eyes glowing in the darkness. There were, she thought, at least four of them. Rebecca had climbed up a tree where she now clung precariously. She was feverish, sore, and tired, so tired.

But her heart raced in fear even while her head reeled. The need for sleep was forgotten from the first moment she'd heard the wolves howl.

Dear God, please don't let me fall, she prayed silently.

The animals were below her, growling and pawing at the trunk of the tree. Rebecca cried out and tried to shimmy up higher, but almost lost her balance. Closing her eyes, she clung tighter, her cheek against the bark, and prayed harder.

Her head hurt. She was afraid of losing consciousness; if she did, she would surely die. *You're going to die anyway,* an inner voice taunted her.

She envisioned her mother's face, contorted with grief. She heard the wails of friends and relatives. The only thoughts piercing her delirious haze was the image of death, of her death, and the fear of the hereafter.

Night Wind had no difficulty finding her tracks. As he'd thought, she hadn't gone too many miles since he'd last seen her. He hadn't thought she would be able to in so much snow. He followed her trail until he heard the growling. He froze, knowing what he'd find when he reached the source of the sound. *Rebecca.* Rebecca was in trouble. He quickened his pace in the direction of the noise.

The sight before his eyes, when he first spied her up in the tree, clinging for dear life, filled him with instant terror. She had her eyes shut tightly as she balanced herself on a huge limb, her arms wrapped around the main trunk, her cheeks pressed against the rough bark. He called her name, but she didn't move. She couldn't hear him. Fortunately, neither could the wolves.

The wolf is forbidden, he thought, and the spirits will be displeased. But he could not let her die. Night Wind thought quickly. What could he do that wasn't forbidden? He stared up at the sky and called to the spirits to assist her where he couldn't. He extended his arms, raising them above his head and closed his eyes as he prayed.

The wind whipped up in a frenzy as he chanted to the spirits that ruled the earth. He called to the spirit of the tree that the limb would hold Rebecca so she wouldn't fall. He prayed to the spirits that governed the rain, the snow, and the sun, asking them to help where they could.

He ignored the continuing howling of the wolves, concentrating on the chant that could bring Rebecca aid. The wind stopped, and he opened his eyes. The first thing he noted was a change in the sky. The day was lit up with the first hint of dawn.

Night Wind felt a rush of gladness as he looked over at the woman in peril. The wolves had calmed some and were circling the ground at the base of the tree. The animals were still there, but Rebecca's time of banishment was done. He could help her.

The brave sprang to the woman's aid, drawing his bow and notching his arrow. His aim was true, and the first wolf fell to Night Wind's skill. The animal yelped as it was hit, drawing the other three's attention to the one who had killed it. Suddenly, Night Wind was the animals' prey.

The beasts came at him, snapping and snarling, their attention successfully diverted from the helpless woman in the tree. There was no time to notch another arrow. Night Wind dropped his bow and drew his knife. He lunged at the nearest animal, who had ventured forward alone. He nicked the wolf above his right front leg. The animal howled with pain, and the others went wild with rage.

Another mistake like that one, he thought, and this Lenape warrior would be gone from his earthly path. Three against one . . . he must kill and kill cleanly. Rebecca still clung precariously from her perch; she wasn't out of danger.

His second strike killed a wolf. He felt a searing pain before his knife hit home, but he ignored it, praying that he wasn't too injured, that his arm would continue to function and that he didn't lose much blood. He had one animal yet to kill, and it was the injured wolf. The animal came at him, knocking him to the ground. Teeth tore at his shoulder as Night Wind fought to gain the advantage.

The snarling of the wolf was a horrendous sound in the otherwise stillness of the night. Night Wind rolled in the deadly tussle, fighting for a position to get a good knife thrust. The wolf had its teeth into his fur wrap, ripping his skin beneath. The brave fought the burning sensation as he plunged the knife into the animal and heard the wolf's howl of pain. The wolf released him, and Night Wind lunged at it again. He watched, his chest heaving, as the animal jerked and then lay still.

His strength renewed by his success, he turned toward the tree where Rebecca hung, hugging the trunk close. He didn't know if he was badly hurt, and he didn't care. The woman was safe.

She heard his voice from a distance and knew her mind was playing tricks on her.

"Come down, Reb-bec-ca."

It can't be him. She was sick and delirious, she

decided, and she was going to die. If she moved, she would fall, and the animals below would attack her.

She could hear their frenzied snarling and growling. She kept her lashes shut, but she could envision their glowing eyes. Her breath rasped within her breast with renewed fear.

I didn't think I would die this way. She clung tighter, her cheek scraping the tree bark. *I want a family . . . children. I want to see my mother again.*

And Elizabeth. What of her poor cousin? Who would care for her when Aunt Veronica died? What if Aunt Veronica was already dead? Who was caring for her now?

"Reb-bec-ca. It is all right. You are safe."

Why, God? she wondered. *Why is my mind playing tricks on me?*

Was it to make her death easier?

Rebecca experienced a warmth about her waist, a firm hand on her ribs.

"Let go of the tree, *Shi'kiXkwe.*"

A new word? she thought. She was crazy and imagining new Lenape words. *No, I've heard it before. Shi'kiXkwe—it means woman who is pretty or woman of beauty . . .*

Could this be real?

"Night Wind?" she asked.

"Kihiila, Reb-bec-ca. It is Night Wind. The *tumme* are dead." There was a silent moment. "You are safe. He moved his hand to her hair, stroking it tenderly. "I will help you down if you trust me."

"I trust you," she said, and meant it. If this was a cruel trick of her mind, then she would submit to it. It was a wonderful delusion that Night Wind was there rescuing her from danger.

"It's a long way down, *Shi'ki.* How did you get up?"

"I don't know," she gasped, afraid to let go. And she didn't know. Fear did strange things to a person, she thought, making them do things they might not ordinarily do. She didn't like heights and yet here she was up high in a tree.

Why was she talking to herself? Night Wind wasn't here. She was dreaming . . .

Night Wind tried to pry Rebecca's fingers from a limb, but she was gripping so tightly her knuckles were white from the strain. She wasn't about to let go.

"Let go of the tree, Reb-bec-ca," he coaxed. "It is Night Wind. I will take you down safely."

"I'll fall!"

"Not if you trust me," he murmured.

He scooted himself higher until her lower body was fully cradled between himself and the tree. He bent close and nuzzled her hair. "Trust me."

"I trust you," she said in a girlish voice. "If you're real . . . Are you real?"

She was rambling, incoherent, he realized, and his concern for her grew. Would she listen to his instructions? If she didn't, they could both fall to their deaths.

Night Wind continued to speak to her in soothing tones as he gently, but firmly undid her fingers from the branch. Her hands felt cold and stiff, and she cried out and fought to regain her grip.

"Feel my arm," he said. "I am real."

She gave a cry of joy and released her hold on the branch. He caught her before she could slide down and knock both of them to the ground. The abrupt change in her behavior had startled him. Now she listened to him as if he could do no wrong, and he was filled with gladness that she trusted him.

"Hold on to me, *Shi'ki*. Turn around and hold tight, and together we will climb down."

He held tightly to the tree as she shifted around, crying out with fear as she did so. She grabbed his shoulders, and he gasped with pain. She had caught his injury, but at his groan, she released him and gripped his neck.

Her breath whispered against his throat. He waited a second for the pain to pass before he started to climb down.

His heart had given him a jolt when he'd first seen Rebecca clinging to the branch like a frightened child.

He winced as he climbed down from the tree, jarring his injured arm and shoulder as he went. The flesh felt warm and wet; he didn't think he was bleeding too badly. But it hurt.

Night Wind released Rebecca after they reached the ground. She looked at him to see if he were real, and this wasn't a dream, and he stared at her with piercing eyes that made little bumps rise on her skin. He was indeed real and alive . . . *and here.*

She experienced an infusion of heat. "Thank you for saving my—"

He grabbed and pulled her into his arms to kiss her hard. His lips were warm and firm as they moved across her mouth, searing her lips.

"Open your mouth, Reb-bec-ca."

She obeyed without thought, and gasped when his tongue entered her mouth. Startled, she started to withdraw, but he held her firm.

He pulled back slightly. "Trust me, Medicine Woman. I will not hurt you."

Rebecca relaxed and gave into the warm, curling sensation that invaded her center and spread out to make her tingle everywhere. He lifted his head and released her. She stumbled and almost fell until he caught her, steadying her. She had wanted the kiss to go on and on, but she was feeling weak and lightheaded from the last day's ordeal. She didn't protest when he withdrew.

Night Wind stared at the women and felt desire as he'd never before known it. She swayed and he caught her. She was ill and here he was kissing her, wanting her. She needed a warm place to rest and recover. She needed food.

"Reb-bec-ca, I am sorry. I should not have done that."

Disappointment flashed in her features, and he was glad.

Night Wind's skin was hot where she held onto his bare shoulder. She was sick and didn't know what she was doing, he told himself.

She fell against him, and he lifted her into his arms. He would go to the village of He Who Came Last. They could take refuge for a time with the people of his clan—the clan of the Wolf. He had a mental image of the murdered wolves, and he was afraid. He forced his fear away . . . for Rebecca.

The village was deserted, abandoned by its inhabitants. All that remained of the Lenape tribe were the empty wigwams and a few cooking utensils that had been discarded or accidentally left behind. Night Wind had carried Rebecca the entire journey to the village, but he wasn't tired or winded. He held her, unwilling and half afraid to put her down. The brave frowned as he looked about the village yard. Something—or someone—had driven his people from their home. The ground here was still fertile; He Who Came Last would never have moved his people without good reason.

There was no sign of a battle; Night Wind didn't believe the enemy forced the Lenape from the area.

What had driven them away?

Carefully venturing inside the nearest wigwam, the brave set Rebecca down on a bed of dried sweet grass.

He would have to spread pine needles on top of the grass, he thought, to protect her from the cold, damp ground. After gathering the pine needles, Night Wind went to search the other wigwams for any abandoned supplies. He found a small pile of firewood, a cracked bowl, a chipped pot, and some dried squash that had been hanging from the rafters of the lodge that had belonged to the sachem. As he approached the big ceremonial house, he couldn't shake the feeling that something bad had happened.

It had been only two full moons since he'd last been to this place. Why hadn't the people of his own village heard of He Who Came Last's move?

Should he take Rebecca from this place? Was it safe to care for her here . . . until she was strong enough to travel again?

Thoughts of the sleeping woman drew him back to the wigwam where she lay peacefully, wrapped in his extra fur. She had made him do the unthinkable. He had killed four wolves, the totem of his clan. What special powers did she hold over him to get him to do it?

Night Wind entered the wigwam and saw her, lying huddled on her side. She was beautiful, and he was captured by her magic. The best thing he could do would be to see her well and take her to the home of her aunt. But could he let her go?

The memory of their kiss made his body burn with desire. Yet how could he live with himself knowing he'd done the forbidden, and while she was near, knowing he would do so again.

He set down his armful of firewood and supplies, and crouched beside her. A feeling of warmth banished the chill in his heart as he stared at her. He reached out to touch her hair. The dark strands felt soft like the fur of a baby rabbit; it was dark like the women of his tribe, yet lighter for it glistened with reddish gold under the rays of the sun.

His arm and shoulder throbbed where the wolf had bit him, but he ignored it. The heat in his loins was stronger.

Rebecca moaned softly in her sleep, and concerned, he felt her cheek. It was hot, yet he knew she was cold by the way she lay with her arms wrapped about herself and her knees drawn up to her chest. He stood and pulled off his own fur, covering her. She gave a little incoherent cry and clutched at the fur, drawing it tighter over her shoulder.

Night Wind built a fire in the center of the wigwam, and then went in search of food. He went out to hunt with his bow and only two arrows. His aim, he thought, must be sure and true. He hoped he'd find game nearby, for he didn't want to stray far from Rebecca, because she might need him.

He saw the deer as the sun set in the evening sky. The trek to the village had taken the better part of the morning and seeing Rebecca comfortably settled had taken until midday. He'd been scouting for game for hours, returning often to the wigwam to check on the sleeping woman, before venturing out again. He'd seen several species of animals, but they were sacred and it was forbidden to hunt them.

The wolf is forbidden. Night Wind couldn't forget that he had killed a wolf, and he was certain that the spirits were angry with him. He was afraid that terrible things were going to happen.

His bad luck started when he missed the buck with his first arrow. He was highly skilled with the bow, and this bothered him. The deer had been the perfect target, yet he had hit it above its right back leg, maiming but not killing the animal. *It is because I killed my totem*. The wolf was the totem of his clan, and, therefore, a sacred animal.

He killed the deer with the second arrow and was appeased some for he was then able to retrieve both arrows. The second arrow hit true, right into the buck's neck, and the animal died within seconds after the strike.

His thoughts returned to Rebecca. He'd been gone too long from the wigwam. He slung the dead animal across his back and shoulders and headed back to the deserted village. Was she all right? Had she awakened and wondered where he'd gone? Or had she become more ill?

She was still sleeping when he arrived. The fire was almost out, and the inside of the wigwam was chilly, but he would soon have it warm again. He went outside to secure the dead deer in a safe place and then worked to rebuild the fire.

"Rebecca? Rebecca!"

She was dreaming. Her mother was there at the door to her room, calling her name, and there was a strange man behind her, standing silently as if waiting to be invited in.

"Rebecca? Come meet your father. See? He's come back to us. He's been waiting a long time to meet you."

"But, Mother—" she cried, confused. "Papa's dead!"

"Yes, dear, I know, but he's come to see you. He's come to escort Aunt Veronica."

"Escort her, Mother? Where?"

Her mother looked away, and Rebecca felt alarm.

"To heaven, Mother?"

The woman who had loved and raised her daughter

on her own met Rebecca's gaze with tears in her eyes. "I'm afraid so, daughter."

"But why has papa come to see me?"

Her mother glanced away again, and Rebecca's alarm increased. "He's come for me, Mother. Am I going to die? No!" she cried. "I don't want to die. Elizabeth needs me, and I don't want to leave you!"

"I'm afraid it's all in God's hands, Rebecca."

"Rebecca."

Her mother moved and the man stepped forward.

"Papa?" He had her eyes, she thought. Or she had his. Eyes of blue, her mother had said, and she'd been right. Her own features were a reflection of her father's, but softer, more feminine.

"Daughter, come."

"No, Papa. I don't want to go! I want to stay here. Elizabeth needs me . . . and Night Wind."

"Elizabeth can stay with your mother," her father said, his voice and expression gentle. He held out his hand. "Come."

"No!" she exclaimed. "I can't leave yet. I can't leave Night Wind!"

"Night Wind?" Her father frowned. "What does the wind have to do with you?"

"No, it's not the wind, Father. He's a man. A good man . . . a caring man."

"A man called Night Wind," her father said thoughtfully. His face darkened. "A savage?"

"No, he's not a savage. He's a Lenape warrior, but he's a kind man. He took care of me."

"Then where is this Night Wind now?"

"I don't know, but he must be nearby." She looked anxiously about for him. "Night Wind?" She reached out as if she could touch him simply by desire. "Night Wind!"

"I am here, Reb-bec-ca." She felt his touch on her shoulder.

"See, Papa? I told you he was here." She felt peace and love and a feeling of security. Night Wind was here. She grabbed out at his hand. "You won't go?"

"No, Medicine Woman, I will not leave you." She released him and felt the warmth of his hand as it caressed her cheek. His fingers stroked her skin gently and she sighed, closed her eyes, and felt loved. She was no longer afraid.

"Night Wind," she murmured. "You came."

"Kihiila, Shi'kiXkwe. I am here."

Night Wind gazed down at Rebecca with tender concern. His breast fluttered with emotion; his heart was full of joy that she'd called his name. At that moment, the brave thought that whatever bad luck he encountered because he had killed his totem animal, it was worth it . . . for her.

Fourteen

The fire crackled as it spit sparks and warmed the wigwam. Outside, the wind howled as it picked up its pace, and the snow fell, cloaking the forest. The golden glow inside the small shelter highlighted the sleeping woman and the man who lay close by her, watching, waiting for her to awaken.

Night Wind had cut up the deer and cooked some of the meat, skewered on a stick, over the fire. He'd made Rebecca a broth, heating it in a chipped bowl he'd found. He'd mixed the meat with some water from his own water skin sack, seasoning it with some herbs from his medicine bag. She had sipped once from the broth, but it wasn't enough. Night Wind waited for her to awaken once again, so that he could feed her some more of it.

He rose and went to the fire to rewarm the broth. Once it simmered, he removed the bowl, setting it outside the flame so that it would be ready for Rebecca when she needed it.

Night Wind sat, eating a piece of venison, feeling it nourish him even while he ate . . . and he continued to watch the woman while she slept. He stared at her intently, fascinated by her beauty . . . her soft, feminine mouth, which he yearned to taste again . . . her thick eyelashes feathering her smooth, pink cheeks.

Rebecca sighed restfully, and he tensed, his blood

rushing through his veins as he waited for her to open her eyes. He set down his venison and moved closer to touch her hair and then her cheek. He smiled when her skin felt cooler than it had previously. She would live, he thought with joy. *She will live.*

She was cold. She shivered and grabbed for the blanket, but it was moved for her, enveloping her with warmth. She felt the heat, heard a soothing voice, and struggled to open her eyes.

She was so tired. Rebecca vaguely remembered feeling frozen and scared, and then a man's face . . . her father. No, she thought, it couldn't have been her father. He was dead. An Indian . . . *Night Wind!*

She'd been dreaming about her father. Had she dreamed about the Lenape brave? Why couldn't she open her eyes? Why did she feel so tired?

I've been sick. Then she must have dreamed everything, she mused. Her capture by the Indians . . . her life with the Cayuga and then the Lenape.

No, it couldn't have been a dream. How else could she know about the Indians?

"Shi'kiXkwe."

She heard his caressing voice, and its seductive pull made her open her eyes. He was there, looking more real, more attractive, than ever before. His expression was soft, his dark eyes glistening with an emotion she was afraid to name for fear it didn't exist.

"Night Wind." She reached up to stroke his face and felt him . . . warm, alive, and wonderful to touch. Her fingers tingled as she cupped his jaw.

"Kihiila." He closed his eyes in enjoyment of her touch. "It is Night Wind."

"You saved my life."

He glanced away, and she thought he looked troubled. She frowned. "What's wrong?" she asked.

He fixed her with his sparkling onyx eyes. "It is

nothing." He gave her a smile, but she didn't believe him.

"Are you hurt?" She wouldn't allow things to drop there.

His grin widened, reaching his eyes. "A little bite, nothing more."

She gasped, her eyes widening. "A wolf bite?"

He nodded, and that strange, haunting look came back to his expression, and then was gone.

"My God!" she exclaimed." "A wolf bit you, because of me." Rebecca searched him anxiously for signs of the bite. He took her hand and placed it on his arm, turning so that she could see the marks.

She drew a sharp breath. There were several small puncture wounds and two long scratches from where the wolf must have drawn his teeth. Rebecca sat up quickly, and her head reeled painfully. Gasping, she put her hand to her forehead and lowered herself down again. Her world righted itself, and she gazed up at Night Wind, her concern focused on the man's arm.

"Does it hurt?" she whispered, aghast. She gently touched the area surrounding the wounds.

Night Wind stared at her and shook his head, his gaze soft and bright.

"It must have bled terribly."

"Maata." He shook his head. "There was little."

Rebecca felt her throat tighten. He was lying. An injury like that one must have bled a lot. He was trying to make light of what he'd done for her. "Thank you. *Wanee'shih,*" she choked out. *"Thank you for rescuing me."*

His lips twitched as he nodded.

He was a strange man, she thought, but a good one. Never in her wildest dreams would she have imagined falling for an Indian. But he wasn't a savage. He had kidnapped her, but only out of love for his young brother. He'd done nothing to intentionally hurt her. Now, he'd saved her life.

"You are worth saving, *Shi'kiXkwe.*" He smiled. "I never knew you could climb trees!"

She blinked. "Yes, the tree," she murmured. Her chuckle was weak. "I thought I'd imagined that part, but it happened, didn't it?" She paled at the thought. "I hate heights."

"But you climbed high in a tree."

"I did what I had to to live."

Night Wind nodded in understanding. "Yes. One must do what one must do."

She thought, from his tone, that he might be thinking of something he'd done at one time. She was curious, but didn't ask. He was still a mystery, but his saving her didn't give her the right to pry.

His expression brightened. "Are you hungry?"

She nodded. She could eat forever and never feel full again, she thought. Food had become more precious to her; she would never again take it for granted. She'd had so little of it during these past days.

Rebecca vaguely recalled sipping broth, and the memory became clearer when Night Wind rose from where she lay and went to the fire to pour her another bowlful. Carefully, he tipped some of the steaming broth into a bowl and came back to where she lay.

He helped her to sit up, and when she assured him that she was all right, he handed her the bowl. "Drink," he told her. "I make you broth. It is hot, but it is good. It will help heal you, make you strong."

She accepted the bowl and brought it to her mouth. The warmth of the steam teased her nose and tempted her taste buds as she placed her lips on the rim of the bowl. Her gaze met Night Wind's as she took her first sip. As he'd warned her, the broth was hot, but she was used to drinking hot things. She didn't have to wait for it to cool, as long as she didn't drink too quickly.

She drew her gaze from his piercing dark eyes and stared down into her bowl. The broth was delicious, seasoned with some kind of herbs or plants. It warmed her throat and belly and made her feel cared for . . . loved.

Her heart beat faster as she stole another glance at her rescuer. He had cared for her while she was sick—and with an injured arm.

He watched her with a look that made her tingle, his onyx gaze having an effect on her like a large hand caressing her skin. She felt herself blush, and she looked away, unwilling for him to see the direction of her thoughts. Why couldn't she forget the memory of his kiss? Why couldn't she forget the searing heat of his touch?

She sipped from the bowl too quickly and choked as the liquid went down the wrong way, burning the back of her throat.

Night Wind was there to rescue the bowl from her hands. *"Hoh!* Are you fine?" he asked with great concern.

Eyes bright with tears, she flashed him a watery smile. His expression made her pulse race and her nape prickle with sexual awareness. "I am all right," she said. "Thank you. I just drank too fast."

Night Wind didn't respond. He stared at her . . . her lips . . . her eyes . . . his gaze wandering down her throat to fasten with brightness on her breasts.

Rebecca's body burned. Her breasts swelled, and her nipples grew hard and sensitive to the brush of her fur cape. Night Wind couldn't see beneath her clothing, but she felt as if she were naked to his gaze.

He set the bowl off to the side, and then he shifted

closer to her. Rebecca's breath caught in anticipation of what he would do next.

Touch me, she thought. *Kiss me like you did before.* Dear Lord, was she a wanton to desire him so?

Damn, but she didn't care if she was. She'd almost died, and without knowing what it was to lie with a man . . . to love *this* man. She wanted him in the full sense and prayed to God that the brave felt the same way about her.

"Reb-bec-ca."

She loved the way he pronounced her name with the slight hesitation between syllables. Should she tell him how she felt? "Night Wind, I—"

"Sh-sh," he murmured. He touched her cheek, and she closed her eyes, tilting her head against his hand, enjoying the wonderfully titillating caress of his fingers against her skin.

She moaned softly as he outlined her mouth with his thumb, tracing the top lip before playfully tugging down her bottom lip. She opened her eyes and they locked gazes. The beauty of his male face, cast in the golden glow of the fire, took her breath away. His ebony eyes burned with desire for her, and she felt the answering heat in her abdomen and in the sensitive tips of her breasts.

Night Wind bent without a word and kissed her, his mouth tender and exploring. Then, his kiss became hot and searing with need, and she gloried in the demanding contact. He raised his head to murmur softly in his native tongue. The low, lilting words were strange, but musical to her. His tone was so beautiful that she could only assume that he was praising her as he bent to nuzzle her neck.

She gasped as his tongue touched her throat. Rebecca experienced a shaft of desire so strong it rocked her to her toes. He nipped and kissed where the pulse beat rapidly near the base of her throat, and she clutched his head. Her hands wove into his silky hair as she pulled his head closer, allowing him to nuzzle lower to the edge of her buckskin tunic.

He undid the fur wrap and slipped it from her shoulders. She stared at him, her gaze bright with desire, her mouth wet and swollen from his kisses.

"Uitiissa."

He placed his hands on her shoulders and gently lowered her to the bed of pine needles and dried sweet grass, following her down as she went, covering her with his body. She felt the weight of him, and her mind spun with doubts of her actions. This was wrong. No, this couldn't be wrong, for she cared for him. And how could anything this beautiful be wrong? She wanted, needed, to feel his touch.

"Do not be afraid, little one."

"I'm not afraid," she assured him.

"You are shivering. You are cold?"

She shook her head. "No not really."

"You are cold," he said. "Let me warm you."

He rose and removed his fur and leggings. He stood before her then, clad only in his loincloth, his smooth muscled chest sleek and golden in the firelight. His thigh muscles looked hard and taut, drawing Rebecca's gaze. She swallowed against a throat that had suddenly become dry. She felt hot and cold, and then hot again as she studied his perfect form.

"You like what you see?" he asked.

She gasped, reddening. The man was blunt. Didn't he know that such things shouldn't be asked?

"We don't speak of such things."

Night Wind frowned. "Why do you not talk of this?"

"It's not proper."

"Proper?"

She nodded, her cheeks burning.

"In our culture, it is proper."

Rebecca was surprised. "It is?" Her heart sped up as she admired his body. *What was wrong with honesty between a man and a woman?*

Night Wind told her it was how things were done in the Lenape culture. While he spoke, his hands went to the strings of his breechcloth. Rebecca drew a sharp breath and looked away. She stared at the wigwam wall, her heart thundering within her breast, and the air was fraught with physical tension in the small shelter.

He said nothing, and Rebecca was afraid to look, afraid that he'd be standing there naked for her to see, afraid that she'd enjoy the sight of him so much she'd not be able to hide it.

And she was scared.

Of loving an Indian.

Of loving Night Wind.

She sensed him move, and she chanced a peek. His loincloth was still intact, and she relaxed, but was disappointed. She got a sudden chill, and she rubbed her arms, gazing at him with expectation. She wanted him to reach out and pull her into his arms. She wanted him to make love to her. Did he want it, too?

"You *are* cold," he murmured as he lay down beside her. It was then that Rebecca realized that she was shivering.

He arranged her fur over the two of them and then drew her into his arms. Rebecca's heart raced at his nearness, at his scent . . . of the forest and the fire . . . and of the night wind.

"Sleep, Reb-bec-ca. Sleep and be warm. Night Wind will watch over you." He began to stroke her hair. "We will talk when the sun rises again in the morning sky."

Sleep? she thought. He wanted her to sleep when

they were lying this close? When she'd had his kisses and felt his touch, but had never known love in the full, physical sense?

He pressed her closer to him, her face against his neck. She could feel the heat of his bare chest against her breast and the solid firmness of his thighs against her legs.

"Kouueen, Nihounshan," he whispered, his low voice drugging her.

Rebecca felt the tension leave her, and a strange lethargy invade her limbs.

"What does that mean?" she murmured sleepily. And then it didn't matter what he'd said. Warm, secure, and safe within his arms, Rebecca fell asleep.

Night Wind gazed down at the woman within his arms, and he felt a possessiveness toward someone he'd never before experienced. He held her tightly, enjoying the sensation of her body pressed close against his own, and he watched over her through the cold night.

Rebecca was dreadfully ill by the next morning. She woke up with chills and muscle aches, and she heard Night Wind's voice calling to her from far away, then she heard no more.

For the next couple of days, she was aware only of the warm arm supporting her head and the soothing voice that pleaded with her to drink the warm broth.

On the fourth day, Night Wind eyed Rebecca gravely. She was burning with fever, and he was frightened. He had done all he knew how for her, but he was no shaman or medicine man. He had fed her and tried to cool down her temperature. What else could he do?

Night Wind had taken off her fur cape, and she lay

in her tunic. When he'd tried to cover her up, she'd thrown off the furs and thrashed about.

They had been in the abandoned village for four days when he began to worry about food. He was afraid to leave Rebecca for fear she'd worsen, but she needed more than the venison broth.

Night Wind stepped outside and stared at the gray sky. Soon there would be a fresh blanket of snow. He should take Rebecca back to his village, to Iron Bear, the shaman, who could help her.

She is a healer. Why doesn't she heal herself?

Was she? Or was she what she'd said—a simple flesh-and-blood woman?

There was nothing simple about Rebecca Morton, Night Wind thought. He, if no one else, knew that.

He had hung up the deer carcass high in a tree where the hungry forest animals couldn't reach it. Night Wind lowered the meat, cut off a section, and secured the deer in the tree again. He took the venison inside the wigwam as he checked on Rebecca, who was sleeping peacefully. Her cheeks were flushed, and he was concerned. What more could he do to break her fever?

Night Wind set down the meat and then gathered firewood inside the wigwam. He didn't want the source of fuel to get wet in the approaching snow-storm. Then, he found some pine needles and dried corn husks left in the fields on the outskirts of the village, and he lined the wigwam against the cold damp ground.

There was a brook nearby, and the brave filled his water skin. The water wasn't too far from the wigwam, but in a blinding snowstorm, a few feet could as well be several miles.

Night Wind hurried back inside with the supplies. He went to Rebecca's side and stared down at her. He had enjoyed sleeping with his arms about her, his face nuzzled in her hair; if only she would get better, so that he could show his love for her.

Would she recover? He was terrified that she might not get well, and he prayed daily to the spirits to help heal the white woman.

She seemed to be improving, but he couldn't be certain. Recalling how she'd cooled Red Fox with the water, he'd done the same for Rebecca, bathing her face and neck, her arms, and her lovely legs.

He stared at her beautiful face and willed her to open her eyes. She moaned softly in her sleep, and he touched her face, felt that she was hot, and frowned. There was only one thing to do. She might not be happy about it, but it was the way left to cool her down.

The party of Cayuga warriors were forced to return to the village because of the snow.

"Why have they come back?" White Flower asked her husband. She was deeply concerned for the White Medicine Woman.

"The snow is too deep and dangerous for Black Horn and his brothers," Killing Bird said. "They will try again to find her when the days become warm and the ice thaws on our great lake. Then, they will find White Medicine Woman and bring her home to her people."

Fifteen

Rebecca's fever broke two days past and she was feeling stronger every day. She had vague memories of Night Wind caring for her, his hands gently lifting her as he coaxed her to drink, his fingers tender on her skin as he bathed her with cold water.

She'd been naked beneath a fur covering when she'd awakened. Surprised and embarrassed, she wondered who had taken off her clothes. Then, she learned that she and Night Wind were alone in an abandoned village. She'd been too sick before to realize this, and after a brief period of being mortified, she began to understand why he'd taken off her clothes. And she was no longer embarrassed if not completely comfortable with the fact that he had intimately cared for her day and night while she was ill.

Another storm three days ago had brought a great deal of snowfall. Glistening white covered the woods in a layer over a foot thick, and the tree branches sparkled under the bright sun as they hung heavy with the snow's weight. The forest seemed quiet, the blanket of snow muffling sounds. The air was cold, but not frigid since the wind had calmed some.

Rebecca sat up and looked about the wigwam. It was early, with the sun still young in the morning sky. Night Wind had gone in the hours of the dark to hunt for food. He had wanted to find something to supplement their diet of deer meat and dried squash. Rebecca knew that he was concerned for her, that she needed more nourishment to fully recover from her ordeal. He hadn't actually said so, but she could tell by the way he gazed at her while they ate during the past two days.

The morning lengthened, and the sun rose higher, shining its light through the smoke hole in the wigwam roof. Rebecca rose and dressed. She slept naked now. Since awakening that way when she'd first felt better, she'd become comfortable with the practice. There seemed no point in putting on clothes. Night Wind, much to her disappointment, had made his pallet on the other side of the fire and was no threat, while she was actually warmer than he sleeping bundled in a pile of furs.

She stoked up the fire before she dressed in her tunic and moccasins. Then, she went about tidying up the wigwam and gathering utensils to cook. Night Wind had found, in the abandoned village, a few other dishes and pots, made of dried gourd, clay, and animal bones. In a lean-to some distance away in the forest, he'd come across furs and blankets and some dry rushes and firewood. The day he'd brought everything to her, he'd told her of his concern for the people who had lived here, how it looked as if they'd deserted their lodges in a hurry.

Rebecca had since recalled the visitors to Red Fox's mourning ceremony, and had asked him whether some of these villagers had come. The brave had thought a moment and then shaken his head. No, he didn't remember seeing any of that tribe. If he'd been thinking clearly then, he might have questioned their absence.

What could have happened to the Lenape who had lived here? she wondered.

Rebecca grabbed a fur from her pallet and wrapped

it about her shoulders, before she found a knife and went outside. Where was Night Wind? Shouldn't he have come back by now?

Her gaze made a visual sweep of the village yard and the woods circling the outer edges of the compound. But there was no sign of the Lenape brave.

She went to the tree where Night Wind had stored their meat, and undid the length of sinew securing the venison to an upper tree limb. After lowering the carcass, she cut away a piece of meat with the knife and sat it on the snow so she could retie the deer. Then, she picked up the meat and went inside the wigwam to make soup. Night Wind would be hungry when he returned. She would have something hot ready for him.

He'll be back soon. He didn't leave you here to die. He's been caring for you so that you will live. He's all right. Nothing has happened to him.

Dear God, she prayed, *please make him come soon.*

He returned as she was stirring the soup. As the day had stretched on with no sign of the brave, Rebecca's spirits had sunk low. She had asked herself if she should go out and search for him, but she had quickly discarded that notion. She would get lost; she knew nothing of these woods. He would return safe and sound if only she were patient.

Night Wind came quietly, raising the fur door flap and slipping inside. She didn't look at him, but she sensed him immediately. She'd been crying, so sure was she that he wasn't coming back, and she didn't want him to see her tears.

He didn't say a word. He just stood there and stared at her. She could feel his regard tingling from her head clear to her toes. She didn't acknowledge that she knew he was there; she pretended an interest in something in the wigwam instead as she surreptitiously wiped away her tears with the back of her hand. She was trembling when she turned to face him, afraid that the sight of him would make her break down.

She spared him a brief glance. "I've made soup," she said, turning back to the pot. She had a giant lump in her throat, and fresh tears blinded her vision. She sniffed as she stirred the broth.

Rebecca felt him move closer. Her body sprang instantly to life at his nearness, her heart picked up its pace, racing hard.

"Reb-bec-ca."

She blinked back her tears.

He watched her silently. And then he said, *"Shi'kiXkwe, k'pet'ching-weh-hih."*

It was a gentle command, but a command all the same. He wanted her to look at him. She rose and faced him with her eyes overly bright and her mouth quivering with her urge to sob.

He looked beautiful. Her gaze checked him for signs of injury, and the lump in her throat eased some when she couldn't see any. His dark eyes glistened with emotion as he stared. His expression held a longing that she prayed she wasn't imagining.

"Lah puk hah teen." He stepped closer, lifting a hand to finger her hair.

"What does that mean?" she asked breathlessly. The urge was strong to flow into his arms and press against him. She wanted to feel his mouth upon her lips.

"Crying," he said. "You are crying." He sounded awestruck. "Do not cry, Reb-bec-ca. I will not leave you."

She gulped back a sob, and he pulled her against him, his arms solid and warm about her waist. He cradled her head against his chest with one hand.

"What took you so long?"

"You think it is easy to find food?"

She shook her head, enjoying the sensation made by rubbing her head against his breast. "No."

He chuckled. *"Kihiila.* Medicine Woman knows what it is to eat little. She has eaten dried berries from the trees that bite . . . and the tiny fish from the *Siipu.* She has run from a frightened deer."

Rebecca laughed softly. "Yes, I—" She tensed and looked up. "How do you know about the fish?"

He met her gaze and smiled. "From the Medicine Woman. You told me of your hunt for food. You told me of the fish and the berries."

But not the deer. She would never confess about the deer, for she'd been foolish. The incident had been too embarrassing to tell about.

She studied his face, saw the knowing gleam in his onyx eyes, and frowned. "You know, because you saw me."

He closed his expression.

"I wouldn't have told you about the deer," she said. "You saw me!" She jerked from his grasp. "You watched while a deer nearly ran into my shelter, and you did nothing!"

He turned away. "I was there."

"And you didn't help me," she said in a strangled voice. "You didn't try to save me."

He faced her, his features appearing as if they had been carved from stone. "I was forbidden."

"Forbidden!"

Night Wind tensed. "You do not understand."

"I understand that you allowed the deer to almost kill me!"

"You did not die. The deer did not hurt you. He ran, because he was frightened." His eyes glittered with anger. "Night Wind took care of you . . . for many suns . . . many moons."

She opened her mouth to argue and then closed it again. He was right, she thought. He had cared for her while she was sick, bathing her, feeding her, massaging her sore muscles when she moaned with pain.

Her eyes widened as the memory of him rubbing her arms and legs came to her. She'd been hurting; she must have cried out with complaint. She had a vague image of a soothing touch and Night Wind's calming voice, and she had felt better . . . so much better.

She touched his arm. He flinched, but she wouldn't release him. "I apologize. You have been . . . wonderful and kind." She swallowed hard. "It's just the thought that you were so close, and I didn't . . ."

He held her gaze. "I was not kind."

The air crackled with energy. The tension between them was not anger, but something else . . . something as equally disturbing to Rebecca's peace of mind.

"I was to blame that you were sick, and I cared for you," he said. "I took you from the Cayuga. I should have left you there. You would not have been cast from my village. You would be well and in your Del-a-ware Colony."

She felt a rush of shame "You are right. But you stole me to help someone you loved." Her voice lowered. "I can't find fault with you for that."

His eyes flamed at her words. "You should hate Night Wind," he said.

"I don't hate you," she softly replied. She went back to the tire to check on her broth, which was boiling. She used a piece of animal skin to remove the pot from the flames and set it on the dirt floor in an area cleared of pine needles and grass.

Rebecca knew that Night Wind watched her. She tried to pretend an indifference she didn't feel and failed miserably. "Would you like soup?" she asked without looking at him. Her voice quivered. When he didn't answer, she was forced to face him.

His expression mirrored pain and an inner sadness. She felt his pain as if it were hers. "Night Wind—"

"I will eat your broth." His face now emotionless, he sat down next to the fire, and she poured him a bowlful of soup. She handed it to him carefully so he wouldn't get burned.

"Was your hunt successful?" she asked, trying to make conversation.

He set down the bowl, rose to his feet, and went outside. He returned with two squirrels, a rabbit, and a small deer. Her eyes widened as she viewed his game. He placed the animals along the wall of the wigwam near the door and then went back out into the cold. He was back within seconds, his arms laden. "I found *pi'sim.*"

He held several husks of sweet corn. "We can make *sa'pan*—and *Ka-ha-ma'kun* for the journey home." He smiled.

Rebecca grinned back. "I found some dried pumpkin in one of the wigwams," she told him, her eyes bright.

He stared at her, and his smile faded abruptly. Rebecca's grin left, and a burning knot settled within her breast.

Night Wind placed the fruits of his hunt on the floor near the door and returned to his seat by the fire. He picked up his bowl and drank the broth.

Rebecca had flavored the soup with small bits of dried squash and pumpkin. He didn't praise her efforts, but he ate it all and then silently handed her his bowl. Taking his actions to mean he wanted more, she poured him another bowlful.

He devoured the second serving in the same way he had the first. She, on the other hand, had suddenly

lost her appetite. Her stomach, which had fluttered
upon his arrival, hurt with the tension between them.
They were alone in an abandoned village with no one
but themselves to rely on to survive. Why then were
they behaving like strangers wary of each other?
Shouldn't they be friends, sharing companionship and
good food, making the best of their ordeal?

Night Wind stopped eating and gazed at her pierc-
ingly. "Are you not hungry?" he asked.

She shook her head.

"Eat," he ordered, setting down his bowl. "You
need to eat to get well."

"I am well," she said, her pulse pounding at his
look. *Thanks to you,* she thought.

He shifted closer, picked up her bowl, and held it
to her lips. "You must finish your soup."

He embraced her shoulders with his other arm as
he encouraged her to eat. His breath whispered against
Rebecca's ear. She felt tiny fingers of pleasure ripple
down her back at his nearness. She obediently drank
from the bowl, pausing to grimace after the first sip.
"This is terrible!"

"It is good," he said, and the return of his smile
warmed her heart. "Come, Medicine Woman, you
must drink it all."

She drank the entire bowl slowly, allowing the hot
liquid to heat and caress her throat on its way down.
When she was finished, he started to pour her another
bowl.

"No," she said. "I've had enough. I'll wait for the
sa'pan," she added quickly upon seeing his look. "I
know how to make that."

He nodded and put down her bowl. "I will go now
and take care of the meat."

"No!" Her hand on his shoulder stopped him from
rising. She blushed and let go. "Do you have to do

it now? You've only just come back. I wanted to talk with you for a while."

An odd look flashed in his dark eyes, but he settled himself down again. He wasn't as close to her as before; she was disappointed.

"What do you wish to talk about?"

Rebecca shifted uncomfortably. What did she want to talk about? "I don't know . . . I—" Her cheeks became a pink several shades darker.

Suddenly, Night Wind was there, closer than before, his large hand cupping her chin. He turned her face up for his inspection and gazed into her eyes . . . at her mouth. "You want to talk?"

She blinked and gazed back. She nodded.

"You want to talk or do you want to touch mouths with Night Wind?"

Her gasp of protest was cut off when he leaned forward and captured her lips with his mouth. Rebecca moaned and reciprocated. His kiss was so good . . . she'd forgotten how wonderful it felt to feel his mouth on her lips.

These past two days when her strength had returned to her and she was cognizant of her surroundings, she'd known a physical tension so great it had made her breasts swell involuntarily and her abdomen ache and pulsate with desire. She'd wanted to taste his lips. She wanted to sleep in his arms again.

His mouth slanted across her mouth, searing her, making her body burn. Rebecca groaned when Night Wind pulled her onto his lap, cradled within his arm. He bent to kiss her again, and she clutched his head, her fingers in his hair, whimpering as he commanded her to open her mouth so that he could deepen the kiss.

His tongue delved between her lips and teeth, thrusting, tasting, making Rebecca moan and burn. He raised his head to study her expression, his eyes slumberous with desire, his breathing heavy. She slipped her hands beneath his clothing to stroke his chest, which was smooth and muscled. She lavished attention to his nipple, which pebbled beneath her fingers, and he groaned deep in his throat.

He muttered something in his native tongue, and she wished she could understand him, for his tone was strained, emotional . . .

"You are much of a woman," Reb-bec-ca," he said in English, his voice thick.

His praise made her heady. His hard thighs beneath her buttocks and his muscled chest beneath her fingertips heightened her desire for him.

Her hands moved to his nape and his dark silky hair, before her caress returned to finger the edge of his fur and the gleaming, bared skin of his right shoulder. She gave into the urge to kiss him, lowering her mouth to the warm column of his throat. He inhaled sharply, and she began to further explore him with her lips, kissing his neck and shoulder, dipping lower to catch a nipple between her teeth. She'd never been with a man before, but she was guided by instinct . . . and the desire to please Night Wind.

He groaned and pulled her head up, fastening his mouth onto her lips, devouring her with his commanding kiss. He raised his head to stare into her blue eyes, and felt himself drowning . . . and enjoying it.

He pressed her back against the bed of pine needles and dried sweet grass, and she reached out, imploring him to follow her. The scent of the grass and the mingled scents of their bodies filled the air. He grabbed her hands and placed them at her sides.

"Lie still," he ordered. "Let me touch you."

He raised the hem of her tunic slowly, all the while watching her reaction closely, prepared to stop if she desired. But she didn't say a word. Her gaze spoke volumes, encouraging him to continue, while she arched her body, assisting him to remove her clothes. She sat up so that he could pull off her tunic, which he folded to make a pillow for her head, and then she lay back down again.

He enjoyed the sight of her. Her white skin gleaming in the firelight. Her small, but full breasts with distended nipples that were begging to be kissed. His gaze lowered to her stomach, and then farther still to the curly nest of hair guarding her womanhood. He felt a jolt of desire so strong he nearly cried out with it.

He wanted to mate with her, to bury himself deep within her soft body, thrusting hard, but he forced himself to go slowly. He wanted her to enjoy their joining as much as he. He placed his hand on her breast, pleased when she closed her eyes and made a sound of pleasure. He saw the contrast of the color of their skins, his dark and hers as pure white as the snow, and it fueled his need of her. He squeezed her breast gently, plucking at the nipple, watching its reaction to his touch, and then he cupped the entire breast, rubbing and palming her until she gasped.

He switched to her other breast, lavishing attention on it in the same way, and then he lowered his head and sucked her. He drew her nipple into his mouth, teasing it with his tongue, before licking and sucking the hardened tip.

"Night Wind!" she cried.

"Nunukunn. Uitiissa," he said. *"Tuulke."* He caressed her breast. "They are beautiful to this brave's eyes . . . to this brave's touch."

She reached up to caress his face, but he grabbed her hand and raised it along with her other hand above her head, holding them in place with one hand. With his other hand, he pulled open his fur cape, baring his chest fully for Rebecca's gaze. And then he lowered himself upon her until their breasts met, hardness against softness. He rubbed himself against her while he kissed her neck, her ear . . . each one of her features. Rebecca writhed beneath him, trapped by his hands and his weight, not roughly, but firmly enough to make her aware of every inch of him that made contact with her.

"Please," she begged. "Let me touch you."

He raised his head. *"Maata.* This moment I will show you pleasure. You will know no pain, only pleasure of Night Wind's body . . . of Night Wind's touch."

He rose slightly and removed his hold. He took off his fur and then stood to undo his breechcloth, his heated gaze never leaving the woman who lay naked and vulnerable at his feet.

Rebecca stared as his loincloth fluttered to the ground and he stood before her in all his glory. She had a contracting sensation in her abdomen as she saw his throbbing manhood, the hard length and engorged tip. She opened her legs, wanting to feel it against her, unsure whether she could accommodate him, scared of doing something wrong, but wanting him to come into her.

Her skin tingled as he came to her. He grabbed her hands, securing them above her head again, and the tiny bud at the base of her womanhood pulsed with feeling and need. They lay naked, him on top of her, as he slid his body against hers to create a friction that heightened their pleasure.

"Please," she gasped. Her breasts were full to bursting with feeling; her woman's core tightened and throbbed with the need to be joined to him.

"Soon, *Nihounshan.* Soon. This brave is *Shaauise,"* he said hoarsely. "He cannot wait much longer."

"Then don't!" she cried. "Come into me. Let me feel all of you."

With a low growl, he slid down and insinuated his knee between her legs, prying them apart, and she opened them wide. He reached down with his free hand and fondled her woman's mound, dipping his finger inside her to judge whether or not she was ready for him. Her reaction to his touch told him she was, and he released her, slid upward and touched his staff to her opening.

"We must go slow," he said when she tried to force him into her. "It will hurt if we go fast."

"Show me," she pleaded, gasping. "Teach me!"

He kissed her, mating her with mouth and tongue, and as he did so, he slowly entered her, inserting his tip into her tight opening. Once he was inside and she seemed adjusted to his size, he began a rhythm of thrust and withdrawal. He kissed her, fondled her breasts, while he kept up the pace of his thrusting manhood.

Rebecca had stiffened at his first thrust, but now she moved against him, arching herself upward, groaning with pleasure when he nipped her breasts. He raised himself to fondle her.

"Kihiila, Rebecca!" he gasped, when she lifted up to catch his nipple between her teeth. *"Kweh! Ala'pi! Yoo'ta-lee!"* He guided her head to his other nipple, moaning when she bit and licked him as she continued to grind against him.

He pulled her head back and then pressed her backward to the ground, kissing her deeply, filling her completely again and again, and the world within the wigwam became a spiraling staircase to the realms of ecstasy as they slammed into each other in that last mind-shattering climb to the top.

Rebecca reached the pinnacle, shrieking as she experienced sexual pleasure for the first time, and Night Wind followed within seconds, shouting out hoarsely as he spilled his seed.

Hearts thundering within their breasts, they hovered in that joyous place where lovers lay for a brief time before floating back down to earth. Rebecca opened her eyes and studied the man whose weight pressed her into the cushioned earth, who had shown her what it felt to be loved.

"Tipaakke Shaakha," she whispered.

His eyelashes flickered open, and he fixed her with his glistening onyx gaze. "You are not hurt?" His tone was heavily laced with concern.

She chuckled. "I did not scream, because I felt pain."

His expression softened, and a smile came to his beautiful male lips. "You want to talk now?"

She shook her head. *"Maata."* No.

"Wul'lut," he said, his hand moving to her breast. "Good."

And he began to stroke and fondle, and love her all over again.

Sixteen

"We must leave this place." Night Wind's soft voice pierced the quiet of the night. Rebecca lay, snuggled within his arms, her head on his chest, her body soft in the aftermath of repeated lovemaking.

She raised her head to gaze at him. "Must we?" she asked. Her eyes glistened with disappointment.

He touched her cheek, studying her face as he caressed her skin. "We have been here many suns. My people will wonder what has happened to this warrior son."

Rebecca nodded and lowered her head back against him. Her throat tightened with her tears as she wondered what was to become of her . . . of the two of them. She was too afraid to ask.

Night Wind stroked her hair, and her scalp tingled. *So this is what it is to love a man?* Had she found love only to have it snatched away?

"What is this?" he asked. He tugged on her hair to raise her face upward. "Why do you cry? Did I not please you?"

She sniffed. "Yes, you pleased me." She blushed and would have looked away, but Night Wind wouldn't allow it.

"Then, why are you sad?"

"Because I'm afraid," she admitted. "What is going to happen to us?"

The brave scowled. Even frowning, he was attractive, she thought. She saw the tiny star-shaped scar on his cheek and wondered again how he'd gotten it. Would life ever be the same for her now that she'd been with this man?

"You are afraid of my people?" he said. "I will not let them hurt you."

She gave him a tender smile. "I know. But don't you see? I cannot return to your village. I have to leave. I must go to Delaware. I cannot forget my little cousin."

"You must wait until the snow clears before you leave. If you go now, you will never make it to your De-la-ware."

Rebecca sat up. "How long?" A tiny bud of joy threatened to blossom in her heart, but guilt about her cousin crushed it down. How could she be happy when she didn't know the fate of young Elizabeth? Her aunt could have died, and her cousin could be staying with strangers.

Night Wind rose up on his elbow. "I know not how long you must stay, but I know that you have been lost and ill. You will never get to your Ver-on-ica's alive."

The fur covering had fallen away, revealing his sleek muscled chest. Rebecca's breath caught at the beauty of him . . . at the memory of how he felt beneath her fingers . . . how he tasted on her lips. She was shocked by the resurgence of desire she felt for him. They had made love many times these last three days, and she had found that with every moment she spent in his company her longing for him intensified.

"If the weather is too terrible for me to go to Delaware, how are we to journey to Turtle-Town?"

Night Wind shook his head. "We are within one day of *Tulpeuta-nai*. Night Wind can take you there

before the sun rises two times in the morning sky.
This brave can see the way without eyes. We will go
to my village, and you will stay until the snow melts
on the treetops and the ice thaws on the great lake."

"But my cousin—"

"You wish to die, Medicine Woman?" The glittering intensity of his dark eyes convinced her that he
was serious. He honestly believed she'd die.

She recalled the days she'd spent trying to keep
warm and hunting for food and she shuddered with
the memory. Did she wish to die? He was right. If
she left now, she'd be condemning herself to a freezing
death.

"Your people," she said, "will they allow me to
come back?"

Did his expression flicker with uncertainty?

"They will allow it," he said, and she thought he said
it with more determination than was warranted, as if he
were trying to convince himself as well as her.

He pulled her down and kissed her hard. Then, he
lay down, tucking her against him, rubbing her bare
back and shoulder. Rebecca's doubts fled as she was
enveloped in his warmth, his scent. She'd be all right;
Night Wind would protect her.

Night Wind held tightly to the woman in his arms
and fought his doubts, his concerns for Rebecca's
safety. Would his people accept her back? Would they
believe she'd survived banishment on her own, or
would they think that he'd helped her? And if so,
would they seek to punish them both?

She'd felt wonderful pressed against his side. When
she'd sat up moments ago, he'd been instantly aroused
by the sight of her. Naked, she was glorious, her full
breasts gleaming in the firelight. He had an instant
recollection of how the lush mounds and hard nipples
felt beneath his tongue. Her long, tousled hair framed

her beautiful face with her glowing sky-colored eyes and her tempting pink mouth. His manhood had instantly hardened as he'd studied her. He wanted her now—badly.

She was more woman than witch, he thought. Not the opposite as he'd first thought. He had witnessed her weakness, her struggle to survive in the forest, and she'd been unable to save herself with magic.

Had she lost her powers when she'd saved the Cayuga child? Is that why she couldn't save Red Fox?

He fondled her shoulder and then slid his hand beneath her arm, down her side to her breast. He gently squeezed the side of the soft mound, before cupping it fully, and then rubbing the nipple. He felt a jolt of renewed desire when she moved against him, moaning with pleasure, the sound coming from deep within her throat. She shifted so that his leg was cradled between her thighs, and rubbed against him. She grabbed his other hand bringing it to her other breast, and Rebecca groaned when the mound filled his palm. He caressed both breasts simultaneously, paying special attention to each. He felt them swell beneath his touch, and as he played with her nipples, he rejoiced to hear her gasp.

"Night Wind," she whispered. "Yes . . . yes."

He wanted to explore her further. His only desire was to bring her pleasure when he rolled over onto his side, pressing her to her back, so he could touch and caress and nibble on her freely. His exploration became more thorough. He took his time, enjoying every inch of her smooth white skin, teasing her senses as he slowly fondled her aroused body.

She tried to caress him, but he wouldn't allow her. He wanted to enjoy the way her eyes lit up and then became glazed with passion. He loved hearing her soft moans and wild cries.

"Tuulke Uitiissa," he murmured, his eyes glowing.

Rebecca closed her eyes as he played with her breast. She had heard him say those words before. "What does that mean?" She gasped as he plucked her nipple, and sensation shot from her breast to her secret core.

He continued rubbing and caressing, and stroking her hardened nipple, and she moaned and writhed in enjoyment of his touch. "Night Wind—" she said.

"It is this," he explained, finally answering her. "You have breasts of great beauty. See how one fills my hand."

She opened her eyes, and their eyes met before her gaze traveled to where his dark hand captured her breast. Then, he lowered his head, and Rebecca inhaled sharply as he began to suckle her. He drew in and sucked her breast. He laved her nipple and licked the full mound, and she went wild with the feeling.

He raised his head, his eyes glowing. "See how one fills my mouth."

He bent again and took the tip of her breast between his lips. He nipped it gently with his teeth and then worshiped the breast fully from top to underside with his lips, teeth, and tongue. Overcome with the sensation, Rebecca alternately moaned and gasped as she clutched his head, holding him to her, telling him without words how much she loved his attention.

He caressed her stomach next, enjoying the way it quivered beneath his fingertips, and then his hand moved lower. It cradled her most sensitive area. Rebecca opened her lips in anticipation of his caress, and then cried with surprise when she felt not his fingers, but his mouth. The hot stroking of his tongue drove her over the edge, and her body arched up off their bed of furs and pine needles, stiffening as she was racked by the earth-shaking tremors of desire.

Wish You Were Here?

You can be, every month, with Zebra Historical Romance Novels.

AND TO GET YOU STARTED, ALLOW US TO SEND YOU

4 Historical Romances Free

A $19.96 VALUE!
With absolutely no obligation to buy anything.

YOU'RE GOING TO LOVE GETTING
4 FREE BOOKS

These books worth almost $20, are yours without cost or obligation
when you fill out and mail this certificate.
(If the certificate is missing below, write to: Zebra Home Subscription Service, Inc.,
120 Brighton Road, P.O. Box 5214, Clifton, New Jersey 07015-5214

Complete and mail this card to receive 4 Free books!

Yes! Please send me 4 Zebra Historical Romances without cost or obligation. I understand that each month thereafter I will be able to preview 4 new Zebra Historical Romances FREE for 10 days. Then, if I should decide to keep them, I will pay the money-saving preferred publisher's price of just $4.00 each...a total of $16. That's almost $4 less than the publisher's price. (A nominal shipping and handling charge of $1.50 per shipment will be added.) I may return any shipment within 10 days and owe nothing, and I may cancel this subscription at any time. The 4 FREE books will be mine to keep in any case.

Name _____

Address _____ Apt. _____

City _____ State _____ Zip _____

Telephone ( ) _____

Signature _____
(If under 18, parent or guardian must sign.)

LP0495

Terms, offer and prices subject to change without notice. Subscription subject to acceptance by Zebra Books.
Zebra Books reserves the right to reject any order or cancel any subscription.

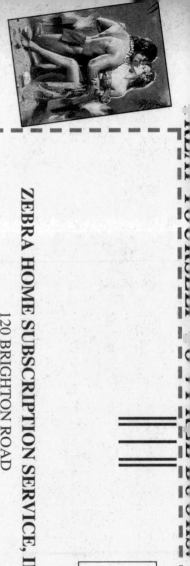

She fell back against the bed, amazed by the experience, slightly ashamed that she had enjoyed physical love without Night Wind's pleasure . . . until she saw his face. Taut with passion and his own pleasure at her release, he was nearing the edge of ecstasy. Rebecca rose up on her side and took a hold of his penis. It was hard and throbbing in her hand, and she smiled and began to fondle its length and tip.

He had unselfishly given her pleasure, and now it was her turn to do the same. She kissed his breast and his belly. She worshiped his neck and throat. She caressed and fondled him much in the same way as he did her, and she knew by his deep groans that he loved what she was doing to him. His reaction lit a spark within her. Startled that it had returned so quickly, she understood the enjoyment he must have felt to kiss her and fondle her and watch her passion.

As his passion rose, Night Wind pulled her onto him, and her eyes widened as he sat her across him and filled her with his manhood. She rode him and the pleasure in their joining was heightened by her wild cries and his deep throaty groans. Night Wind rocked beneath her, while caressing her body freely, and she rose and fell against him, able to fondle him without restraint.

They reached the summit together, crying out at the same time, straining against each other as they climaxed. Satiated, Rebecca fell against him, glorying in the loud thunder of Night Wind's heart beat and the rasps of his labored breaths.

They fell asleep in the sweet lingering aftermath of their lovemaking, their bodies locked in an embrace, their hearts beating as one. For now, they had each other and the loving they shared. There was a heavy snow carpeting the Pennsylvania forest; it would be a long while before it disappeared. Until it did, their love and their lives were safe.

Tulpeuta'nai . . . Village of Night Wind

The heavy snows had confined the Lenape villagers to their lodges. No one ventured outside, except to check the conditions of the weather and to replenish their food and fuel supplies from the storage sheds next to their wigwams.

Gift From Forest had been ill when the first of the snows came, but he had improved each day since the snowfall had kept each family to itself. Ice From Sky and her family had no visitors in their lodge during the inclement weather. The matron cared for her sick son, and under her watchful, loving ministrations, she saw that he drank his broth and ate good meals once he could eat again.

The four-year-old was better, and he had a store full of energy, which was aching to burst free. His mother, grateful for his improved health, tolerated the boy's excess activity. She patiently gave the boy things that would productively occupy his time. Gift From Forest learned how to make meals. The child complained about the woman's work until his father explained to him that a warrior must know how to cook. How else would he eat while he was gone for days at a time during the hunt?

He was taught how to make *ka-ha-ma'kun,* a mixture of parched corn and tree sugar, which when added to water would make a meal substantial enough to satisfy the most hungry of braves. And the boy learned to make succotash, *sa'pan,* and *ah-pon',* which was bread. But he loved *ka-ha-ma'kun* the best, he told his mother, because it was the food of the warrior, and he was a good warrior who would someday be chief.

Gift From Forest was working to make his first bow while his parents looked on approvingly. "Mother," he asked, "where is *Tipaakke Shaakha?* Why hasn't my brother come home to us?"

"You have asked this question many times, my son," his father said with a frown. "He has gone to the sacred place."

"But that was a long time ago," the boy said. "He should have been back by now."

"He will come when he is here," his mother said gently.

Gift From Forest grimaced as he struck his bow. "You said that before," he said.

"And she meant it then as she does now," his father interjected.

The boy's attention went back to his work, and his father's gaze met that of his wife's. The adults shared the child's concern for Night Wind. While Night Wind wasn't the natural son of Ice From Sky, the woman cared for the warrior as one cared for one's own son.

How could she not when Night Wind had so loved her children? Night Wind was her husband's child from a previous marriage. Wood Owl's first wife had died when Night Wind was a young warrior, and Ice From Sky had married *Tahuun Kukuus* shortly afterward. Night Wind was of the *Tuk'sit,* the clan of his mother, which was Round Foot, the Lenape Wolf Band. Ice From Sky and her sons were of the *Pokoun'go,* the Turtle band, the clan of the village chief. Night Wind's father, who was Ice From Sky's husband, was of the *Pe'le* or Turkey band.

Night Wind had always seemed like family to Ice From Sky, and she was worried for his well being. The matron waited for her young son's attention to be deeply involved in what he was doing before she pulled her husband off to the side to speak privately with him.

"My husband," she said. "I am greatly concerned for your son."

Wood Owl nodded. "I too am worried about Night Wind, but what can we do? The snow is thick upon the forest. It falls even as we speak. I cannot search for him until I can see. I cannot find the sacred grave site."

His wife agreed, but her eyes darkened with pain at the mention of Red Fox's resting place. Would she lose two of those she loved?

She had almost lost Gift From Forest to that strange illness. The spirits had looked kindly upon her child. She had prayed and offered sacrifices of burning tobacco. She had cared for her child, and he had become well. She would burn more tobacco for Night Wind; she would close her eyes and ask Manit'to to protect the warrior son and bring him home.

"I will gather supplies when the sun warms the earth and the snow stops," *Tahuun Kukuus* said. "Then I will search for Night Wind."

Ice From Sky caressed her husband's shoulder. "And I will wait for my husband to return with his smiling warrior son."

Confined to their wigwam by the fierce winter storm, Night Wind and Rebecca discovered the joys of loving and forgot for now their concerns for tomorrow.

Seventeen

They left the day after the snow stopped. All in all, they'd spent two weeks in the abandoned village. It had been a time of exploration, a time of love.

Rebecca felt a tingle of alarm when she woke that morning and saw Night Wind up and dressed as if he'd been outside. He was gathering provisions, stowing them into a skin sack.

"Night Wind?" She sat up, blinking.

He froze at her voice, and then turned slowly to smile at her. There was something in his eyes that made her heart trip with fear. Was he leaving her? Had he tired of her and been preparing to go?

"You are awake, Medicine Woman."

"What are you doing?" she asked.

He gazed at her, his expression intense. "I am getting food for us to eat on our journey."

Journey, she thought, and then she brightened at the "we." He was taking her with him.

"Where are we going? To your village?"

He nodded.

"But the snow is deep yet."

"We will get there."

Rebecca was afraid, afraid of returning to a people whom she'd failed. What if they chose not to take her back? What if they decided to punish her again?

They departed in the early hours of the morning.

Darkness still blanketed the land, and the air was nippy, but dry. Rebecca followed in Night Wind's footsteps. The going was rough; the snow was inches deep, and Night Wind had to step carefully. But he seemed to know his way and he traveled as quickly as the height of the snow allowed him.

He said little as they walked, pausing now and again to study the sky and the surrounding woods. Once he stopped and drew his bow, aiming and killing a rabbit for their dinner. They had only a little of the venison left. Night Wind hunted to ensure they kept their strength on their journey.

They continued for hours before Night Wind called a halt to rest and eat. He exclaimed with concern when he saw Rebecca stumble to the ground with exhaustion.

"Why did you not tell me?" he said.

She gave him a half smile. "I'm all right, just a bit winded is all."

He frowned and bent to rub her legs after untying the strings of her leggings. He warmed her skin with the friction from his palms, and she closed her eyes with enjoyment. "We will stay here for the night."

Rebecca raised her eyelashes to glance at him with surprise. He paused in his rubbing, but her legs continued to tingle from his touch. "Here?" she asked. "Already?"

He straightened and studied the area. "We will move to those trees. I will make us a shelter. There is no sense in your becoming ill, when we can rest here and arrive safely."

"How far is it to your village?"

"Many hours."

Chilled, Rebecca longed for the warmth of the wigwam they had left behind in the deserted Lenape village. She had no doubt, however, that Night Wind would see to her comfort.

He told her to sit while he scouted the area for the best place to stay, and when he returned, he was smiling. "I have found us shelter."

She studied him with raised eyebrows. He extended his arm to her and pulled her to her feet, and she followed him through the forest until they reached an opening in a dense thicket of trees. Just past the copse stood a lean-to. Rebecca had to smile when she saw it. She recalled her own efforts to make such a structure; this one was sturdier and had obviously been standing for a long time.

"Why do you smile?" Night Wind asked.

She told him about her lean-to. He didn't share her amusement. The deer running toward her crudely constructed shelter had filled him with terror. He'd felt helpless as he'd watched, knowing that Rebecca was huddled inside.

"We will spend the night here," he said.

"Who built this?"

He shrugged. "Lenape warrior," he said curtly. "Shawnee brave. It matters not." He saw her expression, and he explained. "Lenape built it to sleep during the hunt. He leaves for the next brave. This lodge big enough for one, maybe two warriors, other lodges big enough for many more."

Rebecca nodded and moved in for a closer look.

Night Wind hung furs to cover the open end of the lean-to, lifting them to drape partly over the roof, and then gestured for Rebecca to enter. She slipped past the fur flap and sat against the back wall. The lean-to was an open-ended cabin, built by driving four fork-topped stakes into the ground about three feet high on one side and six feet on the other. Poles had been laid across the forked stakes to make the frame which had a sloping roof. The frame had then been covered with large sheets of tree bark.

Rebecca was pleased to find that Night Wind had lined the inside with boughs from a Balsam tree. They would share a comfortable, fragrant mattress for the night, she thought.

She watched as Night Wind started a fire. When the spark became a steady flame and the scent of wood smoke filled the air, the brave lowered the fur part way over the entrance and then he crawled in beside her.

They ate some dried squash and cakes of corn that they had brought with them, and then they sat staring at the flickering fire, enjoying the warmth. It seemed natural when Night Wind pulled Rebecca into his arms. It felt right that she snuggled against him, feeling safe and secure.

Later, they slept, embracing, with their feet towards the fire, their warm breaths misting in the cold, night air. The next morning they were up early and on their way again. Rebecca tried not to think of reaching the village; she tried not to be afraid.

Night Wind stopped mid-morning, and they shared the last of the venison, sipping from the brave's water skin to wash it down. When it was her turn to take a drink, Rebecca was conscious of placing her lips where Night Wind's mouth had been. She had to fight the frisson of desire that curled in her lower abdomen at the memory of the pleasures his mouth had given her. When their gazes fastened as she handed the skin back to him, Night Wind's eyes flamed, and she knew that he too was remembering.

"We must go now," he said, quickly rising to his feet.

She nodded, and stood.

Hours passed, and Rebecca's legs hurt. "How far is your village?" she asked, gasping as she hurried to keep up in his wake. Her fear of arriving had dissipated in her desire to end the torture to her weary body.

"We will be there when the sun sets in the night sky."

Which wouldn't be long, Rebecca surmised. It was well past noon.

He paused in his tracks and turned to regard her with concern. "You are unwell?" His onyx eyes glistened as he studied her thoroughly.

"I'm tired, but I'll be all right."

"You wish to rest?"

The idea was tempting to her, but she shook her head. "I wish to get to Turtle-Town," she said with a smile.

He nodded and continued the journey. Rebecca studied his back, warmed by his concern for her.

Rebecca smelled the cooking fires before she saw the spiraling coils of smoke drifting up into the clear December sky. Dogs howled as if sensing their arrival, and Night Wind picked up his pace, while Rebecca followed as best she could.

The Lenape surrounded the couple as they entered the village. Voices rose with excitement. Night Wind responded to the barrage of questions as several of the Indians slapped him on the back and expressed their joy at seeing him alive.

Rebecca got shoved aside in the shuffle. She was trying to gain Night Wind's attention when her arm was shackled in a steely grip. She gasped and faced her captor.

"You come," Iron Bear said, squeezing her arm.

"No, not without Night Wind."

"You come now!"

Rebecca held her ground. "Where?"

He gave a jerk, and she stumbled, then was forced to follow him or be dragged bodily across the rough yard. Her breath quickened with fear. She called out to Night Wind, but the chatter of the crowd about him drowned out the sounds of her anxious cries.

Night Wind didn't know she was gone. Would Iron Bear kill her? She could be dead before Night Wind knew that she'd disappeared.

She cried out with pain as Iron Bear pulled her roughly across the square to the edge of the forest and dragged her behind the circle of wigwams.

"Let me go!" she demanded.

"Chitkwe'se!" He paused to glare at her. His expression fierce, he presented a frightening figure of power and brute strength. "Speak again, Medicine Woman, and feel my anger!"

Her eyes filled with tears. Her pulse thundered with her fear, and her muscles protested at the cruel treatment. She'd been kidnapped and made a slave by the Cayuga. She'd been stolen by a band of Lenape and forced to administer to a sick child. She had survived nine days alone in the forest and had recovered from a severe illness, and she had suffered the journey back. Had she done all this only to meet her death?

Night Wind, please realize that I'm gone. Please help me.

"We thought you were dead!" Sun Blossom clutched Night Wind's arm. "You were gone so long."

Ice From Sky held onto his other arm. "When the snow came, we were afraid for you."

He smiled at his father's wife. "I am well, *M' hoo kum a.* You can rest easy now."

"Where did you go, my son?" Wood Owl's features showed signs of strain.

Night Wind's expression was soft as he met his father's gaze. *Tahuun Kukuus* had been concerned for him. "I returned to the sacred ground."

"Where did you find *her?*" Angry Woman inquired disparagingly, coming up from behind.

Night Wind stiffened, before turning to face her. The air became charged as everyone within the gathering waited for Night Wind's explanation. He would have to choose his words carefully; Rebecca's life was at stake. He frowned as he searched the crowd for her. Where was she?

"Where is Medicine Woman?" he asked.

"Pah!" Angry Woman said. "She is no medicine woman. She can cure no one!"

The brave glared at the matron, who flinched beneath his angry gaze. "She has cured a Cayuga child."

The woman raised her chin. "But she killed a Lenape!"

"She killed no one."

"She killed him!" another woman echoed, and Night Wind's fear for Rebecca grew.

Night Wind turned to Ice From Sky, seeking some help from Red Fox's mother. "She tried to help him," he said.

Ice From Sky's expression hardened. "He did not live."

The brave's stomach lurched in fear. "I will take her from our village. She has survived the nine days of banishment, and she should be free to leave."

"Without Night Wind's help?" came a male voice full of insinuation.

Night Wind tensed as Iron Bear joined the group.

"She lived by her own hand," Night Wind told the shaman. "Our paths crossed after the period of banishment."

"How lucky for the white woman," the medicine man quipped.

Night Wind narrowed his gaze. "Where is she?"

"Your white woman is resting comfortably."

"Where have you taken her?" The brave's fists clenched at his sides. "Why have you taken her?"

"Your mind is clouded with the witch's powers. It is up to the council to decide her fate. We cannot trust that you will not help her escape."

"She is no witch," Night Wind said. "She is a healer, nothing more. You had no right to take her away!" He lunged at the shaman, and the villagers gasped and moved out of the way. "She has done nothing wrong! It was I who convinced her to return to the village. She wished to journey south to the land of her people, but I told her to wait until the sun thaws the ice on the great lake."

"You should have left her in the forest, my son," Wood Owl said. "By bringing her here, you have altered her path. If she had returned on her own, she would have been accepted, but since she came with you . . ." Night Wind's father's words trailed off.

"Where did you put her?" Night Wind demanded. He had caught hold of the man's shell necklace, and he twisted it until it tightened to his throat.

The shaman gave him a thin smile. He obviously didn't feel in the least threatened. "I have put her in a safe place where she will stay until the meeting of our council."

The child refused to leave her mother's bedside. The woman had been dead for over an hour, but Elizabeth wouldn't budge from Veronica's side. The little girl stared at her mother's face, which appeared serene in her passing, and silently willed her parent to wake up, to speak to her, like her mother had done so many times in the past two weeks.

"Mama," she whispered, "don't die. *Please* don't leave me. I have no one. Who will take care of me? Rebecca hasn't come. What am I going to do?"

Agnes Martin, the neighbor, who had helped care for the ailing Veronica, stood at the bedchamber door, watching the scene with concern. She conversed quietly with the village minister.

"She refuses to leave her," Agnes said worriedly. "What shall we do? She can't stay there for much longer. We'll have to prepare poor Veronica for burial."

The minister frowned. "Where is this cousin? Rebecca—is it?"

The woman nodded. "I don't know. She was due to arrive months ago. We can only assume she's dead. Veronica thought the girl might have been captured by savages. You heard about those Indians up north? They're a bloodthirsty lot."

"Then you think . . ."

"Yes, I fear so. Rebecca Morton must be dead, killed by savages."

"What is to become of the child?"

Agnes shook her head sadly. "I don't know. You know, Reverend, that I have no place for her in my household with six children of me own. It was a hardship as it was to find the time to be here."

"And you will be thus rewarded handsomely in the kingdom of God," the minister said, patting her arm.

Elizabeth screamed, and then began to sob wildly. Her mother was dead and would never speak to her again.

"I shall have to see what can be done," the minister said, and Agnes nodded before she went in to comfort the little girl.

Eighteen

Iron Bear bound her hands and feet and left her in a wigwam with a gag tied about her mouth. Rebecca's fingers hurt from lack of circulation, and her ankles ached from the odd angle in which she was forced to sit. She'd fought to be free of the shaman's grasp as he forced her to enter, but Iron Bear had struck her across the face. Her jaw had seared with excruciating pain, and she'd known why he was called Iron Bear. *He has fists like bear paws with the strength of pig iron.* And he had used them on her face. She could tell by the way her mouth and cheek throbbed that she was swollen and black and blue.

The interior of the wigwam was filthy, unlike any other Lenape wigwam she'd been in. Dirty rushes lined the floor, and an odor of wet dog fur permeated the air, making her want to gag. Plants, herbs, and dried vegetables hung from the low rafters. A grotesque ceremonial mask leaned against the wall. Spears, rattles, and other strange instruments lying about confirmed what she'd first guessed—the medicine man had brought her to his wigwam.

No one knew she was here. The villagers had taken Night Wind's attention, and he hadn't noticed that she'd disappeared. Cold, frightened, and in pain, she prayed for someone to find her . . . she prayed for Night Wind to come for her.

A flash of light signaled the raising of the door flap, and then the door opening was filled with a man's figure. Rebecca's heart pounded as the masked Indian stepped into the wigwam, allowing the flap to fall behind him.

"Aye!" the Lenape said, removing his mask. He rushed to Rebecca's side, his hands immediately moving to release her mouth gag. *"Shi'kiXkwe,* what has he done to you?" He worked the cloth knot free and gently took off the gag.

"Night Wind!" she breathed. Her eyes glistened with tears of joy. She had prayed for him, and he was here!

"You are all right?" he said anxiously. "He did not hurt you." As he searched her face, something dark entered his features. "He hit you!"

"I will live," she said, not denying it. "But could you untie my hands?"

He made an exclamation of anger and then turned her carefully to undo her wrists. He muttered harshly in his native tongue when he saw the bonds. She cried out with pain as he freed her hands and the blood rushed back to fill her fingers. Instantly, Night Wind was rubbing her hands, helping to restore her circulation.

"You are better?" he asked. He sat and tugged her onto his lap, but she screamed when her legs shifted beneath her, pulling on her ankles bonds. He gave a sound as violent as an Englishman's curse as he set her down gently and then worked to untie the lengths of sinew binding her ankles. Next, he carefully undid her moccasins and tenderly rubbed her feet.

She gazed at him, her heart warmed by his ministrations, her eyes soft with her love for him. As the pain eased, she felt a rush of pleasure at his touch and the overwhelming desire to caress him. But she held back. This wasn't the time for loving.

You prayed for him, and he came, she thought.

He sat back and pulled her onto his lap, cradling her within his arms. He held her silently, her head nestled against his chest, his face buried in her hair. She closed her eyes and sighed, satisfied with his holding her. *He is here. He will care for you.*

She didn't know how long they sat that way. Her senses were filled with Night Wind . . . the sound of his breathing . . . his scent . . . his warmth, and his hard, muscled form. She turned her face into his neck, tasting the skin above his clothing. She heard him inhale sharply, felt his hold tighten, and unable to help herself, she kissed his throat.

She felt the tremor that went through him, and she heard the increased rhythm of his heart. But then he abruptly shifted her from his lap. He sprang to his feet in an obvious state of agitation.

Disappointed but not devastated, Rebecca saw his inner struggle and was pleased. *He cares for me.* But how much? Enough to save her? Even if it meant defying his own people? Enough to love her until the end of time?

Rebecca stood and touched his arm. He flinched away, and she was hurt. A knot of unease settled in her stomach.

"When the sky grows dark and the moon rises to light up our village, the council will meet." He didn't look at her as he spoke quietly. He stared at the wall instead.

Her heart thumped. "To decide what?"

He fixed her with his gaze. "Whether the White Medicine Woman lives or dies."

She paled, swaying. "But I suffered my punishment. I survived the nine days!"

"Iron Bear thinks you lived because of Night Wind." Night Wind saw her face and experienced a burning in his belly. He didn't tell her that he too would be on trial, that because of the medicine man's accusation and his influence over the tribe that he too could be punished . . . punished or put to death.

His concern was not for himself, but for Rebecca. Whatever decision was made concerning him, he would find a way to live—live and survive the better for it. But he feared that Iron Bear wouldn't be satisfied until Rebecca died.

"Will you help me to escape?" she asked.

He looked at her, his face grave. How could she ask this of him? To defy his people? "I cannot." He saw her shock, and her pain.

"You will not, you mean!"

The brave shook his head. "If I help you, they will know. They will believe that we did wrong and seek to hide it. And if I help you the Lenape will no longer be my people. I will be forced to roam the forest alone for the remainder of my white path."

She grabbed his arm. "You can come with me!" She clutched him hard. "We can be happy together."

He scowled. "And live with your English?" His scowl became a grimace. "Your people will not allow this man to live with the white! And Night Wind would not be happy in a house of bricks with a floor of wood."

"Doesn't what we've done mean anything to you?"

His scowl deepened. "What we have done?"

She blushed and looked away.

"Because we have shared the same sleeping mat?"

Rebecca looked at him, and he regarded her with raised eyebrows. "We did not only sleep," she said.

He inclined his head. "This is so."

"But it means nothing to you."

Night Wind's expression flickered with emotion. "We enjoyed each other's body. We shared each other's hearts. Is that not something?"

"Go then!" she shouted. "I don't need you!"

Night Wind stared at her. "You wish me to leave?" he said, startled by her request.

She nodded, her eyes bright with unshed tears. Perhaps it would be best if he left, he thought. He had told the truth. Until the council decided his own fate, there was nothing he could do for her.

And he was angry. She was trying to use her magic to get him to do what she wanted. He would do what he could, but he didn't like being ordered to do so. Did she think she could use her body to manipulate this brave?

"Go!" she cried. "Leave me! You don't care about me. I thought you had feelings for me, but you don't, because you have no feelings!"

Night Wind became furious. He glared at her before he turned and left her. Was this the same woman who had kissed him softly? Was this the same woman who had cried out at his touch?

She was in the hut of a man who wanted to see her put to death and she'd sent away her only ally and friend . . . the only man she'd ever loved. Rebecca stared at the door flap through a haze of tears.

"Night Wind?" she whispered. *"Tipaakke Shaakha!"* she shouted.

The flap raised, and the brave stepped in. Night Wind had not left her. *"Shi'kiXkwe,"* he said huskily.

She beamed at him with her heart in her eyes, and he rushed forward to take her into his arms.

The drums began after darkness fell. Rebecca trembled when she heard the first sound, for she knew the time had come. The drums signaled the gathering of the council. The Lenape were meeting to decide her fate.

Earlier, Night Wind had arranged to have her moved. She was back sharing the wigwam of She Who Sees Much and the matron's daughter, Sun Blossom. If the matron felt the same as Iron Bear, then she gave no sign of it when Rebecca had been brought before her. She had smiled at the white woman, nodded her welcome, and then had gone about preparing a place for Rebecca to sleep.

Sun Blossom, on the other hand, was openly hostile to Rebecca. The white woman had no idea whether it was because the Indian maiden shared the shaman's views and wanted to see Rebecca punished or whether her hostility stemmed from Rebecca's involvement with Night Wind. It had been obvious to Rebecca from the first that the beautiful Lenape woman had feelings for the brave. It must have been equally evident to Sun Blossom from his defending Rebecca that Night Wind had feelings for the white woman.

Rebecca had no intention of questioning the maiden about her feelings. Her life was complicated enough as it was and to openly argue with Sun Blossom might jeopardize Rebecca's welcome in She Who Sees Much's wigwam. Here, at least, Rebecca was away from the bear-like man who hated her. Her safety might be temporary, but for now she could rest easily, assured of her well-being in this kind woman's lodge. Here she could safely wait the decision of the Lenape council.

She rose from the fire and went to the door flap. She Who Sees Much had left at the first beat of the ceremonial drums, and her daughter had glared at Rebecca and then followed her mother.

Here, Rebecca was not bound. She had promised Night Wind that she wouldn't run, so in She Who Sees Much's lodge, she was allowed to move about freely. With the fiercest part of winter on its way, Rebecca wasn't about to escape. In this weather, she'd never survive the journey to Delaware. Those nine days in the forest had shown her that.

She peered out into the yard and saw the Lenape coming out of their wigwams and heading toward the Big House. Someone had built a huge fire in the center of the yard, and the fire roared upward as one Lenape brave fueled it with dry wood. The flaming wood highlighted the men and women as they crossed the yard. An Indian matron stood waiting near the fire with a huge cooking kettle, ready to heat up food for the community.

She could hear the raised voices of some of the men. She recognized the faces of those she knew in the village. She Who Sees Much was conversing with Wilting Flower, the oldest matron of the tribe, but Rebecca could see no sign of Sun Blossom anywhere. A brave called Feather Coat sat outside the Big House, tapping his drum in time with the other drummers inside, a call to all to come quickly. Ice From Sky, Red Fox's mother, exited her wigwam and hurried toward the meeting that would decide the fate of the one who failed her son. Rebecca's chest tightened when she saw her.

Soon, the center yard was empty, but for several small children who were supervised by an older child, still too young to be part of the adult meeting. The children were playing a game with sticks and rocks, chanting a song as they ran about in a circle.

The drums inside the Big House beat faster, more fiercely, and then all became silent. Rebecca's heart stopped for a beat and then started up again. These

Indians were deciding her fate. How could they expect her to wait here calmly?

Rebecca, anxious about the meeting, started to leave the wigwam.

"Saa!" an angry voice exclaimed. *"Ekesa'. K'tuh-shing'huh. E'kaiu'. Ala'pi."*

She felt a burning in her stomach as she turned. The warrior was an ugly brave with tattoos across his face and neck. The Lenape had posted a guard outside the wigwam. Night Wind didn't trust her to keep her word.

The Indian pointed to the door. She could tell that he was ordering her back inside, and for a moment, she contemplated ignoring him. What would he do to her if she refused to obey?

Kill her. The thought came to her quickly, and she backed inside, her heart pounding with dread. She was hurt that Night Wind had felt it necessary, despite her promise, to post a guard.

You were leaving the wigwam, an inner voice taunted her.

"To go to the Big House," she muttered. "Not to escape!"

But they don't want you there.

"I have a right to know what they're saying about me!"

You'll learn soon enough, the voice argued. *There's nothing to do, but be patient.*

Rebecca sat on her bed and waited nervously, again, for the Lenape to decide her fate.

The Indian wore beaver pelts and bearskins on his massive body. His headdress was a bear's head with eagle feathers attached to the fur at the back of the head, and several necklaces of beads, shells, and porcupine quills hung about the man's thick neck. His face was painted with vermilion; his skin was oiled heavily with bear's grease. He carried a large spear in his left hand and a turtle shell rattle in his right one. His earrings were huge, of beads strung on a long piece of sinew threaded through his earlobe. Each time he turned his head, his earrings clicked together, making noise. He was the shaman of the tribe in Turtle-Town, and he was the focus of all eyes as he entered the Big House and came to the center of the room.

Night Wind sat near his father, his muscles knotted with tension, his mind anxious with thoughts of the white woman's plight. Wood Owl had been overjoyed at the return of his son, and Night Wind had been happy to see his father. They had talked well into the night. Night Wind had told Wood Owl of his adventures while he was gone, how he'd come across the Medicine Woman, who had been in danger. He'd confessed of his desire for the white woman, how he'd been tempted to interfere and help her before it was time, but that he'd held back, because he'd been forbidden to give assistance.

"But, *noX'han,*" Night Wind said, "I cared for her when she became ill. Was that wrong?"

Wood Owl frowned. "This was after the ninth morning?"

The son nodded.

"Then there was no harm in your actions."

Night Wind had not told his father everything, but he could tell that his father had drawn his own conclusions about the relationship between his son and the white woman.

Wood Owl had looked upon his son without condemnation, but with a sadness that said more. "You must watch the yearnings of your heart, *ne gwis*. A warrior must keep his head . . . or lose his life."

His father's words came back to Night Wind as he sat, waiting for the meeting to begin. He knew it was wrong to want the white woman, but he also knew that the wrong seemed right all the same.

"We are here once again to speak of the White Medicine Woman." It was the sachem who spoke first. Beaver Hawk, Ice From Sky's brother, was a good man and a fair chief; Night Wind wasn't concerned that he would allow his relationship to the dead boy to influence his people's decision on the future of the White Medicine Woman.

". . . The white woman had returned to us alive, bringing with her our warrior brother." The sachem paused, before continuing. "Iron Bear has come to me with great concern. He believes that the Medicine Woman did not live by her own wits. He believes that our brother, *Tipaakke Shaakha,* has helped her."

Several of the villagers gasped, and Night Wind became the focus of all eyes.

"But let us not make hasty judgments," Beaver Hawk said. "Let us question our brother and learn the truth. If the warrior disobeyed the decision of this council and helped the Medicine Woman, then we shall have to decide whether or not to punish him. We must decide whether or not the white woman should die!"

The sachem paused to study Night Wind and allow his message to sink in. "We shall all speak. We shall allow Iron Bear to go first, since it was he who made the accusations against *Tipaakke Shaakha.*" Beaver Hawk turned to the shaman. "Iron Bear," he said, "what have you to say?"

The shaman looked like a hulking bear as he came forward to speak. The fur of his headdress glistened in the glow of the flames from the two fire pits; the fur draped over his shoulders dragged against the ground as he walked. He wore fringed leggings and highly decorated moccasins. He cut an impressive figure as he prepared to address his audience.

Iron Bear walked about in the center of the Big House, stopping to gaze at each section of the tribe. His gaze fastened first on the *Pe'le* or Turkey band, before moving to meet those of the *Poko-un'go,* which was the Turtle band, the clan of the chief and the main sect within the village. Finally, his eyes fell on the *Took' seet,* or Roundfoot band, the clan of the Wolf, the clan of Night Wind.

"My brothers . . . grandfathers—we are here to talk of a great wrong made to our people." He moved about as he spoke, his gaze returning to each one of the tribal clans. "Many days ago, Night Wind brought to us the White Medicine Woman. He brought her from the Cayuga, our enemy, yet he promised that she would heal our young brother, who was sick and in need of help. But the White Medicine Woman did not heal our young brother. Red Fox died."

There was an astonished murmur about the Big House. Iron Bear had broken custom by speaking the name of one who was deceased.

"When the White Medicine Woman failed to heal our young brother, she was brought before council and her fate was sealed. We chose to banish her from the village for a period of nine days.

"Night Wind was chosen to take the White Medicine Woman out to the forest and leave her there . . . without food and water . . . without furs to sleep on and extra clothing to keep her warm. And this he did." Iron Bear paused dramatically. "And so he said.

"The woman was left there to make her own way. If at the end of her banishment period, the White

Medicine Woman survived on her own, we would know that the spirits did not hold her responsible for our young brother's death . . . and the white woman would be free to go or return to us as she pleased.

"The White Medicine Woman was gone for more than nine days and so too was our warrior brother, Night Wind. The snows came, keeping us to our lodges, making our food difficult to get to, making wood hard to burn, but we survived." Iron Bear tapped his spear and paced as he spoke, his expression somber.

"Night Wind did not immediately return to us. When he came, he stayed for only a short time, before venturing out into the forest again. He was gone for a long time, and we all worried what had happened to him. It was thought by us all that Night Wind had gone again to our young brother's sacred burial place, where he could pray over his brother's grave for the days left of his mourning period. It was no secret how much Night Wind cared for his father's son, so no one questioned his need to do this.

"But when *Tipaakke* didn't return to us, our people began to wonder. What had happened to Night Wind? Why didn't he come back to us?

"After many weeks and many days, Night Wind returns to us, but he brings with him the White Medicine Woman. One can't help but wonder how, in heavy snows, when it is difficult for us to survive in our village, that this inexperienced white woman could return to us unharmed."

Night Wind stared at the shaman, unwilling to allow the man's words to unnerve him. He knew of the influence of this medicine man over his people, and he feared for Rebecca's life.

"Night Wind," Iron Bear said, "had a hand in the Medicine Woman's safe return. Did they not come back together? Is it not strange that this should be?

It is strange only until you see the truth! That our brother, Night Wind, broke the law of our people. He helped the White Medicine Woman to live past the nine days. He helped her, and now his presence here says that he is unconcerned by his actions!"

"I ask you, grandfathers . . . brothers, and matrons of our tribe. We must question Night Wind, and we must decide if the warrior had a hand in the Medicine Woman's safe return. If it is believed that he did, then we must decide if Night Wind should be punished, and whether the White Medicine Woman should be punished. Only then will we be assured that Red Fox made the haven of the Afterworld."

Iron Bear banged the ground with the end of his spear as he continued. "Night Wind, what have you to say of these charges."

Night Wind rose, his expression somber, his voice quiet as he addressed the crowd. "I have been out to my young brother's grave site where I have prayed many days for his safe journey to the Afterworld." He paused. "Yes, it is true that I have been with the Medicine Woman for many days, but I did not help or save her until after the nine days of her banishment. Then, it would have been against all that we believe if I did not help the Medicine Woman, when she became ill. I cared for her. As she tried to save my young brother, I tried to save her."

"But you were successful!" someone cried.

"The Medicine Woman is alive, while our brother is dead!" Iron Bear exclaimed.

"It is so because the spirits wish it!" Night Wind said. "The woman survived the nine days of banishment. In the eyes of our Great Spirit, *Kit-ta-hik'kan,* she was innocent of harming our young brother. Why shouldn't I have helped her when she was ill?"

The brave's gaze rested on each band of the tribe

as he spoke. "As the Medicine Woman is innocent of any wrong, so am I—Night Wind. Should you punish someone who is not guilty of a crime?"

Night Wind turned to address Iron Bear. "Iron Bear, you are shaman of our people. Would you not help an injured warrior? Would you not pray over a sick matron or a young maiden who is very ill?" He faced the Wolf clan. "Yes, I cared for the White Medicine Woman, but I see no wrong in that for she was free to come and go when I did so. Why are we questioning the spirit's wishes?"

Iron Bear was angry. "How do we know that you did not help the woman before the end of her nine days?"

Night Wind glared at him. "Because I have said this. Have I ever given you cause to doubt my word? Have I ever done wrong to my people? Yes, I brought the Medicine Woman to Turtle-Town, and she failed to heal. But I believe she tried to save him, only the spirits called home their son.

"Remember how our young brother woke and sat up during the Medicine Woman's care. He was much better. It was only after he was up and about and the Medicine Woman was out of the house and in the lodge of She Who Sees Much that he became deathly sick again."

Beaver Hawk intervened and addressed his people. "It is my belief that the one who should decide the truth is Ice From Sky. It is her son that was taken from his earthly path. If anyone was wronged, it was Ice From Sky. And yet Ice From Sky is not only the mother of the deceased child, she is the wife of Night Wind's father. Her decision would be a fair one." Beaver Hawk approached the Indian woman and asked her to stand. "Matron, what are your thoughts on this?"

Ice From Sky rose slowly. There were tears in her

eyes as she gazed at the chief, for mention of her dead son had given her pain. The memory of how she'd almost lost a second son, Gift From Forest, made her anxious and afraid. She looked at Night Wind, saw his face and the sadness in his eyes, and then her gaze returned to the sachem.

"Well, matron? Is Night Wind guilty or innocent? And what of the white woman?"

Ice From Sky closed her eyes and bowed her head, and all were silent within the Big Ceremonial House. As the silence lengthened, the tension grew, until finally Ice From Sky spoke.

"Night Wind has not committed any wrong," she began. "He brought the Medicine Woman here to save my son. Is it his fault that she failed to do this? No." She fingered her beaded necklace while she spoke. "I have suffered a great loss—the loss of my son. Will punishing an innocent man bring back my child? It will not."

The village chief accepted her decision about Night Wind, for it was clear by the woman's words that she did not want to punish her husband's son. "What of the White Medicine Woman?" the sachem asked Ice From Sky.

Ice From Sky's lips tightened, for she had hoped and prayed that the White Medicine Woman could save her son. "The white woman did not help us. She did not save my child. She saved a Cayuga child, but she failed a son of the Lenape." Her dark eyes flashed with anger. "The White Medicine Woman must be punished for her failure, but she must not die. I will take the White Medicine Woman into my lodge as slave. She will be replacement for my lost son. She will do the work that my son might have done, but she will not be a daughter. She will be a servant to Ice From Sky."

The Indians all began talking at once in reaction to the matron's decision. The village sachem clapped his hands and shouted above the noise until all was quiet again.

"You have heard Iron Bear's accusations, and you have heard Ice From Sky's wish. It is my belief that we, the members of Council, should honor Ice From Sky's decision in this matter."

Tahuun Kukuus, the matron's husband, stood. "I say the White Medicine Woman becomes slave."

Angry Woman rose from her rush mat. She was sister to Ice From Sky. "I say the white woman should die! Why should she go free when our young son reached the end of his white path?"

Another brave spoke up. "Ice From Sky is the one who has suffered by the white woman's failure. If she wishes a slave, then a slave she should have!"

"Then it is done," Beaver Hawk said. "Night Wind will not be punished, and the White Medicine Woman shall be a slave to Ice From Sky. If you agree, please rise."

A number of the Indians stood, and soon others joined them, until the decision was final.

With that decision made, the chief went on to other matters within the village, and Night Wind slipped out of the Big House. The brave went to see Rebecca to tell her the decision of the tribe.

He lifted the flap to the wigwam and peered inside. Rebecca sat on her sleeping platform and stared blankly. Tears glistened on her cheeks; her dark hair was a soft cloud about her shoulders.

"Reb-bec-ca."

She gasped and rose upon seeing him. "Night Wind!" She came to him. "Is it over?"

He nodded. He did not tell her that his own life had been at stake. He did not tell her that he had been on trial for caring for her when she was ill. . . . And he did not—could not—tell her of his strong feelings for her.

He studied her and felt his heart thump at her beauty. His only concern those last hours had been for her. He had killed the *tumme,* which was forbidden. Whatever came his way he deserved.

Not even his father knew of the *tumme.* Only the spirits knew of his sin.

He cupped her face. Her skin was soft and smooth. He stroked her cheek, enjoying its texture, as he studied her lips. He threaded his fingers into her hair and brushed it behind her ear tenderly. He played with her silken strands, glorying in the shiny softness.

"You will not die," he said.

Rebecca exhaled with relief and closed her eyes.

"But—"

Her eyes flashed open, anxiety returning to cloud her features.

"You are to be punished, Medicine Woman."

"Punished? Why? How?"

"You are to become slave to Ice From Sky. You will replace the son that she has lost."

"Slave to Ice From Sky?" she echoed blankly.

He nodded.

"But you told them the truth? You spoke on my behalf, didn't you?"

Night Wind averted his glance. She took his silence as an admission of guilt, and tears filled her eyes as she turned away.

She took several steps from him and stopped to face him again. "Ice From Sky hates me. She believes I killed her son. How can I be a slave to her? She will not want me in her lodge!"

"Ice From Sky is the one who made the decision. Iron Bear wanted you dead. Ice From Sky said no."

Night Wind's expression was unreadable. "You will live with my father's wife."

"For how long? You know I need to leave here. I must go to Delaware as soon as I can . . . when the spring thaws the ice . . ."

Night Wind stared at her, his lashes flickering. Rebecca's heart pounded, for she knew then that he would not, or could not help her. Would she ever be free?

"Come," he said. "Gather your things. We go to the house of Ice From Sky. I will take you to the house where my father lives and his little son, Gift From Forest."

Rebecca was angry. She had been brought here against her will, and she had tried to save the child. When she'd failed she'd been banished in the cold, without food, without water, and she'd done her best to live. Then there was Night Wind. He had cared for her when she was sick, and he'd shown her the joys of womanhood. Now, he was abandoning her, leaving her to be a slave. She was lowered from a medicine woman to the lowest position in an Indian village—a slave.

Night Wind would no longer have anything to do with her. She knew this, because she knew the ways of the Lenape were much like the ways of the Cayuga. Was her fate to forever be a slave? Would she never be free to find Elizabeth?

She must get free. When the sun warmed the earth and the snow melted, she would escape. Somehow she would leave this tribe and Ice From Sky. She would leave Wood Owl and Gift From Forest. And she would leave the man she loved without regrets, a man whom she would love no longer. Night Wind was forbidden to her now, and she must forget him.

Nineteen

Life with Ice From Sky was difficult for Rebecca. In contrast to the Cayuga woman, White Flower, who was Rebecca's last owner, the Lenape matron was a hard taskmaster. Rebecca decided it was because Ice From Sky still blamed her for Red Fox's death. Ice From Sky had pinned all of her hopes on the White Medicine Woman, and her child had died anyway. And now Rebecca was paying for the woman's pain.

She slept not in the wigwam with the family near the fire, but in the *apicheka'wan,* which was the storage shed. The structure was small, built next to the wigwam to hold the family stores, and she had only enough room for her to sleep. Items had been pushed to one side for her rush sleeping mat. There were no windows in the building, a fact that Rebecca later decided was a blessing in this cold weather. As she lay on the ground that first night, her only barrier against the frigid fury of the winter wind the four thatched walls of the *apicheka'wan,* she was glad there were no windows. She slept with the wind howling through the rafters of the hut and a single bearskin pelt to shield herself from the cold.

She saw little of Night Wind. Either he kept to himself on purpose, or he was forbidden to speak to her. Either way, she felt the loss keenly as the days passed and the winter cold intensified. Rebecca was allowed to join the family in the wigwam during the day when she was put to work, mending clothing, making moccasins, and other various chores that Ice From Sky gave her.

She worked until it was time to retire when she headed for her sleeping pallet, tired, her spirits low, and she felt more lonely than ever before without the comfort of sharing quarters with another human being.

Rebecca had been with Ice From Sky and her family for two weeks when their young son, Gift From Forest, became ill. There had been a break in the winter weather. There was activity in the yard again as families came out of their homes and replenished their food and fuel supplies. The Indians chatted happily amongst the tribe, glad to be out and about.

Gift From Forest first showed signs of being sick when it was time for him to go to bed on the first warm day. He had been playing with other boys in the village and then he'd eaten at the community cooking pot, cheerfully expending his energy by visiting everyone in the camp. When he finally came home, he complained of stomach pain. His mother fixed him a special tonic and then put him to bed for the night. By the next morning, Gift From Forest was worse. When Rebecca was aroused from her sleep, Wood Owl told her of his son's ailment and ordered her to fetch Iron Bear to see what the shaman could do.

No one asked for her help, and she was glad. If she did anything to help Gift From Forest, and he vomited or worse, she'd be in great danger, perhaps put to death, for she had already failed one Lenape child.

She was uncomfortable as she reached the shaman's wigwam, for she didn't like the man. He had made no effort to accept her. His hostility toward her made him a dangerous adversary.

By the time, she and the shaman returned to Gift From Forest, Rebecca realized that the boy was extremely ill. He continued to worsen for the next three days. The shaman came to visit him daily, bringing with him rattles and ceremonial masks and other tools of his calling.

Night Wind came to see how the little boy was faring on the third day, and it was the first time Rebecca had seen him since she'd been made a slave to Ice From Sky. He had gone on a hunt with other braves in the village, and the party had only returned that afternoon.

It was dusk, and she was outside the wigwam, scraping corn from the husk into a clay bowl. She sat on a woven mat beside the door.

The light masked Night Wind's features, but Rebecca's heart leapt when she saw him. He glanced at her briefly as he passed her to enter the wigwam. She felt her belly flip-flop as their gazes locked, but then he looked away.

She strained to listen to what the Indians inside were saying, but she couldn't hear well enough. She knew, though, that the tone of conversation was grave. After a while, Night Wind came out of the wigwam. He brushed past her without a glance or a word.

"Night Wind!" she called, needing to see him, speak with him. She just wanted to hear his voice.

He froze and turned slowly to face her, his face unreadable in the dusk of night.

"How is he?" she asked.

He came closer, his expression concerned. "He is not good. Ice From Sky says that he was ill before, while we were gone, but he became better. He is as his brother . . ." He stared at the ground.

Were those tears in his dark eyes? she wondered.

But when he looked at her again, she saw no tears, although his eyes appeared overly bright.

"I'm sorry."

He became angry. "He is not dead!"

She was horrified. "No . . . he isn't . . . and he'll get well. Perhaps it is something he ate?"

Night Wind studied her thoughtfully. "Ice From Sky says you do not cook."

Rebecca felt as if he'd struck her. "I can cook, but she will not let me." She glared at him. "You thought it was my cooking?"

He shook his head. "It is not my thoughts that gave me worry, but Ice From Sky's."

Then Rebecca understood. Ice From Sky might have blamed her for Gift From Forest's illness. "You were concerned for me," she said.

She wanted to take him into her arms and soothe away his worry lines. She wanted to comfort him and tell him that the boy would be fine. But everything between them had changed since returning to Turtle-Town.

"I am concerned for Gift From Forest," he said with lack of feeling.

Rebecca's cheeks burned with embarrassment. "Of course."

He was gazing at her reflectively. "You should go to the house of She Who Sees Much. You must stay there until my young brother is well."

"No!" Rebecca had no desire to stay with the matron and her hostile daughter, Sun Blossom. There had been such venom in the young woman's attitude toward her lately that she knew she'd feel concern for her own life there. Ice From Sky was not openly vindictive or cruel to Rebecca. Here, Rebecca knew, she'd be safe.

"You wish to stay with Ice From Sky?" He sounded surprised.

She nodded. "Ice From Sky will need my help. Who else will do her mending or her chores?"

Night Wind inclined his head. "This is so," He prepared to leave her.

"Night Wind."

He turned back.

"Are you . . . all right?"

His expression softened with a smile. "I am fine, *Shi'ki,*" he said, his voice soft. His smile vanished. "It is Gift From Forest who needs *Manit'to's* help."

Rebecca murmured her agreement. Night Wind left her, but she felt warmed inside. He had smiled at her and called her pretty. Perhaps he cared for her after all.

The weather became brutally cold and the families were once again forced to their homes. Gift From Forest showed signs of improvement, and Rebecca was glad for the boy and his concerned parents. As the child sat up and started to eat, Ice From Sky's attitude toward Rebecca softened. While her sleeping quarters didn't change, she was given more furs and blankets to keep her warm, and she was allowed to stay with the family late into the night.

Rebecca sat with the family around the fire and watched Ice From Sky working on a pair of moccasins. The young Englishwoman had been trying to keep herself busy to hold back her growing fears for the future. Her life with Ice From Sky was better, but she didn't deserve to be a slave! She was anxious to be on her way to Delaware.

One day the matron finished the moccasins and

gave the highly decorated pair to Rebecca. The white woman gaped at the woman and then at the moccasins.

"Lenhoksi'na will keep you warm," the matron told her in her native tongue.

Rebecca knew enough Lenape to understand the woman. She was learning more each day thanks to Ice From Sky and the child, Gift From Forest. Even *Tahuun Kukuus,* the boy's father, was patient enough to speak slowly so that Rebecca could understand.

"Wa-nee'shih," Rebecca said, thanking her in Lenape. She accepted the moccasins and removed her old pair which displayed signs of wear and were far from as warm as Ice From Sky's gift to her.

The Lenape woman had lined the moccasins with soft fur, and Rebecca, noticing the difference immediately, smiled as she donned first one and then the other shoe. "These moccasins are *shiitte.* They will keep my feet warm and dry. *Wa-nee'shih, M' hoo kum a,*" Rebecca said, thanking the matron again.

The woman smiled, pleased with Rebecca's gratitude.

Ice From Sky was taken aback by the white woman's happiness. The Medicine Woman was very pretty when she smiled. The matron had never before noticed this. Now that her son was up and eating again, she was too happy to be angry anymore. Perhaps the presence of the Medicine Woman had helped her son.

"The days have become very cold," she said to Rebecca. "You will sleep here."

Tears filled the white woman's eyes as she nodded and thanked her. Ice From Sky felt a pang of conscience as she waved her slave to follow her out to the storage shed to gather Rebecca's meager things. She would have to make the girl another tunic. The girl had worn the same tunic since she'd first come to the village; she would need another pair of leggings and perhaps a heavier cape. Winter had just begun; there would be many frigid, cold days ahead of them.

The matron entered the storage shed first and felt a blast of cold air as she bent to pick up Rebecca's sleeping mat and furs. She suffered another wave of guilt as she turned and gave the mat to Rebecca.

"Go back to the wigwam," Ice From Sky said. "I will follow." She handed the young woman the furs from the bed. "I must get some things."

Included in the things she wanted were two pieces of doeskin, corn, beans, and some dried fish. *Tahuun Kukuus,* she decided, would return for the firewood while she prepared the evening meal.

Rebecca was preparing her sleeping pallet on the ground to one side of the fire. Ice From Sky put down her bundle and touched the woman's shoulder.

"No, Medicine Woman, you will not sleep on the ground. You will sleep here—on the *Xa'sun.*" The Indian matron gestured toward the sleeping platform, which was currently covered with various family belongings.

Ice From Sky, with Rebecca's help, began to clear off the wooden platform. The platform was built more than a foot off the ground, protecting the Lenape from cool drafts and the cold, damp ground of winter. They stored the cooking utensils and other personal items, including Gift From Forest's bow and quiver of arrows, under the platform. There were similar items under the other platforms; under *Tahuun Kukuus* and his wife's was where the firewood was kept dry.

Rebecca sat on the platform, noting the difference immediately. She accepted some dried corn from Ice From Sky and started to grind it with the matron's mortar and pestle. Ice From Sky was soaking the dried fish in her clay pot, and as the two women worked to prepare the meal, the inquisitive little boy, Gift From Forest, asked his mother numerous questions.

"Is it going to snow, *Onna?*"

"It is possible, my son."

"Dark Eagle says it's going to snow hard, and that it will cover our wigwams, and we'll not be able to get out again."

Ice From Sky frowned. "Dark Eagle is teasing you, *Ne gwis.* I have lived through many winters, and I have yet to see the snow so deep."

Gift From Forest had a small round rock which he tossed up in the air and caught, playing with the rock like an English child might amuse himself with a ball. "I would like to see the snow so deep."

His mother clicked her tongue. "You would like to see us buried beneath white powder?" she asked with a scolding tone. "How would we breathe?"

He caught the rock and paused in the act of throwing it again. Grinning, he said, "We would make a hole in our *week'wam* roof and dig a tunnel to the sky!"

The matron couldn't help smiling. "Such a smart boy I have for a son. He thinks he can solve every problem." She reached over to ruffle the child's hair, which was silky black, falling to his shoulders. "What if the weight of the snow breaks the roof of our *week'wam?*"

He laughed as he tossed up the rock. "Then we wouldn't have to dig through the roof—would we, *Onna.*"

His mother laughed with him.

Rebecca was entranced by the relationship between mother and son. She could feel the love flowing between them. There was no ignoring Ice From Sky's affection and devotion to her child. Rebecca could picture how it must have been when Red Fox was alive and there was much banter between the mother and her two sons, and she understood how devastating it must have been for the matron to have lost her oldest son.

She herself had become attached to the ill Red Fox in the brief time she'd spent with him, and now Gift From Forest had worked his way into her heart with his chubby cheeks and little boy's smile. It made Rebecca long for a family of her own.

Unbidden into her thoughts came the mental image of Night Wind. How would it be to have his sons? Would he be a good father? Would they make a happy family?

Rebecca silently scolded herself. How could she be so foolish as to be thinking of such things?

She shook away her thoughts of Night Wind and focused instead on Gift From Forest. The child was still asking questions. Only it was his father—*Tahuun Kukuus*—who patiently answered his son's queries.

"Father, when will we hold *Ow'tas Kin'te-ka?*"

"We will have *Ow'tas Kin'te-ka* when it is time."

"The *Ow'tas Kin'te-ka*," Ice From Sky explained to Rebecca, "is the dance of the doll. Each year we honor *Ow'tas,* the medicine doll, by holding a feast for her. It is enjoyable for everyone within the tribe, especially the little ones," she said with an affectionate smile in Gift From Forest's direction. "That is why the boy is anxious for *Ow'tas Kin'te-ka.*"

Night Wind entered the wigwam just as Ice From Sky had completed her explanation. Rebecca had yet to arrange her furs on the sleeping platform. Her pulse racing at his entry, she busied herself smoothing them on top of her rush mat.

She heard his deep voice greeting his father's wife and child, and then she felt his gaze watching her. She glanced over, and their eyes met. He looked down, saw what she was doing, and spoke rapidly to Ice From Sky. The matron responded with a defensive tone. Soon, *Tahuun Kukuus* entered the conversation, and it seemed as if the three were arguing.

Gift From Forest had stopped playing with his rock, and he stared at the adults with big eyes. When the child's gaze transferred to Rebecca, the young woman guessed that she was the subject of the argument.

Gift From Forest got up from the rush-covered floor and crawled up to sit next to Rebecca on her sleeping platform. "They are fighting about you," he said matter-of-factly.

Rebecca nodded. "I thought so."

The boy's gaze narrowed as he turned back to study Night Wind.

"What are they saying?" Rebecca couldn't help asking.

"Tipaakke Shaakha is angry with *Onna*," the boy said. "He did not know that you had slept in the *apicheka'wan.*"

Storage shed, she thought. Her heart skipped a beat. She didn't want to be the cause of anger between Night Wind and his father. . . . Night Wind and the family that meant as much to him as his own clan.

Rebecca stood to interrupt, but Gift From Forest grabbed her arm. "Do not go," he warned. "They are angry and will turn their anger on you."

She studied the child with awe at his wisdom. Gift From Forest would someday be chief. If his wisdom continued to grow with his years, he'd be a wonderful leader of the Lenape people.

The conversation ended abruptly, and Night Wind signaled to Rebecca to come outside with him. Rebecca glanced at Ice From Sky for permission, and the matron nodded. The older woman seemed composed, not angry as Rebecca had expected.

Rebecca started for the door flap, but Ice From Sky stopped her. The Indian woman handed her a heavy fur mantle. "It is cold," she said.

The white woman smiled. *"Wa-nee'shih,"* she said. Her heart was beating fast as she went out to meet Night Wind.

Night Wind motioned her over to the storage shed, where they could speak privately out of the wind and cold. They entered the shed, and the Lenape brave secured the door behind them. He turned to her, his face stern, but there was a glimmer of concern in his dark eyes.

"Until this day, this had been your shelter," he said stiffly.

She nodded.

"I didn't know."

She couldn't think of a reply.

Night Wind took her by the shoulders and gazed into her eyes. His expression made her breath catch. His nearness made her body react as if every nerve ending had been jolted wide awake. He looked upset, worried . . . and apologetic.

"I am sorry for this, Reb-bec-ca," he murmured. She swayed against him, overcome by her attraction to him. "You are slave, but you should not have been sleeping here."

"It wasn't too terrible," she lied, recalling the freezing nights when she'd shivered and couldn't sleep, when the chill to her bones had made her muscles cramp up and stiffen during the daytime.

"You make a bad liar, Reb-bec-ca." But he was smiling. His features became serious. "Why do you lie?"

"I don't want you to feel bad," she murmured, looking away.

He tensed. "What is it you said?"

She gazed at him. "I don't want you to feel responsible. It's all right. Ice From Sky is not a mean woman, but she was—"

"Angry," he finished for her.

She inclined her head.

Night Wind tenderly cupped her chin, rubbing her jaw with his thumb. "Medicine Woman," he murmured. And he bent to kiss her mouth.

She closed her eyes, sighing in enjoyment of his kiss, and then she heard someone clear his throat. Night Wind released her hastily and stepped back.

"Tipaakke Shaakha."

Tahuun Kukuus eyed the two from beneath lowered lids. "Medicine Woman, my wife needs you."

Cheeks flushed, Rebecca nodded, and then after a brief glance at Night Wind, she scurried away.

Father and son stared at one another searchingly.

"You are attracted to the white woman," *Tahuun Kukuus* said.

Night Wind opened his mouth to deny it, and then abruptly closed it again. *"Kihiila."*

His father's lips tightened. "You are walking a dangerous path, my son. Be careful of your foot falls."

Night Wind knew what his father meant. "I have denied my heart's lead."

Tahuun Kukuus raised his eyebrows. "Have you?" he said with skepticism.

The young man nodded. "If she were not a slave, she would return to her people."

His father agreed. "I know not what you see in her pale face, but she is basically a good woman, I suppose."

"She is brave and has spirit. She lived by her wits in the forest cold."

"You did not help her?"

Night Wind shifted uncomfortably. "Not as you think. If I have helped her by praying to Manit'to, then I am guilty. If not . . ."

Wood Owl's face brightened. "The spirits help those whom they desire. Do not concern yourself that prayer is a sin, for it is not."

Tahuun Kukuus spun to exit the hut. "My wife has prepared food. She invites you to eat with us."

Night Wind froze. "She is not angry?"

His father stopped to regard him from the opening of the hut. "Ice From Sky stays angry for as long as it takes a warrior to skin a deer." He grinned, and Night Wind returned it with a smile.

"Come, *Ne gwis*. Each day brings a new beginning. Let us enjoy the moment of this earthly life."

Twenty

December became January, and January rolled with a bluster into February. For Rebecca, life with the Lenape was not unpleasant, but there were days when the harsh freezing temperatures made her long for the comfort of an English home.

Her days, although spent mostly in the closed quarters of the wigwam, were full. Ice From Sky treated Rebecca well, and the two women worked together, preparing food, making clothing and various other chores that kept Indian women occupied during the long winter months. Rebecca learned a lot from Ice From Sky, about the matron's family, the Turtle clan— the lineage of the chief. Currently, it was Beaver Hawk, Ice From Sky's brother, who held the position of sachem. Before him, it had been her uncle, Man With Crooked Nose. Rebecca listened as she was told about the uncle's life . . . how brave a warrior he was, how he lost his life to a Mohawk tomahawk. She became fascinated as each new aspect of his tribal reign was revealed.

Rebecca studied Gift From Forest. The child would one day succeed Beaver Hawk as sachem. She said a silent prayer that the boy would fare better than his ancestor. Gift From Forest was a charming child, and her heart skipped a beat on occasion when she looked at him. His features were much like those of his other brother; only Red Fox's face had had the maturity of six more years.

Gift From Forest had a wisdom well beyond his four summers, but his frequent bursts of playful activity were typical of a very young child. Rebecca enjoyed the boy, and the child seemed to like her. When she wasn't kept busy helping his mother with chores, she was encouraged to play with the boy and keep him busy. Ice From Sky appreciated times when she could work without the constant inquisition of his alert mind.

Rebecca found herself forming an attachment to the child. She knew she shouldn't, because it would be hard once her time came to leave. But she couldn't help it. Gift From Forest kept her entertained; he made her feel like she was a member of his family. It was only when the night came and everyone was asleep, that she felt lonely for her old life. As she lay on her sleeping platform, snug and warm in a bundle of furs, she would stare at the wigwam roof and think of the life she'd left behind her . . . recall her cousin Elizabeth and the life she should be leading now. Her concern for Elizabeth plagued her constantly, increasingly each night, and although Rebecca knew she was helpless to find her, it brought her little comfort to know that the child might be all alone.

And then there were her feelings for Night Wind.

There wasn't a day, a moment, that she didn't think of him . . . remember. She missed the passion they had shared, and his companionship. She loved him. She had admitted it once before, but the fact hit her harder each day she woke up and he wasn't beside her. She knew there was no hope of a future together, but she couldn't stop longing for him.

But how did he feel about her?

He had enjoyed making love with her, but she doubted he felt a serious attachment. He would come to visit her, if he had. His absence from her new life told her that his feelings for her had been rooted in the flesh.

Rebecca couldn't forget what had happened yesterday. The memory made her stomach lurch. It had been several days since Night Wind's last visit to his father's family. The winter wind had died down enough to allow families to visit other lodges, and She Who Sees Much and Sun Blossom had come calling on Ice From Sky.

Sun Blossom had entered the wigwam, her eyes flashing briefly with surprise, when she saw how Rebecca fared in Ice From Sky's home.

"You have forgiveness in your heart, Ice From Sky," she said with a hint of anger.

The matron smiled. "Hatred hurts the one who hates more than the one who is hated."

Sun Blossom had mumbled some appropriate reply, but it was her look that Rebecca couldn't forget. The maiden had been furious that Rebecca was being treated kindly.

She Who Sees Much and Sun Blossom had sat by the fire to exchange news with Ice From Sky. Gift From Forest's mother had been pleased to see her friends, and she had listened raptly as She Who Sees Much had imparted the latest word.

Months with the Lenape and help from Ice From Sky had taught Rebecca their native language, which she followed quite easily now. She had understood their conversation, a part of which upset and displeased her.

"Night Wind has gone to search for He Who Came Last and his people," She Who Sees Much said.

Ice From Sky nodded. "He was greatly concerned

to find they had left their village. It seemed most strange."

"Feather Coast has gone with him, so have Deer That Runs and Raven Feather."

Rebecca pretended an interest in Gift From Forest's new bow, but her ears were perked as she listened to the women talk.

"Night Wind is a brave warrior," Sun Blossom said, her tone drawing Rebecca's glance to the girl. The maiden smirked at the white woman, before turning back to Ice From Sky. "When he came to me before he left . . ."

The rest of what Sun Blossom was saying had been lost to Rebecca. The only thing she'd heard was the phrase "When he came to me" over and over again inside her head.

Sun Blossom's smile had remained on her face as she continued to talk to the two matrons. "He says he will return in two days."

"And if he doesn't find He Who Came Last?"

Sun Blossom shrugged her shoulders. "Night Wind will find him."

Ice From Sky smiled. "He is a good hunter," she agreed.

"And a handsome brave with strong arms," Sun Blossom said in what Rebecca had thought was a knowing tone.

Night Wind came back later that day. Rebecca, hearing his hailing cry, hurried outside along with the other villagers to greet the returning braves. She was anxious to see Night Wind again.

He was immediately surrounded by inquisitive family and friends. Sun Blossom wasted no time in getting to him, Rebecca noted with annoyance. Ever since the young woman had come to the wigwam earlier that morning, Rebecca had been plagued by thoughts of the two of them together—Sun Blossom and Night Wind.

Was that why he never came to see her? Rebecca wondered. Had he been spending his time with the beautiful Lenape maiden?

The image of Night Wind kissing Sun Blossom made Rebecca burn with jealousy. Had the brave been satisfying himself with the Indian girl? Had she, Rebecca, been simply a vessel for a man to satisfy his physical desire?

She hung back from the crowd and studied Night Wind with longing. She rejected the idea that his only interest in her had been a sexual one. He had been so caring . . . so loving . . . so warm.

Then why hadn't he come to see her?

Because now she was a slave and it wouldn't be acceptable? She knew that was probably the reason. She knew, too, that the sooner she left the village the better she—and her aching heart—would be.

The remaining months of winter would be difficult with Night Wind so close . . . yet far out of her reach.

"We found He Who Came Last," Night Wind told the sachem of Turtle-Town. "He and his people fled to the valley past the great mountain."

Beaver Hawk frowned. "Why did they leave their home?"

"Iroquois."

"Cayuga?"

The question hung tensely in the air between the two men. The Cayuga were the people of the White Medicine Woman. Had they come to claim their daughter?

"Mohawk," Night Wind said. He sought Rebecca among the others. Her presence in his village had been a continued source of pleasure-pain for him.

"Did you not say that there had been no sign of

war in the village of He Who Came Last?" Beaver Hawk asked.

Unable to see her, Night Wind's gaze returned to his chief. "They moved before the Mohawk could attack. Word came to them of an Iroquois raiding party, and the sachem had few braves to protect his villagers. He moved them to their new home, but they will return again—when the spring thaws the great snow."

Night Wind searched the yard for Rebecca again. He'd been unable to get her out of his mind, even while he was on the trail.

He saw her emerge from Ice From Sky's wigwam. As their gazes met, he felt an instant fire, and he wanted to be alone with her, to take her into his arms. He missed spending time with her, missed sharing with her his lodge and his food. He longed to lie beside her once more and worship her with his body . . . his hands . . . his mouth.

"Night Wind." Sun Blossom tugged his arm.

The brave forced his gaze from Rebecca to the Indian maiden who was smiling up at him. He felt guilty and so his smile was brighter than it might otherwise have been.

"May I speak with you?" Her dark eyes glistened as they gazed up at him. She was really quite beautiful; he wondered briefly why no one had taken her to wife.

He nodded, and she pulled him to one side. Night Wind left Deer That Runs and Feather Coat to tell the tale of what they had seen.

"What is it, Sun Blossom?" he asked with concern. It wasn't like Sun Blossom to single him out this way.

"I must speak with you," she said. She glanced

about the yard as if she'd something important to impart but didn't want to be overheard.

"What is it?"

She reached up to stroke his jaw, and his eyes widened. "I cannot tell you now," she said. Her voice was like a caress. "You must allow me to come later."

Her fingers rubbed his cheek and trailed to his shoulder.

"When?"

Her touch tingled as anyone's soft trail across one's skin, but he was unaffected by her nearness. It would be so less complicated if he were attracted to the lovely Lenape woman, but his soul yearned for the white woman.

"After the sun sets and our people are in their lodges—" She paused to glance over the gathering before she met his gaze. "—and when the moon is high in the night sky, I will come to your *week-wam.*"

Night Wind opened his mouth to protest, but quickly closed it again. He had hoped to see Rebecca, to visit lodge of Ice From Sky, but he couldn't refuse the Indian maiden. Whatever she had to say must be important for her to want to meet him this way. "I will be there," he said.

Then, to his surprise, Sun Blossom leaned up and kissed his cheek. *"Wa-nee'shih,"* she murmured. Her breath was a warm caress against his skin. The maiden walked away, leaving him to stare thoughtfully after her.

Rebecca saw when Sun Blossom and Night Wind left the crowd to stand alone, and she experienced a burning in her stomach. The couple conversed quietly away from the other villagers, their heads close together, their bodies nearly touching.

She felt a constriction in her throat when Sun Blossom caressed Night Wind's jaw, and when the maiden kissed him . . . Rebecca turned away, feeling physically ill.

It could be nothing. Why am I doing this to myself?

Because she loved him and she didn't believe he loved her. *I'm slowly dying inside, for I know there's no future in loving Night Wind.*

Eyes blurred by tears, Rebecca stumbled inside the wigwam and went to her sleeping platform. She lay, quietly sobbing her anger and her grief. She was angry at her situation, her position and presence within the tribe . . . and she was mourning the loss of the man she loved.

She was composed by the time the family came in a short while later. After much thinking, she'd decided to bide her time until the spring, when she would leave the village and never once look back at what—or whom—she'd left behind.

The sun set, announcing the end to another day, and Ice From Sky and her family shared the nightly meal with their slave. When they were done, Wood Owl told stories, and they all listened, enthralled. Ice From Sky had a tale to tell of her own—of her father during the hunt for bear. Gift From Forest and Rebecca hung on to her every word. Wood Owl listened with a smile, and then he attempted to tell a more exciting story. It was a pleasant evening, and Rebecca forgot her troubles and enjoyed herself.

It was late when Rebecca collected the dishes and went outside with the scouring brush. She scrubbed off the bowls and then brushed them with wet snow. Her gaze strayed from the job as she worked . . . toward Night Wind's wigwam. She remembered with a pang a time when she had shared the brave's lodge and his food. She yearned to do so again.

He wasn't right for her; why couldn't she forget him?

The door flap to his wigwam lifted, and Rebecca stood, staring, her pulse pounding. Would he see her and approach?

She moved closer, wanting to speak, not waiting for him to come to her, and the door flap shut again. That was when she heard the woman's voice and then soft laughter. There was a long, silent pause, and Rebecca could picture Night Wind and Sun Blossom kissing, caressing, lowering onto his sleeping pallet.

Then, she heard Night Wind's deep voice louder than before, and Rebecca ran and hid behind someone's storage shed. She made it in time to see the door flap being raised a second time.

Her heart tripped with pain, and her belly burned with fire as Sun Blossom exited the wigwam. The Indian maiden glanced toward Ice From Sky's wigwam. Rebecca sensed that the Lenape woman was looking for Rebecca and that Sun Blossom was smiling smugly.

The truth hit Rebecca with a force that stole her breath away. She'd been right in her suspicions. Night Wind had been finding release with Sun Blossom. She had been a fool to hope that he missed her, that he cared for her. It was Sun Blossom, he was enjoying now.

When Night Wind came to the door and stared after the beautiful maiden with what Rebecca decided could only be longing, Rebecca experienced pain as she'd never before known it.

The knowledge of Night Wind's relations with Sun Blossom hurt Rebecca worse than she'd ever dreamed possible. Devastated by what she'd seen, Rebecca knew she'd never be able to stay until spring. She must leave the village tonight. Guided by emotion rather than reason, she made plans to escape, convinced that she preferred the dangers of a winter forest to the searing pain of seeing Night Wind and Sun Blossom together.

She waited until the family was asleep before she got up and gathered some supplies for her journey. She took only enough food to last her a few days, for she didn't want to take from Ice From Sky and the family that had generously forgiven her for their son's death.

Rebecca was grateful for Ice From Sky's gift of fur-lined moccasins as she slipped from the wigwam and into the frozen yard. The snow on the ground had been packed from village use, but Rebecca went to the storage shed anyway and "borrowed" shoepacks or overshoes. The Lenape called them "Mahkt-chee'pak-o." They would help her to walk easily over the deep snow.

Ice From Sky had also made Rebecca a new doeskin tunic and fur mantle, and she wore them, taking her older clothes with her. There would come a time, she thought, when she would need several layers to keep her warm. She decided she was well prepared for her escape as she headed across the yard toward the woods.

Her doubts resurfaced as she left the familiarity of the village and entered the forest, but she forced her concerns back. The mental image of Sun Blossom's triumphant smile spurred Rebecca on, and she quickened her pace along the trail.

Night Wind couldn't sleep. Sun Blossom's visit had disturbed him, for it made him realize how much he wanted Rebecca . . . a woman destined to remain a slave.

He had heard Sun Blossom's arrival before she entered his *week'wam*. She wore tiny bells on bands about each ankle, and when she walked, one could hear a musical, tinkling sound. Curious about the reason for her visit, he had smiled at her as she'd sat by his firepit. Once he'd seen her serene expression, his concerns that something was terribly wrong disappeared, and he'd waited patiently for her to speak.

"Yun," she said, handing him an object. "Ma!"

He was momentarily taken aback when she gave him the *Ah-pee'kawn*. Sun Blossom had always been like a sister to him; that she wanted something more between them came as a shock. It was so much a shock that when she'd first given the flute to him, he'd asked to whom it belonged.

Sun Blossom had smiled. "You," she responded. Then, after a brief pause, she said, "I would like you to play it for me."

He had known her since she was a tiny babe. She was of the clan of Raven Feather, the *Pe'le* band, whose totem was the Turkey. Sun Blossom was eligible to be his wife by the tribe's standards, but he had never thought of her that way. Her request for him to play the flute was a request for him to court her. He couldn't, but he didn't want to hurt her tender feelings.

"Sun Blossom—" he began.

"Think about it." Her gaze was flirtatious, knowing. He had enjoyed flirting mildly with her in the past, but they'd always known it was just a game. At least, he had *thought* she felt as he.

"You honor me with your request," he said, meaning it. It was the Lenape custom that when a man was interested in a woman he would play the *Ah-pee'kawn* outside her parents' lodge, wooing her with his musical talents. Then it would be up to the maiden to decide to accept or reject his suit. By giving him the flute, she was accepting his suit before it had ever been offered.

"If I honor you, then you will think on it," she said with quiet dignity. She sounded more grown up than he'd thought her to be, more womanly and beguiling with her seductive smile.

Sun Blossom had been forward by taking the initiative herself, but then he knew her well. She'd never been one to sit and wait idly for something she wanted. Apparently, she wanted him.

She wants to lie with me, he thought with surprise. But he wouldn't—couldn't—play for her, although it would make life simpler if he did care for Sun Blossom in that way.

He loved Rebecca.

It was foolish to love the white woman, but he couldn't help his feelings. And he wouldn't do Sun Blossom the injustice of taking her to wife while he longed to hold—to love—the White Medicine Woman.

Restless after Sun Blossom's departure, Night Wind rose from his sleeping platform and went out into the night. He had built the *Xa'sun* recently, envisioning sharing the sleeping platform with Rebecca, recalling an earlier time when she'd sickened because of a chill. It was warmer to sleep on a *Xa'sun,* and he had made it comfortable to lie on by covering it with two rush mats and several layers of beaver pelts and thick furs. It had taken two rush mats because it had made the platform big enough for two.

As he stepped into the night air, his mind was filled with the image of Rebecca naked upon his bed, waiting for him to join her. The vision seemed so real that when he closed his eyes he felt his loins harden. He

opened his eyes and stared at her wigwam, drawn to
the lodge by the desire to see her.

Was she sleeping? Awake?

If he called to her softly, would she come?

In his need to see her, he had planned a visit to Ice
From Sky's family, but he'd been called earlier to the
lodge of the chief about He Who Came Last and his
people. Beaver Hawk had only released him in time
to meet Sun Blossom.

How was Rebecca faring? He'd been furious to
learn that she'd slept in the storage shed. She was a
slave, but she deserved better treatment, and it wasn't
like Ice From Sky to be so mean. His father's wife
had corrected the wrong to Rebecca, but Night Wind
had been angry with Ice From Sky and so he had
stayed away from her lodge.

He wandered toward the wigwam and froze as
someone raised the fur flap. Night Wind hung back
until he saw it was Ice From Sky.

"M' hoo kum a," he said, coming out from the shadows of another lodge. "Why are you not sleeping?"

The matron was, at first, startled, and then she
seemed glad—or relieved—to see him. "It's the slave.
She is not on her *Xa'sun.*"

Night Wind glanced toward the woods. "Perhaps
she had gone to seek relief."

The Indian woman agreed. "This is so, but she has
been gone too long. She was gone when I awakened,
and my eyes have been open for some time. I fear
something bad has happened to her."

The brave touched her arm. "I will find her and
bring her back. Sleep and do not worry."

She smiled with relief. *"Wa-nee'shih."*

Taking his advice, she went back inside.

Night Wind stared at the forest and frowned. Was
she in danger? Or had she escaped? He alone knew

how badly she wanted to leave Turtle-Town. His frown became a scowl when he found her tracks and realized that she was wearing snowshoes.

Rebecca moved quickly, silently, through the woods. She'd been successful! She had traveled for almost an hour and no one had come after her. There had been no cries to stop.

She knew she was foolish for leaving the village, but she had convinced herself she simply couldn't stay. She couldn't bear the sight of *them* together, knowing the truth of their relationship.

The forest was lit by a full moon. She could see her way easily, as the snow on the land was glistening with light. The woods beckoned her; the terrain seemed less sinister with the glowing orb brightening the night sky, and she hurried on, bolstered by a confidence unhampered by fears of the dark.

Her *overshoes* made it easy to move quickly. Rebecca wasn't certain if she had chosen the right direction, but she didn't allow it to bother her, to sway her from her resolve.

Would the Lenape search for her? Would Night Wind care that she'd gone?

She was a slave. They would search for her, if only to punish her for escaping. As she covered more ground, that fact was brought home to her, and she began to see just how foolish she'd been to leave.

Her footsteps slowed as her doubts returned. She had journeyed for over two hours when she decided she had to go back. She had let her heart rule her mind. She'd be no good to her young cousin dead.

She stared at her own tracks, knowing that she could get back to the village without difficulty. She'd be back before sunrise if she followed the prints made by her *mahkt'chee'pak-o*.

Clouds came up to block the moonlight, and Rebecca shivered as she began to retrace her steps. The forest appeared sinister and black, and it was a long way back to the wigwam of Ice From Sky.

Twenty-one

Night Wind frowned as he entered the forest and saw her tracks in the snow.

Ah, Shi'ki, how could you be so foolish?

He had to find her, before she was hurt . . . before the people of Turtle-Town realized that she had gone. He returned to his wigwam for his overshoes and then set out at a quick pace. He was both hurt and angry with her. She had deceived him. She hadn't said goodbye.

You've been ignoring her. It was true, but he'd felt compelled to avoid her. He would ignore her no more.

Rebecca stopped to rest off the main trail. Cold, she started a fire. She'd brought with her a Lenape fire-making kit. She carried dried kindling and food in her satchel; for this trip she was better prepared.

She didn't know she'd stumbled on a bear's den until she heard the angry growl. The scent of burning wood must have aroused the animal from its winter shelter. As the beast prowled through the snow toward her, Rebecca gaped at it and slowly backed away.

"Ku-les'ta, Shi'ki," a familiar voice said. He had seen her from a distance and saw the bear before she did.

"Night Wind! Oh, Night Wind!" she cried. She was

terrified. Was she dreaming of Night Wind's voice?
She tried to find him, but could see nothing.

"You must not move, my love. You must stay very
still."

She nodded, her heart filled with gladness. He was
here. Night Wind was here! She shook so badly with
her fear that she couldn't remain still.

"I must lure the bear from your path, Reb-bec-ca."

"But he'll hurt you!"

His chuckle was soft. He moved out into the open
where Rebecca could see him. "He will not hurt me,
Shi'ki. I have hunted the black bear before . . . and
this is a small one. Hunting bear is what Night Wind
does best."

"Not best," she said softly.

He inhaled sharply when their gazes met, for they
were both remembering their intimate moments together. She wanted him again, he could see this.

The bear was growling low in his throat. His actions
were sluggish, for he had been hibernating. Soon,
Night Wind thought, they would have plenty of fresh
fur as well as a good supply of meat and bear's grease.

"Mahx' W!" He drew his weapons and crouched,
his spear in one hand, his knife in the other. *"Mahx'
W! Yu'taLi!"*

The bear turned and roared furiously.

"Night Wind!" Rebecca gasped.

"It is all right, *Shi'ki!*" he called back. The animal
reared up on its hind legs, and the brave jumped back
several feet.

The next half hour was the longest Rebecca had
ever endured. Frightened for Night Wind, she watched
helplessly as the Indian thrust his spear toward the
beast and retreated as the animal growled and moved
forward.

Later, once the horror was over and the bear was

dead, Rebecca recalled the encounter between man and animal as a scene resembling an Indian dance. Night Wind, crouched low, his arms raised with weapons in hands, had circled the animal slowly, gracefully, teasing the animal while he moved in for the kill.

Rebecca recalled the mourning dance for Red Fox and saw the similarities to this skilled motion of the hunt. Night Wind had been magnificent. Calling to the bear in his native tongue, he managed to stay clear of the animal's massive paws as the bear attempted to hit him. The moon had escaped the cloud cover, and the forest was again illuminated by a crystalline glow. Rebecca could see the action clearly.

The brave waited until he could get a true aim, and then he speared the animal in the neck. The bear rose up on its hind legs in its final death throes, bellowing with pain, as his front came down a last time. Night Wind stayed clear of the beast as the animal fell to the snow, its life force staining the white carpet a bright crimson.

"Night Wind!" Rebecca, thinking the animal dead, started to run toward Night Wind.

"Stay back, Rebecca! *Maata!*"

She obeyed him, her heart pounding, her pulse roaring in her ears as loud as the bear's growls had been. She cried out as the bear suddenly rose up, half off the ground. The creature, oblivious to all but his pain, fell back, and attempted to pry the spear from his neck with his huge paw. His attempt to do so only made things worse for him, and the blood oozed freely from the spear wound.

The animal roared one final time before he fell backward into a pool of red.

When the bear was still, Rebecca ran forward.

"No, *Shi'ki! Maata!*" Night Wind warned. "I must see that he is dead."

She froze. Night Wind moved toward the animal slowly. He placed his hand before the animal's nose and then listened at the bear's chest for breathing. "It is all right, Rebecca," he said. "The *Mahx'W*—he is *Ong ul.*"

Dead. The bear was dead. Rebecca ran into Night Wind's arms, hugging him, kissing his face. The brave groaned and embraced her tightly. He captured her mouth with his own and kissed her with all the weeks, the days, of pent-up longing, giving his passion free reign.

They were both gasping when he raised his head. "Oh, *Tipaakke Shaakha!* I thought I'd never see you again."

"You could have been killed," he exclaimed. Night Wind released her, his features dark, and stepped back. "Why did you leave Turtle-Town?"

She averted her glance, unable to confess the truth. He grabbed her arms. "Why, Rebecca, why?"

"Because I'm a slave!" she yelled.

He clamped his hand over her mouth. "You must speak low! Our enemy may be near. The Mohawk. There could be others." He released his gentle grip.

She shuddered and hugged herself with her arms. She had visions of him and Sun Blossom. She could barely control her fury.

Night Wind studied her, his expression tense, filled with anger that she had left the village.

His face didn't soften. "You have dishonored Ice From Sky. You have dishonored me."

She gaped at him. "I have dishonored no one!"

"You left *Tulpeuta-nai.*"

"Because I was unhappy!"

"You prefer to die?"

She shook her heard. "I did not think." She spun

from him. "Until later." Her voice became soft. "I was coming back," she said, meeting his gaze.

He appeared skeptical.

"I was!" she cried. "Look for yourself if you don't believe me!" She gestured toward a set of tracks in the snow made by her Lenape shoepacks. "The village is that way," she said, surprising herself with her sense of direction. "Look and see. The tracks tell that I was returning to Turtle-Town—not running away."

She saw with a pang that he didn't believe her. He followed the tracks some distance, before he returned to her, his face dark and unreadable in the bright moonlight.

"Come," he said, his voice husky. "We will go to the village." He caught her arm and his touch seared her like lightning. She resisted him, determined to make him admit that he believed her. She wanted him to admit he was wrong.

"You saw my tracks?"

His fingers continued to burn through the sleeve of her tunic. "I saw them."

She was outraged that he still refused to say more. "And?"

He released her, facing her fully. He crossed his arms over his chest. "What is it you wish, Medicine Woman?"

"An apology!"

He raised one eyebrow. "You ran away. You promised not to run. You owe *me* a-po-log-y." He effectively put an end to the conversation by leaving her for the dead bear.

Rebecca's mind spun with mixed feelings. On one hand, the man was right, on the other. . . . She watched tensely as Night Wind removed his spear from the bear's neck. The man was infuriating! He must have guessed why she'd tried to escape. For

God's sake, she had a cousin that needed her. She was a slave. Did he think she'd be content?

She marched up to where he worked. He tied the bear's paws together. "Wouldn't you have tried?" she asked.

He gave her a questioning look. "Tried?"

She sighed with exasperation. "Would you be happy if you were me? A slave? What if Gift From Forest was captured by the Cayuga and waiting for you to rescue him, and you were a slave to the Mohawk? Wouldn't you try to escape to get to the child?"

Rebecca saw a flicker of emotion cross his face. *See?* she thought. *You must understand now!*

Night Wind rose and tucked his knife into his legging string. "If I were Iroquois prisoner, I would be dead."

She shuddered, knowing he spoke the truth. She had seen what the Iroquois did to their male captives. She had heard their wild cries of pain.

Closing her eyes, she recalled the family her mother had arranged for her to travel with, the Richmonts—a man with his wife and two sons. Rebecca felt dizzy with the memory of the father's death. It had been horrible what they had done to the poor man. He'd been tortured, burned, and so had his eldest son. His wife had been made a slave like Rebecca, but she had died in the end. Grief-stricken by the loss of her husband and son, she had gone mad and turned on the Indians. She'd been stabbed trying to spear the matron who had owned her.

The youngest boy, Samuel, was six years old; he'd been spared death, because the Cayuga people loved children. He'd been taken as slave into an Iroquois family, but it had seemed that Tall Turtle and his wife had taken a special liking to the child. Rebecca thought that the Indian family would someday adopt Samuel as their son.

Yes, she knew what the Indians did to adult males. She'd never be able to forget the horror, the blood-curdling screams that had made her cover her ears and pray while tears squeezed out from her tightly closed eyes. It seemed hard to believe that the people she'd learned to live with amicably could behave so heart-lessly.

It hadn't helped to learn that the Richmonts' deaths had been part of a religious rite, that what they did with the bodies afterward gave the Iroquois braves the courage and strength of the deceased. To her, their acts had been beastly, and she would never believe that such behavior was anything less than savage.

Still, Rebecca was maddened by Night Wind's apparent lack of sympathy for her plight. He didn't care for her, she thought. Not when there was Sun Blossom waiting to fulfill his more basic needs.

He was gutting the bear, pulling out its vital organs. She swallowed against bile as she watched him. His actions reminded her that he was a savage—just like the rest of them.

"Damn you!" she cried. "I wouldn't have left if it weren't for you."

He tensed and rose slowly from the bear. "What is this truth?" he asked.

Her cheeks were hot with her ire. Her hands cramped; she was clenching her fists so tightly.

"You! It's your fault."

He approached her, towering over her like some vengeful god. "How is this so?"

Incensed, she spoke without thinking. "Because you never came. And you chose her over me!"

He appeared startled, then puzzled. His face cleared. "Sun Blossom."

She nodded, her eyes filling with tears. "I saw her . . . you. When you came back after you were gone, she was there—and you . . ." She spun away. Her anger was gone; only the hurt remained.

"Sun Blossom is to me as Angry Woman is to Ice From Sky." His tone was soft. He was behind her, close enough for her to lean back and touch, but he didn't reach out and neither did she.

"She's your sister?" Rebecca faced him, her breath suspended in anticipation. "She is of the Wolf clan?"

Her stomach burned. She could tell by his expression that Sun Blossom was not of the Wolf clan; therefore, they were not considered kin.

"You're lying!" she exclaimed, aghast.

His eyes flashed with black fury. "I tell the truth. I look at Sun Blossom as *Num ees.*"

She believed him. "But Sun Blossom doesn't see you that way."

The flicker of guilt told her that he knew this, that something had happened to convince him.

"What was she doing in your *week'wam?*" Rebecca wanted, needed, to know what occurred. Had he succumbed to temptation? He must have been moved by the maiden's beauty; he wouldn't be a man if he hadn't been. But how moved? How tempted by the wide dark loveliness of her eyes and the lush womanly curves of Sun Blossom's form?

His eyes widened. "You saw Sun Blossom."

She inclined her head, her throat tight.

The brave exhaled loudly as he turned away. "It is true that Sun Blossom wants . . . more." He spun back to face her. "She said she wanted to speak with me, and so I let her. I was surprised to hear what she had to say."

"And what was that?" she asked softly.

"She gave me *a'pi'kan*. She wanted me to play it for her."

Rebecca's blue eyes flashed with understanding. She'd lived with the Indians long enough to know that Sun Blossom had asked Night Wind to court her. "Are you?"

He shook his head.

Her relief was so great that her head spun. She averted her glance to hide her reaction. She was overjoyed; she couldn't hold back the tears.

Night Wind turned her and pulled her into his arms. She leaned against him, burying her face against his neck, sniffling.

He pulled back and lifted her chin, a tender look softening the glistening onyx eyes. "I will play the *a'pi'kan* for one woman," he said.

She closed her eyes, and he kissed her eyelids . . . her cheeks. Finally, he captured her mouth. She could taste her tears on his lips, and she moaned as he held her. She leaned into him fully, surrendering herself to his demands.

She broke away. "No!"

Night Wind was taken aback. *"Shi'ki,* what is it?"

"Why do you do this to me?"

He furrowed his brow.

"I can't think when you hold me," she said.

Night Wind smiled. "Then come, and we will not think together."

Rebecca retreated a step. "Shouldn't we be getting back?"

He narrowed his gaze. "It is your wish to return?"

"I told you I was on my way back," she said. "I had only stopped to rest and get warm."

He nodded. "Then we should go." Dismissing the last moments as if they had never happened, he handed her the satchel. Then he lifted the bear carcass to carry it across his shoulders. He stumbled slightly under its weight and then straightened.

Rebecca took one look at the bear's entrails in the white snow, and she choked back vomit.

"A gift for the gods," he told her.

She looked away, unable to bear the blood.

They completed their journey while it was still dark. Night Wind set down his kill and then took Rebecca to Ice From Sky's lodge.

He gazed at her as he waited for her to enter the wigwam. Rebecca shifted, feeling suddenly shy.

"Wa-nee'shih," she murmured. She felt embarrassed. They had kissed earlier with exploding passion, and she had ended it like a fool.

His ebony gaze seemed to search her soul. "Tomorrow when the sun has gone and the moon has risen to light up the night sky, I want you to come to me."

Her blood flowed like wild fire. "I don't know—"

"Kihiila, Reb-bec-ca. Please come to *Tipaakke Shaakha.*" His face was intensely emotional, his eyes beseeching.

She wanted to go. Did he mean what she thought? She wanted, needed, to lie close with him again. Yes, he wanted her, too, and he was begging her to come.

Head bowed, hair curtaining her face, she nodded. He wasn't satisfied until he saw her expression, for he cradled her jaw and made her look into his eyes. "You wish to come?"

"Kihiila," she said, trembling. He looked triumphant, but she didn't care. Having made the decision to go, she was glad.

"What about Ice From Sky?"

Night Wind appeared thoughtful. "She will not know." He paused. "I will speak with her—"

"No!" she exclaimed, aghast by the idea.

"Why?" He frowned. "Are you ashamed of what we share?"

Was she? Rebecca shook her head. "No, I'm not ashamed. It's my culture. It is not right to openly . . ."

"Ah!" Understanding lit up his features, softening them. "In my culture, it is good."

Her belly fluttered. "Because I'm a slave?"

He shook his head. He was so beautiful, she thought, fighting the urge to touch him. She wanted to stroke his angular jaw, run her finger down his ruggedly shaped nose; her hands tingled as she kept them at her sides.

"It is different with slave," he confessed. "But as long as we meet late . . ."

She was bothered by the implied meaning. She thought she should tell that she'd changed her mind. But had she? Wasn't this what she wanted? To hold him? To love him again? And hadn't she just complained that she didn't want the others to know?

"It is all right if Ice From Sky allows it," she guessed.

"I will speak with my father's wife. You will have nothing to fear from *M' hoo kum a.*" And with that, he encouraged her to go inside.

The family was sleeping when she entered, which made it easier for her to come back and slip into bed. Everything was all right, she thought. No one knew that she'd escaped. No one but Night Wind . . .

He had been her lover.

And tomorrow night, he'd be loving her again.

Twenty-two

Rebecca could barely control her excitement as she anticipated going to Night Wind's wigwam. Ice From Sky had looked at her strangely the next morning, but she hadn't said a word, for which Rebecca was grateful. If the matron suspected that Rebecca had tried to escape, she gave no sign of it. The two women went about their chores as they usually did these winter days.

About midday, Rebecca felt the effects of a sleepless night. Everyone had seen Night Wind's bear, and the animal was shared first with the Wolf clan and then the other two bands—the Turtle and the Turkey. There was plenty of meat for all. Night Wind kept the bear's skin, but the head he gave to Iron Bear, who was pleased by the gift of a new headdress.

Rebecca was out in the yard helping the Lenape to cook their meat for the grease and food, and she had difficulty keeping her eyes open. She thought she had managed to hide how tired she felt, but she was wrong.

"You are ill?" Gift From Forest asked.

She smiled at the child. "No, I'm tired." The boy had a supply of boundless energy; it was a wonderful thing to see, but it made her own lack more evident.

"Why do you not sleep?" Ice From Sky had come up from behind them.

Rebecca was surprised by the question. "It would be all right if I lie down?"

The matron nodded.

"You don't need my help?"

Smiling, Ice From Sky pointed toward the wigwam. She was cooking her share of bear's meat.

"Thank you," Rebecca said. She rose, and as she passed Ice From Sky, the matron grabbed her arm.

"Do you not think I don't know why Night Wind got the bear? You got lost and disturbed it."

The Englishwoman inclined her head. It was the truth, she thought, but not entirely.

"Sleep, and I will wake you later," the Lenape woman said.

Rebecca went to her sleeping pallet and lay down.

Night came quickly. Rebecca had slept most of the afternoon, and amazingly, Ice From Sky had allowed her. She was awakened in time to help with the late meal. She was cheerful as she worked and ate; the early evening passed pleasantly.

The last hours before the family fell asleep were difficult for Rebecca. As the time came closer for her to meet Night Wind, her body tingled and her thoughts raced.

Soon the moment she had anticipated arrived, and she rose from her bed, grabbed her fur mantle, and crept toward the door. Had Night Wind spoken to Ice From Sky? If he had, then Rebecca had to commend the matron for displaying no sign of it. Rebecca lifted the flap and went out into the night.

The air was crisp and cold, but not brutal. The moon was bright, making the snow sparkle and the village glow like a fairy land. Rebecca started across the compound when she heard voices, and she hung back, watching. A woman left a wigwam and then disappeared into another lodge—the shaman's.

Rebecca heard a soft giggle then the deeper tones of masculine laughter. The shaman's laugh. Night Wind was right, she thought. It was acceptable in the village for men and women to lie together before marriage. The Lenape wouldn't be shocked if they knew that she and Night Wind were lovers.

But would it be different because she was a slave?

The yard was again empty, and anxious, she hurried toward Night Wind's lodge.

Rebecca felt the heat immediately as she entered Night Wind's wigwam. He had built up the fire in the pit in the center, and the interior of the shelter was golden and toasty warm. She pulled off her mantle and dropped it. As it fell to the floor, she searched for Night Wind, only to find him watching her. Her breath quickened. He rose from his sleeping platform where he'd been waiting for her. His muscled chest naked, he wore only the cloth covering his loins. His skin was sleek, the strength of him evident in his arms and thighs. His copper-colored skin was enhanced by the flickering flame of the orange firelight. But it was his eyes that caught her attention. His glowing gaze lured her closer. She could read the emotion in the black orbs, his desire for her.

"Kweh, *Shi'kiXkwe.*" His deep seductive voice vibrated down her spine and produced ripples of sensual pleasure.

"Tipaakke Shaakha, it's good to see you again." She paused. "You built a *Xa'sun,*" she said, her eyes mirroring her surprise.

Night Wind nodded. Before, when she'd slept here, it had been on the ground. The nights had been cold, but not as frigid. He had built it with the vision of sharing it with her. Concerned for her comfort, he'd cushioned the *Xa'sun* with mats and furs.

She seemed to float toward him when he held open

his arms. Excitement shivered along his skin, making it tingle. He had waited so long . . .

Rebecca studied his beloved face and experienced warmth, a sense of rightness about her being here. Desire pulsated to the core of her as she glided across the wigwam and flowed into Night Wind's arms.

He didn't kiss her, but gazed into her eyes with his arms about her waist and his lower body pressed close. The heat of his skin burned her like fire, seared her fingertips as she placed them on his chest. She experienced a tightening in her abdomen and a sensitive fullness in her breasts.

"It has been a long time, my love," he said in Algonquin.

She nodded. "Too long," she answered in kind, wondering what he'd called her.

"I was afraid you would not come."

Rebecca stared at his mouth. "I almost didn't." *Liar,* she thought. She wanted him so badly; nothing could have kept her away.

"Then I would have come for you."

She blinked. "You would have taken me from Ice From Sky?"

He smiled slowly, his dark eyes gleaming, and she believed that he'd meant it.

Her throat went dry, and she swallowed. Excitement welled within her breast, and she wanted to cry out with pure joy, because Night Wind wanted her, wanted her enough to openly take her from Ice From Sky.

"Night Wind, I—"

He cut her words off with a kiss, a deep sensuous kiss that curled her toes and made her body tingle. He pulled her closer, his hands in the small of her back, and he devoured her mouth.

She swayed when he released her, but he steadied her with his arms.

"Do you believe the truth?" he asked.

Rebecca inclined her head. "You want me." She'd become brazen, she thought. Or more like the Indians. Hadn't Night Wind said that Lenape men and women spoke freely of their feelings and desire for each other?

She slid her hands up over the smooth, sleek muscles of his chest, enjoying his hardness, the power of his breast and shoulders. He was not bulky, but his body was finely honed from running and hunting, and other heavy work. She recalled the load he'd carried on his shoulders when he'd brought back nearly a hundred pounds of freshly killed bear. And when he'd first kidnapped her, hadn't he carried her for miles before letting her walk? The days of kidnapper and captive seemed long in the past.

I love you, she was about to say when he kissed her again, effectively putting an end to all rational thought. She could feel the firm tenderness of his moist lips . . . the warm velvety length of his tongue as he deepened the kiss.

When he raised his head, she put her fingers on his throat at the pulsing, sensitive hollow at the base. She trailed her index finger up to his Adam's apple, watching with pleasure as he swallowed and it moved.

She heard his breathing change as she touched him. She became bolder in her caresses, rubbing his nipple, watching the passion in his expression as he closed his eyes.

Rebecca explored his shoulders and his chest, her fingers slowly, tantalizingly, encircling his nipples. She touched a nipple with her mouth, and Night Wind gasped, and his hands gripped her waist harder, but he didn't stop her, and Rebecca was pleased.

"Do you like it when I touch you?" she asked, emboldened. Her gaze lifted from her explorations to lock with dark glittering twins of fire.

"Kihiila," he admitted huskily. He jerked her closer, but she wedged her arms between them so that only their lower bodies touched.

"Maata," she said. "We must go slowly. You must allow me to touch you." She could feel that Night Wind was hard and ready for her. His tumescence bulged against his loincloth; she could feel him beneath the two layers of deerskin that separated flesh from flesh.

She was heady with the experience. Before he had always been the one in control, and now she was enjoying the power, the privilege, of setting the pace. He opened his eyes and Rebecca held his gaze as she shifted her hands lower. She ran her fingers delicately over his stomach muscles, which were flat and taut, but sensitive to her touch. She enjoyed watching his face change as she caressed him. She heard her effect on him in the altered rhythm of his heartbeat. His breath quickened and became loud.

"You have a beautiful body, *Tipaakke Shaakha,*" she murmured, lowering her gaze to follow her hands. "So strong . . . so smooth . . . so hot beneath my hands."

He jerked as she leaned back to trace along the upper edge of his breechcloth. He seemed fascinated by what she was doing, by the direct bold way she was complimenting him. Before this, she'd always been somewhat shy.

His ebony eyes appeared glazed as Night Wind regarded her from beneath lowered eyelids. She continued to stroke along his waist area, and he closed his eyes. His head fell back slightly. Yes, she thought, he was enjoying her boldness, her new-found courage while they were making love. And she enjoyed it as well—perhaps too much.

Rebecca paused in her caressing and pulled back. When he tried to reach for her, she stopped him by holding up her hand. "You must be patient," she told him.

She stepped back and took off her moccasins, removing them slowly and dropping them to the floor. His eyes gleamed as her hands went to the hem of her tunic and she lifted off the garment and held it aloft between three fingers. She wore nothing underneath. The fire burning in Night Wind's gaze intensified, searing her golden skin, sensitizing her breasts and making her nipples harden. She looked away to set her tunic aside.

The air grew thick with sexual tension as desire pulsated throughout Rebecca's body. She stood before him naked. Her hair was unbound, and the long silky strands were tousled from undressing. Finally, returning to meet Night Wind's gaze, she felt a moment of extreme awkwardness as she straightened, suddenly conscious of being nude and vulnerable.

He has seen you before, she silently reminded herself. But never before in the light of a bright fire.

"Uitissa," he rasped. *"Uitissa wulluts."*

The tension, the doubts, left her. He had just told her how lovely, how beautiful, her breasts were to him. And he went on to compliment her stomach . . . her legs and feet. Apparently, he found pleasure in every inch of her.

The effect of his words was instant—a shaft of physical desire so intense that it made her hot. She felt as if she'd been created for Night Wind, to love and lie with him . . . to house and nurture his seed. She felt a longing to have his child and share with him the joys of being a parent.

A flicker of doubt. A moment of truth. She made a valiant effort to banish her concerns, but they wouldn't go away. Her need to hope, to believe in their future, made her continue . . .

Rebecca went to him and tugged the strings of his breechcloth, allowing the garment to fall to the floor. He was hers to fondle and enjoy.

"Woman," he groaned. Night Wind closed his eyes as he braced himself with feet apart. She cupped his manhood and stroked him lovingly. Her fingers encircled the engorged tip, and she rubbed over the opening, pleased when he sighed and moaned, his lashes fluttering against his cheeks.

She kissed his chest, heard the heavy thundering of his beating heart, and she trailed her mouth downward, taking the time to kiss and nuzzle his belly. Night Wind jerked and clutched her head as she licked and nipped his firm stomach muscles. His reaction was honest, so complete that Rebecca's desire heightened. She moved her lips lower.

"Maata!" Night Wind gasped, dragging her upward. He captured her mouth with his own, and their lips mated. Their tongues dueled and thrust. Rebecca whimpered and pressed closer. Flesh burned flesh. Hardness met soft curves.

Rebecca moaned against his mouth when he shifted and he was situated between her legs, the hot throbbing tip of his shaft brushing the moist pulsating heat of her womanhood.

She was frustrated with their positions. Standing they were limited in their ability to press close, and she gasped her complaint, which he immediately heeded.

Night Wind released her and then lifted her into his arms as effortlessly as if she weighed no more than a child. He carried her to the sleeping platform.

"Each night I hoped, dreamed, that you would come," he confessed in a husky voice. "I dreamed that you would lie on my *Xa'sun* with me beside you, touching you."

She was moved by his admission, seduced by his words. He placed her gently on the thick pile of soft furs on the platform, and then he stepped back to study her. Judging from his expression, she thought that he enjoyed seeing her naked. But did the picture meet his expectations? The image in his dreams?

"Night Wind."

"Kihiila, Reb-bec-ca. It is as I dreamed." He came to her then, covering her with his length. As their skin touched, Rebecca trembled and felt the tremor that racked Night Wind.

They kissed, and she enjoyed it, surrendering to the pleasure. She cried out as he touched her, caressing her breasts and belly, running his fingers down her thighs and legs. Their caresses became frantic, their kisses wild. They stroked and kissed on and on until gasping, unable to wait any longer, Rebecca reached for his staff and guided it inside her.

She inhaled sharply as he filled her. She arched her hips and rocked upward against him, and Night Wind pressed down, grunting his enjoyment.

Caught in their web of passion, they moved together, their hips grinding, their breasts and bellies touching. They loved rhythmically, lunging together and moving apart, thrusting and withdrawing and thrusting in their search for release.

Man and woman found the pinnacle of their desire simultaneously. Rebecca gave a little cry as Night Wind stiffened above her, climaxing with a deep groan. Clutching each other, they soared for several seconds, suspended above the world in ecstasy before slowly, pleasurably, sailing back to earth.

They lay, locked in each other's arms. Rebecca loved the weight of Night Wind on her breasts, her lower body. She closed her eyes, inhaling his scent, and sighed happily while stroking his back.

Night Wind touched her face to make her look at him. She saw something in his features that she'd never seen before . . . a vulnerability and an emotion that hinted at deep feelings for her.

She smiled and leaned up to kiss him.

"Medicine Woman," he murmured, his eyes darkening with passion.

Rebecca gently rolled him to the side. She rose up on her elbow and kissed him . . . on his mouth and his chest . . . on his navel . . . and lower. She returned to pay homage to his lips, and he deepened the contact and pushed her to her back, following her with renewed desire.

The kiss ended on a tender note. She was ready to love him again, but he turned over to lie on his back, pulling her to lie on her side against him. He caressed her shoulder.

She didn't want the night to end. She wanted to suspend time and continue their loving, but Rebecca knew she couldn't, and the dark seed of doubt returned to silently torment her.

Night Wind shifted and kissed her forehead, a gesture that was so gentle, so loving, it banished all of Rebecca's fears.

She sighed and snuggled against him. Safe and secure in his embrace, she slept, her concerns forgotten.

Night Wind lay awake. Somehow he must find a way to take Rebecca into his wigwam. He didn't want to live as before . . . alone . . . without her.

Perhaps Ice From Sky would sell her?

And guess the truth? That he wanted Rebecca not as a slave, but as his woman? He hadn't told the matron of his desire for the slave. He couldn't put his feelings into words. They were . . . strange . . . to him. He felt vulnerable, and he was unwilling to share what he felt with anyone, but Rebecca.

And he hadn't yet told her. Because he didn't want to give her the power, the means to manipulate him.

But would she?

What if she was as enthralled with him as he was with her?

Until he knew for certain, he must keep his love a secret. A man and woman didn't need to love to enjoy each other's bodies. She need never suspect that he wanted more from her than having her share his sleeping mat.

Twenty-three

Rebecca slipped back to her wigwam in the early hours of morning when it was still dark. Night Wind had awakened her with a lingering kiss and the memory of what followed brought a smile to her lips and joy to her heart as she crawled onto her bed. As she covered herself with furs, her body tingled in spots she had been unaware of before Night Wind's touch, and her lips were swollen from his demanding mouth.

Would they notice? she wondered. Wood Owl and Ice From Sky?

Would Gift From Forest? The boy was observant. If he noticed something different about her, he would openly ask questions. And what was she going to say?

She turned to face the wall. She was worrying about nothing. She could always make up an excuse. For the marks on her breasts where Night Wind had suckled her? Her cheeks burned. Who but her was going to see them? As long as she didn't have to bathe when the village women did, no one would know.

She relaxed, and a smile gently curved her lips again as she fell asleep.

Rebecca was startled awake by the sound of coughing against the murmur of anxious voices. She sat up, saw who was ill, and immediately went to the boy's side.

"When did this happen?" she asked the child's mother.

Ice From Sky shook her head. She was obviously frightened. "When you were gone——"

Rebecca tensed. Gone, she thought, at Night Wind's wigwam?

"During the time you were not with us. Gift From Forest was ill, and we thought we would lose him. Later, after I watched over him, never leaving his side, preparing him broths, he became well again."

"Is this the same illness as . . ." Rebecca allowed her voice to trail off. She wouldn't hurt the family and speak Red Fox's name. To do so would risk the dead child's soul.

The Indian woman inclined her head. "Only this is the first that my son has had difficulty breathing."

The white woman crouched beside the bed and touched the boy's face. "How do you feel, little warrior?" she asked softly.

"Moot a he hurts," he said, rubbing his stomach. "And my *weel,*" he added, referring to his head. The boy tried to rise and fell back on his sleeping mat, groaning. A spasm of coughing overtook him, and he rose up, gasping and choking, until the episode passed.

"Poor *Pee-lah-a-chick,*" his mother crooned.

"Has he eaten?" Rebecca asked.

Ice From Sky shook her head. "Not since he went out to play with the other children."

Rebecca was concerned. Gift From Forest hadn't eaten since yesterday morning. Why hadn't she noticed? She cared deeply for the little boy, and her heart went out to him. The child had charmed her, making her long for sons of her own . . . with Night Wind.

"Where is *Tahuun Kukuus?*"

"My husband is with our *sakima,* Beaver Hawk.

The men have been called to council." The matron appeared worried. "One of our braves saw signs of the Mohawk. I fear that there will be fighting."

The news filled Rebecca with dread. Would Night Wind leave and fight with the other warriors? Dear God, what would she do if he was killed?

She had to remain calm. There was an ill child who needed help. And his mother needed her support and assistance. What could have caused the boy's illness?

Something he ate or came in contact with? Were any of the other Lenape children sick?

Rebecca asked Ice From Sky. The matron told her that she'd heard of no other children who had become ill. It seemed suspicious to Rebecca that only the sons of Ice From Sky suffered this strange sickness.

Ice From Sky went to inquire about the other children in the village, leaving Rebecca with Gift From Forest. Rebecca was warmed by the knowledge that the matron trusted her enough to allow her to remain with the boy alone.

"I am sorry you are ill, little one," Rebecca said, her voice gentle.

The boy gazed up at her with dull eyes. "You will stay with me, Rebecca? You will stay here and help *Onna?* I want you to care for me like you did for—" He hesitated. "—my brother."

Rebecca grew still. "But I did not save your brother."

The child dismissed that with a weak wave of his hand. "He was better while you cared for him. Night Wind said so, and I believe it, too."

Night Wind defended her? Her head spun with a rush of exhilaration.

"I will care for you," Rebecca answered him in his tongue, "so you will get well and teach me to play snowsnake."

Gift From Forest managed a grin. "I will have to get better quickly, before the snow melts. Snowsnake can only be played while the ground is covered with the frozen white."

Ice From Sky returned, out of breath, her gaze anxiously seeking her young son. She saw the child's smile, and the gentle expression on her slave's face. She relaxed as she joined them.

"You are healing him already, Medicine Woman. It is said that a smile is magic that heals the body from the heart out."

Rebecca rose from where she·had been crouched next to the boy's sleeping platform. "If a smile is like medicine, then imagine what laughter can do for this brave warrior." She ruffled his hair. "We shall have to see."

She faced the child's mother. "I think this little warrior should try to eat something."

And the two women worked together to prepare soup.

News of Gift From Forest's illness reached the men during their meeting. Night Wind along with Beaver Hawk, Wood Owl, and the war chiefs of each of the Lenape bands were discussing attacking the Mohawk before they reached Turtle-Town. They were concerned for their families.

"We must find the Mohawk and see their numbers. If they are few, we can kill them and remove the threat," Feather Coat said. He was a ceremonial drummer and the war chief of the Turkey band.

"The Mohawk will not be alone," Night Wind warned. "They are brothers to the Cayuga and the Onondaga. They are friends with the Seneca. If we strike, we must kill with no traces of what we've done.

If one of the brothers learns of our deed, they will find us . . . and there will be many of them. The people of Turtle-Town will not have a chance."

"My son speaks the truth," Wood Owl said. "I have been with the Seneca. I have the marks of their knives on my back and chest. I have the burns from their fire on my ankles and feet. If not for Beaver Hawk—" He paused to smile gratefully at the sachem. "I would have died at the Senecas' hands. But Beaver Hawk—brother to my beloved Ice From Sky—used his powers and skill as chief to bring in a Lenape raiding party . . . to rescue this injured Wood Owl."

The memory of the incident made *Tahuun Kukuus* visibly shudder. "It was a long time ago, but I will never forget it. Night Wind was but a little child when his mother and I were captured on our way from Village-By-the-Lake to my mother's clan in Turtle-Town. My mother had gone ahead with our son, so *Tipaakke* was not captured by the Seneca tribe.

"Ice From Sky had never met this Wood Owl, but she pleaded on his behalf, convinced her brother to find the mother and father of the little boy . . . And when the father was rescued alone, bleeding, burnt, and out of his mind with grief, the lovely maiden had spoken gently to him. She had visited him often, caring for his wounds, helping his mother look after his son. She healed this Owl with her tender caring. It took awhile, but he learned to live a day without suffering . . . of hearing his dead wife's screams. He learned to sleep without crying out the horror of his dreams."

Wood Owl's eyes were bright with love for his second wife and the pain for one who had lost her young life. His relationship with Silver Rain, Night Wind's mother, had been a good one, but it seemed as if it were part of another lifetime. Only Night Wind was left of his first marriage, but Ice From Sky's love had been so complete that the young *Tipaakke* had become one of her own sons.

"I know these Iroquois," he said. "We must act fast and take nothing by chance. We must think of our wives and our little ones. By all costs, they must be spared the horror of the Seneca's rage!"

"Then let us be swift and accurate," Beaver Hawk declared. "Let us send out a scout to find these Mohawk and learn their numbers."

The men agreed with their sachem and discussed who would go. They were deep in their discussions when suddenly a young brave, barely out of boyhood, rushed in to disturb them.

"Wood Owl! *Tipaakke Shaakha!*" he gasped. "It's Gift From Forest. The boy is sick. Ice From Sky is worried."

Father and son stood. Night Wind's gaze met his sachem's. "Beaver Hawk—"

"Go, Night Wind. See to my sister's son. We will decide this matter and let you know."

Wood Owl left, but Night Wind hesitated. "If you wish me to go," he began.

Beaver Hawk shook his head. "Your head is with the little brave. Better Deer-That-Runs or Raven Feather go alone this time."

The brave nodded and then hurried away.

Night Wind's gaze met Rebecca's when he entered the wigwam. Her blue eyes glowed briefly before she returned his attention to Gift From Forest. The warrior saw the child's fingers clutching the woman's hand, and he marveled how good Rebecca was to have earned the boy's love. He had done nothing since last night but try to think of a way to keep her with him. But seeing her with the boy, knowing that the child was ill, he had to forget his desires. Rebecca would have to stay in the lodge of Ice From Sky.

"How is my little brother?" Night Wind gently asked the child.

"Tipaakke!" The boy's face lit up, his eyes sparkling with joy. "You came to see me!"

Night Wind felt guilty. "You are my favorite young warrior. Why wouldn't I come?"

"You've been busy lately."

The older man sighed. "Mohawk, Seneca," Night Wind said with a hint of exasperation. "One must worry about the Iroquois."

The child sat up in his excitement. "You were fighting the enemy?"

Night Wind came to sit next to the boy on his sleeping platform. Rebecca stood to give him room, but he waved her into her seat, and she shook her head.

"A brave is our enemy only if he means us harm," the man said.

"Do not the Seneca mean us harm, *Tipaakke?*" Gift From Forest asked, his eyes wide. "I saw our father's back. I saw where they beat him."

The brave touched the boy's arm. "Yes, those Seneca are our enemy. They did wrong to hurt *Nukuaa,* but we must be careful we do not fight those who would befriend us."

"Like who?"

Night Wind shrugged. "The Shawnee. They are grandfather to us . . . and there may be others who wish only to live in peace."

"Yes," the boy said. "I believe this is true." He was overcome by a coughing spasm, and Night Wind raised him to sit up straight, rubbing his back until his breathing cleared.

"You must rest, *Niimut.*" Night Wind studied his

father's youngest son with concern. "You must eat well and listen to *Onna*."

"And Medicine Woman," Gift From Forest added.

"Kihiila, it is important to do what Reb-bec-ca tells you."

Rebecca watched and listened as Night Wind spent time with the sick child. He was tender and affectionate with the boy; yet he made the child feel grown up by listening to him carefully and treating the boy's questions with respect. Night Wind would make a wonderful father, she thought. So loving, caring, and patient.

When the boy appeared tired, Night Wind rose and convinced the child to rest, promising to return to visit later. Rebecca was moved when the man and the little boy hugged.

I love this man, she thought. But how could she stay here and be a part of his life and care for Elizabeth, too? Why was she even contemplating such a foolish dream?

Night Wind waved her outside as he was leaving the wigwam. He had spoken briefly with Ice From Sky and before that his father. Now he wanted to speak with Rebecca. Her breath quickened as she preceded him under the door flap.

"You will . . . care for him?" His tone was hesitant, pleading as they stood beside the wigwam.

"I will care for him," she promised, "as if he were my own son."

Night Wind smiled and tenderly caressed her cheek. *"Wa-nee'shih."*

"The pleasure is mine, *Tipaakke Shaakha.*"

"I will miss you."

Her heart skipped a beat. "You will not visit?"

He frowned. "I will visit the family, but it will be you I miss. I want to kiss you, but I know it will hurt your English proper if I do. I want to . . ." His voice dropped. ". . . love you with these fingers." He held up his hands. ". . . with this body." He gestured down his long, lean length.

"Night Wind," she breathed, swaying toward him.

He looked tortured as he gently pushed her away. "You must go in, *Shi'ki,* for already this warrior is ready for you."

Her gaze dropped involuntarily to his breechcloth, and she saw by the strained deerskin what he meant. Night Wind turned to leave.

"Night Wind!"

He halted and regarded her warily over his shoulder.

"I want you to kiss me," she mouthed. "I want you to love me."

He closed his eyes with a silent groan. His dark orbs glittered with longing when he opened his eyes again. "Soon, Reb-bec-ca," he said.

And she held on tightly to his whispered promise.

Days passed and Gift From Forest's condition improved before it grew worse again. Rebecca was puzzled. The child had been well on the mend, eating and sitting up, playing happily with the other children, when the boy's illness returned.

What is making him sick? Rebecca wondered. She was convinced that something about the village was adversely affecting him. She didn't believe that Gift From Forest was just a sickly child. He'd been healthy while Red Fox was alive . . .

Night Wind came in daily to see the boy, and Gift From Forest eagerly awaited the brave's visit. Rebecca understood the child's eagerness, because she too was anxious for Night Wind's visits. Her heart beat rapidly at the time of each day that she expected him to come.

The brave was friendly toward her, but not loving. No one seeing them would suspect by his actions that they had shared a sleeping mat. She, on the other hand, might have given the fact away. She was nervous and jittery whenever he was near. She could feel the color rising in each cheek whenever he looked at her.

One day his visit took her by surprise. It was one of Gift From Forest's well periods, and the child happened to be inside when Night Wind came. He entered the wigwam so silently that she was startled by Gift From Forest's cry of joy. Rebecca spun from the fire too quickly, and she spilt the bowl of *sa'pan* she'd just filled, burning her hand.

She exhaled with a hiss of pain. Night Wind was beside her immediately, lifting her hand to inspect the damage. Rebecca's body sprang to life. Her breath quickened. She could hear the thunder of her heart beat roaring in her ears. Tingles of pleasure crawled up her arm.

"Rebecca!" Gift From Forest was upset to see she was hurt. He regarded her worriedly. "Your face is red. Are you ill?"

Rebecca exchanged glances with Night Wind. "No, I am fine, little warrior. I was clumsy."

"You need to take care of this." Night Wind's deep voice added shivers of sensation down her spine.

She nodded. Why had she suddenly become shy of him?

"I will get something," he said. She didn't protest; she wanted him to help her. A memory flickered of his caring concern when she was ill.

Night Wind left the wigwam. While he was gone, Ice From Sky returned. *"Tipaakke* said you burned your hand," she said.

Rebecca showed her the burn and had to bite her tongue from protesting when the matron said, "I have special root for burns." How could she refuse the woman's help? It would seem odd if she did.

Night Wind returned then, and Rebecca's flesh warmed with pleasure. "I have brought medicine," he said.

Ice From Sky nodded approvingly. "That is good," she said, reaching for the salve.

"I must help her," the brave insisted, drawing a strange look from Ice From Sky. "It is my fault that she is hurt," he explained.

Rebecca was pleased. Gift From Forest suddenly demanded Night Wind's attention, and so it was the boy's mother who spread the specially prepared paste-like substance over the slave's burn. The white woman was disappointed, yet pleased that Night Wind had wanted to help her.

Night Wind remained for a meal. Rebecca had made plenty of *sa'pan,* so she was glad when Ice From Sky asked him to stay. His ebony gaze settled on her briefly before he accepted the invitation with a nod.

To Rebecca's surprise, Gift From Forest ate little. She watched him carefully, recognizing the recurring signs of his illness.

"Forest," she said, "what did you do today?"

Her gaze met his mother's, and they shared concern over the child's loss of appetite.

"We were warriors," the boy said.

"Do you eat anything today, *Ne gwis?*" his mother asked.

The boy looked defensive. "I ate when Dark Eagle did."

"What did you have?" Rebecca asked gently.

"Sa'pan."

Rebecca sighed. The child had eaten *sa'pan* before and not become ill. Was he not eating now, because he'd had it earlier? No, she thought, watching the boy cradle his stomach.

"Are you feeling poorly again?" Night Wind said.

Gift From Forest inclined his head, his face pale.

"Maybe you should lie down," his father suggested.

Rebecca rose to help him. She could feel Night Wind's piercing gaze and his concern for his father's son.

Wood Owl stood and left the wigwam.

"Where did he go?" Night Wind asked Ice From Sky.

"To get Iron Bear."

Rebecca looked over and locked gazes with Night Wind in shared concern.

Iron Bear came quickly. He burst into the wigwam and shoved Rebecca aside in his attempt to get close to the boy.

Angered, Rebecca left the wigwam to wait outside.

"Why did you leave the lodge?" Night Wind had followed her into the night.

"I would only be in Iron Bear's way." She stared at the ground. "He doesn't like it when I'm near."

The brave touched her face, lifting it upward tenderly. "And this concerns you."

Rebecca's eyes flashed with angry fire. "My concern is with Gift From Forest."

He released her. "And you think Iron Bear would hurt him?"

"Something—or someone—is hurting him." She wasn't accusing, but said it with such concern that Night Wind couldn't help but be moved. "I wish I knew what was making him sick!"

"What is your thought?"

She faced him, her blue eyes glistening. "I believe he's eating something he shouldn't. I've done a lot of thinking on this—he gets sick after he's played with the other children."

Night Wind was thoughtful as he studied her. "It is possible," he conceded. He had noticed a pattern in the boy's illness.

Rebecca grabbed his arm. "Do you not find it strange that only Ice From Sky's sons have taken ill?"

He experienced a jolt. It was true, he thought. It was odd that the only sick ones had been the two boys.

"I'm worried," she confessed. She hadn't released his arm, and he could feel the heat of her hand tingling his skin. He had a sudden mental image of her naked, lying beneath him, her eyes glazed with passion, her lips soft. Her full curves pressing into his hardened muscles. . . . Desire hit him like a lightning bolt. He wanted her on his sleeping mat. Now.

"Night Wind?"

Rebecca's eyes widened as she saw his face. A bright glitter had come to light up his onyx eyes. He stared at her, his features mirroring his desire, and her body burned.

"*Shi'ki* . . ."

She swallowed and pulled away. She envisioned Red Fox, remembered his illness, and she knew that their only concern now should be for Gift From Forest's health.

"Medicine Woman." Ice From Sky called her into the wigwam.

"I am coming, *M' hoo kum a.*" Her gaze broke contact with Night Wind's, and she turned to go.

He caught her shoulder. "I miss you, Reb-bec-ca. My mat seems cold without your warm beauty."

She closed her eyes. When she lifted her lashes, she knew that her love would be there in her eyes for him to see. "I must go." Her voice was husky. He nodded. She took several steps and spun. "I miss you, too, *Tipaakke Shaakha.*" And she entered the wigwam.

Night Wind stared at the door flap where she'd disappeared and realized that Rebecca was right. Gift From Forest's sickness was caused by something. But what?

Or who? Who would want to hurt the child?

Who would want him dead?

Twenty-four

"Onna—"

"Chitkwe'se!" the boy's mother said. "I am busy. Can't you see?"

Angry Woman stared down at her dwindling supply of poisonous roots, and she scowled. It had been months since Red Fox's death, and his brother, Gift From Forest, was still alive.

The wigwam was filthy. The dirty floor rushes were littered with old mats, broken dishes, and food waste that even the dogs wouldn't eat.

The slovenly crone clenched her fists with fury. She couldn't poison the child quickly; someone might suspect. Yet, every time she'd managed to get a little of the root powder into the child, something would happen to isolate Gift From Forest, and she had to start all over again.

Red Fox had been a weak child, the toothless squaw thought. Gift From Forest was strong. She would have to use more of the special root. Where was she going to get more of it? She was running low, and the ground was frozen, the roots encased in ice.

"Onna." Her son called to her a second time.

The woman exploded with anger and rose to backhand the child across the face. Dark Eagle fell back, hitting his head on the cluttered sleeping platform. Stunned by the blow, he lay on the dirty rush floor.

"I told you not to bother me!"

The boy gazed at his mother, his dark eyes brimming with tears. "I wanted to tell you about Gift From Forest," he mumbled.

Angry Woman tensed. Suddenly, her face softened as she pulled her son to his feet and then cradled him comfortingly against her sagging chest.

The child sighed as he snuggled against his mother's breast. This was how he loved his *Onna,* when she treated him kindly and gave him hugs. He wrinkled his nose. She smelled of rancid bear's grease and dried venison stew, unlike the other matrons within the village who had the scent of the clean forest air. But he loved his mother anyway, despite her horrible smell.

He'd wanted to tell her the news about his clan brother, Gift From Forest, because *Onna* had seemed so interested in the child lately, so much so that he himself had become jealous. But then his mother never took Gift From Forest into her arms like she did him.

Angry Woman clumsily stroked Dark Eagle's head as she questioned him about Gift From Forest.

"Gift From Forest is ill, *Onna.*"

The woman stiffened and stopped stroking. She set her son away from her and grabbed his shoulders, squeezing hard. "When did this occur?"

"This morning, *Onna.* It happened early when the sun first lit up the sky." He grew frightened at his mother's changing expressions. He jerked from her hold and backed away.

She stared at the wall, her features contorting as she thought. When she regarded her son, the boy flinched.

Angry Woman smiled. "You have done well to tell me this, Dark Eagle."

"Wa-nee'shih, Onna."

"We shall have to make Gift From Forest a special medicine to see that he gets well." Her dark eyes bore a calculating gleam. "Will you take it to him, my son?"

He couldn't deny her anything when she spoke to him tenderly. He didn't want to give Gift From Forest anything; it bothered him that his mother displayed such concern for the boy. But he wanted her to go on being nice to him, so he would do it for her—bring Gift From Forest a special medicine made by his mother's hands. But he would take his time about it, he decided stubbornly.

"I will bring it to him, *Onna*," the child said.

His mother beamed at her eleven-year-old son and then gave him a hug, kissing him on the head.

Dark Eagle closed his eyes in happiness. He loved his mother when she wasn't mean.

Gift From Forest was sleeping. Rebecca sat near his sleeping platform, mending a tear in the child's jacket. She kept a careful eye on him as she worked. Her gaze strayed from the buckskin garment to light on the boy more often than it remained on her lap.

Ice From Sky was out in the sweat lodge. It was something the Lenape women did often these days. Rebecca had only been there once, and the memory of her experience made her cold.

She had gone to the steam lodge with Ice From Sky, where she and the other village women who had gathered there had stripped off their garments and sat naked in a room filled with hot steam. The steam was made by pouring water over hot coals, and one woman did this until the air was thick. The temperature had risen with the intensity of the vapors, and Rebecca had sat on the platform with the others, feeling her skin warm and her body open up to the heat. They had stayed in the building until Rebecca felt that she couldn't breathe and then they had run outside into the winter cold, the Indian women giggling, as they had lain down and rolled their naked bodies in the snow.

The shock of the cold after the heat had made Rebecca gasp. And although her entire body had tingled and felt more alive than ever before, she hadn't been sure she'd enjoyed the experience. When Ice From Sky had approached her with going the next day, Rebecca had nervously, politely, declined. To her relief, the Indian matron had seemed to understand, and while Ice From Sky's gaze invited Rebecca to come as she left each day, she'd never pressed Rebecca into joining her.

Wood Owl was gone. He was attending a meeting in the lodge of the chief, and Ice From Sky had only just recently left for the sweat lodge. There was only Rebecca to watch over Gift From Forest, but she didn't mind. In fact, she enjoyed it, enjoyed the Indians' trust in her ability to care for the boy.

The child rested comfortably. He had suffered no fever this particular time, and Rebecca thought it wasn't the same illness which had plagued him earlier.

Iron Bear must have thought so, too. He had left after being with the child only a short time, and he hadn't returned these last three days.

Night Wind had stopped in to check on the boy daily, and Gift From Forest, when awake, had laughed at the things the brave did to entertain him.

When the door flap raised this morning, Rebecca expected to see Night Wind. The rhythm of her heart sped up, until she saw it was a child who stood hesitantly at the door. Rebecca set down the jacket and approached.

"You are Dark Eagle," she said.

The child stared at her. He was quiet so long that Rebecca was discomfited. The boy's hands cradled a small bowl. Steam rose from the clay dish, surrounding the child with vapor.

"Did you bring that for Gift From Forest?" she asked.

Dark Eagle inclined his head.

"Then, would—"

He thrust the bowl at Rebecca and fled, the door flap shutting in his wake with a puff of a cold draft. Rebecca smiled at the boy's shyness as she took the bowl over to the sick child's sleeping platform.

She would set the bowl on the floor near Gift From Forest's bed, she thought. It would be close and ready when the boy woke up to eat it.

Curious as to the bowl's contents, Rebecca held it to her nose and sniffed. A vile odor assailed her nostrils. She made a sound of disgust and pulled the bowl away.

What on earth was in the broth?

It was sweet of Dark Eagle to bring it. His mother—

Angry Woman, she thought with a shiver. She had a vision of dark, wrinkled skin, a toothless mouth, and eyes that were evil-looking and too small for the woman's face.

She is Ice From Sky's sister, her inner voice reminded her.

"But I don't like her," she said aloud. Something about the woman made her skin crawl, and Rebecca was unable to put a name to it. It was hard to believe, she thought, that Angry Woman was related to Ice From Sky.

She sniffed the soup again and gasped. Whatever

the woman had put in the brew smelled like it was rotten. *Yes,* she thought. *It smells like the decaying carcass of a dead animal!*

Rebecca glanced quickly toward the door, before she poured the bowl's contents in the fire-pit. The flame hissed, and the odor grew stronger as the liquid soup turned into steam. Choking, Rebecca had to open the door flap to air out the wigwam.

Gift From Forest would thank her if he knew about the soup. If she told him, which she had no intention of doing. The boy would be happy that she'd dumped it.

What person would willingly drink such a vile broth?

"Did you bring over the broth, *ne gwis?*" Angry Woman regarded her son with bright eyes.

"Yes, *Onna,*" the child replied. "Only Gift From Forest was sleeping. I had to give to the slave. The white woman."

A loud crack resounded about the wigwam as Angry Woman struck her son. "I told you to give it to Gift From Forest, to make sure you saw that he drank it."

"But, *Onna*—"

"Maata! You have been a bad boy." Angry Woman's lips convulsed as she spoke. Her eyes glittered with a wild light. "You know what happens to bad boys."

The child nodded, and his hands visibly shook as he took down the switch from where it hung on a rafter.

"Turn around."

The boy obeyed. Slowly, trembling, he lifted his shirt.

His mother lashed him across his back again and

again. Grimacing, holding back tears, Dark Eagle endured the pain in silence. He had learned from the past that if he cried out or begged her to stop, she would only hit him longer and harder.

Angry Woman's features brightened with enjoyment as she inflicted pain on her young son.

Twenty-five

Dark Eagle returned with the broth twice more, and it was more difficult for Rebecca each time to keep Gift From Forest from eating it. The second time the boy came, Gift From Forest had been sleeping again, which the white woman thought was fortunate. But Dark Eagle wasn't easy to get rid of on this occasion. This time he refused to leave, telling her that he wanted to wait for Gift From Forest to wake up. He sat for several minutes, squirming uncomfortably, until Rebecca suggested that he share some of his mother's broth. Then, the child made his excuses and bolted.

Gift From Forest had woken up and seen the bowl. "Medicine Woman, is that for me?"

"No, little warrior," she'd told him. "It is bad waste. I must get rid of it."

The boy had believed her—thank God.

On the third instance, Dark Eagle came, again in the morning while Ice From Sky was gone, but this time Wood Owl was in the wigwam. One look at the man sent Dark Eagle scurrying away.

Wood Owl eyed the steaming bow. "Angry Woman has made broth for Gift From Forest. Good," he said.

"I'm not certain it is good, *Tahuun Kukuus*," she said feeling alarmed.

The Indian looked at her oddly. "Why is this so?"

"It smells bad."

He laughed. "Angry Woman's soup always smells bad."

"Like rotten animals?"

"Hmmm." Wood Owl waved his arm dismissing the soup's importance, his mind already on other things. "Do what you think best, Medicine Woman," he said.

And so Rebecca poured out the malodorous soup.

On the fourth morning, it was Angry Woman herself who came to the wigwam. Ice From Sky was late in going to the sweat lodge, so she was there when her sister came. The women greeted each other, and Rebecca wondered again how these two women could be blood-related.

Ice From Sky took the bowl from Angry Woman's hands, and Rebecca panicked that the matron would give it to her child.

"I'll take it," Rebecca said, moving up quickly to take it from Ice From Sky.

Angry Woman glared. "His mother can give it to him."

"No," Ice From Sky said, "I must get to the lodge. Angry Woman, will you not join your sister? Rebecca will see that my son eats."

Rebecca felt a moment of triumph after the women left. She stared at the broth and sniffed. It still smelled the same, terrible, but not as strong as on the previous days.

Was she right in believing it wasn't good for Gift From Forest? She held it to her mouth, squeezed her eyes tightly, and tasted it. It was bitter. After one swallow, she threw it away. Shortly afterward, Rebecca felt sick to her stomach. She was sure then that Angry Woman was putting something in the broth to make the child sick. But what?

Had she done the same for Red Fox? Had she killed him? Did she want his brother dead? Why?

Her stomach roiled with nausea. She barely held on, waiting for Ice From Sky to return. Once Ice From Sky came back, Rebecca ran outside into the forest and vomited. Sweat broke out on her forehead. She felt clammy and alternately hot and cold.

"Reb-bec-ca." A firm arm cradled her shivering form. "You are ill."

She blinked and focused on Night Wind's beloved face. "Poison," she whispered.

He released her as if burnt. "What do you mean by this?"

"Angry Woman has been poisoning Gift From Forest, giving him bad medicine. She must have poisoned Red Fox, too," she choked, swaying. "She killed Red Fox and now she's trying to kill little Forest!"

The brave's face darkened. "What lies are these? Angry Woman is family. She wouldn't kill Gift From Forest!" He was more angry than Rebecca had ever seen him.

"It's true!" Her belly made a grumbling noise. She inhaled sharply and clutched her stomach until the cramp eased. "I drank some of the broth meant for your brother. They tried to give it to him four times, but I threw it all away."

Her head swam as she gazed at him through a film of tears. "This last time I drank it. Just a mouthful. And now I'm sick!"

Darkness descended as if she would faint. She bent, nearly stumbling onto her head, but Night Wind steadied her. *Please God make him believe me!*

"You have the boy's sickness," he said, refusing to believe anything else. He paused. "Angry Woman would never hurt anyone."

Rebecca knew then that she'd never be able to convince him. He chose to believe in a toothless crone rather than her. He chose to distrust her—the woman he'd spent many nights loving . . . joining in the flesh.

Night Wind helped her back to the wigwam and Ice From Sky exclaimed when she saw her slave. The matron was full of tender concern as she helped Rebecca get into bed. Night Wind and the woman spoke briefly, their voices too low for Rebecca to hear. Sick both in body and at heart, Rebecca didn't really care what they were saying.

Night Wind left, and Ice From Sky was bending over her.

"You are sick like my son," she said, "but he is better." She smiled. "You will get better, too."

Rebecca looked at her, but had difficulty keeping her eyes open. How could she tell Ice From Sky that the woman's own sister was trying to kill her son?

And what if Night Wind was right and she had, in fact, contracted Gift From Forest's illness? No one else had gotten sick so far, but then Rebecca had barely left the child's side.

After declining an offer of soup, Rebecca closed her eyes. No, she was sure she was right. Angry Woman had killed Red Fox, and now she was trying to kill Gift From Forest. The question was why? And what was she, an Englishwoman slave, going to be able to do about it?

Rebecca recovered and made a silent decision to guard Gift From Forest closely to ensure that the child stayed safe. It was something that would prove difficult as the weather had warmed and the boy wanted to play with the other village children.

She did everything she could to work outside so she could keep an eye on him. She saw how he ate and where he got his food; she was satisfied when he ate little from the community cooking pot, eating most of his meals at home. But Rebecca knew she couldn't keep doing this forever. Eventually she would have to leave Turtle-Town and Angry Woman would get to the child.

Still angry with her, Night Wind was a stranger to her these days. She had insulted one of his people with her accusation, and to dishonor another Lenape was to dishonor him, apparently. He avoided Rebecca, ignoring her when they passed in the village square, never acknowledging her existence with a look or word, not even when he came to the wigwam to visit his father's family.

His behavior wounded Rebecca deeply. She had given her all to him—her body and her heart, and to be rejected so cruelly, so completely, was almost more than she could bear. But she knew she was right; she refused to give up her belief that Angry Woman was responsible for the boy's illnesses.

"You are quiet, Medicine Woman," Ice From Sky observed. "Are you ill again?"

Rebecca gave her a slight smile. "I am fine, matron." She was unhappy, heartbroken, and worried about Night Wind's people. Most of all she missed the brave's presence . . . his caring . . . and the loving warmth of his muscled arms.

"It is good to know that you are well," the woman said. "As it is good to see my son running about again."

Rebecca's smile widened. "You have a wonderful son, *M' hoo kum a.* He will make a fine sachem someday."

Ice From Sky nodded, but her eyes were sad. Rebecca realized the woman was thinking of her first-born, Red Fox. The Englishwoman touched the matron's arm in comfort.

"You are unhappy," Ice From Sky said perceptively.

"I am . . . longing for my family," Rebecca admitted. "My home."

Something flickered in the Indian woman's eyes. "You miss your *Onna*."

Rebecca inclined her head. "My father died when I was but a babe. My mother and her sister raised me. We were poor, but we got by, for my mother knew how to sew, and my Aunt Veronica—she helped out at the vicarage, cleaning and cooking for our minister. It was a good life. I miss both of them."

"Kihiila, I know how it was with Angry Woman and me. We were close when we were small, but now . . ."

Rebecca's attention perked up. "Things are not the same between you and your sister?" Her heart pumped with excitement.

"Not since we had children, and Angry Woman learned that my son was to be chief."

The white woman frowned. "Why yours and not Angry Woman's?"

"I am the eldest daughter of the Turtle clan," she said. She smiled at Rebecca's shock. "I know. Angry Woman looks old, but it is because her life has not been easy, I think. Her *uikkiimuk* treated her unkindly, then he died, leaving her alone to raise their child. In our village, we love all of our children equally, but still we have those from our bodies who live with us."

Rebecca nodded with understanding.

"Because I am oldest," Ice From Sky continued, "my sons are first in line." Her eyes filled with tears. "My *son*," she corrected.

"And if you didn't have sons?" Rebecca's breath suspended with anticipation.

"Then Dark Eagle would be chief."

"And after Gift From Forest, who is next to be chief?" she asked, her heart pounding.

"Dark Eagle."

Rebecca knew then why Angry Woman wanted Gift From Forest dead. The woman was ambitious for her own son; she wanted Dark Eagle to be the next chief of Turtle-Town.

But if she told of her suspicions, who would listen to her? She couldn't tell Ice From Sky; the woman loved her sister, despite the tension that had cropped up between them over the years. No one else in the tribe would listen to a slave. *No one,* Rebecca thought, *but Night Wind.*

But he hated her.

She'd tried talking with him once. How could she possibly speak of it again?

She had to try. She had to do it for the child's sake, even if Night Wind's response caused her pain.

Rebecca cornered him outside his wigwam late at night when the others had gone to bed. She would have barged into his lodge if she'd had to, but as it was, he was returning from the forest when she saw him coming around toward the door from the back.

"Night Wind."

He glared at her and went to enter his wigwam.

She grabbed his arm. "Night Wind, please!"

He tensed beneath her fingers, but she refused to let go. *"E'kaliu'.* Go away. I wish not to talk."

"Maata!" she cried. "I must speak with you." Her stomach burned like fire. Tears filled her eyes, making them sting.

"I do not wish to speak with you!" he said, breaking away. He spun and, instead of going inside, he walked away in the opposite direction.

"Tipaakke Shaakha!" she called. "You did not tell

me that if Gift From Forest dies, Dark Eagle will be chief."

He froze, his back stiffening, and slowly faced her. "Why should it matter?"

"Because Angry Woman wants her son to be sachem! How far will she go to see that he is?" Rebecca challenged him, her blue eyes bright with tears. "As far as murder?"

He came back and caught her shoulders. "Angry Woman would not murder."

"No?"

"Maata!" he exclaimed.

"Then why won't you watch her? Why won't you see if what I say is true? If I am wrong, then the only one who will be dishonored is me."

Night Wind released her. "Angry Woman would not kill," he said.

Did it sound as if his confidence was weakening?

She touched his arm. "Do you think I want to hurt you? That I intentionally make accusations to cause you pain? It's Gift From Forest that worries me. He's a wonderful child. He'll make a good chief." She paused. ". . . If he lives long enough to become one."

Twenty-six

The snow on the forest ground was melting. Night Wind bent and picked up some of the slushy substance, and it warmed and dripped through his fingers. The temperature was rare this early in the year. He frowned at the muddy path before him. Soon, the days would all be warm and the green would come: tiny buds on the bushes . . . leafy foliage on the trees. Then the grass would grow and there would be flowers lining the forest floor.

And Rebecca will want to leave, Night Wind thought. He'd been angry with her; he still was. She'd made bad accusations against one of his people, Angry Woman, but she'd been wrong. It had been days since she'd pleaded with him to listen, and Gift From Forest was alive and well.

Medicine Woman was wrong.

It was the early hours of the morning. The sun was not yet visible, which made the warm air all the more unusual. Night Wind couldn't sleep. He hadn't been sleeping well for a long while. *Since Medicine Woman left my sleeping mat,* he thought, angered by his feelings.

Why did she lie and tell him such things about Angry Woman? In defense of the woman, he had told Rebecca that Angry Woman wouldn't hurt anyone, which wasn't altogether the truth. But he'd been so sure that Ice From Sky's sister was innocent of murder.

Kill his brother? How could a Lenape mother kill one of their own children? The Lenape women loved and cared for all the children within the tribe, treating each of them lovingly as if they were their own. To think that a mother could kill a child so that another would take position of chief was—Night Wind's chest constricted painfully—*possible*. If someone wanted it badly enough. Which was why he was standing watch near Angry Woman's wigwam. That and the fact that he'd been noticing things about the woman lately. Disturbing things. Like the way she treated the other children of Turtle-Town.

His people would be rising soon. Beaver Hawk's wife, Moon On Water, would light the fire in the village center, and many of the women would go to the river to bathe. But not Angry Woman. Sister to Ice From Sky had always been an odd one, although he'd never questioned her loyalty before. Until now. Until Rebecca had planted the seed of doubt.

Smoke billowed heavily from the roof hole of Angry Woman's wigwam. Ice From Sky's sister must have stoked the fire in preparation for the day. She was up early, which surprised Night Wind. She usually slept later than the other women. He was further surprised when she left her wigwam, carrying a basket, and crossed the yard toward the woods.

Night Wind kept himself hidden as he observed her, then he followed her as she disappeared into the forest. He hung back, watching, as she stopped, set down her basket, and began to dig in the soil with a piece of deer antler. Angry Woman dug in several places, and he thought nothing of her behavior until her actions turned frantic. She appeared upset that she couldn't find what she needed. There must be others within the village who would share with her, he thought. Why was Angry Woman so upset?

He heard her exclaim harshly, and astonished by the curse, he tensed. In her fury, Angry Woman picked up her basket and threw it against a tree. Then, cursing, she retrieved the basket and stomped back to the wigwam.

Night Wind was right behind her. He stood outside her wigwam and listened.

"Onna," her son greeted.

Night Wind heard a crack and a whimper. Had she struck the boy?

"You are bad! Now I have little to make good broth, you fool! You will never make a good *sakima* if you do not listen to your *Onna*."

Appalled, the brave held back to see what she'd say next. He heard a second slap louder than the first. Night Wind burst into Angry Woman's wigwam, shocking both her and the boy.

"Tipa-ak-ke Sha-akha," she stuttered, "why are you here?"

"I was near when I heard someone cry out. I thought one of you was in trouble." He narrowed his gaze as he studied Dark Eagle, before transferring his attention to the child's mother. Angry Woman shifted uncomfortably under Night Wind's regard.

"Is something wrong?" the brave said.

"No," the woman said with a bluster, "nothing." She moved as if to block something with her body that she didn't want revealed.

"Dark Eagle," Night Wind asked. "What happened to your face?"

"The boy fell, *Tipaakke*. It is nothing; he will live."

Ignoring Angry Woman, Night Wind waved the child forward. After an anxious glance at his mother, Dark Eagle hesitated.

"Come here, boy," he said in a gentler tone. "I will not harm you. All within the village love you; we do not want to see you hurt."

Night Wind flashed the child's mother a look that warned Angry Woman that he knew the truth; she'd best beware.

Dark Eagle took several steps. Night Wind completed the distance and raised the boy's chin to inspect his face.

"Your cheek looks angry, little warrior."

"It is fine, Night Wind," the child said. "I am hurt, because I was clumsy."

Night Wind didn't believe that Dark Eagle had fallen. "We are all clumsy, ah?" He touched the cheek, and Dark Eagle flinched. "You must take care of this, Dark Eagle."

The child nodded. *"Onna* can fix it," he said, beaming.

His mother appeared relieved as she quickly agreed. "We are happy you are concerned, *Tipaakke,* but I know what to do for my *ne gwis."*

Dark Eagle, innocent of his actions, went behind his mother, picked up a bag, and held it up to show Night Wind. *"Onna* can make me broth," he said proudly, "just like she does for Gift From Forest." He was obviously pleased that he would finally have what his mother had fixed for Gift From Forest.

Night Wind saw Angry Woman's reaction. She appeared horrified by her son's words. "What is in the bag, Angry Woman?" he asked.

The woman snatched the bag from her son. "Only some special roots and herbs for my broth, *Tipaakke."* She looked nervous; her hands shook as she cradled the small satchel against her breasts.

"May I see?" Night Wind held out his hand.

"Maata!" Angry Woman exhaled sharply. "It is a matron's secret how she heals her children."

And how she hits them? Night Wind thought. Murders them?

"I asked to see the bag." He grabbed the satchel from Angry Woman's fingers.

"Maata!" She struggled frantically to get back the bag. "The medicine is mine. You have no right!"

"And because Dark Eagle is your son, does that give you special rights . . . like the right to strike him!"

Her strength was no match for his. Night Wind held tightly to the bag and waited patiently for Angry Woman to tire of the fight.

"I will go to Beaver Hawk," she threatened, releasing the bag.

"Good," he said. "Then together we will all see what is in the bag. What it is that Angry Woman must hide from her people."

Dark Eagle frowned as he came forward. "It is medicine, Night Wind," he defended his mother. "It smells bad, but it is goo—"

Angry Woman backhanded him across the jaw. "You bad child! This is your fault—all of it! I tried to make you chief, but you are too stupid to be *sakima!*"

Night Wind growled low as he caught the woman's arm. "Do not ever hit this child or any other, Angry Woman," he warned. "For this, you will appear before the council!"

"For disciplining my child?" she taunted, but he could tell she was afraid.

"That and for the death of my brother," he informed her. "And for attempting to kill Gift From Forest!"

Dark Eagle gasped. *"Onna,* tell him it isn't true. Tell him you were helping our brother! Tell him how you made Gift From Forest well!"

"You stupid child," his mother said, "are you blind? Do you know why I killed Red Fox? For you! For you to be chief!"

The child looked as if he'd been struck again, harder. "No, *Onna*," he whispered with horror.

"Yes! Yes, I did it and would have succeeded if not for you." Angry Woman glared at Night Wind. "And that slave—Medicine Woman!" Her face contorted with anger, and her hands clenched into fists. "She kept me from killing Gift From Forest. She guarded the boy like a *Mahx' W* protects her young!"

Then the woman went wild, screaming her words as she confessed what she'd done. She seemed to take pleasure in hurting her son with her words. Her shrill cries aroused others from their wigwams. There was a gathering waiting at her door when Night Wind emerged, dragging the cursing Angry Woman behind him. Dark Eagle followed, stunned. An old matron took one look at the child and pulled him into her comforting arms. The boy's broken sobs were drowned out by his mother's loud curses.

When the truth became known, Beaver Hawk, the village sachem, was summoned along with other members of council. The village residents gathered in the Big House, where the story was told in front of the whole tribe.

"Death!" was the cry about the village. "Death for Angry Woman!"

"Maata!" her son screamed. The woman had been evil and cruel to him, but she mustn't die. She was his *Onna!*

It was decided then to banish Angry Woman from *Tulpeuta-nai*. Ice From Sky, horrified by the revelation of Angry Woman's crime, refused to look at her sister while the decision was being discussed. A woman who could kill a mother's child was no sister, no kin to Ice From Sky. She was no member of the clan of the Turtle.

The child, Dark Eagle, was taken from the scene. Rebecca was called in to take Gift From Forest, Dark Eagle, and the other small children to the river where they could take their daily bath.

"It is not right that Angry Woman should live," Iron Bear said. The woman had made a fool of him, and he wanted to see her punished. He held up the matron's bag. "See this satchel. It contains root. Touch it and smell the odor. It is bad medicine! Poison! The poison she used to take Ice From Sky's first son!"

"We must not kill her for Dark Eagle's sake," some-one said. "We must not allow the child to suffer for his mother's deeds."

"But the boy helped her!" another said. "He brought broth to Gift From Forest!"

"But the child is innocent," Night Wind said. "He thought only to please Angry Woman and help Gift From Forest. He wanted his *Onna* to make the broth for him."

"Banishment alone is not punishment," Feather Coat, one of the ceremonial drummers, said. "Angry Woman should know what she has done. Medicine Woman was cast out into the forest for her failure to heal. Angry Woman intentionally killed. She wanted to kill again. Her punishment should be greater than Medicine Woman's."

Beaver Hawk stared at his sister with disgust. Angry Woman had taken the life of his loved one. Throughout the proceedings, Angry Woman had cursed at his people. She was no longer a member of his village . . . a member of his family.

"Angry Woman will suffer the loss of her hands," he said as a hush came over the crowd. "She will be cast into the wilderness to make her way with no fingers to find food or build shelter. If the spirits are wise, they will spare her no mercy as she spared no mercy for our beloved sons. If it pleases the gods, let her soul wander forever in the dark regions of this earth."

Angry Woman screamed.

Everyone else cheered Beaver Hawk's decision. Night Wind was silent; his concern was for the sachem's other sister. Ice From Sky had lost her son, had almost lost her youngest, and now she had no sister. How much pain could one endure?

Angry Woman went wild at her brother's decision. She cursed and hit and kicked the two braves who held her captive by her arms. She saw Iron Bear approach with his sharp flint-head ax, and she thrashed about in terror.

Ice From Sky turned away. Night Wind went to her, meeting his father's gaze with sadness as Wood Owl stood next to his wife.

"M' hoo' kum a . . ."

She glanced at Night Wind and then toward the square. Angry Woman's cries had become screams as she was dragged off into the woods.

Ice From Sky was visibly shaken when she met Night Wind's gaze. *"Tipaakke."* She attempted to smile at her husband's son. "Thank you for saving *ne gwis."*

Night Wind's face was solemn. "That is what I must talk with you about, *M' hoo' kum a.* I did not save your son."

The high-pitched wail of pain reached Rebecca and the children at the river. Rebecca wanted to block out the sound with her hands, but she didn't want to upset the children, especially Dark Eagle and Gift From Forest.

Her eyes settled on Angry Woman's son. He stared at her with dark eyes that were teary and pain-filled. The other children, who had bathed and were playing a game with Sun Blossom and another Indian maiden, seemed oblivious to the woman's tortured cries.

How often did these children hear such sounds that they could remain unaffected?

Dark Eagle was affected. It was his mother's wild screams.

Rebecca's face softened with sympathy. She opened her arms to the boy. Dark Eagle ran to her, dissolving into tears, as she held him close. The other Lenape children started to tease and taunt Dark Eagle until Gift From Forest, their future sachem, ordered them to be quiet in a very adultlike manner. Rebecca sent Ice From Sky's child a silent message of gratitude. The boy smiled back and then organized another game to keep the children occupied.

Rebecca flinched at the *thud* and the blood-curdling scream that followed. When it happened again, she clutched Dark Eagle tightly, her hands over the boy's ears.

Tears came to her eyes at the child's agony, but when she remembered that the woman screaming had killed Red Fox and had tried to murder Gift From Forest—and she had abused her own son, she felt no sympathy for the woman's pain. Angry Woman deserved it and more. It was a miracle, she thought, that the Indians hadn't killed her. She wondered how long it was going to take before it was over, how much longer she'd have to keep the children here.

A group of matrons approached. One of them was Ice From Sky.

Twenty-seven

Rebecca released the boy as Ice From Sky came to her. Dark Eagle was embraced by the old matron, Laughing Eyes.

"Medicine Woman."

"Ice From Sky," the Englishwoman murmured, her heart pounding. "Are you all right?" The Indian woman nodded. "I am sorry for your pain."

The matron looked surprised. "The one who hurt my sons is found. I am glad."

"But your sister—"

"I have no sister."

Rebecca looked away. "Yes, of course."

"Night Wind tells me it is you who discovered the truth. He says you protected my son when the rest of us were blind."

Night Wind said that? Rebecca thought, amazed. "Night Wind found out what happened. I had no proof." She bit her lip.

"But you told my husband's son about your fears. You watched my son like the hungry hawk watches a rabbit."

Rebecca's laughter was soft. "I never thought about eating your son."

To the Englishwoman's pleasure, Ice From Sky smiled. "That is good." Her expression became solemn.

"I wanted to tell you."

"But who would believe a slave?"

Rebecca inclined her head.

"I wish to thank you for your help, Reb-bec-ca," Ice From Sky said. "In return for your honor, I wish to give you a gift."

"It's not necessary—"

"Your freedom."

Rebecca's heart skipped a beat. "Freedom," she whispered.

"From being slave," the Indian woman said. "I wish instead that you become my daughter—a true daughter of the Lenape Turtle band."

The white woman was touched—and elated. She would finally have what she desired. As a daughter of the Lenape, she'd have the freedom to come and go just as she would have if she'd been adopted into the Iroquois Cayuga tribe!

"I am deeply moved by your gift, Ice From Sky. But what of the others? What does the Council think?"

"This is my decision. I have spoken with Beaver Hawk, and he agrees." The Lenape woman gave her a slow smile. "There is more to the gift."

Rebecca was overwhelmed. What more could they possibly give her?

"The matrons of my village have spoken. Night Wind likes Medicine Woman," the woman said, and Rebecca blushed. "Ice From Sky believes that Medicine Woman finds Night Wind a handsome brave." She hesitated. "You follow him with your eyes." Rebecca's cheeks burned.

"It is our choice that *Tipaakke Shaakha* of the Wolf Clan and Medicine Woman of the Turtle Clan will marry, and that their children will run happily and freely about our village, bringing joy and hope into our people's hearts."

Marry Night Wind? Rebecca's stomach tightened. "But Night Wind—"

"He will agree when we tell him. He will honor our choice." She paused. "And he will make Medicine Woman good husband."

"But marriage?" the white woman gasped.

"You do not like *Tipaakke Shaakha?*" She Who Sees Much said. She sounded offended.

"No—I mean, yes, I like him . . ."

The village matrons exchanged grins. "Then it is done!" Laughing Eyes said. She hugged Dark Eagle closer and stroked his hair. "Medicine Woman will marry *Tipaakke Shaakha,* and the two will live together in peace and love."

Love? Rebecca thought. Night Wind desired her. He didn't love her. He hated her; his recent treatment of her showed her that. *He won't want to marry me, and I can't possibly marry him!* She had to leave and find Elizabeth. An Indian husband wasn't included in her plans.

"Go," Ice From Sky instructed. "Go to the wigwam and we will come for you."

Rebecca hesitated, concerned.

The matron touched her arm. "You must first become daughter of Turtle band."

"Yes," the white woman agreed. She wanted to become a daughter of the Lenape. It was the only way she'd obtain the freedom to leave.

How could she be free if she were married to Night Wind? It wasn't that she didn't care for him. But how could she go?

And she didn't want a reluctant husband. Yes, she and Night Wind had been wonderful together while she shared his sleeping mat, but husband and wife? Forever and after?

Night Wind will not want marriage and that is good,

for *it will make it easier to convince the others . . . to leave when it is time.*

Rebecca was in the wigwam, anxiously awaiting Ice From Sky, when Sun Blossom came to the door. She stood and eyed the Indian maiden warily. "Sun Blossom."

To her astonishment, the young woman smiled. "You must come with me, Medicine Woman."

"Where?"

Sun Blossom wouldn't answer.

"No," Rebecca said, digging in her heels. "I won't go until I know where you're taking me."

The maiden grinned. "You must not be alarmed. Ice From Sky wishes to thank you for saving little *sakima.*" She hesitated and looked slightly shamefaced. "Sun Blossom thanks you for saving *sakima* child."

Did Sun Blossom not know what the matrons had in mind for Rebecca? Was that why the maiden was being nice, because she was unaware of the women's decision that Rebecca and Night Wind would marry?

"Come. Ice From Sky awaits." Sun Blossom's look became knowing. "Night Wind awaits. Your future husband."

"You are not angry?"

The Indian maiden shook her head. "I am to marry Thunder Arrow. He is good brave. He is of the Wolf clan like *Tipaakke Shaakha.*" Her expression was soft. "He is handsome Lenape."

Rebecca blinked. "I am happy for you."

The girl grinned. "And I am happy for White Medicine Woman."

The Englishwoman was taken to the river where all of the women of Turtle-Town had gathered to wait for her. Ice From Sky smiled in greeting as she came forward.

"Medicine Woman," she said. "I am glad you are

here. You have come so that we may prepare you to become Lenape daughter."

Rebecca saw that the village women included young girls barely into their teens. She studied their faces; she attempted to smile, but failed. She was too nervous. She had an idea of why she was here. The Iroquois adoption ceremony of a female included a communal bathing ceremony, during which the matrons of the tribe washed and prepared the one who was to become the daughter.

Rebecca had been kidnapped before she'd gone through any part of the Cayuga adoption ceremony, but she'd bathed often with the Iroquois women. She'd never before been the focus of such attention, however, while unclothed. The thought of being stripped of her tunic and inspected by all the women who were present made her uncomfortable. Still, she would gladly endure it for her freedom.

The other women removed their clothing while Ice From Sky along with She Who Sees Much helped Rebecca out of her garments. It was warm for the season, but it was early March. As the air brushed her naked body, Rebecca's skin rose like feather-plucked gooseflesh. She covered her breasts with her arms, for her nipples rose with the cold, and she was self-conscious. Her embarrassment faded when she saw that the other women were all in the same condition.

While Sun Blossom smeared red paint on Rebecca's cheeks, Ice From Sky and She Who Sees Much took off their own deerskin capes and skirts. Sleeping Turtle, the young girl who had brought Rebecca water while the Englishwoman was tending Red Fox, placed about Rebecca's neck several necklaces of shells and beads like those found in their wampum belts. Then the girl combed the white woman's long, silky dark hair with a porcupine tail.

When she was adorned to the matron's satisfaction, Rebecca was led into the cold river water until she was waist deep. She gasped and shivered. Her skin turned slightly blue. The Indian women seemed oblivious to the chill. Since the advent of winter, Rebecca had been heating water for washing over the fire in the wigwam, and amused, Ice From Sky had allowed her to bathe inside. But now Rebecca was to become a Lenape; from this day she'd be expected to honor the practicing of bathing in the river, no matter the time of year, unless the water had turned to ice.

The women surrounded Rebecca, laughing and chatting, and it was much like their normal bathing routine. Ice From Sky dipped below the surface of the water, bending until she was submerged up to her neck, and she gathered sand from the river bottom. She Who Sees Much followed suit, her copper-colored breasts bobbing to the surface, as she rose. Then, the two women used the sand to scrub Rebecca's body until her skin became pink.

Rebecca gasped at the friction, but it warmed her. When the women were done, they dunked her completely—red paint, jewelry, and all—pulling her up to wash her hair. She was so cold, her teeth chattered, but she knew that it was almost over.

Ice From Sky and She Who Sees Much then escorted Rebecca to the shore. While the others followed, the youngsters giggling, Rebecca was dried and wrapped in blankets and furs. She was seated on a rock next to the water, and she waited, shivering, for them to tell her that she was done.

Wilting Flower, the oldest matron in the village, came forward. She had a grease bag, which she handed to Ice From Sky. Rebecca closed her eyes and raised her face, thinking that the woman was going to coat her skin with bear's grease. Wilting Flower caught up Rebecca's hair instead, and the white woman lifted her lashes and tilted her head back as she waited for another practice—to have her hair rubbed lightly with the grease.

The matron rubbed Rebecca's hair dry and then combed it from her face. Wilting Flower's hands on her hair and scalp were soothing, and Rebecca shut her eyes. Suddenly, the woman's fingers were at her right ear. Rebecca felt a sharp needle-prick pain as Wilting Flower pierced her ear with an awl made from a thin sliver of deer bone. She endured the same to her other ear. The matron greased two short lengths of sinew and threaded them through the holes in Rebecca's ears. When the old woman was done, Rebecca's earlobes were burning and throbbing with pain.

The Englishwoman endured it without complaint. She saw that the women were smiling at her, pleased. Except for her lighter skin, she looked and acted like a true daughter of the Lenape.

"Rise," Wilting Flower instructed. Rebecca rose.

She Who Sees Much took off Rebecca's blankets and furs, and Ice From Sky slipped a lovely white doeskin tunic over Rebecca's head. The soft sleeveless garment fell over her breasts and brushed her hips. The fringed hem came to below her knees.

She Who Sees Much adjusted Rebecca's necklaces, pulling them from beneath the tunic so that they could be seen. Sun Blossom gave Rebecca a copper bracelet, which the maiden slid up Rebecca's bare arm. Sleeping Turtle tapped Rebecca's foot, and Rebecca raised first one and then the other while the girl put moccasins on her feet. Sleeping Turtle exclaimed at the beauty of Ice From Sky's handiwork.

Rebecca was ready for the ceremony in the Big House.

The whole tribe was assembled in the Big House.

Rebecca was conscious of being the focus of all eyes as she was led inside. Beaver Hawk, the village chief, stood in the center of the large room between the two poles with the painted faces and the two firepits. Iron Bear was behind him, looking—much to Rebecca's surprise—pleased.

She felt one person's regard more than the rest, and she turned toward the east and the Wolf clan. Rebecca saw Night Wind seated next to Deer-That-Runs, the look in *Tipaakke*'s ebony eyes intense as he stared at her. She had not seen him since the last council meeting, and she had not spoken to him since the night when she'd tried to make him see that Angry Woman was dangerous.

Did he know about the marriage? Was that why he was staring at her so strangely?

Shaken, Rebecca looked away. *I don't want to marry him.* But the thought rang hollow like an untruth.

She was placed directly in the center of the long ceremonial building. Beaver Hawk announced why they were all here as Iron Bear took Rebecca's shoulders to turn her to the west so that she faced her new clan.

Rebecca tried not to react as she felt the pressure of the shaman's hands, and she must have been successful, for as he positioned himself beside her, he didn't appear to be angry.

Beaver Hawk addressed his people, directing most of his statement to his own clan—the *Po-ko-un'go* or Turtle band.

"Who takes this woman as proud daughter?" he asked.

Ice From Sky rose from her seat in the west section of the Big House. "I, *M'hoo'kum a,* take this woman as daughter," she announced loudly. Iron Bear moved, and the matron came to stand in his place at Rebecca's side.

"Who is she to replace?" Iron Bear asked in a booming voice.

"She will replace my first son, who died by the hands of another," Ice From Sky answered.

"Who will speak for this woman to be daughter of the Lenape?" Beaver Hawk said.

She Who Sees Much rose. "I speak for her!" she exclaimed. The matron joined the other two women in the center of the room.

Beaver Hawk was satisfied. He spoke to the three women as he stood before them. "New Daughter of the Lenape, you shall be of the Turtle clan. Your blood will be of mine and my sister will be your mother. Is this acceptable to you?" he asked Rebecca.

"It is acceptable." She Who Sees Much spoke for her as was intended.

"Ice From Sky," Beaver Hawk asked, "how will she be named?" He turned and his gaze encompassed the entire tribe. "How will she be named?"

"Medicine Woman!" someone cried out.

"No, White Healer!" decided another.

Night Wind stood. *"Shi'kiXkwe,"* he said.

Woman of Beauty. *Pretty Woman.*

A child snickered, and his mother quickly silenced him. Rebecca wasn't insulted, for she knew that by the Indians' standards, she fell far short of beautiful. Night Wind was the only Indian who had considered her beautiful, and now he wanted everyone to call her such . . . Rebecca was deeply moved.

Beaver Hawk listened to the suggestions of names and then asked Ice From Sky for her thoughts. "Sister, how shall you call her?"

"I agree with Night Wind," she said. "I will call

her *Shi'kiXkwe*. My daughter has many beautiful qualities that make a woman proud to be called *Onna*."

Rebecca's eyes filled with tears. A lump rose to tighten her throat as she glanced at the brave who had stood up for her and spoken.

"Then let it be so!" Beaver Hawk proclaimed. "From this moment on, the white woman, Reb-bec-ca Mor-ton," he said, stumbling over her English name, "shall be white no more, but a true daughter of the Lenape. A daughter we shall call *Shi'kiXkwe*. Let us all wish Pretty Woman a long and happy life. May we all love and accept *Shi'kiXkwe* as member of the *Po-ko-un'go*, family to your sachem!"

Twenty-eight

"Pretty Woman, what is wrong?" her new adoptive mother whispered.

Rebecca gave her a slight smile. "There is nothing wrong, *Onna*," she said, keeping her voice soft.

"It is Night Wind," the older woman said perceptively. "He has said little to you."

It was late. The Indians had gone to their wigwams. Wood Owl and Gift From Forest were asleep. Rebecca couldn't sleep. She sat by the fire with Ice From Sky. This was the first night that Rebecca was a daughter of the Lenape, and Night Wind hadn't said a word to her.

"I haven't spoken with him," Rebecca said.

"Ah . . ." Her Indian mother's voice sounded knowing. "He will come."

"Does he know?" Why did she care if he knew about the proposed marriage? What did it matter when she wasn't going to marry him?

"Maybe," Ice From Sky replied. "Maybe not."

Rebecca stared into the flames. "I want to thank you for . . ." Her gaze met her Indian mother's, ". . . You've been kind."

The woman's expression was soft. "I am glad to have a daughter." They exchanged smiles.

Ice From Sky scrambled to her feet and added wood to the fire from the stack beneath her sleeping platform. A log rolled and jarred the others, making noise. *Tahuun Kukuus* and his son slept on, undisturbed.

"These men," she said, "they fight hard and play hard. This one of mine sleeps hard, too." She regarded her husband with affection.

Ice From Sky pulled off her tunic and slipped naked beneath her husband's blanket. "Are you coming to sleep?" she asked Rebecca.

Rebecca had looked away while Ice From Sky was undressing. Would she ever get used to the Indian's openness? At her new mother's question, she tore her gaze from the fire. "Not yet," she said. "But soon."

"You must not worry about *Tipaakke Shaakha,*" her mother advised. "He will come for you."

A while later when Ice From Sky had gone to sleep, Rebecca was still awake. She hadn't moved from her seat next to the fire. She watched the way the flames danced in the firepit, and she closed her eyes to listen. It was a peaceful time, a time for reflection. With no sounds within the compound but for the sound of Wood Owl's snores, it was a time for Rebecca to come to terms with the fact that she'd soon be leaving Turtle-Town to find Elizabeth.

She thought of her mother—her real mother in New York, and she wondered how the woman was faring. Had word filtered back to her of her daughter's disappearance? It had been months; it must have, she realized with a painful pang.

Dear God, had her mother grieved for her, believing her dead? *Poor mother, has she gotten over the shock, the pain?*

She blinked back tears. "Mother," she whispered, "I'm sorry you're suffering. But I'm alive . . . and these last months—it hasn't been too terrible."

The tears escaped to dampen her cheeks, and Rebecca rubbed them away with the back of her hand.

She sniffed, and her gaze fell on her fingers. Her hands looked no worse than before she was captured by the Indians. She'd always worked hard in the New York Colony, helping her mother to keep money in the house and food on the table.

"You might think that the Indians live like animals," she mouthed as if speaking directly to her mother, "but they don't." She smiled. "Some of the Indians might seem like savages, but they are people, Mother. The women, here in the village, are treated well. Better than Mr. Brennick treats his wife. Better than most of the families we know." Her smile widened. "You and Aunt Veronica were strong, independent women. I believe you would enjoy the Lenape way of life."

Rebecca yawned and stood. She had best get to bed before it was time to get up. Tomorrow she would talk with Night Wind. Find out what was bothering him so much that he avoided her. She climbed into bed, pulling the furs to cover herself. She closed her eyes, crossed her arms over her chest, and attempted to go to sleep. Then, she heard the sound. She thought she was imagining it, but the noise came again. The sweet melodic trill of a musical instrument. It came from directly outside the wigwam on the other side of the wall from her bed.

Night Wind. The brave was playing the *a'pi'kan* for her. He was courting her, wooing her with his music. The notes rose and fell, making her shiver. She sat up and hugged her knees, listening, and debated whether or not she should go outside.

Rebecca lay down again. It wasn't the Lenape custom to go outside. What if she was wrong and it wasn't Night Wind? She closed her eyes, enjoying the strange melody and was soothed by the dulcet tones.

It *was* Night Wind, and he was courting her!

Did that mean he was interested in the marriage?

She should speak with him and find out, before all within the village knew that she'd rejected him. . . .

She didn't know what to do! Rebecca was torn between loving Night Wind and her desire to help Veronica's child. Elizabeth had been through too much; she needed a stable home—an English home. How could she marry Night Wind?

As if he'd sensed her dilemma, Night Wind changed his playing. The new song created images for Rebecca of the times they had made love.

Night Wind stroked her with his music. He caressed her with each note, soothing away her fears, so that finally Rebecca slept her dreams filled with visions of the handsome brave.

The next morning Rebecca woke up, wondering if she'd imagined the flute. Had the music been real? And had it been Night Wind, expressing his feelings— his desire—for her to be his wife?

Her new Indian family said nothing. Either the flute had been a figment of Rebecca's dreams or Ice From Sky and the others had slept through the music. How was she going to know if it had been real or a part of her dreams?

Ice From Sky was preparing for a visit to the sweat lodge. Rebecca rose with the thought that now that she was a daughter of the Lenape, she'd be expected to join her Indian mother in the steam. Ice From Sky went outside while Rebecca gathered some things to follow her. The matron returned within seconds, her face beaming.

"A present has been left for the mother of Pretty Woman," she said, holding up several blankets. "From *Tipaakke.*"

"Night Wind?" Rebecca asked, feeling breathless. She tried to see past the half-opened door flap for a glimpse of the brave.

"Thunder Arrow brought gift on behalf of Night Wind. It is Lenape custom." Ice From Sky studied her new daughter with a smile. "Night Wind has requested to marry you."

Rebecca's stomach flipflopped.

Ice from Sky's smile was knowing. "Last night," she said, "I hear the *a'pi'kan* of Night Wind. He plays for my daughter, Pretty Woman."

"You heard it, too," Rebecca murmured, stunned by the fact that the music had been real. She flushed, embarrassed by her reaction to his songs. Had Ice From Sky heard and guessed how . . . moved . . . she'd been? "I thought I was dreaming," she confessed.

Her new mother laughed softly. "The music was real, my daughter." She paused and handed Rebecca the blankets. "As these are real. As *Tipaakke* is a handsome brave."

Rebecca's cheeks burned brighter.

Ice From Sky became serious. "You must think and decide, Pretty Woman. Night Wind would make good husband, but it is your decision."

Night Wind had been playing his flute for her! She thought as she followed Ice From Sky to the sweat lodge. Did that mean he truly wanted to marry her? Or was he "courting" her because he'd been told he must?

As Rebecca stripped off her tunic, her mind whirled. She heard giggling and saw two young girls watching her. Her first instinct was to cover herself with her arms.

"Last night they heard *Tipaakke*'s music," her Indian mother said. "They knew it was for you."

Rebecca was embarrassed. Did everyone in the village know that Night Wind was paying court? How? When even she herself hadn't been sure?

She didn't see him until that afternoon when he was in the yard, helping himself to something to eat from the community cooking pot. Her heart leapt to her throat. Would he say something to her? She grabbed a bowl and went to the community pot. Night Wind glanced at her briefly and then looked away.

Rebecca's heart pounded like a rhythmic Lenape drum as she took some food—beans and corn with broth. She flashed him a look out of the corner of her eye as she headed back to her wigwam. Her breath quickened when she realized that he was staring at her. He didn't smile when she turned, he just watched, and Rebecca's stomach insides burned as she wondered if the others were mistaken. He didn't look like someone who was studying the one he wanted to marry. He appeared . . . curious. Yes, she thought, like he was trying to read her mind and perhaps understand her.

Why did it feel as if they were strangers when they'd lived together, slept together, and shared the most intimate act of loving between a man and woman? Why didn't he approach? *Why don't I?* she wondered.

Rebecca turned on her heel and headed back. Night Wind was speaking now with Thunder-Arrow, Sun Blossom's intended. Thunder Arrow saw her and said something to Night Wind while gesturing in her direction. She saw Night Wind stiffen and then turn to face her as she was near.

"Thunder Arrow," she greeted the other brave first. *"Tipaakke,"* she murmured. "May I speak with you?"

Night Wind nodded, and Thunder Arrow left the two alone. Rebecca saw the children playing in the yard. Dogs ran about, yapping and howling. Suddenly, the village center seemed noisy and a terrible place to talk.

"Come," he said, as if reading her mind. "We will walk in the forest."

She fell into step beside him. They were both quiet as they left the village for the woods. Rebecca felt the tension between them, and she wondered from where it had come.

They walked for awhile, the earth dry beneath their feet. The air temperature was warm. There was a scent about them that reminded Rebecca of spring. It called to mind that she must soon leave Turtle-Town. She had to find Elizabeth.

Rebecca stopped. "Night Wind."

He halted as soon as she had. He waited silently for her to speak. His ebony eyes glistened. She admired his features . . . the masculine nose . . . his angular jaw . . . the lips that she knew could bring her wild pleasure. Her gaze brushed briefly on the tiny star-shaped scar.

"Is it true?" she asked, sounding out of breath. "Did—you—play the flute for me?"

His gaze flamed as he inclined his head.

"And you gave the gift?"

He again nodded.

"But you know I have to leave," she said. "There's Elizabeth to consider—"

"I know this."

"They why are you . . ." She blushed. "Courting me?"

"It is destined that we must marry."

"But I can't marry you!" She caught his arm, embarrassed by how badly she was handling the conversation. "It's not that I don't find you . . . attractive. And you know we . . ." Her cheeks burned. "We . . ."

He smiled. "We enjoy sharing sleeping mat."

"Yes," she said, nodding vigorously. "We enjoy sharing a mat."

"Then what is bad for us to marry?" he asked.

"I have to leave!"

"Why?" he said.

"Because Elizabeth needs me!" she cried with frustration.

"Elizabeth can come to Turtle-Town."

Her pulse jumped. "She's English. She'd been through a great deal. I don't think—"

"We are to marry." He frowned.

"I can't," she whispered.

"If I help you find Elizabeth, then you will take me to husband?"

Rebecca opened her mouth to refuse. She loved him. Why shouldn't she have him for a little while? *Because it will hurt worse when it's time to part.*

But could she find Elizabeth without him? He knew the forest and would protect her. Why shouldn't she let him help her? Why shouldn't they marry . . . for a little while?

"I will marry you, and you can help me. But I cannot promise to stay." She had to be honest; she wouldn't intentionally deceive him for her own purpose. "I have to think of Elizabeth," she told him. "What's best for her."

He stared at her, his jaw tense. A muscle ticked at his temple. He nodded, an abrupt jerk of his head, which said that he agreed, but he wasn't happy.

"We will marry," he said, as if a deal had been made and agreed upon by both.

Two days later, Rebecca found herself being dressed and adorned for her wedding to Night Wind. Each night since he'd first played for her, his music had come again, and so had another gift to her Indian family each morning that followed.

She wore the doeskin dress that Ice From Sky had made her, and which she had worn for the first time at her adoption ceremony. After bathing, Ice From Sky had brushed Rebecca's hair until it crackled and shone. When She Who Sees Much handed Rebecca's Indian mother a wooden bowl filled with bear's grease, Ice From Sky pushed it away. Rebecca's hair looked pretty enough like it was, she said.

Rebecca's ears were still sore from the piercing. Each day, Ice From Sky had doctored the area with a salve made from the Tamarack plant.

"I wish you could wear bead earrings," her new mother said. "But ears not healed enough yet."

The bride was given bracelets and necklaces and a fancy hair comb, which Ice From Sky put in her hair. Her cheeks were smeared with red pigment, after the women had dusted Rebecca's face with a powder of finely ground dried corn.

When Rebecca was ready, everyone left the wigwam except Ice From Sky.

"Daughter," the woman said, "you have chosen wisely. Night Wind will make good husband. He is fine brave, mighty warrior. Many maidens would wish to be in your place."

Rebecca murmured her agreement and waited with racing heart for her Indian mother to continue.

"In Lenape tribe," Ice From Sky said, "it is the woman and man who perform ceremony. I asked you to make *sa'pan,* because it is part of marriage. You must take *sa'pan* to Night Wind's wigwam, and he will eat, and then you will eat, sharing from the same bowl. Then you will be husband and wife."

"Here," her Indian mother said, "I wore this arm band on day I married Wood Owl. It belonged to my *Onna.* Now it will belong to my daughter, Pretty Woman."

Rebecca accepted the arm band, which was made of copper. It was beautifully crafted with a design hammered into the metal. She studied the gift, her eyes filling with tears. This woman had been wonderful to her. She would never forget Ice From Sky's kindness after she left Turtle-Town. Her first thought, however, was that she should refuse the arm band. It wouldn't be fair to Ice From Sky to take the arm band and then leave. But she knew she'd hurt her Indian mother much worse by not accepting. Rebecca made a silent promise to give the arm band to her own daughter someday just as Ice From Sky had given it to her.

"Wa-nee'shih," she murmured, her blue eyes misting.

Ice From Sky smiled. "Go. Go and find your brave. He is waiting for you."

Rebecca paused at the door, removed the bracelets, and put on only the copper arm band. It felt warm as it encircled her bare upper arm. Then, she went to get married.

Twenty-nine

The woman stumbled, and the Cayuga war party heard her as she fell.

"Black Horn," a brave exclaimed, "over here. It is a woman!" He kicked her, rolling her over with his foot.

She groaned as she flipped over, and the brave and his war chief saw her arms. Bloody stumps. Someone had cut off her hands.

The two Iroquois eyed her curiously. "Old woman," the young brave called to her. "Old woman, who are you? Why are you here?"

Black Horn, the Cayuga party's war chief, narrowed his gaze. "She cannot understand you," he said, as the woman moaned. "She is not one of us. She is of the 'stutterers,' I think."

The brave drew his knife. "I will kill her then!"

"No," Black Horn said. "We will find out why she is here. Why she has no hands." His gaze sought the young warrior's. "She can be useful to us. It is the stutterers who took Medicine Woman. This woman," he said with a hint of disgust at her soiled condition, "will help us find her."

The younger man's eyes gleamed. "I will carry her over to the fire."

Black Horn nodded. A smile slowly curved his mouth, for he was sure her people had done this to her. The Cayuga would not have bothered to spare her life. If the Lenape had done this to her, she would want vengeance. He would use her anger to get information, to find Medicine Woman. And if he was wrong and the woman's people were not responsible for her condition, there were ways, he thought, to make someone talk.

When she entered the wigwam, the first thing Rebecca noticed were the gifts: wooden bowls and blankets, firewood, furs, and food. Ice From Sky had divided the gifts brought to her by members of Night Wind's clan, giving them to those of the Turtle clan, who in turn gave the gifts to the bride and groom.

Her gaze fell on the sleeping platform and the huge pile of soft furs that cushioned the wood and made the bed comfortable. Rebecca recalled the last time she'd slept there, and her abdomen tingled at the memory. Loving Night Wind had been an experience that surpassed all others. But would it be different once she was his wife?

What on earth had prompted her to agree to marry him? Would he really help her to find Elizabeth? It wasn't that he'd have power over her by marrying her, unlike the white women under English law. If an Indian wife wasn't satisfied with her husband, she could put an end to the marriage by simply putting his belongings outside the wigwam. Of course, she didn't own a wigwam, Rebecca thought. If she wanted, she could have one built, she supposed.

Night Wind had been called outside by his father, Wood Owl. He came in as she was studying the gifts. Her whole being recognized her attraction to him. She didn't realize until this moment how much she wanted Night Wind, wanted to marry him.

Rebecca turned slowly to face him. His eyes shone brightly as he approached. The flickering light from the fire danced across his features, making him more beautiful to her. She waited with suspended breath for him to touch her. She wanted to touch him, but didn't. The silence lengthened until Rebecca knew that she must say something.

"I've brought *sa'pan*," she said, gesturing toward the pot on the fire. She felt foolish; he'd seen the pot. Of course, she'd brought *sa'pan*. She was here to marry him.

Night Wind sat on a mat next to the fire and waved for her to sit next to him. Rebecca knelt on the same mat and sat back. Should she serve him? She should have asked her Indian mother more questions about what to do.

She was so nervous her hands were shaking. She had known this man intimately. Why couldn't she relax?

Because you don't marry a man every day!

She spooned some *sa'pan* from the pot into a bowl and set it on the mat before him. Night Wind picked up the bowl and, holding her gaze, he dipped his spoon into the hominy and raised it to her lips. Rebecca tasted it. He stared at her mouth as she ate the *sa'pan* and then at her throat as she swallowed her food.

Her skin tingling, Rebecca reached for his hands and gently removed the bowl and spoon, her fingers caressing him as she did so. Passion flared in his features, and she felt an answering jolt of fire in her body and limbs. She fed him much as he'd fed her. Her gaze watched him as he consumed the hominy. They fed each other alternately until all of the *sa'pan* in the bowl was finished.

"Nux ah o shum," Night Wind murmured.

Her breath caught. My wife, he'd said.

"Neet il ose," she whispered with a smile.

He grinned at her, and she felt as if the wedding was meant to be. The marriage might be temporary, but she would love this man forever.

Night Wind set down the empty bowl and stood. He held out his hand to her and she took it. Her new husband assisted her to her feet and led her to their sleeping platform. He seemed in no great hurry, although it was the final part of the ceremony, binding their ties with physical love. Rebecca felt no urgency to rush now that he was hers.

She studied the beloved plains of his face . . . his eyes . . . the tiny scar on his cheek. She outlined it with her finger, her touch feather-light.

"How did you get this scar?" As his wife, it was her right to know more about him. In an Iroquois attack? she wondered. A bear hunt?

His mouth twitched as if he'd read her mind. "I got it as a boy . . . playing snowsnake."

"Snowsnake?" She wasn't disappointed to hear how he had gotten the scar. She'd watched Gift From Forest play the game with the other children. The image of Night Wind as a child fascinated her. She wished she'd known him then, and wondered if his son would look as he had. Pain constricted her chest. *His son.* Who would carry her husband's son? Not she . . . she would be leaving Turtle-Town.

Rebecca hated the thought of him touching, loving another woman. She was already jealous. She closed her eyes to hide her feelings.

Night Wind caressed her cheek. "Wife, why do you look so hurt?"

Her lashes fluttered open. She forced a smile. "I was thinking about Elizabeth."

His features darkened. "I will help you to find her,"

he said, sounding offended that she'd doubted his word.

She cupped his face, stroking his jaw soothingly. "I know, my husband," she said. "I do not doubt your word." She swallowed as she looked away. "Actually I was thinking of your son." *Our son,* she thought, *the one we will never have together.*

"And this causes you pain?"

She shook her head. *"Maata, Tipaakke.* I long for the day I can hold our child."

He pulled her into his embrace. "I too long for such a day, my wife." He kissed her and the world beneath her eyelids exploded into a flash of bright color.

"Shi'ki," he murmured as he raised his head. "Woman of beauty."

"Why did you tell the tribe that I should be named Pretty Woman?" she asked in English, suddenly struck by the memory. "You know that your people don't believe I'm pretty."

"Our people," he corrected her in Lenape. His fingers toyed with her hair. He played with the little tendrils that had escaped the hair comb at her nape. "You are pretty," he said. "Every Lenape brave thinks so."

"No," she scolded with a smile, "I don't believe that."

He returned her grin. "Every Lenape brave that matters." His hand brushed the length of her hair to the hair comb, which he pulled, allowing her dark silky strands to fall free.

"I wish to see you on my sleeping mat," he said huskily. His fingers reached for the hem of her tunic. With her cooperation, he lifted it from her body. Then, he stood back and removed his own clothes.

The warmth of the fire caressed Rebecca's naked body. She stood proudly, her breasts full and her nipples erect. His gaze glittered with fire as it brushed the nest of soft black curls shielding her womanhood.

"Come, wife." He held out his arms. "Let us be one."

Without shame, Rebecca went to lie with her new husband.

The Indians came in the night. Rebecca heard the first wild cry and woke up believing the Mohawk were attacking. She sprang out of bed.

"Night Wind!"

"Iroquois!" he said. He was up and grabbing his weapons. "Stay, *Shi'ki!* Do not leave *week-wam.*"

Their gazes met, and he kissed her hard. Then, he ran into the yard, naked, protected only by his knife and his spear.

Rebecca searched the wigwam for something to fight with and found Night Wind's bow and quiver of arrows. With shaking fingers, she notched the arrow onto the bowstring. Pulling the sinew back, she tested the feel of the weapon. She was inexperienced with the bow, but she felt she could use it.

Screams filled the compound. Her heart racing with fear, Rebecca ran to the door and peered out. The sight chilled her. Night Wind and several Lenape warriors were engaged in battle with the Iroquois. The enemy wore war crests and had painted faces.

A woman shrieked from a nearby wigwam. A child started to cry as another shouted and screamed. Rebecca's heart jumped to her throat when she thought of her Indian family. Everything in her being urged Rebecca to go to Ice From Sky, to see if she and Gift From Forest were all right.

Her gaze sought Night Wind. She had lost sight of

him in the confusion, and she stopped breathing as she searched for, but couldn't find him.

A man howled with pain. Rebecca spun just as an Iroquois warrior clutched his bloody chest where Night Wind had plunged his knife in the region of the man's heart. Her husband looked up and saw her. She started to go to him, but his gaze silently commanded her to go back inside. She did, but she continued to watch with increasing horror.

A child ran out of her mother's lodge with an Iroquois warrior in pursuit. Rebecca hated to think what the Indian had done to the girl's mother. Night Wind threw his spear, catching the warrior in the neck just as the Iroquois lunged toward the little girl. Crimson spurted from the man's throat, and she heard him make a garbling sound before he fell, dead.

Rebecca stared in mesmerized horror as the battle continued. Night Wind was spectacular in the fight. Naked, his coiled muscles gleaming in the light of dawn, he crouched and circled his opponent, before picking the right moment to strike. His movements were graceful like they were in his dance. He fought skillfully and killed each one of his opponents earning only a few scratches to himself, while his friends battled beside him.

A hand latched onto her arm, making Rebecca gasp. She saw the brave's face, recognizing a Cayuga warrior from White Flower's village. Caught by surprise, she dropped her bow, and was dragged from the wigwam. She cried out, kicking and fighting to be free.

She broke away and ran back inside, scurrying for the bow and arrow. The Cayuga was there, stalking her, as she scrambled to her feet and raised the weapon high.

"I'll kill you!" she warned. After these months with

the Lenape, the Cayuga words felt foreign to Rebecca's tongue.

"We have come to bring you home, Daughter of the Cayuga," he said.

"I am at home. I'm Lenape now."

The Indian's face contorted with anger. "No! You belong to Iroquois. Killing Bird says you must come."

"No!" she cried. "Come closer and I will kill you!"

He laughed, and she drew back on the bowstring. Her hands shook, and the bow wobbled, affecting her aim.

"You cannot shoot bow," he scoffed. "You are woman!"

She released the string, and the arrow hit Black Horn's arm. Clutching his injury, he bellowed with rage and advanced. Rebecca picked up a clay pot and smashed it against the brave's head. The Indian reeled on his feet, but remained conscious.

She searched wildly for another weapon. He grabbed her arm, dragging her, screaming, from the wigwam.

"Night Wind!"

Her husband froze when he saw her. Angered, he killed his opponent with one swipe of his knife and then, after jerking it from the man's body, he ran to rescue her.

The Iroquois released Rebecca to fight Night Wind. The two braves circled each in a deadly dance. Night Wind was naked, but his skill with weapons made up for his vulnerability. Black Horn was a worthy adversary. He was the war chief of the Deer Clan, and one of the Cayuga tribe's finest warriors. Rebecca watched fearfully as the men fought.

"Tell this brave that if he lets you go, I will not kill him," Black Horn said.

Rebecca translated. Night Wind stared at the Iroquois, and the man took a strike at him with his war club, barely missing Night Wind's left shoulder. Like a skilled dancer, Night Wind had maneuvered himself out of harm's way with lightning speed.

"Tell him I will not give you up," Night Wind said. "You are my wife."

The Iroquois froze when he heard this, nearly dropping his war club. "This is true?" he asked Rebecca. "You are wife of this Lenape warrior?"

She nodded.

"I will not fight him if it was your choice to be his bride," Black Horn said.

"It was my choice," she said, her voice soft. And it was true, she realized. She had wanted nothing more than to marry Night Wind.

"What is he saying?" Night Wind asked with a scowl.

Rebecca's gaze swung to her husband as the Iroquois turned to speak to his men.

"He will not fight for the wife of another," she said.

Night Wind shouted to Deer-That-Runs and Raven Feather, who in turn called to the others to cease fighting.

The Indians stopped battling and backed away from each other warily, ready to strike again should the other side attack.

"I will leave you to your people, Medicine Woman. I do this because you saved Life From Above. White Flower would not want you taken against your will."

Rebecca's eyes filled with tears at the mention of the woman who had once been her master, who had cared enough for Rebecca to send a search party.

"Tell White Flower that I am happy," Rebecca said. "Tell her that I am grateful for her friendship."

Black Horn nodded and turned to leave.

The tension was thick as the Iroquois were leaving the Lenape village.

"Black Horn," Rebecca called. "How did you find me?"

"An old woman," he said. "With no hands. She was glad to tell us where to find the village of the Lenape with the White Medicine Woman."

"Angry Woman," she breathed in Lenape.

Night Wind caught her words, and he stiffened.

Black Horn smiled. "She did not live," he said with a sly grin. "She died quickly . . . from her injuries."

Rebecca shuddered. "Angry Woman is dead," she told her husband. Night Wind nodded, his eyes narrowing as he continued to watch the Iroquois war chief.

"You must go now," Rebecca said to Black Horn. "My people will not wait much longer."

The war chief stared at her. "You would have been happier with Cayuga, Medicine Woman. These women stutterers," he said referring to the Lenape, "they will all be killed by the Iroquois one day. Soon you will die with them."

"Pretty Woman," Rebecca said, purposely ignoring Black Horn's warning. "There is no Medicine Woman. I am Pretty Woman of the Lenape Turtle band."

"Pretty?" The man laughed, and then after a word to his men, they departed.

Rebecca ran to Night Wind, pulling him inside the wigwam, making him sit so that she could inspect him for injuries. Night Wind lay on his side and hugged her when she knelt beside him. Rebecca started to cry as she realized that because of her, Night Wind could have died.

"I'm sorry," she sobbed, burying her face in his neck. "It's my fault."

"You shot Cayuga with bow and arrow," he said. He sat up, his fingers gentle, his expression soft, as he stroked her hair back from her face.

"But I missed," she said. "I only hit his arm."

He leaned forward and kissed her. "You shot Cayuga and stayed with Lenape." He grinned, and she smiled widely in sudden understanding.

Night Wind's amusement faded. "It is not safe here for Pretty Woman. Cayuga will be back."

"No, Black Horn said—"

"Cayuga will be back," Night Wind insisted. "Warrior will return to his *sakima*, who will be angry. Cayuga will return and bring brothers. The Mohawk."

Rebecca was alarmed. "I don't want to bring trouble to your people."

"Our people," he said.

"Yes," she murmured. She bit her lip. "You promised to help me find Elizabeth. You promised to let me go." She rubbed his cheek. "The snow has melted. The Cayuga came here without difficulty. There's no reason we can't leave for Delaware now."

The air was thick with silent tension and the reminder that their marriage was only a temporary one. Rebecca would have to leave. Night Wind had stopped touching her. He released her and lay down, his head propped up on his elbow.

"You are not happy here?" he asked, his voice soft.

"It has nothing to do with being happy or not," she said, raising her chin.

Their eyes locked. His face was unreadable, but she could sense—feel—his pain. She raised her hand to touch him. He moved out of her reach.

"Night Wind," she pleaded. She needed him to understand. "I promised my aunt . . ."

"Honor," he murmured, nodding. He rolled onto his back. He didn't look at her, but stared at the ceiling. "My word . . ." he said. "We will leave Turtle-Town when the sun rises in the morning sky."

Thirty

It wasn't until they were on their way that Rebecca fully realized that Night Wind's accompanying her would place him in great danger. Here, in the forest, he could handle whatever threats came his way, but in Delaware, in an area of white men . . .

They traveled for days, and it was a bittersweet time for Rebecca. Night Wind knew they would part at the end of the journey. He was quiet at times, and she found him watching her with a strange look in his beautiful ebony eyes, but he said nothing about their marriage or their impending separation.

Thanks to her husband, Rebecca ate well, slept well, and covered many miles each day. As their destination drew near, Rebecca felt her throat tighten with emotion. How could she leave him? Yet, how could she not when there was Elizabeth to consider? It would be best for the child to be raised in an English home, preferably her own—the one Aunt Veronica had shared with Elizabeth until the day she'd died. How could she take a child who had been through so much and expect her to live with the Indians?

Night Wind had become unusually quiet that day, hardly speaking at all. Rebecca realized that they must be close to her aunt's village. Then, she saw the open farm fields.

She couldn't allow him to go into the village with her. If the residents—anyone—saw him . . .

Rebecca halted and grabbed his arm. His flesh burned beneath her fingers, and she felt the urge to cry. "Night Wind," she said in a choked voice, "you must go no farther."

He stared at her. "I promised to take you to E-liza-beth," he insisted.

"But it's too dangerous for you!" Rebecca cried. He looked so handsome, she thought. His black hair glistening in the afternoon sun, and his golden copper skin was sleek, smooth—she wanted to touch all of it. Why did he have to look so good?

His dark eyes glittered. "I will not leave you."

He turned to continue, but she wouldn't release him. How could she argue with him? She knew she'd never win.

"Then we will wait until dark," she said. "My people—" She saw the way his eyes narrowed. "—the whites if they see you . . ." She sighed and closed her eyes. "They won't understand."

"You are ashamed of Lenape husband."

"No!" she cried. "Never." She swallowed against a lump. "I'm afraid for you," she whispered, her eyes filling with tears.

His expression softened. "Do not be afraid for Night Wind," he said. "I have hunted many an animal larger than a white man."

Rebecca opened her mouth to argue and then closed it. *But the white man is more cunning than a bear or a deer,* she thought. *And there are many more of them. They have weapons. Guns.*

"We will wait until dark," he said after she refused to move. "And then we will find your Elizabeth."

* * *

Darkness cloaked the land, shadowing the woods and fields. Only a thin sliver of the moon was visible; Rebecca was glad. They needed no bright light to further add to the danger for Night Wind.

They had spent the remainder of that afternoon and the better part of the evening in a woods by a farmer's field. They had no fire, so they had eaten *ka-ha-ma'kun,* which Night Wind had brought with them. They had enjoyed the corn dish and some dried venison strips her husband had saved for the time that it was unsafe to hunt or cook meat.

The extra time with her husband had been precious to Rebecca, forever locked inside her, a wonderful memory of companionship and sharing . . . of kissing and tender touches . . . of making love. The moments had been fraught with a wariness that someone would come upon them. But no one had, and she would carry with her the joy of their last days together to sustain her after they were apart.

They left the woods and crossed the field, staying clear of the brick farmhouse. Night Wind led the way as they began to search for her aunt's home. Rebecca had been in the area once after Veronica had married, but she'd been young and her memory of Kent County was a vague one.

Rebecca began to feel frantic. She had no knowledge of Elizabeth's whereabouts, and with her Indian husband, she couldn't just knock on someone's door and ask questions. One look at the warrior with pierced ears, loincloth, and leggings, and they would shoot first and ask questions later . . . when it was too late.

How could she convince Night Wind to let her go on alone?

A crude signpost pointed the way to the local minister's house.

"The Reverend will know where Elizabeth is," she said, stopping Night Wind. She turned to him, placing her hands on his shoulders, her blue eyes pleading with him to listen. "I'll go on alone."

He shook his head, his dark eyes a flash of angry light in the shadows. He set her aside and continued on.

She exclaimed with frustration. *"Tipaakke—"*

He halted. "I will come or you will not go."

"You'll get yourself killed."

"You will die if I do not go."

"These are my people!"

Night Wind scowled. "Look at Pretty Woman. She looks Lenape not English," he said, fingering the leather strips through her ears.

Rebecca was startled. He was right, she thought. Who was going to let her have Elizabeth while she looked like this? Who was even going to answer her questions?

"You are right," she admitted. "I have to find other clothes."

They stopped at a house whose owner had forgotten to take in their wash. Night Wind wanted to get the garments, but Rebecca insisted. If she were caught, the risk wouldn't be as great.

With racing heart, Rebecca went and removed the clothes. The garments were damp, but she didn't care. A dog inside the house barked, and she froze with fear. When no one came to the door, she worked faster. Pulling the garments from the line, she made a silent promise to return them if possible. Once she had what she needed for both of them she ran from the yard to Night Wind.

The gown was simple, of plain muslin dyed blue. She procured a shirt and a pair of breeches for her husband, and she gasped when she saw him in the

English clothes. The shirt was small, but not too much. If she wasn't so aware of his muscled shoulders and chest, Rebecca thought she probably wouldn't have noticed the fit at all. His breeches fit his thighs snugly, tapering down to hug his firm calves.

She frowned as she studied his bare feet. "You cannot wear your moccasins."

Night Wind raised an eyebrow. "You want me to go without *lenhoksi'na?*"

Rebecca shifted uncomfortably. "Would you?"

He gave a jerk of his head. "I will go with naked feet."

She slipped off one of her necklaces—a simple strip of leather; she would use it to bind her Indian husband's hair. She loved his long dark hair and often wondered why he'd chosen to wear it long when all of the village men but a few, like the shaman, had plucked their heads free, leaving only their war crests. Rebecca asked him.

"I like hair long," he said, and she had to smile.

Rebecca combed back the silky ends, using her fingers, and tied them at his nape with her leather necklace. When she was done, she stood back to admire him, satisfied that he wore his hair now like an Englishman.

"When we get near the Reverend's, keep your head low. Maybe no one will see you." She frowned as he nodded, which drew attention to the strips of beaded sinew in his ears.

"Night Wind—"

"Maata! I will not remove them."

Rebecca sighed. "All right, but then you had best stay back while I ask the Reverend questions."

"Rev-er-end?" he asked.

She blinked. How could she explain this? "The

Reverend is a man of God. Like a shaman, only he doesn't practice medicine."

"Reverend prays to the white man's Great Spirit," Night Wind said.

She smiled. "Yes."

There was no village church, and Rebecca began to wonder if they had taken the right road when she saw the wooden benches in a clearing in the woods next to a house. A small cross had been constructed of wood, raised high on a wooden pole.

"That must be Reverend Thomas's," she said, recalling the name that Aunt Veronica had mentioned in her letters. "Wait here—"

"I will come!" Night Wind said.

"No!" She clutched his sleeve and felt his arm muscles. "Please, I beg of you, Night Wind. Let me question the Reverend alone!"

He wasn't happy, but he let her go. Rebecca was gone about a half hour. It seemed a long time to Night Wind who waited in the silent dark behind a wooden storage building.

The Lenape brave stared at the house and wondered whether or not he should go after her. *Pretty Woman asked me to wait. I will wait longer before I go inside.*

He tensed as he heard a sound, but he saw nothing. His palm warmed the handle of his knife as he gripped the weapon tighter and waited.

"Thank you, Reverend Thomas," Rebecca said. "You don't know how relieved I am to know that Elizabeth has been well cared for all this time."

"Agnes Martin has six children of her own, Miss Rebecca. She is a poor woman, although her husband farms successfully. No one else here could take the child, I'm afraid, and it's been a hardship. Agnes will be most happy to see you."

Rebecca was concerned by something in the man's expression. "My cousin . . . she's all right, isn't she?"

"Ah, yes, yes," he said, looking away. "She's fine." Rebecca wasn't convinced when his brown gaze returned to hers. "She took her mother's death hard."

Her eyes filled with tears. "Yes, I imagined she would." She swallowed against a lump. "I loved Aunt Veronica. I wanted so much to see her before . . ."

The minister patted the young woman's shoulder. "Such a dreadful experience getting lost and then kidnapped by those Frenchmen. How ever did you get away?" He eyed her intently. Too intently, Rebecca thought.

"A young woman, a wife of a French soldier, helped me," she lied.

"And they didn't hurt you . . ." he said, moving closer.

Rebecca shook her head and stepped back. The Reverend appeared relieved, she noticed. "I must go," she said. "I'm anxious to see Elizabeth."

"Yes, you must," the man agreed. He escorted her to the door. "You came here all alone . . . amazing."

"Not all alone, Reverend," she reminded him of the details of her fabricated story. "I traveled with a family. The Richmonts. We separated just north of here." The only part that wasn't a lie was that she'd once traveled with the Richmont family.

Reverend Thomas smiled. "Yes, yes, how could I have forgotten?" He opened the door for her. "Your aunt's house is vacant. You may stay there if you like. Veronica Webster . . . left a few debts so I don't know if the place will be sold, but—"

"Thank you, Reverend," she interrupted. "We'll do

that. Elizabeth and I can always go to New York to live with my mother."

The man frowned. "You must get word to your mother quickly. When your aunt died, we sent her a letter. It's been months. I'm sure she's heard of Veronica's death and your disappearance by now."

Rebecca was upset. "Yes, I'll write to her right away."

"Bernard Hanlick goes north often. If you plan to stay here for a while, you may want to send word through him." He gave her directions to the Martin house. "It's just up the road." He hesitated. "You must be careful. There's been two murders in the area recently."

"Murders?"

The minister's face was grim. "Terrible incidents. A man and a woman. Both strangers here, but everyone in Kent is concerned." He eyed her speculatively. "Do you have a weapon?"

"A knife," she said. He looked surprised. "I use it when I cook," she explained.

In a hurry to leave, Rebecca thanked the Reverend again and was conscious of the man's gaze as she left his house. *Night Wind don't show yourself,* she thought. *The man is watching.*

But Rebecca didn't have to worry. She couldn't find him; Night Wind must have seen the English man of God.

There was still no sign of her husband as she reached the road. Her chest tightened. Had he given up and left? He had known that they would soon be parting, that she had to stay while he returned to his people, to Turtle-Town.

Rebecca headed down the road toward the Martin house, where her young cousin had lived since Aunt Veronica's death. *Couldn't he have stayed a while longer?* She had wanted, needed, to kiss him one last time.

Night Wind still hadn't made an appearance by the time she saw the light in the Martin cottage window. Perhaps it was better this way, she thought. Perhaps he had wanted to make their parting easier.

She tensed. What if something dreadful had happened to him? What if he'd been captured by white men? Or shot?

Rebecca scolded herself. She would have heard a gunshot. But the murders that the Reverend had mentioned. How did those people die? What if the killer had gotten Night Wind?

She was within yards of the Martins' door when she turned and ran back. *Night Wind, where are you? Please be all right!*

Night Wind watched his wife walk away, down the road, and he knew she was leaving him. She hadn't looked for him; she had made her choice. His eyes blurred as he turned away.

The village would not be the same without her, he thought. He swallowed against a tight throat. Life would not be the same without the woman he loved. He rubbed his tears with the sleeve of his shirt. He must get back to Turtle-Town, but what was his hurry when Pretty Woman wasn't there?

And then he heard the faint cry. Her cry.

"Night Wind! *Tipaakke Shaakha!*"

He spun and saw her. She was running toward him, her cheeks streaked with tears, her arms open. She ran into his embrace and hugged him, sobbing incoherently into his white muslin shirt.

Rebecca looked up after she'd quieted down.

"There's a murderer out here somewhere. I thought you'd been killed, and I couldn't bear it!"

Night Wind grinned. "I am alive as the wind on a stormy night."

She laughed. "I love you." She kissed him on the mouth. His eyes flamed as she pulled back.

"I love you, bride of Night Wind."

Rebecca's eyes brimmed with tears of happiness. It was the first time he'd actually said the words. They sounded like sweet music. She sobered. "Elizabeth—I know where she is. She's been through a lot."

"We will get her."

She pressed him close. "I don't know if she'll like living in Turtle-Town."

"You did not like *Tulpeuta-nai,*" he reminded her, "and you—"

"Love village life," she whispered with renewed hope. "But what if she won't come? What if she doesn't know me?"

"We must find her and see," her husband said.

Night Wind waited outside while Rebecca went to get Elizabeth from the Martin household. Startled by Rebecca's sudden appearance, the woman was nevertheless happy to see Elizabeth's long awaited cousin.

"She's a difficult child," Agnes Martin warned, after Rebecca had retold her fabricated tale of her kidnapping. Rebecca studied Agnes and saw an Englishwoman of middle age who had kind eyes but a face that belonged to one who had a hard life.

"I'm sure I'll be able to handle her," Rebecca said. She felt her lie was justified, sparing everyone a good deal of worry and grief. As for Elizabeth, she was Veronica's child, and knowing her aunt, the child was a warm, loving girl with an ingrained streak of independence which most people would find unacceptable.

Agnes looked relieved that Rebecca was willing to cope with the child. "Elizabeth," the woman called.

From what Rebecca could guess, the house had three rooms—the largest main room where the couple slept, a bedchamber in the back, and a kitchen of sorts. Rebecca saw from the iron kettle that they might use the fireplace in the great room to do some, if not most, of the actual cooking.

Six children, Rebecca thought, *which meant that seven children were sleeping in the back room, unless there was an attic loft.*

Two children burst in from the back bedchamber. "Elizabeth's being mean," the young boy cried.

"I hate her!" announced the little girl. "She won't give me back Emma!"

Agnes glanced at Rebecca apologetically. "Emma is my daughter's doll," she explained. "I'm afraid Elizabeth has taken a liking to it."

"She keeps calling it Rebecca!" the child complained. "But her name's Emma!"

Rebecca paled. "Tell Elizabeth that she won't need your doll anymore," she told Agnes's daughter. "Tell her the real Rebecca has come to take her home."

The child ran toward the bedchamber, happily shouting Rebecca's message.

The young girl who came out of the back room had large gray eyes that sparkled with defiance as she clutched the doll tightly to her breast. Her hair was a golden brown, lighter than Rebecca's, but darker than the child's mother.

"Elizabeth," Agnes said. "Someone is here to see you."

Her long lashes flickered as she searched the room. Rebecca stepped from the doorway, making herself known.

Elizabeth stared at her, and Rebecca saw the emotion that crossed the child's face as she must have noted the resemblance to Veronica. Her heart went out to the little girl.

"Elizabeth," she said, her throat tightening. "It's so good to finally meet you. I'm—"

The girl gave a wild cry and ran to her, throwing her arms about Rebecca's waist, hugging the woman tightly. "Rebecca," she exclaimed, "you finally came!"

Thirty-one

A knock on the front door woke Rebecca. She got up from bed and threw on one of her aunt's dressing gowns. Then, after closing the bedchamber door, she went to answer the knock.

Her pulse raced with alarm as she crossed the parlor. If any of the local residents found out that there was an Indian sleeping in the next room . . .

We'll be on our way before morning, she thought. They were just spending the night in the house, and Elizabeth was asleep in her own bedchamber. Rebecca's gaze fell on her aunt's clock as her hand touched the door. *Three o'clock in the morning. Who on earth would be visiting at this time of night?*

Rebecca hesitated before opening the door. "Who's there?" she asked in a trembly voice. Should she get Night Wind? No, people wouldn't understand.

"Rebecca Morton, is that you?"

Her heart skipped a beat. "Mother?"

"Yes, dear, now will you please open the door. It's co—"

The door flew open, and Rebecca launched herself into her mother's arms. The two women cried and hugged each other, rejoicing in the reunion.

"You thought I was dead!" Rebecca gasped.

"Dead?" her mother said. "Of course not. Now why would I think that?"

"Didn't you get the Reverend's letter?"

Margaret shook her head. "No, I didn't receive any letter. I hadn't heard from my sister or my daughter, and I was wondering how you both were . . ." Her expression fell when she saw Rebecca's face. "Veronica is dead," she whispered, her eyes filling with tears.

"Yes, Mother, I'm afraid so, but there's something else you must know . . ."

Night Wind heard his wife's wild cry and sprang from the bed, grabbing his spear. He burst from the bedchamber into the other room, naked, his hair mussed, his spear in hand.

Rebecca's mother pulled from her daughter's arms and stared. Rebecca's breath caught as she watched the reaction of two people she loved—her husband and her mother.

"Shi'ki," Night Wind said in Lenape, "I thought you were—"

Rebecca's gaze fell on her parent. "Mother—"

"Daughter," Margaret Morton said, "I do hope you're married to this man. Fine specimen or not, he is without clothes."

Rebecca giggled. "Mother, this is my husband, Night Wind." She turned her loving glance on the naked man across the room. "Night Wind, this is my *Onna*. Margaret Morton."

Night Wind stared at the woman hard, but he relaxed his stance, dropping his spear arm.

"Son," Margaret said, recovering from her shock quickly, "it's a pleasure to meet the man who has captured my daughter's heart."

Epilogue

The village echoed with children's laughter. Spring had come to the land, and the earth was green with tiny shoots of new growth. It was a season, Rebecca thought, for happiness and thanksgiving.

The Lenape tribe had traveled far to the shore where they would stay through the summer months. There the men fished, caught crabs, and dug for clams. The women gathered shells for jewelry and wampum belts, while the Indian children enjoyed the warm sunshine and the saltwater of the bay. It was the time within the village that Rebecca loved most, and now that her whole family was with her, this time was even more precious to her.

She sat outside her wigwam, nursing and cradling her tiny son. Robert Wind-Song had been born to the couple three weeks earlier. He had come, healthy and making a lot of noise, in the middle of the night with her husband and her two mothers beside her. After seven years of being barren, Rebecca had finally given Night Wind a son. She had almost given up hope of conceiving and had gifted her wealth of her motherly love to Elizabeth during those months each year that the girl had been with them.

And then one morning, Rebecca had awakened with

tender breasts and a sick stomach. She'd been afraid
to hope . . . to believe that she might be with child.
When the morning illness continued for days and then
weeks, Rebecca knew that her prayers had been answered. She was carrying Night Wind's child.

For nine months, she carried their babe with a radiance that convinced even the most hardened Lenape
that Pretty Woman was beautiful. And then the babe
came . . . a healthy boy with five fingers and five
toes and all of his other parts. Night Wind had cried
silent tears, and Rebecca had learned of his hidden
fears. He had blamed himself for her barrenness, because of his sin. He had done the forbidden and killed
his totem animal. He'd been sure that the spirits were
punishing him for the wolves' deaths.

With the birth of a healthy son, Night Wind was
no longer afraid. He was convinced that the spirits
had forgiven him, and that they had shown him by
giving him Robert Wind-Song.

Rebecca smiled down at her suckling son. Her
world was complete. She had all of her family with
her now, and she couldn't have asked God for another
thing.

She heard a girlish laugh. Seeking the source, she
saw Elizabeth walking across the compound, her sparkling gray eyes defiant, her chin raised high. Nearby,
two young braves watched the fourteen-year-old girl;
one young man in particular was gazing at her with
moonstruck eyes.

Rebecca was concerned. After years of living most
of her young life in New York with Rebecca's mother,
Elizabeth had finally rebelled. Instead of spending
merely a month or two in the Lenape village, Elizabeth wanted to live there—permanently. Margaret
Morton had finally given in. Rebecca's mother had
spent time in the village over the years herself, and

now that Elizabeth was older, she saw no harm in granting the child her wish. She had already done all she could for Elizabeth, and still the girl preferred the life of the Indians.

The first years had been difficult. Little Elizabeth, having waited a long time for Rebecca, had not wanted to go with Margaret. The child had consented only with the adults' promise that she could visit for at least one month out of every year. She was a spirited child with a mind of her own, just as Rebecca had expected Veronica's daughter to be. Just as she herself had been, but her stubborn independence had been to a lesser degree, Rebecca thought.

Margaret Morton was still with them, having been here since two days before the babe's birth, but soon Rebecca's mother would be returning to Delaware, where she had purchased her sister's house a year ago from its last owner. She had sold her late husband's property in the New York Colony and gone south where, she claimed, it tended to be warmer. Her new home wasn't even a full day's traveling distance away, and Rebecca was pleased, knowing her mother was close.

Rebecca studied the child whom she loved like her own daughter. In the past, each time Elizabeth had left to return to Delaware and the tribe had moved farther inland in preparation for the winter months, Rebecca had managed to say farewell without crying, until the child had actually left . . .

She'd been excited when Elizabeth had made the decision to stay, even more so when Margaret had agreed to her niece's choice, until now. . . . Until Rebecca had realized the full responsibility of Elizabeth's well-being. What if she was wrong in allowing the girl to live among the Indians? What did it matter if

Elizabeth seemed to fare better in the wilderness with her Lenape family?

Rebecca gasped when Night Wind sat down beside her. She hadn't heard his approach.

"Golden Dove is growing," he commented.

Rebecca glanced at her husband with concern. "Yes, but she is too young."

He knew what she was saying. Elizabeth was too young, his wife thought, for capturing the eye of Lenape braves. "Lenape maidens marry young," he said.

"But not Elizabeth," Rebecca insisted, her eyes never leaving the girl. "Elizabeth is—"

"Different," he said. He grinned. "Like her Lenape mother."

Rebecca saw the way the girl walked across the yard with her head held high as if daring anyone to cross her. Elizabeth was naked from the waist up, another of Rebecca's concerns, for now she was afraid the girl was brazen. The young woman thrust out her chest as if proud of her body and its effect on the young Indian males. Elizabeth certainly enjoyed the freedom of her new life, Rebecca thought worriedly.

What was a mother to do with such a child?

"Elizabeth is strong. She will not hurt easily," Night Wind said. "She will handle her own."

His wife relaxed as she looked at him. His gaze was on his son, whose head he caressed with his large copper-skinned hand. Rebecca saw the love her husband gifted upon their son, felt the warmth of his love surround and protect her every moment of every day, and she felt a peace come over her. Night Wind had won the affection of Veronica's child. He had earned the respect and love of Rebecca's mother. He was a wise man, a caring man. She would be equally wise to believe him.

Rebecca touched his cheek and smiled. "*Kihiila,*

neet-il-ose." Yes, my husband, she'd said. "I believe you are right. Golden Dove will make out fine."

They exchanged looks of love. And the baby continued to suck at Rebecca's breast as the laughter of the village children filled the air with its merry sound.

Zebra Books and Kensington Books
proudly announce . . .

*SUMMER DARKNESS,
WINTER LIGHT*

by Sylvia Halliday

Coming from
Kensington Books Hardcovers
in early May, 1995

The following is a preview of
*SUMMER DARKNESS,
WINTER LIGHT* . . .

One

The wrought-iron gate was newly painted. Allegra ran her fingers over the smooth curliques, followed the cool, sinuous curves to the oval medallion that held the Baniard coat of arms. The carved leopard still raised a broken front paw. But after more than eight years of fresh paint—glistening black layers piled one upon another—the jagged metal edges had become rounded, gentle.

"Curse them all," Allegra muttered. "Every foul Wickham who ever lived." She clenched her teeth against the familiar pain. If only sharp memories could be as softened and gentled as the old iron gate. She reached into the pocket of her wide seaman's breeches and pulled forth a worn, lace-edged square of linen, yellow with age and mottled with stains the color of old wine, the color of dead leaves. Papa's blood—staining the proud Baniard crest embroidered in the corner.

Wickham. Allegra's lip curled in silent rage and bitterness. If there was a God of vengeance, a just God, her prayers would be answered today. Her stomach twisted with the pangs of hunger, and her feet—in their broken shoes—ached from the long morning's climb through the Shropshire hills, but it would be worth it. She reached under her shabby coat and waistcoat and fingered the hilt of the dagger tucked into the waistband of her breeches. All her pain would vanish when she confronted John Wickham, Baron Ellsmere, false Lord of Baniard Hall. When she saw his look of surprise, then fear, then abject terror in the breathless, time-stopped seconds before she plunged her dagger into his black heart.

A sour-faced manservant came out of the lodge next to the high stone wall that enclosed Baniard Park. A thickly curled gray peruke covered his round head, and he wore a handsome livery of blue velvet trimmed with crimson—the Ellsmere colors, no doubt. He squinted up at the morning sun, peered through the bars of the gate and shook his fist at Allegra. "Get off with you, boy. You have no business here."

Allegra jammed her three-cornered hat more firmly over her forehead to shield her face from the gatekeeper's gaze. Her masculine guise had protected her clear across the ocean and through the English countryside all the way north from Plymouth. Still, to be discovered now, when vengeance lay so close at hand . . .

"I ain't doin' no harm, your worship," she mumbled, keeping her naturally husky voice pitched low, her accent common. "Just come up from Ludlow, I did. It were a long climb. And I'm fearful hungry. Thought I might beg a farthing or two of His Lordship."

"Pah!" said the gatekeeper with a sneer of contempt as he scanned her stained and ragged clothing. "Do you think milord can be bothered with the likes of you? A dirty-faced whelp?" He scowled at her dark eyes, her raven-black hair braided into a tousled queue, and her face still deeply tanned from the Carolina sun. "Leastwise not someone who looks like a black Welsh Gypsy," he added. "Be off, lest I give you a good rap on the ear."

Years of cruel servitude had taught Allegra how to

feign humility, even while her heart seethed with rebellion. "Have a crumb o' pity, your worship," she whined. "I be but a poor orphan lad."

"Be off, I say." He pointed across the narrow, dusty road to a footpath that wound its way through a small grove of trees. "That way lies the village of Newton-in-the-Vale. There's a fine workhouse that will do well enough for you. A good day's work for a good day's bread, and none of your sloth and begging."

Allegra rubbed at her hands, feeling the hardness of the calluses on her palms and fingers. She wondered whether this self-satisfied, overfed man had ever known *real* work. Heigh-ho. There was no sense in quarreling with him. She shrugged and plodded across the road. The trees were thick in the coppice, crowded close together; their dark, summer-green leaves and shade soon hid her from the gatekeeper's view. She waited a few minutes, then stepped off the footpath and doubled back through the trees, treading softly so as not to alert the servant. Just within the shelter of the coppice, she found a spot that concealed her presence while commanding a clear view of the gate.

By King George upon his throne, if she had to wait all day for Wickham she would!

She heard the noise of a coach from somewhere beyond the gate—the rattle of harness, the squeaking of wheels—as it made its way down the long, tree-shaded drive that led from Baniard Hall. In another moment, the coach appeared in view and stopped at the gate; the team of horses snorted and stamped, eager to proceed. At once, the gatekeeper hurried to take hold of the iron gate and swing it wide. Allegra heard the word "Milord" uttered in deference, noted the blue and crimson she was certain now were Ellsmere colors on the coachman's ample body. Wickham's very own coach. Without a doubt, the villain himself was within.

Allegra's heart began to pound in her breast, like the thud of distant thunder before a storm. After all this time . . . She started to rush forward, then checked herself. No. No! She mustn't let her impatience cloud her judgment; she must think clearly. The coach was moving quite slowly through the open gate. Out of the view of the gatekeeper and coachman, she might be able to hoist herself onto the empty footman's perch in the rear and cling to the coach until it stopped and her enemy alit. But that might not be until they reached a village and the coach was surrounded by crowds. And then the job would be impossible.

She remembered a crumbling section of the wall that surrounded the park, where the stones had loosened. Perhaps she could make her way onto the grounds from there, wait for Ellsmere to return. No. The wall might be repaired after all this time. And, besides, she couldn't wait another minute. She laughed softly, ruefully. She had endured the long, slow years, the years of nurturing her hatred in patient silence. And now, to her surprise, she found that the thought of a few hours' delay had become unbearable.

What to do? The frown faded from her brow as a sudden thought struck her. She would accost him now, present herself as a harmless lad, win his sympathy, worm her way into his favor. He wouldn't recognize her after all this time. And then, when his guard was down, her dagger could do its work.

"Milord!" she cried, and dashed in front of the carriage. The coachman shouted and tried to avoid her; she held her ground and leapt away only at the last second. It had been such a narrow escape that her shoulder burned from the friction of rubbing against a horse's flank, and a passing harness buckle had torn the sleeve of her coat.

She began at once to howl. " 'Od's blood, but my arm be broken!"

She heard a string of foul curses from within the coach, then a deep voice boomed, "Stop!"

As the coach drew to a halt, Allegra clutched at her arm and bent over in seeming pain. Though she continued to wail, all her energies were concentrated on observing the man who sprang from the coach. She'd seen him once before—that long-ago, sweet summer at Baniard Hall. The summer she'd turned nine. The summer before the nightmare had begun. A man of stature, proud and haughty and cruel.

He was even taller than her misty memory of him, and the years had clearly treated him with kindness. His dark-brown hair was still untouched by gray. He wore it simply, unpowdered and tied back with a black silk ribbon. His pugnacious jaw had a bluish cast, as though he'd neglected to take a shave, and his dark and somewhat shaggy brows were drawn together in a scowl, shading pale-brown eyes. His well-cut coat and waistcoat of fine woolen cloth covered a solid, muscular torso, and his legs were strong and straight. The fact that he looked so young made her hate him all the more: Papa had aged a dozen years from the time of the trial to the day they had been herded aboard the convict ship.

"Damned fool," growled the man. He sounded more annoyed than angry, as though it was a bother merely to deal with the lower classes. "Why the devil did you run into my coach, boy? I should break your neck, match it to your arm." He stepped closer and thrust out his hand. "Show it here."

The simmering hatred became a red mist before Allegra's eyes: the red, bloody dream that had kept her going through all the hellish years, through the shame and the suffering and the loss of all she'd held dear. She felt strength coursing through her body—the strength of righteous anger that poor Mama had never been able to find.

Now! she thought. For her pledge to Mama. For all the lost Baniards! There would never be a better opportunity. The gatekeeper was busy with his gate and the coachman was too fat to scramble down from his perch in time to save his master.

Allegra snaked her hand inside her coat. A quick thrust with her dagger and then—in the chaos of the unexpected, the confusion of the servants—she'd make her escape into the woods. "Die like the dog you are," she choked, and drove the knife upward toward his breast with all her might. With all the fury in her pent-up heart.

"Christ's blood!" he swore. He wrenched his body to one side and just managed to dodge the murderous blade. At the same moment he caught Allegra's wrist in a punishing grip and twisted it until she was forced to drop the knife. His lip curled in disgust. "Good God. You're not a fool. You're a bloody lunatic! Do you fancy the gibbet, boy?"

She bared her teeth in a snarl. "It would be worth it, to see you dead."

He laughed, an unpleasant sound, lacking in humor or warmth. "What a tartar. How does a boy learn such passion at such a young age?" He drawled the words, as though strong emotions were scarcely worth his own effort.

"I learned from villains like you," she said. She eyed her dagger lying in the dusty road. If she could just reach it . . .

"Oh, no, boy. You'll not have a second chance."

Reading her intentions, he quickly stooped and retrieved the knife.

"Curse you!" Allegra felt her stomach give a sickening lurch. She had failed them all. All the ghosts waiting to be avenged. How could she have been so hasty and careless? Would there ever be another chance to redeem herself? Another chance to do what she must, and, after, learn to live again? In her frustration, she raised her hands to spring at the man's throat; she grunted in surprise as she felt her arms caught and pinioned behind her back. She struggled in vain, then twisted around to glare at the man who held her—a somber-looking young man who had stepped from the coach behind her. He was dressed in a plain dark suit, the garb of a steward or clerk.

"Hold your tongue, bratling," he said, "unless you mean to beg His Lordship's mercy."

"His Lordship can rot in hell, for aught I care!" She turned back and spat in the direction of the tall man. "In *hell*, Wickham! Do you hear?"

"Wickham?" The tall man laughed again and idly scraped Allegra's blade against the stubble on his chin. It made a metallic, rasping sound. "Wickham? Is that who you think I am?"

"You're the Lord of Baniard Hall, aren't you?" she challenged.

"That I am. But Wickham was ruined by debts nearly two years ago. The last I heard, he was in London."

"No!" She shook her head in disbelief, feeling her blood run cold. "Curse you, villain, you're lying to save your skin."

The steward gave a sharp jerk on her arms. "I told you to hold your tongue, boy," he growled in her ear. "This is Sir Greyston Morgan, Viscount Ridley. Baron Ellsmere sold the Hall to His Lordship a year ago."

"I don't believe you." But of course there was no

reason to doubt him. She examined the tall man more closely. What a fool she'd been, allowing her passion to blind her to reality. He didn't just appear younger; he *was* younger, and considerably so. Perhaps in his early thirties. Wickham would be almost as old as Papa would have been today, or at least nearing fifty. She'd forgotten that, still seeing the man through the eyes of her childhood.

All the fight drained out of her. She sagged in the steward's grip, filled with an aching disappointment. To have come so far, and then to find another obstacle in her path, another barrier before she could sleep in peace . . . She stared at the viscount, her dark eyes burning with frustration and resentment. He should have been Wickham. "I curse you as well, Ridley," she said bitterly. "A pox on you."

"Now, milord," said the coachman, climbing down for his box, "if this isn't a rascally lad who needs a few hours in the stocks to teach him manners! Shall we deliver him to the beadle in the village?" He looked for agreement toward the gatekeeper, who had finally joined them.

Ridley looked down at Allegra's petite frame and shook his head. "He's just a slip of a boy. The stocks would kill him. A mere ten minutes with a mob hurling garbage and filth . . ."

"But you can't let him go, milord. He tried to kill you!" said the gatekeeper.

Ridley smiled, a sardonic twist of his mouth. "So he did, Humphrey. And I note you took your time coming to my rescue." His icy glance swept his other servants as well. "The lot of you. Slow as treacle on a cold day. Very shortsighted. If you'd let him kill me, you'd have had to seek honest employment for a change." He shrugged, ignoring his servants' sullen frowns. "Well, the lad wasn't the first to wish me dead. However"—he slapped the broad width of Allegra's dagger against his open palm—"the boy does have an insolent tongue, and for that he should be made to pay." He nodded at his steward. "Loose him, Briggs. I'll deal with him myself."

"But . . ." Briggs hesitated. "Do you think you're fit, milord?"

A sharp laugh. "Sober, you mean?"

"I didn't mean that at all," said Briggs in an aggrieved tone.

Ridley's eyes were cold amber. "What a damned bloody liar you are, Briggs. Now, do you want to keep your position? You'll not find another master willing to pay so much for so little. Loose the boy, I said."

"As you wish, milord." There was pained resentment in the steward's voice, but he obeyed.

The moment her arms were freed, Allegra looked wildly about, seeking a path to safety. There was none. The three servants hemmed her in, and Lord Ridley stood before her, a cold smile of determination on his face. He slapped the flat of Allegra's knife more sharply against his hand. Again, and then once more—a decidedly menacing gesture, for all his smiling. "Damn me to hell, will you, boy? Spit on my boots, will you? Someone has neglected your education, it would seem. I intend to remedy that." He slipped the knife into his boot top and advanced on Allegra. His long arm shot out and wrapped around her waist. With the merest effort, he lifted her and tucked her under his arm, like a farmer carrying a squirming pig to market.

Allegra writhed in his strong grip. "Bloody villain. Spawn of hell! Put me down!"

"If I were you, boy, I'd hold my tongue," he said dryly. "I have all day to educate you, and every fresh

insolence will only earn you another painful lesson."
He turned toward the woodland path.

"Where are you going, milord?" asked the gatekeeper, Humphrey.

"To find a suitable 'schoolroom.' Don't follow me.
Grant the lad privacy in his humiliation." Ridley
laughed, a sharp, sardonic bark. "Besides, you shall
hear his howls anon."

He carried Allegra into the grove of trees and
stopped at last when he found a fallen log in a small
clearing. He sat down and slung her across his knees
with such force that her hat flew from her head and
landed in a patch of bright green ferns.

Allegra grunted and wriggled in powerless rage,
punching at his legs, his thighs—anything within
reach of her flailing fists. It was like beating back a
tempest with a lady's fan. His strong arm held her
firmly against his lap. She felt his other hand at her
rump, turning up the skirts of her coat; then his fingers were curled around the top of her breeches.

She struggled more violently to free herself. She
didn't fear the thrashing—not even with the flat of
her own knife, which the villain clearly intended. Punishment was nothing new to her. But if he saw the
pale flesh of her backside, the womanly curves, he'd
guess at once. And then what? What could she expect
from this cold-hearted devil of a viscount? God save
her, she hadn't guarded her virtue against the greatest
adversities only to be raped by a man with nothing
better to do on a July morning! With a superhuman
effort, she wrenched herself from his lap and tumbled
to the ground.

He reached down to pull her back. By chance, his
hands closed over her breasts. "Christ's blood," he exclaimed, and dropped down beside her. "A *woman,*
begad!" While she struggled in helpless frustration, he

rolled her onto her back, straddled her and pinned her wrists over her head. With his free hand he explored her body, threw open her coat and tattered waistcoat and fondled her breasts through her full linen shirt. It was a leisurely, searching examination that clearly amused him. His mouth twisted in a smirk. "A very pleasing shape. May I assume your other parts are equally feminine? Or shall I find out for myself?"

She squirmed in disgust at his touch, her eyes flashing. "Let me up, you plaguey dog!"

He shook his head and laughed. "To think I very nearly beat you like a child. I should have realized . . . all that passion. Not childlike at all. But why waste your fire in anger? Why foul your lips with curses, when they could be put to better use?" He bent down, his face close to hers. His breath smelled of liquor, sour and pungent.

"Cursed rogue," she muttered. "Drunken sot. I would rather the beating than the kiss."

"Perhaps I can oblige you with both," he said, and silenced her mouth with his.

His lips were hard and demanding, rapacious in their greed, the desire for self-gratification. And when she groaned and bucked beneath him, Ridley chuckled deep in his throat, as though her struggles only increased the enjoyment of his mastery over her. Without releasing either her lips or her hands, he shifted his body so his considerable weight pressed upon her breast and his free hand rested on the juncture between her legs.

Allegra had a sudden, terrifying memory of Mama, gasping in pain and grief as Squire Pringle violated her frail body. She could hear again the animal sounds she'd heard, night after night in the dark. Hear her mother's heartbroken sobs as the master, satisfied once more, slunk away to his own bed. *No!* It mustn't happen to her. She was stronger than Mama. Hadn't she survived until now?

Despite her rising panic, she forced herself to think clearly. If Ridley wasn't completely drunk, he'd certainly had a great deal to drink this morning. His senses would be dulled, his reflexes numbed by alcohol. Surely she could outwit him if she put her mind to it.

With a sigh, she relaxed under him in seeming surrender. She even managed a moan of pleasure when he began to stroke her inner thigh, his large hand hot through her breeches. He grunted his contentment, softened his kiss, eased his hard grip upon her wrists. How easily gulled men could be, she thought. And if he was anything like the lecherous pigs in Carolina, no doubt he enjoyed kissing in the French manner. She prayed it was so. She parted her lips beneath his, hoping he'd understand and respond to her invitation. To her satisfaction, he immediately opened his own mouth and thrust his tongue between her lips and teeth. She waited a second—fighting her disgust— then bit down with all her might.

He let out a bellow and flew off her as though he'd been shot, sitting up to clutch at his bloody mouth. "Damned bitch!" he roared.

She gave him no chance to recover. She scrambled to her knees and drove her fist into his diaphragm with all her strength. He recoiled in agony and doubled over, gasping for breath. She was on her feet in a flash. She snatched up her three-cornered hat, pulled her knife from his boot top and turned toward the footpath. Her mouth was bitter with the taste of his blood; bitterer still with the knowledge that time was passing and she was no nearer her goal. Her stomach burned with hunger, and London and Wickham were long miles and days away. Somehow, that made her hate Ridley all the more. Ridley, with his careless, shallow lechery. What did he know of true suffering?

She retraced her steps to where he still sat, rocking in pain. "Filthy whoremonger," she said, and spat his own blood upon his bent head. When he looked up at her, she was pleased to see that the cold, indifferent eyes were—for the first time—dark with rage. "Laugh that away, Ridley," she said. "If you can." She turned on her heel and made for the safety of the trees . . . and the direction that would take her eventually to London and Wickham.

And bloody vengeance.

Sir Greyston Morgan, Lord Ridley, late of His Majesty's Guards and survivor of many an incursion against the Mogul Empire, gingerly rubbed the sore spot beneath his ribs and muttered a soft curse. He pulled out a handkerchief and wiped the spittle from his hair, grunting at the pain that small effort cost him. The absurdity of the whole episode served to temper his anger. "Ambushed, begad," he said, beginning to laugh in spite of his discomfort. He stuck out his tongue and dabbed at it, marveling at the amount of blood on the snowy linen. It was a wonder the virago hadn't bitten his tongue clean off!

"Are you hurt, milord?" Jonathan Briggs stood on the edge of the path, frowning in concern.

Grey struggled to his feet and glared at his steward. It was one thing to be outwitted by a wench. It was quite another matter to be caught at it by a servant. "Damn it, I thought I told you not to follow."

"We heard you cry out, milord." Briggs looked around the small clearing. "Where's the boy?"

Grey took a tentative step forward, relieved to discover that the could breathe almost normally again.

"The 'boy,' Briggs, turned out to be a woman." His tongue was still bleeding; he stopped to spit a mouthful of blood against the base of a tree. "And a damned shifty bitch at that."

Grey watched in dismay. "Was it the wench responsible for this? I'll send Humphrey after her."

"No. Let her be. I'll wager she's halfway to London by now."

"What's to be done now, milord?"

Grey moved swiftly to the steward and leaned his arm on the man's shoulder. "Help me back to the coach and open that bottle of gin."

Briggs shook his head in disapproval. "But, milord, do you think it wise, so early in the day?"

He swore softly. "You tell me what's worth staying sober for, Briggs, and I'll stay sober. Until then, you'll keep me supplied with all the drink I need. And no insolence. Is that understood?"

Briggs pressed his lips together and nodded.

By the time they'd reached the coach, Grey was feeling a good deal better. At least his tongue and his ribs were feeling better. He wasn't sure of anything else. There was something disturbing about the woman. Something about her eyes, so large and dark and filled with pain . . . "Damn it, Briggs," he growled, "where's that gin?" He snatched the small flask from the steward's hand and took a long, mind-numbing swallow. Why should he let the thought of a savage creature with a dirty face get under his hide?

"Do you still want to go down to Ludlow, milord?"

"Of course. The blacksmith promised to have that Toledo blade repaired by today."

"Are you sure you don't want someone to go after the woman?"

"I told you, no!"

"But she tried to kill you. What if she should return and try again?"

"She wants Ellsmere, not me." He smiled crookedly. "I pity him if the witch should find him." He took another swig of gin and shrugged. "Besides, if she should return to kill me, I'm no great loss."

"Nonsense, milord. You're a great man, admired and respected by your tenants and servants. Everyone in the parish honors Lord Ridley."

Grey threw back his head and laughed aloud. "Such kind flattery, Briggs. You do it well, as befits a man of honor. But how difficult it must be for you. To serve a man you don't even like. You're the second son of a knight, aren't you? You were predestined to inherit nothing from your father except his good wishes. Well, a house steward is a fine calling for a man with few prospects and a good education. And money speaks with a loud voice, as I've learned." He leaned back in his seat and tapped his long fingers against the bottle of gin. "How much am I paying you?"

"Forty pounds, milord," murmured Briggs. He watched in silence, his solemn eyes registering dismay, as Grey downed the last of the gin.

The liquor stung Grey's injured tongue, but he was beginning to feel better and better. He chuckled softly. "What a disappointment I must be to you, Briggs. I think your upbringing was better than mine, though I, too, was the second son of a title. I regret that I don't suit your ideas of proper nobility here in Shropshire. But if you can learn to hide that look of disgust on your face, I give you leave to take another thirty pounds per annum. If not"—he shrugged—"it's simple enough to buy loyalty elsewhere, if one has the money." He laughed at the sullen look Briggs shot at him. "God's truth, I think if my brother hadn't died and left me his fortune and title, you'd be pleased to knock me to my knees at this very moment. But you're too much a gentleman for that. Too respectful of a man's rank, even if he's undeserving. Eh, Briggs?" He laughed again as the steward reddened and turned away.

Grey closed his eyes. The rocking of the coach soothed him. And the gin had done its work. It was good to feel nothing but a comfortable hum in his brain. There was a surfeit of passion in the world, a stupid waste of emotion. He hated it. Hated caring, hated feeling. It was better to be numb than to suffer with rage and pain, one's soul exposed to the agony of the human condition. Raw flesh held to an open flame. Like that ragged, dark-eyed creature, who burned with an intensity he couldn't begin to understand. That he didn't *want* to understand.

"Briggs," he said suddenly. "Do you remember the red-haired serving wench at the Kings Oak tavern in Newton? Find out if she's still as agreeable as before. If so, pay her double what you did last time. Then see that she's waiting in my bed tonight."

"Yes, milord." Briggs's voice was sharp with disapproval.

Grey opened his eyes and smiled cynically. "She's a shallow, greedy whore, Briggs. I know. But—like the gin—she gives me what I want. Forgetfulness."

And plague take all sad-eyed creatures who overflowed with more passion than their hearts could safely hold.

* * *

SYLVIA HALLIDAY has written a dozen highly praised historical romances under the pseudonyms Ena Halliday and Louisa Rawlings. Her Louisa Rawlings books include *Forever Wild*, a finalist for the RWA Golden Medallion, *Promise of Summer*, which received the *Romantic Times* Reviewer's Choice Award, and *Wicked Stranger* which was a finalist for a 1993 RWA Rita Award. Born in Canada, raised in Massachusetts, Sylvia Halliday now makes her home in New York City.

* * *

Look for
SUMMER DARKNESS, WINTER LIGHT
Wherever Hardcover Books
are Sold in
early May, 1995

SURRENDER TO THE SPLENDOR OF THE ROMANCES OF F. ROSANNE BITTNER!

CARESS	(3791, $5.99/$6.99)
COMANCHE SUNSET	(3568, $4.99/$5.99)
HEARTS SURRENDER	(2945, $4.50/$5.50)
LAWLESS LOVE	(3877, $4.50/$5.50)
PRAIRIE EMBRACE	(3160, $4.50/$5.50)
RAPTURE'S GOLD	(3879, $4.50/$5.50)
SHAMELESS	(4056, $5.99/$6.99)

Available wherever paperbacks are sold, or order direct from the Publisher. Send cover price plus 50¢ per copy for mailing and handling to Penguin USA, P.O. Box 999, c/o Dept. 17109, Bergenfield, NJ 07621. Residents of New York and Tennessee must include sales tax. DO NOT SEND CASH.

THE SEARCHLIGHT

From an anti-aircraft battery

In smug delight we swaggered through the park
and arrogant pressed arm and knee and thigh.
We could not see the others in the dark.
We stopped and peered up at the moonless sky
and at grey bushes and the bristling grass
You in your Sunday suit, I in my pleated gown,
deliberately we stooped (brim-full of grace,
each brandied each rare-steaked) and laid us down.

We lay together in that urban grove
an ocean from the men engaged to die.
As we embraced a distant armoured eye
aroused our dusk with purposed light, a grave
rehearsal for another night. The field
bloomed lovers, dined and blind and target-heeled.

SUMMER REMEMBERED

Sounds sum and summon the remembering of summers.
The humming of the sun
The mumbling in the honey-suckle vine
The whirring in the clovered grass
The pizzicato plinkle of ice in an auburn
uncle's amber glass.
The whing of father's racquet and the whack
of brother's bat on cousin's ball
and calling voices call-
ing voices spilling voices . . .

The munching of saltwater at the splintered dock
The slap and slop of waves on little sloops
The quarreling of oarlocks hours across the bay
The canvas sails that bleat as they
are blown. The heaving buoy bell-
ing HERE I am
HERE you are HEAR HEAR

listen listen listen
The gramophone is wound
the music goes round and around
BYE BYE BLUES LINDY'S COMING
voices calling calling calling
"Children! Children! Time's Up
Time's Up"
Merrily sturdily wantonly the familial voices
cheerily chidingly call to the children TIME'S UP
and the mute children's unvoiced clamor sacks the summer air
crying Mother Mother are you there?

PART OF THE DARKNESS

I had thought of the bear in his lair as fiercely free, feasting
  on honey and wildwood fruits;

I had imagined a forest lunge, regretting the circus shuffle and
  the zoo's proscribed pursuits.

Last summer I took books and children to Wisconsin's Great
  North woods. We drove

one night through miles of pines and rainy darkness to a garbage
  grove

that burgeoned broken crates and bulging paper bags and emptied
  cans of beer,

to watch for native bears, who local guides had told us, scavenged
  there.

After parking behind three other cars (leaving our headlights on
  but dim)

We stumbled over soggy moss to join the families blinking on
  the rim

of mounded refuse bounded east north and west by the forest.

The parents hushed and warned their pushing children each of
  whom struggled to stand nearest

the arena, and presently part of the darkness humped away from
  the foliage and lumbered bear-shaped

toward the heaping spoilage. It trundled into the litter while we
  gaped,

and for an instant it gaped too, bear-faced, but not a tooth was
    bared. It grovelled

carefully while tin cans clattered and tense tourists tittered. Pains-
    takingly it nosed and ravelled

rinds and husks and parings, the used and the refused; bear-
    skinned and doggedly explored

the second-hand remains while headlights glared and flashlights
    stared and shamed bored

children booed, wishing aloud that it would trudge away so they
    might read its tracks.

They hoped to find an as yet unclassified spoor, certain that no
    authentic bear would turn his back

upon the delicacies of his own domain to flounder where mere
    housewives' leavings rot.

I also was reluctant to concede that there is no wild honey in the
    forest and no forest in the bear.

Bereaved, we started home, leaving that animal there.

AT A SUMMER HOTEL

I am here with my beautiful bountiful womanful child
to be soothed by the sea not roused by these roses roving wild.
My girl is gold in the sun and bold in the dazzling water,
she drowses on the blond sand and in the daisy fields my daughter
dreams. Uneasy in the drafty shade I rock on the verandah
reminded of Europa Persephone Miranda.

A LOUD SONG, MOTHER

My son is five years old and tonight he sang this song to me.
He said, it's a loud song, Mother, block up your ears a little, he
said wait I must get my voice ready first. Then tunelessly
but with a bursting beat he chanted from his room enormously,
>   strangers in my name
>   strangers all around me
>   strangers running toward me
>   strangers all over the world
>   strangers running on stars
A deafening declaration this jubilant shout of grief
that trumpets final fellowship and flutes a whole belief.
Alone and in the dark he clears his throat to yawp his truth
that each living human creature's name is Ruth.
He sings a world of strangers running on the burning stars
a race on every-colored feet with freshly calloused scars.

Our stark still strangers waited back of doors and under beds
their socket eyes stared at us out of closets; in our heads.
We crawled on hob-nailed knees across our wasted starless land
each smugly thinking his the only face that wore a brand.

Sons, may you starve the maggot fears that ate our spirit's meat
and stride with brother strangers in your seven-league bare feet.

THAT PRINCELING

"Here is a candle to light you to bed
here comes the chopper to chop off your head"

That princeling bland with dapper smiles for daylit danger,
that dauphin gay as a dolphin at high noon,
in the purring night, pawed by the furry darkness,
howls mutely at the looming loneliness.

In his cold comfortable cage (unguarded)
bulging with beasts, pulsing with strangers,
in a ferocity of silence, it is his own
soft breath that pads and pants and pauses.

Bereaved and unbelieved, beset, be-nighted,
wincing from the awaited and insupportable pounce,
his little tender burrowing bones
bury him to bed.
    No lance no bow of burning gold
    No ewe no shepherd and no fold
    No jerkin of green nor coat of mail, no grace nor grail
    Can celebrate or succour him. Fearful and frail
that trembling desolate and dear prince cringes on his cot
while down unending corridors behind an arras (innocent and not
unarrogant with unicorns) the dauntless King and Queen
waltz sumptuously to sleep.

CANZONETTA

for a god-son aged five

Swim little king-fish   Leap small salmon
Sally from the sea and up the stream Fling
Game as Isaac and gold as Mammon
Plunge April fishlet Sprintheart dash
Drought's the drowning though love is rash
And anglers bait to poach your dreaming
    Cheat that larder, Beat that Chowder, Splash!

Gambol Gamble Easter lambling
Adam as Ram and mortal as Mother
Baa your benison   Ding your damning
Bruise and blessing bell your bleating
Carillon lambkin rousing routing no retreating
Hurtle into wolf and spring's bell-wether
Spiel your glock and,   spell your flock, and Ring!

Gallivant giddyap bantam Will-joy
Bold as bugle and brave as bunting
Trumpet! Furl out! Bannering boy
Gallop to the hill-top. Strut your stride
Raising praising choosing losing never hide-
ing, heeled by the hope that hounds your hunting
    Sound your horn   Astound your dawn and   Ride

There was never any worry about bread or even butter
although that worried me almost as much as my stutter.
I drank coffee with the others in drugstores and then went
back to my room for which I paid a lower rent
than I could afford and where I was proud
of the bedbugs, and where I often allowed
myself an inadequate little Rhine wine. Two
or three times a week after seeing the producers who
were said to be looking for comedy types I wandered
off to the movies alone and always wondered
if anyone in the mezzanine knew me by sight, or might
know me by name or have kissed me and I felt an itch
to stand right up and ask, like swearing out loud in church.
Only one agent agreed to be rude to me every day, a
cross cockeyed woman who had acted in her youth.
I was not union because I had never been paid and the truth
is no other agent would speak to me or even see me until I was
     Equity . . .
a vicious circle but not unpleasing to me.
I smoked for hours in producers' anterooms where
I prayed that interviews I had come there
to beseech would be denied.
Usually my prayers were granted and I stayed outside.
I was a tense imposter, a deliberate dunce,
in a lobby of honest earnest seekers. Once
or twice thanks to a letter of introduction I
got to see the man, but instead of "chin up" and "do or die"
I effectively slouched and stammered in disorder in order
to thus escape the chance to read I might be
offered. An English director once said I was the
"perfect adorable silly ass," due in part to a part
he saw me do in which I had to lisp and giggle.

But that of course was in another country. I did not boggle
at summer stock, and somewhere north of Boston I had
at last become a paid member of a company where sad
to relate I was successfully grotesque in numerous unglamourous
bit parts (usually dialect for I did not stutter
in dialect) and I was always differently grotesque, utter-
ly; but people laughed and/or cried, always saying I was playing myself, that I was a 'natural'. Through the good offices of a
well-connected friend I at last read for a producer who was
     Broadway
and was given the part of a Cockney maid, afraid
and eager, who moved and talked in double-time.
But I was fired. The stars complained for no rime
or reason that they became confused when I was 'on' (there was
     no basis
for their saying that the audience laughed too much and in the
     wrong places)
although it is possible that I just did everything faster and faster.
I had come to depend on the laughs and dismissal was a disaster.
My next job was a haughty lady's maid with a faint brogue
and a strip-tease walk. One night (in Hartford) I was more rogue-
ish than usual and the college boys broke up the show
banging their feet on the floor and whistling. Not long ago
I portrayed a madwoman (but gentle and sentimental)
I curtseyed, sang a short song as I did not
stammer when I sang, and fondled a telescope that
had belonged to a sea-going ancestor. It was agreed
that at last, despite previous successes, I had indeed
and finally found my niche. It was declared
that I could go on and on doing that kind of thing, but I dared
myself to attempt only straight parts although it is hard (playing
     with fire)
for a character actress to play herself and only too true
that the audience response is not at all what one is used to.
Nevertheless it is a challenge and no reason to retire.

SUMMERS AGO

For Edith Sitwell

The Ferryman fairied us out to sea
Gold gold gold sang the apple-tree

Children I told you I tell you our sun was a hail of gold!
I say that sun stoned, that sun stormed our tranquil, our blue bay
bellsweet saltfresh water (bluer than tongue-can-tell, daughter)
and dazed us, darlings, and dazzled us, I say that sun crazed
(that sun clove) our serene as ceramic selves and our noon glazed
    cove,
and children all that grew wild by the wonderful water shot tall
as tomorrow, reeds suddenly shockingly green had sprouted like
    sorrow
and crimson explosions of roses arose in that flurry of Danaean
    glory
while at night we did swoon ah we swanned to a silverer moon-
    light than listen or lute,
we trysted in gondolas blown from glass and kissed in fluted
    Venetian bliss.

> Sister and brother I your mother
> Once was a girl in skirling weather
> Though summer and swan must alter, falter,
> I waltzed on the water once, son and daughter.

is one game that no-one quits while he or she's ahead. The
stakes are steep. Among the chips are love fame life and sanity.
The game's risk is that winning one chip often means the forfeit
of another but despite the penalties there is a surfeit
of players. Some are only kibbitzers, others play it safe
(their chips are counterfeit) cheating, they may not come to grief,
or so they hope, and hoping keep their places near the pot.
There are other gambits deployed to trick the croupier's hot
eye and hand. For some in terror for their reason and their rhyme
There's a disguise in style to rent or borrow or assume:
hair-shirts, brocaded waistcoats (the gilt is slightly tarnished)
sackcloth interlined, embroidered chasubles refurbished,
helmets turbans caps (with bells) wreaths high silk hats cockades . . .
and for women Quaker bonnets wimples coifs and sun-shades,
long blue stockings hawking gloves a fan a hobnailed boot.
But it's the gamblers wearing their own hides who shoot
the moon rocketing on unprotected feet to outer space
where (out of pocket, having no sleeves up which to hide an ace)
they fall bankrupt or being down to their last chip are stran-
ded. No-one has pocketed the moon since the game began . . .
or . . . sooner than they did
they died.

JEAN SANS TERRE
WRAPS HIMSELF IN A RED COAT

Coming toward you in my red coat
Do not ask me if I wear the mantle of the king of Tyre
Or the cloak of the beggar of Benares
My coat is lined with love

The song of love goes before me as crimson dust
Preceded the sirocco which trails the sulphurous storm
It breathes above the seven couching hills
Before astounding the valleys of thirst dried up by Satan

For it is a wind of anger that swells my bloody coat
And flares my pine torch from the forest's depths
I carry vengeance to the people who still dream
In the strangled slums, in the hangars of nightmare

In the flophouses of the Beggar's Court
In the bazaars where hang the carpets blood-stained
By the thousand-year-old hand of slaves
In the prisons cemented by tears and petrified skulls

I light I light with my dancing torch
The tarnished skies of the cities
For the poor who exist on the thirst of others
And have not the right to be thirsty

Those who peddle the song of apples
Of milk of rain of air and the coca of the Trusts
Those who sell exactly enough to die,
To dress the abscessed wounds of their children

I come I come on my red horse
Whose wings are put together with flaps
Torn in strips from my heart, from my vagabond's coat . . .
His hooves flower the rock to a rosebush of love

His nostrils breathe fire from the stars to you
I come from the depths of the forever virgin forest
And I kindle for you all the birds of my crown
The fire of the lyre-bird and the golden fire of the phoenix

A universal Saint Elmo's fire
To spark men's dust
To portion joy to all the corners of the world
To wrap you, my brothers, in a crimson coat

JEAN SANS TERRE
THE CHEST OF DRAWERS

I am a chest of drawers
Open to the passerby
Containing enough to eat and drink
And above all to die

Here is the bunch of mouldering keys
The bouquet of keys to fields and dreams
Here is the key which locks the door of grace
And the one which will open my tomb again

In this drawer I have the essence of rain
And the spices of the earth
Pepper for killing memories
And shadow—dissolving salt.

In another a gold ancestral watch
The watch time cannot break
Anger Love Nothing stops it
No hammer shatters this dial

Here is the keen edge to sever trust
The wool for mending friendship
But alas I have dropped the stitch
Which could re-weave the wing of innocence

The pack of cards from which my wife emerged
The accountings which prolong the lunar year
And my will written in invisible ink
Will see the notaries of Tartar age.

This compass measures the angle of sincerity
And this bell pings for every lie
And here is a life-supply of nails
To crucify the guilty.

There I have the bleached heart of my mother
Who always knitted socks for the condemned
And I have the ivory hand of my love
Lost as she leant to wave farewell

The seventh drawer contains the tools of prayer
The gimlet for the worm of temptation
The file against the growth of impoverished thoughts
And the pliers to screw tight the piety of my hands

I am a chest of drawers
Locked from the passerby
Containing enough to doubt and trust
And above all to die